The Merchant of Venus

The Merchant of Venus

ELLEN HART

ST. MARTIN'S MINOTAUR ✴ NEW YORK

www.minotaurbooks.com

ISBN 0-312-28905-7 (pbk)

First St. Martin's Griffin Edition: February 2002

10 9 8 7 6 5 4 3 2 1

In loving memory of my parents,
Marjory Rowena Boehnhardt
1914–2000

and

Herman Charles Boehnhardt
1912–1976

Cast of Characters

Jane Lawless: Owner of the Lyme House restaurant in Minneapolis. Friend of Cordelia.

Cordelia Thorn: Artistic director for the Allen Grimby Repertory Theatre in St. Paul. Friend of Jane. Sister of Octavia. Hiram's daughter.

Octavia Thorn: Broadway actress. Cordelia's younger sister. Hiram's daughter.

Peter Lawless: Jane's brother. Cameraman at WTWN.

Roland Lester: Hollywood movie director. Buddy's older brother. Grace's great-uncle.

Grace (Gracie) Lester: Internet artist. Buddy's granddaughter. Roland's grandniece.

Ellie Saks: Documentary film artist.

Lew Wallace: Actor/movie star. Friend of Roland and Verna.

Christian Wallace: Lew's son. Movie producer.

Verna Lange: Actress/movie star. Friend of Roland and Lew.

Dr. Hiram Thorn: Octavia and Cordelia's father.

Hilda Gettle: House manager at Innishannon.

Buddy Lester: Roland's brother and personal assistant.

John Toscano: New Haven homicide detective.

The only thing new in this world
is the history you don't know.

—Harry Truman

History is a romance that is believed;
romance, a history that is not believed.

—Horace Walpole
English Author
1717–1797

Prologue

If life can be said to have its own unique rhythm, so too can death—or, in this case, murder. It was just past seven P.M. on the first day of the new year when Jane Lawless hailed a taxi in Times Square, heading for LaGuardia and the long flight home. As the glittering lights of New York sped past her, she leaned her head back against the seat, closed her eyes, and thought about life and death in Hollywood, about old wounds and new grievances, about hatred, bitterness, the desperate desire for retribution, and finally, about the most powerful emotion of all: love.

Roland Lester's story would always haunt her. Piece by piece, she'd put the puzzle together, sifted through the layers of lies and secrets until she'd developed a reasonably clear picture. It was far more complex than the simple slip of stationery she'd discovered—a page stuffed inside an old shoe, a paper with a few numbers and letters scratched onto the surface. She'd merely done what she was good at—followed her instincts. But while she'd been busy tracking down a fascinating bit of Hollywood history, someone had stepped right out of that history to end a life—two lives, before it was all over.

There were no simple answers, thought Jane, hearing the cab driver fiddle with the radio. He'd been listening to a religious station, but now seemed to be in a mood for jazz. Jane's story, her Christmas trip to Innishannon, had ended in one shattering moment inside a ramshackle house in Wister, Connecticut. The Merchant of Venus had led her there, and like a fool, she'd followed. But was it love or hate? Fact or fiction? The only question she'd been concerned with that night had to do with life or death. The search for complex truths paled when you were staring down the barrel of a gun.

Late August
Innishannon, on the Connecticut Shore

It must be a statue of Venus, thought Octavia, parking her Volvo in the circular drive next to the mansion. Easing out of the front seat, she crossed the matted, dying grass to a crumbling stone fountain, one obviously no longer in use. In the growing twilight, she gazed up at the bronze sculpture, noticing that the face and body were heartbreakingly beautiful. Venus, the goddess of love, the symbol of physical perfection. Venus had also become the symbol of a man who'd made a name for himself by examining—some said exploiting—the subjects of love and beauty in his films. What Hitchcock had been to suspense and Frank Capra to the more innocent American values, Roland Lester had been to romance. His films were world famous, even though he himself, now in his eighty-third year, had become a recluse.

Weeds surrounded the base of the once magnificent fountain, climbing the carved stone until the tops lay flattened and decomposing in the filthy water. As Octavia took it all in—the wild, untended grounds, the woods in the distance, the tall grass leading down to Long Island Sound, the huge Tudor manor—she knew this might be her first and last visit to the famous Innishannon. She also couldn't help but feel that something was terribly wrong.

Decay, the kind that came not just from the passage of time but from neglect, was everywhere apparent on the multiacre estate. The house, once considered one of America's great Eastern castles, looked forlorn and deserted. Octavia wasn't sure what she'd expected, but this wasn't it. Why would a man reputedly worth millions allow his grounds and his home to descend into such a state of disrepair? It made no sense.

As the sun inched deeper behind the once grand manor house, a chill wind off the sound blew dry leaves across the cracked and pitted drive. So bleak was the scene that had her curiosity not been shamelessly piqued, she would have returned to her car that moment and driven back to New York. But she couldn't, not until she learned why she'd been summoned.

The invitation had been precise. Cocktails at six. Dinner at seven. Formal attire. She assumed that at least a *few* others had been invited, but since there wasn't another car in sight, it seemed that she was the only guest. A postscript had been added by Roland Lester himself. Written in a hand that appeared shaky with age, it had said, "If you love old movies as much as you've said you do in all your interviews, I have something to discuss that may very well change your life. Don't fail me, Ms. Thorn. I shall count the days until we meet." The note was signed, simply, "R."

The whole thing had a vaguely scripted feel to it—heavy on the melodrama. She'd almost expected to see Klieg lights set up on the front lawn waiting to light her arrival. Just the eyes, of course. Shadow and light, the physical as well as spiritual duality from which the old black-and-white movies had been created. Directors always told her she had amazingly expressive eyes. She was born too late for Klieg lights, but hey, she still appreciated a good lighting designer.

As Octavia walked up the broad sweep of steps to the arched front door, the air of desolation grew even more powerful. The mansion's peaks and gables stood high above her, erect and forbidding. The coldness of the crumbling stucco and wood exterior made her feel as if she were about to enter a ruin, not a living person's home.

Since there was no doorbell, Octavia assumed she was to use one of the two brass door knockers. One was cast in the shape of the Greek mask of Comedy, the other of Tragedy. Perhaps Roland Lester was giving his guests a choice. Deciding not to tempt fate, she selected the Comedy mask, but as she tried to pull it away from its hinge, she found that it was stuck fast, rendering it useless. Not a good omen.

Pounding on the door with her fist, Octavia waited. She adjusted the neckline of her evening gown, then checked her watch. When nobody answered, she swallowed back her superstitious nature and used the mask of Tragedy to announce her arrival. Moments later, the door swung back and a woman stood before her. Her short, dumpling shape and pleasant smile put some of Octavia's more overt fears to rest.

Octavia handed her the invitation.

After studying it silently for a few moments, the woman said, "Come in, please," taking Octavia's wrap and draping it over her arm. "I'm Hilda Gettle, Mr. Lester's house manager."

"Nice to meet you."

"Did you have trouble finding us?"

"No, the map Mr. Lester sent was more than adequate."

The front foyer was large and dark, paneled in oak and filled with antiques. Through a wide corridor that ran beside the stairs, she could see all the way to the back of the house, where a series of multipaned windows looked out on a veranda, one that faced the sound. To her immediate right was the dining room. To her left, another long corridor led off toward the west side of the house. The interior, while still breathtaking, was every bit as dank and dilapidated as the exterior. The Oriental carpets and heavy drapes appeared frayed and smelled faintly of mildew. The furniture—circa 1920's—looked faded and undoubtedly full of the dust of decades. If only someone would throw open the windows and let in some fresh air, but then, that would break the spell. Innishannon was seductive in its disintegration. Like her older sister, Cordelia, Octavia had been born with acute intuitive abilities. This was a house of darkness and secrets, nothing she wanted any part of. For a brief instant she wondered if she shouldn't just offer an excuse, say she wasn't feeling well, and leave. But before she could formulate the right malady, she felt the elderly woman's eyes on her.

"Is something wrong, Ms. Thorn?"

"No, I . . . ah—" She gave a weak smile.

"Please. If you'd follow me?"

Like Jane Eyre, caught between fright and fascination, she couldn't leave until she'd met the lord of the manor. As they left the front door and proceeded down the west hall, Octavia became aware of the smell of wood smoke. The scent seemed to center her and calm her down. So did the walls filled with framed photos of famous actors and actresses. Get a grip, she told herself. Coming here tonight couldn't put her in any personal danger. It was simply one of life's little adventures. Sometimes she mistook her rather fertile imagination for intuition. Just

7

because the estate was old and falling apart didn't mean there was anything truly amiss. She'd come here at the request of one of the most beloved film directors in Hollywood history. What could be more delicious?

While Octavia had made a big splash on the legitimate stage, she'd never been able to break into movies. Oh, she'd done a couple of minor films, but nothing anybody would remember. She admitted to a certain hope that tonight's meeting would change all that. At thirty-four, her luck had better change soon or Hollywood's brass ring—and the money and fame it represented—would pass her by forever.

When they reached the living room, Hilda nodded politely and then left. Octavia found herself alone. Since her host hadn't appeared yet, she decided to use the time to survey her surroundings. The room itself could easily have swallowed all of her apartment in Manhattan, and then some. Heavy oak beams crisscrossed the ceiling, while the tall windows were draped in velvet gloom. Clusters of tapestry chairs and couches were spread throughout. The room was spacious, even inviting in its own austere way, and yet it had a certain worn and empty air about it.

She prowled around for a few minutes, touching things, looking at the pictures, brushing a finger along the fringe on a lamp, but never ventured far from the fireplace. For some reason, she felt the need to be close to its warmth and comfort. This close to the ocean, the evening had turned chilly. As she stood staring at the burning logs, she suddenly felt something touch the back of her dress. When she turned around, she found a bundle of white fur sniffing her shoes.

"And who are you?" she asked, crouching down to let the little bichon examine her hand.

"Busby, you idiot. Come here!" shouted an annoyed voice. The dog's owner appeared a few seconds later. It was a woman again, this one a good deal younger than the house manager. She appeared to be in her late twenties, with short tufts of green and magenta hair sticking out from under a baseball cap, a tattoo of a chain around her neck, and four nose rings. The long, gauzy dress seemed to be a trifle 1960's but then Octavia figured the woman liked to wear period clothes.

She stopped dead when she saw she wasn't alone. "Who the hell are you?" she asked, clapping for the dog to come to her.

Busby turned and jumped into her arms.

8

The woman stared at Octavia with such naked curiosity, she wasn't sure what to say. "I, ah . . . I'm here at the request of Roland Lester." She knew she sounded way too formal, but the damn house was making her feel like she'd entered a time warp.

The woman stroked the dog's fur, digesting the information. "What's your name?"

"Octavia Thorn."

"You an actress?"

She nodded.

"You look like one."

"Thanks. I think."

"Where's Uncle Roland?"

"Roland Lester is your uncle?"

"Well, great-uncle, but I'm not big on detail."

"I don't know where he is," said Octavia, rising from her crouching position. "I just got here."

"You staying for dinner?"

"That was the plan."

She continued to stare. "Are you a friend?"

"No, we've never met."

"Then how come you're here?"

Octavia wanted to say that it was none of her business, but held her tongue. The woman hadn't even introduced herself and here she was administering the third degree. She wasn't big on detail *or* manners. "It's . . . a private matter."

"Really. Private."

"And you are?"

"Oh, sorry. I'm Gracie." She held out her hand and shook Octavia's with gusto.

"Do you live here?"

"Yup. Upstairs. The entire third floor is mine."

Octavia had a few of her own questions. "How long has your great-uncle owned Innishannon?"

"Let me think." She scratched her head through her cap. "He bought it in 'fifty-seven, but didn't move in until years later. I guess he wanted a house where he could get away from his work in Hollywood, but since he was such a workaholic, he asked my gramps and his family— Gramps is his brother—if they'd move in and caretake it. Since Gramps was Rolo's personal assistant, he did what he was told. Gramps thought for sure he'd want to renovate the place, but Rolo insisted it remain just the way it was. I call it the Museum. It's gone downhill in the past few years, but I think the shabbiness is kind of funky." She smiled amiably.

"Is your grandfather still alive?"

"Sure. He has rooms upstairs on the second floor. Gram died about twelve years ago. He spends a lot of his time in New Jersey with our family, but he's still the great man's right arm, I guess you could say."

"I assume your uncle entertains quite a bit."

"Not really. Not since Peg died. Except for a few close friends, of course. Old cronies from his movie days. You're the first stranger we've seen around here in ages."

"Who's Peg?"

"His daughter. She died, must be a good seven years ago now. It was real sudden. Rolo went into a complete funk. Wouldn't eat. Couldn't sleep. That's when I arrived. I was finishing my graduate degree at Yale. I had an apartment in New Haven, but I came back here most weekends. Eventually, I just stayed. And then, when I graduated, I moved in. Gramps thought my presence might help."

"And did it?"

She shrugged. "Grief takes time. Believe it or not, I've grown kind of fond of the old guy. I'm sorry I'm going to miss dinner, but I've got a date with some friends in town."

"In New York?"

"St. Albans. It's not far." She kept her eyes fixed on Octavia, which only served to heighten Octavia's sense that she was some sort of rare fungus everyone wanted to get a good look at before Hilda Gettle rushed back in with the disinfectant.

"Well, I guess I better hit the bricks. Enjoy your dinner, Ms. Thorn. Hope I see you again sometime." She backed out of the room with her dog in her arms and disappeared around the corner.

Once Octavia heard a door close deep in the belly of the house, she returned her attention to the fireplace. She hoped Lester would show up soon to put her out of her misery. At this point, the fist of tension inside her stomach had grown so large, dinner seemed out of the question. She needed to find out why she was here. It was probably just a pipe dream, but Octavia harbored a secret hope that the elderly director

10

had some project he was working on—some new movie—and he wanted to cast her in the leading role. Even the remote possibility sent shivers up her spine.

As she moved to a window seat under one of the tall windows, deciding whether sitting down on the upholstered cushion would do any permanent damage to her designer gown, she noticed a thin stream of smoke rising from a wingback chair on the other end of the room. Since the chair was facing away from her, it never occurred to her that someone might be sitting in it.

Before she could think what to say, an elderly man with snow-white hair and a thin mustache stood up and turned around. He was wearing a tuxedo with a red cummerbund. Octavia's startled look must have caused him a moment of amusement because he smiled. Lifting the cigarette he was holding to his lips, he said, "Welcome to Innishannon, Ms. Thorn. I'm Roland Lester."

What struck her first was his elegance. The way he stood reminded her of a character in a Noel Coward play. He wasn't as tall as she'd expected, but his presence was still commanding. "I . . . didn't know you were here. Do you always eavesdrop on your guests?"

"My apologies if I've upset you. I was just curious to see which of my family and staff would want to get a firsthand look at the reigning queen of Broadway."

Now he was flattering her. Embarrassing though it was to admit, she'd always been a sucker for flattery, even the most obvious kind.

"As my grandniece said, we rarely have guests anymore, certainly not someone with your . . . qualities."

"My qualities?" Had she really fluttered her lashes just then? God, the play had switched to Tennessee Williams. A Southern accent would come next.

"Please don't take this the wrong way, Ms. Thorn, but I've been watching you and your career for several years. I have a chauffeur drive me into New York several times a month so that I can catch a play. Off Broadway, on—it doesn't matter. I watch and I learn. You may think I'm just an old man, someone who's lost his creative edge and his lust for life, but you'd be wrong. I still know a thoroughbred when I see one. The sad truth is, I've felt for years that there are no real *Hollywood* actors and actresses around anymore—nothing like the icons of the thirties and forties. And then . . . well, you went and proved

11

me wrong." Again, he smiled. "You've got star quality, Octavia. The kind that can take even an old man's breath away." He moved slowly toward her. "You have the fire of a Bette Davis, the beauty of a Joan Fontaine, and the intelligence of a Kate Hepburn. And, my dear, you have natural timing, the kind it takes to become a great comic actress. Your range continually astounds me."

She wasn't sure what to say. "Did you say . . . Joan Fontaine?"

"You could be her daughter." He moved even closer, this time taking one of her hands in his.

Only now did she notice the two hearing aids, and the filigree of wrinkles that covered his face. But the eyes—they were so clear . . . so mesmerizing.

"Very simply, Octavia, even though you've made very few movies and your talent has never been fully recognized, you're the direct descendent of that enchanted Hollywood legacy I've dedicated my life to keeping alive." He held her hand to his lips. With a sudden and amused lift of his head, he added. "And since you're the heir apparent, you might as well have the rest as well."

"The rest of what?" she asked, almost in a trance.

Leading her over to a couch, he said, "That's what I've called you here to talk about."

They sat down in front of the fire.

"Let me start by giving you something." He removed a small box from his pocket.

My God, thought Octavia. This was getting more bizarre by the moment.

"I want you to have this."

"What is it?"

"Open it and see." He waited, his amused smile turning expectant, even eager.

Inside she found a key attached to a chain. The key itself wasn't decorative in any way, but it was old—a skeleton key. The chain, one meant to hang around the neck, looked like it was made of gold. "I'm confused," she said, cupping the key in her hand. "What's it for?"

"That has to remain a secret—for now. But if you agree to my terms, Octavia, I promise, you'll have the wealth and power you deserve. With that key, you can write your own ticket. Be whatever you want."

12

Were these the ravings of a man who'd gone over the edge? If he had so much money, why did his home look like it was ready for the wrecking ball? Something didn't smell right. "What terms?"

Before answering, he got up and walked over to a table filled with liquor bottles, glasses, and a container of ice. "First I need your promise that you'll stay with me here for a few months."

"Stay? For *months*?" She was stunned.

"I know your most recent play closed last night. Your time is your own, at least for a while. Would staying here with me be so bad?"

"But . . . why would I do that? I don't even know you. Besides, I have a life in New York. A career. Friends."

He poured them each a brandy. Returning to the couch, he handed her a glass, then raised his in salute. "Forgive an old man for taking his time, but if you'll be patient with me, Octavia, all will be made clear." Sitting down next to her, he crossed his legs, stared into the fire and said, "I want to tell you a story."

Mid-December
Minneapolis

2

Cordelia sat before the lit dressing table in her fifth-floor loft, carefully applying a new glitter shadow pencil she'd recently bought at Dayton's. Selecting a small fluff brush from the makeup tools in the top drawer, she began to experiment with the color—Midnight Magnolia. Sort of lavender meets pink trailer-park trash, one of Bon Femme's older, more sedate shades.

She'd arrived home a few minutes ago, in a mood to celebrate her good news, though if she popped a bottle of bubbly and invited a bunch of friends over to share the moment, she doubted any of them would show.

Since morning, a good eight inches of snow had fallen on the city. The radio said three more would fall by midnight. It was the kind of night to stay home in front of a roaring fire and drink cocoa, not take your life in your hands by braving the wind, the frozen roads, and the idiot drivers who roared around town skidding through stoplights in their SUVs, behaving as if it were mid-July. Even though the winter weather had nixed her plans, at least she could dress for the non-occasion. Once her eyes were glittered to her complete satisfaction, she intended to party down.

For months, Cordelia had been kept in suspense about her contract at the Allen Grimby Repertory Theatre. Would she be asked to continue as the artistic director, or would she be out on the streets come January first?

Minnesotans might be an idiosyncratic breed, one foot planted firmly in Lake Woebegon and the other in cyberspace, but they loved the arts. Cordelia couldn't imagine that any other regional theatre would allow her the creative latitude the Grimby had. Not only had she been keeping her fingers crossed, but her eyes and ears open, hoping to ferret out the board's final decision before the official announcement at the end of the year. Earlier tonight, she'd received word—via the highly reliable janitor's grapevine—that she was going to be offered another three-year contract. She felt instantly triumphant. She'd been deeply worried that her critics would starve this winter. Now they'd have so much crow to eat, they wouldn't need to leave their caves until spring.

Also, the news couldn't have come at a better time.

Over the years, Cordelia had risen to the status of theatrical diva in Minnesota. She loved being one of the local glitterati, being a mover and shaker in this nationally respected theatre scene. She might be a transplanted New Englander—she'd lived in Minnesota since her parents moved from Boston to St. Paul before her junior year of high school—but this was home now. If she'd been forced to look elsewhere for a similar position, she most likely would have had to relocate. That would mean leaving her friends—and most importantly, her best friend, Jane—behind. Jane was still recovering from a serious head injury, as well as the loss of a lover. She needed Cordelia right now, needed her steady hand and sage advice.

Cordelia was *nothing* if not sage.

Back in the seventies, when Cordelia had been attending the University of Minnesota, she'd written a column for the school newspaper—"Ask Auntie Cordelia." In it, she'd brought to bear the full weight of her nineteen years of wisdom on the problems of student life. Jane, of course, thought Cordelia merely liked telling people what to do. Cordelia forgave Jane that unflattering characterization, as any good friend would, but as her penance, she made sure that Jane read every column from beginning to end. If she recalled correctly, she dealt with such fascinating topics as:

Should I try a bong, or just use the traditional roach clip?
Why don't my parents understand how much I need my space?
If I own a Paul Anka record, is it best to keep it under my bed where no one can see it, or should I destroy the evidence?

What should I say to my mother now that she's discovered I've tie-dyed all my underwear—the expensive stuff she bought for me at Dayton's?

All questions of great pith and moment. But Cordelia felt she was at the peak of her form when it came to matters of the heart. She'd always known she was a free spirit living in a world of dreary Calvinists. She felt *that* perspective gave her a definite edge in the advice biz. Even today, she still possessed an uncanny ability to bring forth order out of romantic chaos. She might not have the best track record with her own love life, but that didn't mean she couldn't give advice—help the needy. That's why she couldn't leave Jane, not until her love life was back on track. At the rate Jane had been going, it might take years.

With one last fluff of her makeup brush, Cordelia got up and sashayed into the kitchen. She knew she had a bottle of champagne somewhere, she just had to find it. She simply *had* to celebrate, even if the forces of nature forced her to do it alone. She might even make a ham sandwich to go with the . . . ah, yes. A bottle of Asti Spumonti. Perfect. Just as she popped the cork, she heard the doorbell ring.

"Uno momento," she called, rushing back through the living room. Tipping the scales at well over two hundred pounds, Cordelia wasn't much for aerobic exercise, though the size of her loft kept her on her toes.

It didn't matter who'd come to call. Neighbor or delivery boy, she intended to drag the poor sap inside and insist on sharing a drink. Quickly lighting two candles, she switched on the track lighting, softly illuminating the entire loft, then picked up Lucifer and Blanche Du Bois, two of her cats. Fortified by mounds of fur, she flung back the door.

Her smile faded instantly.

"You don't look very happy to see me."

"What are you doing here?"

"Not much of a welcome. Aren't you going to invite me in?"

"Why should I?"

"Try simple manners."

Cordelia glared.

"How about . . . we haven't spoken in eight years."

"There's a *reason* for that," said Cordelia, eying her sister, Octavia, wondering just what fresh hell had brought her to Minnesota. Octavia

19

looked good, as usual. Healthy. Exceedingly blond and glamorous. She might impress an audience, but she didn't impress Cordelia. Octavia had always been able to break people's hearts with that innocent, tragic look of hers. Sad that such talent belonged to a woman of overpowering shallowness. Glancing down, Cordelia spied a suitcase. "Let me guess. You've become a Fuller Brush man. You're selling hairbrushes now, door-to-door."

"Cute. Guess again."

"If you think you're staying here, I suggest you turn around and head back to New York."

"Can't. The airport's closed."

"Then call a taxi and find a hotel."

"Can't."

"Why?"

"Because I *can't*." She picked up her luggage and barged past Cordelia into the living room.

The cats squirmed out of Cordelia's arms. "You're not staying."

"I have to."

"Why?"

Octavia flipped off the track lighting and moved over to the long bank of windows, peering carefully down at the street.

"What?" said Cordelia, her hands rising to her hips. "The drug busters after you again?"

"Nothing like a little bitterness to get things off on the right foot."

Cordelia just stared at her. "Age cannot wither nor custom stale your infinite acerbity."

"Oh, great." She whirled around. "I travel all this way and all you can do is toss bastardized Shakespeare quotes at me like an adolescent theatre major. Can't we communicate like human beings—like sisters?"

"And how would that be?"

"Straight. Without all the sarcasm. For your information, I'm not using anymore."

"Right. Tell me another."

"I'm *not*. I haven't touched alcohol or cocaine since—"

"Since when? Since Mom died?" Cordelia could feel the anger building in her chest.

Octavia looked away. "Cut me a little slack, will you? I wouldn't be here if I didn't need . . . if I didn't want—" Her voice faltered.

20

"You always want something, Octavia. What is it this time?"

"You're my sister! We're family."

"And you're in trouble."

"No," she said, gazing forlornly down at her hands. "It's not like that . . . exactly."

There it was. The look that could launch a thousand handkerchiefs. "Save the tragic act for your audiences in New York."

"You're a hard woman, you know that?"

"*Au contraire.* I am the soul of compassion. Just not where you're concerned."

Octavia paused, glanced around the room, then started again. "I came because . . . because I wanted to mend fences. It's about time, don't you think? I know what I did was horrible. Inexcusable. If I could take back any of my actions, I would. I'm clean, really. I have been for years." She paused, then tried on a hesitant smile. "Hey, don't you ever read *Variety*? I'm the toast of New York. Your little sister. Think of that."

Cordelia drew herself up to her full six-foot height. "After what you did, I can't believe you'd think I'm even the least bit interested in your career."

"You used to care."

"That ended eight years ago." Cordelia stood her ground as Octavia moved restlessly about the room.

Finally, Octavia said, "Dad's forgiven me."

"Then he's a fool. I'm not."

"How would you know? You haven't been home since Mom died."

"We talk on the phone."

"Not much you don't."

"How would you know?"

"Because I'm there, Cordelia. I drive up to Boston every chance I get. Dad's all alone now. He needs us."

The phone suddenly rang.

Octavia jumped. "Don't answer that."

This was too much. "It's my loft. You don't give orders here."

Octavia lunged at the phone, preventing Cordelia from picking it up. "Please! Just this once. Do what I ask."

"What's the big deal?" demanded Cordelia. "All this talk about forgiveness and reconciliation. You're here because you're hiding from

21

someone, right? You never change. When you're in trouble, you come to me to bail you out."

"That's not true. It's just . . . we were having our first real conversation in eight years! I don't want to be interrupted."

"What *real* conversation? All I heard were the usual excuses."

"Cordelia, give me a break!"

Ignoring her sister's pleas, Cordelia pried Octavia's hand off the receiver and clicked it on. "Thorn here," she said abruptly. "Speak."

3

Put Octavia on the line, please."

Cordelia didn't recognize the voice, but the man's lack of formality matched her own. She was irritated that her sister had been in her loft less than five minutes and she was already receiving phone calls. "It's for you," said Cordelia, handing back the phone. She sat down on the couch, draping her jewelry-encrusted arms across the cushions. She had no intention of giving her sister any privacy.

Octavia turned away and walked to the windows overlooking downtown Minneapolis. "Hello?" she said quietly. "Oh, hi." She listened a moment, then said, "Yes . . . sorry . . . I, ah . . . I needed to get away. I was going to tell you, but then I couldn't find you. I got in my car and started driving. Before I realized it I was back in New York. My apartment felt so claustrophobic, I couldn't stay there, so I packed a bag and headed for the airport." She paused. "How . . . how did you know I was here?"

Cordelia couldn't help herself. She was intrigued.

"I see," said Octavia, resting her forehead against the glass. "Yes, I should have known you'd put it together. What?" She touched a hand to the back of her hair. "I've already contacted him. He'll be coming on Sunday night." She turned and dropped her eyes to Cordelia. "Yes, I thought I'd ask her in person, and no, I don't know what she'll say." Another pause. "I'm fine. Really. It just got kind of crazy around there, especially when Christian arrived. I'm used to that documentary person always being around, but——" She listened. "No, Roland, you never said anything about houseguests."

It had to be boyfriend trouble, thought Cordelia. She hadn't read anything in the papers about her sister getting married again, though the nuptials could have taken place privately, perhaps in Europe. Octavia was partial to Italy—and Italian men. Cordelia liked Italy too, though she preferred Italian women.

"I know that," continued Octavia, "but I just felt funny, like they were all watching me. It's not easy, you know. This is all so new." She held a hand to the side of her face. "I don't *know,* okay? I just . . . I had to get out of there. But don't worry. Nothing's changed. I'll see you soon. Yes . . . yes, I promise." After a few more seconds she added, "Me, too. Bye." She clicked off the phone and set it down on an end table, then glanced at her sister. Some of her normal confidence was missing.

"What was all that about?" asked Cordelia, an amused smile pulling at the corners of her mouth.

"You enjoy seeing me squirm, don't you? You always have."

Now Cordelia looked stricken. "That's not true."

"Oh, cut the crap. It's just you and me here."

"You and me and your little secrets. Sounds like you've caught yourself another live one. Who is he? Another producer who's going to make you the next Meryl Streep?"

"Meryl Streep has been box office poison for years. I know that's a ghastly comment on a ghastly industry, but there it is."

Cordelia shrugged. "I believe you said something about asking me a question in person. Well, here I am, big as life, and I'm *all* atwitter thinking what it might be. Does my sister need money? A character witness for some criminal lawsuit? Or a place to hide? If the latter, I think you better bag that idea. Your cover's been blown."

"God, but you're transparent." She bit the nail on her little finger, glowering. "But this time, you can be as snide as you want, I'm not going to rise to the bait."

"Like the predictable small-mouthed bass I used to know and love."

Sitting down across from her, Octavia hesitated a moment, then continued, "Promise me you'll think about this. You won't say no just as a matter of course."

"I'm not promising anything."

"Okay . . . be that way." She took a slow, calming breath, then said, "Do you know who Roland Lester is?"

"You mean the famous Hollywood director? Sure, who doesn't?"

"He's asked me to marry him."

Cordelia didn't think her sister had any shock value left in her, but here she was, lighting her usual firecracker. "Isn't the man dead?"

"If he is, he's rather animated about it. He's eighty-three."

"And he actually proposed?"

"Right."

"Three words, Octavia. *Anna Nicole Smith*."

"You think I'm a gold digger? That I'm marrying him for his money?" Cordelia flung her arms in the air. "Well, duh!"

"Look," said Octavia indignantly, "it's not immoral or illegal."

"Or fattening."

"Exactly."

"So, is this also a passionate love match?"

"Not passion. But love . . . in a strange way, yes. It is."

"Have you been dating long?"

"A few months."

"And, of course, an extended engagement is out of the question."

Again, Octavia glowered. "If you're going to make a bunch of stupid age jokes, I can leave right now."

"Good. You remember where the door is." Cordelia started to get up.

"Just give me a break, will you? Give me one measly second of your precious time."

"I have. Why should I give you more?"

"Because you're my sister. And I care about you, god knows why. And also . . . well . . . I came here to ask you to be part of the wedding. My maid of honor."

If Cordelia had ever consciously given anyone the evil eye, she was doing so now. "You've *got* to be kidding."

"Dad's coming. He's going to give me away."

It took her a moment to realize her mouth was open. "Not only is that concept archaic, but this would be your *fourth* marriage. Hardly the time to waltz down the isle of a big church, maids and maidens in tow. Why don't you just fly to Las Vegas, find yourself a chapel and a vaguely unsavory justice of the peace, and hire some Elvis impersonator to hum the wedding march?" She paused—but only for a second. "I suppose next you're going to be telling me you're wearing white."

"My stylist suggested off-white. Or . . . cappuccino."

"Well, there you are!"

Octavia looked hurt. "Can't you be happy for me just this once?"

"Who's idea was it to get married? Yours or Lester's?"

"His."

"You swept him off his feet."

"Not exactly, although he does find me fascinating. He thinks I look like Joan Fontaine."

Cordelia rolled her eyes. "If you're so happy with the man, why did you run away? And why on *earth* would you want me around knowing the way I feel about you? I'm still so angry I could put my fist through a brick wall. I would think my presence would cast a pall on your happiness."

"But, don't you see? This will give us the chance to mend fences. Work our differences through. You left in such a huff after Mom's funeral, we never had time to talk. And then you wouldn't take my phone calls. You never answered my letters. Come on, Cordelia. Wouldn't you like to meet Roland Lester? He's everything you'd expect—and more. I thought maybe Jane could come too. We'd all fly back together. I haven't seen her in ages. We could all stay at Innishannon—that's Roland's mansion on the Connecticut shore. It's really . . . atmospheric. Kind of run-down, maybe, but still amazing."

Under her breath, Cordelia whispered, "I dreamt I went to Manderlay again last night."

"You and Jane could catch a show in New York while you're there. I already checked your schedule at the Allen Grimby. You're free until after New Year's. Are your holiday plans so set in stone that you couldn't come back with me, meet a man who's dying to meet you, and spend the holidays with your family? I know I could talk Dad into coming for Christmas if you were there. And Jane's always been welcome at any family event. Please, Cordelia, just think about it."

"No," said Cordelia, flatly.

"But—"

Stiffening her shoulders, she folded her arms over her ample bosom and said, "You heard me. There's not a single thing in this world you can say to make me change my mind."

4

So, it's actually going to happen. You're flying to Connecticut for the holidays," said Peter Lawless, Jane's younger brother. He was sitting on an upholstered bench in her bedroom, watching her pack. "You know, when you told me yesterday, I thought for sure Cordelia would never change her mind. I mean, she's not all that tight with her sister anymore, right? Or did I miss something?"

"No, you didn't miss a thing," Jane said as she folded a sweater and tucked it into the side of her bag. As a matter of fact, she thought Peter's assessment was an understatement.

Jane and Cordelia had been as close as sisters for almost twenty-five years, and certainly for the past eight of those years, Octavia had not been a part of Cordelia's life. To even bring up her name in Cordelia's presence was to be met with a withering stare and a clipped reminder of the definition for the word *anathema*.

When Cordelia phoned Jane at home last night with the news of her sister's impending wedding and an invitation to join the festivities, Jane thought at first it was a joke. Octavia had been married two or three times already. Jane didn't even know she'd been divorced from her last husband, let alone that she might be thinking of taking the plunge again. And when she heard who the groom was to be, that settled it. Cordelia had to be pulling her leg.

Fortunately or unfortunately, however you wanted to look at it, Octavia's hope had once again triumphed over her experience. Through gritted teeth, Cordelia explained that it was entirely true. And while she didn't exactly beg, she made it clear that she expected Jane to accompany her to Innishannon, Roland Lester's estate on the Connecticut shore. Cordelia was like that. Imperious, demanding, opinionated, and yet incredibly loyal and loving. She expected nothing less from her friends.

Ever since Jane and Cordelia had first met back in the eleventh grade, Cordelia had added a kind of spontaneous insanity to Jane's more normal existence. Jane had always been drawn to the outrageous and the artistic, so their friendship developed almost overnight. Because Octavia was also a budding thespian, Jane assumed early on that the two sisters were close. Nothing could be farther from the truth. Octavia and Cordelia had always been like oil and water. Both were unusually attractive, but while Octavia was blonde and delicate, Cordelia's darker, more massive form belonged on an opera stage belting out Wagner. Jane was completely in the dark about what had happened between the two of them shortly after their mother's death. Whatever the story, Cordelia steadfastly refused to talk about it.

Since Jane had been leaning on Cordelia's friendship rather heavily of late, she could hardly say no to her request. The bizarre odyssey that had become Jane's life since late summer had taken a turn for the worse when, in October, she'd been hospitalized after being attacked in her home. She'd sustained a serious head injury that had left her weak and partially paralyzed. Physically, the worst of it was over now, but in the aftermath she'd become estranged from the woman she'd been dating, one Julia Martinsen. Julia was now in Paris. From comments in her rather upbeat postcards it was clear that she hoped to resume her life with Jane on her return to Minneapolis at the beginning of the new year. Jane didn't view matters quite the same way. After much soul-searching, she'd come to the conclusion that, even though she still had feelings for Julia, their relationship wasn't going to work. The reasons were complex and painful, but the bottom line was, Jane's trust in Julia had been shattered. She had to move on. The idea of spending time away from Minnesota right now, from her daily routine, from all the memories, did have a certain appeal.

For the past few weeks, Jane had been putting in only eight- to ten-hour days at her restaurant, instead of the usual twelve. She'd spend her early mornings at the Y, trying to pound her body back into shape. Her left leg still continued to give her the most problems. She'd return home in the evenings by eight so she could work on a culinary memoir of her childhood in England, one she'd started last summer. With all that to keep her busy, she didn't think much about Julia these days. At least, that's what she told her friends and family. The truth was, she hadn't entirely been able to get Julia out of her mind. She assumed it was simply going to take time.

"So," continued Peter, absently scratching the side of his beard, "where's your pooch?" He clapped his hands. "Beany, where are you?"

"He's already over at Evelyn Bratrude's. She's going to take care of him while I'm gone."

"When do you leave?"

"We're catching an afternoon flight to New York. Octavia left her car at the airport, so she's going to drive us up to Connecticut. We'll arrive sometime tonight." She glanced over at her brother, wondering why he had such a faraway look in his eyes. "Hey, bro. You okay?"

"Me? Sure. Never better."

Jane knew her brother well enough to know he wasn't telling the truth. Sitting down next to him, she said, "You never did say why you stopped by." It was Wednesday. Normally, he'd be at work on Wednesday morning.

"Just to say bon voyage."

"You didn't know I was actually leaving until you got here."

He tried a smile, but it wasn't convincing. "We'll talk when you get back."

"No you don't. If you've got something to tell me, I want to hear it now. Is it about you and Sigrid? Have you two reached a decision?"

Jane's brother and his wife were having some problems. Peter desperately wanted to start a family, but Sigrid, having grown up taking care of her younger siblings, had no interest in motherhood—now, or at any time in the future. It was a matter they should have discussed before getting married, but for whatever reason, they hadn't. That omission and the battleground it created now dominated their relationship. Both had confided to Jane that they weren't sure the marriage would survive.

Peter looked down at his hands, then breathed in deeply. "It's not good news, Janey. The truth is . . . I left Sigrid this morning. Packed my bags, got in my car, and took off."

29

Even though Jane knew something like this might be coming, she was still shocked. "Left for good?"

"I don't know. We haven't talked about divorce, but I suppose that's the next step."

"But . . . your counseling sessions—"

"We're at an impasse. A counselor can't alter reality. I understand where she's coming from, and she understands me. I mean, I don't hate her. That's just the problem. I still love her. I want to spend the rest of my life with her. But . . . how do we compromise on a child? We've discussed every potential option and it always comes down to the same thing. We want to live very different lives."

Jane could hear the heartbreaking sadness in his voice. And the anger. He may not hate Sigrid, but he certainly hated the situation.

"I knew I was going to leave her before Christmas. It's just too painful to be together."

"But . . . I thought you two were spending the holidays in Montreal—like you did on your honeymoon."

He shook his head. "I'm sorry, Janey. I never meant to mislead you. Sigrid and I did toy with the idea for a while, but we never booked the trip. We both knew where we were headed. I can't tell you how glad I am that Dad and Marilyn decided to spend Christmas in New Orleans with her family this year. It gets me off the hook. I won't have to make any big explanations."

"Not until after New Year's."

He gave a weary nod. "But see, I got this crazy idea when I was getting ready to leave the apartment this morning."

When he didn't continue, she asked, "What idea?"

"It doesn't matter. You're going off to Connecticut. That will be good for you, Janey. A change of pace."

"Hey, if you need me—"

"No, really, I'll be fine. It was just a silly thought."

"Tell me."

He hesitated. "Well, see, I knew you and Cordelia planned to spend Christmas together at her loft, so I thought I'd stop by and ask the two of you to come up to the lodge with me. I figured we could all use some time away. I'd split up some wood in the barn. We'd build fires and roast marshmallows—just like when you and I were kids. Eat junk food. Sleep late. I thought the three of us could find the perfect tree in the woods, I'd chop it down, and then we'd decorate it together. Then, on Christmas Day, we could get wrecked and watch old movies."

"Peter, I had no idea—"

He took hold of her hand. "It's no problem, Janey. Really. I knew you might've made other plans. We haven't talked much lately. But with or without you, I'm still heading up to the lodge. I need to get away. Being out in the country will feel good."

Jane's family had owned a large cabin on Blackberry Lake since the early thirties. Many of her fondest childhood memories were of winter vacations spent there. Building snowmen. Playing hide and seek in the woods. Lying on her bed, reading *The Brothers Karamazov, Emma,* and *God Bless You, Mr. Rosewater.* Sitting by the fire in the evenings embroiled in a game of checkers. It sounded so idyllic now, and in many ways, it was. "What about your job? Can you get away?" Peter was a cameraman at WTWN-TV in Minneapolis.

"I'm taking some personal time. It's not a problem."

"And Sigrid? Does she know where you'll be?"

He nodded. "When I left she was in tears. She cried pretty much all night. God," he said, his gaze drifting away, "how could I have made such a mess of my life?"

"Look, Peter, maybe I should call Cordelia and tell her that I can't come."

"No." He squeezed her hand, then let go. "I wouldn't be much company for you, unless you just *love* being with depressed men. And besides, this trip will be fun for you. You deserve it. Your life hasn't exactly been wine and roses lately."

Jane had an idea. "What if you came to Connecticut with us? Cordelia would love it. She adores you."

He shook his head. "Thanks, but no thanks. I need time alone— time to think."

"But . . . if we came up to the lodge with you, you wouldn't be alone."

He smiled at her attempt to win him with logic. "I don't need to be in the middle of some wedding frenzy, Janey." He shuddered at the thought.

Okay. He was probably right. Still, she was torn.

"Listen, sis. You go and have a great time. I'll be fine. When you come back, maybe we'll build that fire and spend some time together."

"How long are you going to stay up at the lodge?"

"A few days."

"Where will you live when you get back to Minneapolis?"

"I hadn't thought that far ahead."

"Then you'll stay here. You've got a key, right?"

He nodded. "But——"

"It's settled. Hotel Lawless. A landmark of elegance in the Twin Cities since 1982."

When he smiled this time, Jane could tell he meant it.

Connecticut

5

The drive up to Innishannon took a couple of hours. It wasn't a pleasant experience. As soon as they'd left LaGuardia, Jane noticed that Octavia wasn't a particularly good driver. She was nervous and tended to take the straightaway slowly while speeding up on the curves. A light drizzle had been falling ever since they'd hit the outskirts of Stamford, so when they stopped for dinner in Bridgeport, Jane suggested that she drive the rest of the way, just to give Octavia a break. After a quick sandwich at a restaurant near the water, they started off again, following the interstate through the darkness. Cordelia, who'd wedged herself into the back seat of Octavia's Volvo C70, did her best to get comfortable, but had kept up a running patter all the way from New York City about the ridiculously small size of "some of these idiotic sports cars." Now, she seemed to quiet down.

After a few minutes, Octavia glanced into the backseat. "She's asleep. Finally. She's just like a baby. You feed her, she burps, then she needs a nap."

"I'm a little like that myself sometimes," said Jane, turning down the volume on the CD player. Perhaps Cordelia found the B-52's soothing, but she didn't.

Octavia fumbled around in the glove compartment until she found the map. After switching on a small light, she said, "New Haven is the next big town. After that, it's about thirty miles to Roland's estate."

Except for Cordelia's peaceful snoring, they rode in silence until they came to the Asbury exit. Octavia directed Jane through the main streets of the small town until they reached the Country Road 37 turnoff.

Ten minutes later, Octavia announced, "We're here," loudly enough to wake Sleeping Beauty in the back seat. "Turn in where it says Private Drive, just up ahead on your right. The iron gates are usually open. If you stay on the main road, we'll eventually run right into the house."

The paved estate road was a mass of potholes. This was to be Jane and Cordelia's inauspicious introduction to the once magnificent Innishannon.

"Hey," said Cordelia, bumping along in the backseat. "What's the deal? Doesn't your boyfriend pay his taxes?"

"The road is privately maintained," said Octavia.

"Maintained being the *in*operative word." Cordelia's auburn curls jerked in pothole rhythm as she rubbed the sleep out of her eyes. "I think I'm going to be sick."

"We're almost there," said Jane, swerving the car to avoid a particularly large hole.

After another bumpy few minutes, they reached the circular drive in front of the house. Jane parked the Volvo, then got out to stretch her legs. She'd been cooped up with two princesses since early afternoon and needed a breath of fresh air.

Seen from far away, Innishannon simply looked like a big house. But up this close, the massive structure had an almost medieval aura about it. Jane's eyes traveled along the outline of the building, a dark etching against an even darker sky. She counted eight gables of varying sizes, four separate chimneys, and dozens of tall mullioned windows. The mansion was everything she'd expected and more, and yet it was clearly run-down. Cracked and crumbling white stucco. Dark half-timbering that needed a good paint job. Beauty mixed with decay. A cozy glow came from inside, and yet the light by the front door hung at an odd angle, suggesting it was broken. There was nothing to welcome the weary traveler home.

"And so the drama begins," said Cordelia as she squeezed out of the backseat.

"The drama began a long time ago," muttered Octavia.

"Then, maybe this is where it will end."

Jane wasn't sure what they were talking about, but now wasn't the time to get into it. "I think we better unpack the trunk," she said, stepping around to the rear of the car.

"I guess," said Cordelia, gazing up at the house. After another few seconds, she turned back to Jane. "Hey, let the butler do that."

"There is no butler," said Octavia, pulling her camel hair coat more tightly around her thin body. She leaned against the front fender, her eyes fixed on a second-story window. For whatever reason, thought Jane, she wasn't rushing inside to greet her fiancé.

"A mansion without a butler?" blustered Cordelia.

"The staff is pretty minimal. That's the way Roland likes it."

"Are you saying that your millionaire boyfriend has . . . shall we say . . . a cheap streak?"

Instead of getting mad, Octavia laughed. "I've wondered about that myself."

"Well, the bags aren't going to walk inside by themselves," said Jane, tossing Cordelia her purse.

"Cordelia Thorn does not *haul*."

"We know," said Jane and Octavia in unison.

"In this case, you'll have to make one of your rare exceptions," said Jane, retrieving Octavia's overnight bag from the trunk. The last suitcase to come out was her own. Thank God, she'd packed light.

"Isn't there some exceedingly sweaty yet sensual stable boy around here who can take these up to our rooms?"

"You read too much D. H. Lawrence," said Octavia. She started up the steps with Jane and Cordelia in tow.

"At least tell me there's a maid."

"House manager. She manages the staff. Her name's Hilda Gettle. She's quite old—in her early seventies, I suppose. There's also a handyman who appears occasionally, and a guy who shovels the walks and plows the roads. They live in town."

"What about a cook?"

"Hilda again."

"And I suppose she mucks out the stables in her spare time."

"Roland shut down the stables years ago." Allowing her suitcase to thunk to the ground, Octavia used the brass door knocker to announce their arrival.

Cordelia continued to sputter. "How can an old woman clean this place *and* do the cooking?"

"She can't."

"So . . . what are you saying?"

Before Octavia could answer, the door was drawn back, revealing a startled Hilda Gettle in her bathrobe and slippers. With her hair done up in curlers and an oily liquid covering her face, it was hard to tell what she really looked like.

"Oh, Ms. Thorn. I wasn't expecting you. If I'd only known—"

"Didn't Roland get my fax?"

She seemed surprised. "He hasn't been home all day. I didn't go into his study because . . . well . . . with the extra guests in the house, I haven't had time." She glanced at Jane and Cordelia with trepidation. "Will you all be staying the night?"

Octavia made introductions, explaining that Jane and Cordelia would be remaining at Innishannon until after the wedding on Monday.

"Oh, dear," was all the old woman managed to squeak out. Except that she squeaked it twice, the second time with much more feeling.

After lugging their suitcases inside, Octavia took off her gloves and asked, "When do you expect Roland home?"

"I don't know." Hilda tugged at the tie on her bathrobe, looking embarrassed.

"Where did he go?"

"I don't know that either. You know Mr. Lester, Ms. Thorn. He's so very private. If he wants me to know something, he tells me. Otherwise, I don't pry."

Cordelia moved over next to Jane, lowered her head, and whispered out of the side of her mouth, "Sounds like a personality just *born* for divorce court."

"Well," said Octavia, slapping her leather gloves against her hand and looking around, "I guess we'll have to make the best of it."

"If you're hungry, there's some cold turkey and smoked salmon in the refrigerator. We had a bread delivery just this morning, so there's lots of fresh buns for sandwiches. Oh, and there's eggnog and Christmas cookies, compliments of our documentary person."

Octavia nodded. "Is she around? Ellie, I mean?"

Hilda spoke more quietly this time. "She came up for dinner, but she's taken up residence in the tack house. A man from the telephone company was here this afternoon. I think she had another phone line installed down there. Something about a computer." Lowering her voice even further, she added, "She said her crew would be arriving after the first of the year. I'm not looking forward to it. I don't know why Mr. Lester agreed to this documentary business. It sets my teeth on edge."

"And Christian?" asked Octavia. As an explanation, she added, "Christian is Lew Wallace's son. You remember Lew Wallace? The old actor?"

Cordelia nodded, her eyes traveling down the central hall, where photographs of Hollywood stars filled the walls.

"He comes every year for the holidays," continued Hilda. "He's been such a help to me today. He even made dinner for the five of us tonight. Omelettes and roasted potatoes. He's up in his room now. He said he had a headache and might go to bed early."

"And Gracie? That's Roland's grandniece," said Octavia, amused by Cordelia's obvious interest in the photo gallery.

"Oh, I assume she's up in her third floor lair. I don't know what that child does up there all day, but she keeps busy."

"Well, I'm sorry we surprised you," said Octavia, giving her gloves one final slap against her hand. "I'll make sure my guests get settled in tonight. Don't worry about a thing."

"There's a bedroom in the east wing, facing the sound—that one's all ready. And then, in the west wing, the room just down the hall from Mr. Lester's study is all made up." Giving Jane a knowing nod, she added, "Unexpected visitors at this time of year aren't unusual. You never know when one of Mr. Lester's friends from the old days might drop in. I like to have extra food in the house, just in case."

"That's good of you," said Octavia. She was about to head up the central stairs when she stopped and turned around. "I have to say, I find it hard to believe that Roland would just take off—not tell anyone where he went. You really have no idea when he'll be back?"

"None."

"Is Buddy around?"

"He was, but he left after dinner. He has a meeting in New York tomorrow. Something to do with the wedding. You have to understand, Ms. Thorn. Sometimes Mr. Lester can be absent for days. I realized he hasn't been gone once since you've been staying with us, but it's not unusual. It's just the way he is."

Jane could tell this penchant for disappearing didn't sit well with Octavia.

After thanking the old woman, Octavia turned and led the way up the broad, carpeted stairs. Over her shoulder she called, "If he gets back tonight, will you tell him I need to talk to him right away?"

"Oh, I'll do that," said Hilda, switching off all the downstairs lights for the night.

With the old wooden stairs creaking under their weight, Cordelia bent close to Jane again and whispered, "The no light policy's got to be more of Roland's austerity program. My sister, the last of the big spenders, is going to have a simply marvelous time being married to Ebenezer Scrooge. I give it a month."

6

Jane woke suddenly to the sound of footsteps in the hall outside her room. Leaping out of bed, her heart pounding, her pulse racing, she tried to orient herself in the dark. She grabbed the travel clock off the nightstand and saw that it was just after two in the morning. She'd been having another one of her bad dreams. Running a hand through her hair, she sat back down on the bed, trying to calm her nerves. She supposed it was possible that Cordelia was up for her two o'clock feeding, but since they'd both had a turkey sandwich and a beer before they turned in around midnight, it seemed unlikely.

Switching on the lamp next to her bed, she found her slippers, tied her robe snugly, then tiptoed over to the door and opened it a crack. Tiny, diamond-shaped metal wall sconces provided the central hallway's only light. She took a moment to get her bearings. She knew Cordelia's room was all the way on the other end of the house. Octavia's bedroom adjoined Roland's somewhere in the middle. Beyond that, she had no idea what was behind the rest of the closed doors, although she re-membered Hilda's comment that Roland's study was just down the hall from Jane's room. Thinking that the master of the house might have finally returned, Jane crept away from her bedroom door. She merely wanted to observe, not be observed.

The dark, carpeted passage made her feel as if she were in an ancient cathedral full of vague echoes and gloomy shadows, a place where any noise would register not only as clumsiness, but sacrilege. The house had the ancient, musty smell of an old church. As she passed a rather flamboyant, round, Deco mirror, she glanced at her image. The face she saw looking back at her stopped her cold. Backing up, she studied her reflection for a moment.

Several weeks ago, feeling the need for a change, Jane had cut her long, chestnut hair short. She was sure it had been a mistake. For days she felt like hiding in her house and never coming out. But tonight, gazing at this strangely new creature, she wasn't so sure it had been such a bad idea. She actually liked what she saw.

Her eyes looked much larger now. Large and soft, and filled with . . . what? The frankness was still there. So was the humor. But there was something else—a new texture, or perhaps a quality that had gone missing. She struggled to define it, but couldn't, and for some reason that inability frightened her, as if she were staring into the face of a stranger.

"Mirror mirror on the wall," she whispered, realizing how silly she must look. She'd never been the kind of person who worried much about her appearance, so this nocturnal inspection was out of character. And yet she knew that what she'd lived through during the past few months had somehow altered her conception of who she was. If she could feel the change inside, it had to be reflected in her face. "So what's wrong with my universe?" she whispered, trying to make sense of this new, foreign world, a place where nothing was quite the same as it used to be.

She stood in quiet contemplation for a few more minutes, but her lack of clarity frustrated her. Continuing on down the passage, she stopped suddenly when she heard a noise. Not footsteps this time, but a faint clicking. She couldn't imagine what was causing it, but it appeared to be coming from a room about ten feet away on the other side of the corridor. As she moved closer, she realized a dim light was coming from inside.

Trying to be as unobtrusive as possible, Jane edged cautiously into the open doorway. Her caution turned out to be wasted. The woman standing behind the desk was so caught up in her own work that she seemed unaware of anything else around her. She just kept turning pages in an old photograph album, then aiming her tiny camera and clicking.

Jane leaned against the door jamb and watched. The woman was certainly being thorough, though she did skip certain photos, sometimes whole pages. She was after something definite, all right, and wasn't wasting any time getting the shots she wanted. If Jane had to guess, she'd say this was Roland's study, and the woman was the documentary artist, the one who'd come to Innishannon to do a film of the director's life. Apparently, the woman also liked to burn the midnight oil—or, perhaps this little photographic expedition hadn't been authorized. Whatever the case, Jane found herself instantly fascinated.

As the woman bent to take more pictures, the desk lamp threw a wedge of yellow light against the side of her face. Jane put her age at somewhere in the mid-forties. She was attractive in a ruddy, athletic sort of way, with unruly copper-colored hair and a broad, friendly face that was full of concentration at the moment. She was dressed casually in jeans and an old Stanford sweatshirt. Once she'd turned the last page in the photograph album, she put the camera away in a leather case, then turned to examine one of the filing cabinets. She tugged on each of the drawers, but found them all locked.

"Damn," she whispered, brushing a thick shock of hair away from her forehead. She sat down in the chair, her attention suddenly caught by a large framed photo on the wall.

Jane crooked her neck to view the picture herself. It was a commercially done photograph of Roland Lester with an attractive woman about the same age, and a little girl. No doubt a family photo.

The woman stared at it for almost a minute, then stretched her arms high over her head and lost interest. Shuffling some papers into a briefcase, she started to get up, but stopped when she saw Jane standing in the doorway. Her body tensed. It might have been simple surprise, but Jane thought she detected something more.

"How long have you been standing there?" the woman asked casually, stuffing the briefcase with one last folder.

She lied. "Not long. I was looking for the bathroom."

"It's right down the hall. Two doors on your left."

"Thanks."

Attempting a friendly smile, though keeping her voice just above a whisper, the woman said, "I haven't seen you here before. My name's Ellie Saks." Looking as if more explanation might be needed, she added, "I'm doing a documentary on Roland Lester."

"And you like to work late."

"Sometimes." She hesitated, then asked, "You here for the holidays or the wedding?"

"Both. My name's Jane Lawless. I'm a friend of Cordelia Thorn's, Octavia's older sister. We just got in a few hours ago."

"I'm here for the duration, too. Actually," she continued, "Lester's asked me to shoot the wedding as a personal favor to him. I could hardly say no. I may be wrong, but I think he plans to direct the footage, with me doing the camera work. We've already been to the church and talked about specific shots and camera angles. I mean, can't you just *see* it? Octavia says, 'I do,' but then she stops and says, 'I need a second take. What's my motivation here, Roland?' He hollers, 'Cut!' The minister calls for makeup. The script girl runs in. The producer— that would be Roland's brother, Buddy—screams that the production is going over budget." Ellie was clearly amused by her scenario.

Jane found it pretty funny herself.

"When all the footage is in the can, Lester says he's going to edit it himself. It's kind of a strange approach to holy matrimony, if you ask me, but then he's used to viewing the world in manageable scenes captured on celluloid. From my standpoint, it will be a real coup. I mean, how many people my age can say they've worked with Roland Lester?" She walked around the front of the desk and sat down on the edge.

Since she didn't seem to be in a hurry to leave, Jane asked, "I don't suppose you know where he is? When we found out he wasn't home this evening, Octavia was pretty upset."

Ellie shrugged. "I figured he went off to buy his bride a wedding gift. I know he's very excited about the forthcoming marriage."

Jane's eyes rose to the peeling wallpaper.

Ellie followed her gaze. "Yeah, the place is kind of a disaster. That surprised me too."

"I wonder why he's allowed such a magnificent house to fall into such a state of disrepair. Doesn't make sense."

"Actually, I did a little digging and there is a reason. His daughter, Peg, died several years back. She was a highly successful independent producer and was shooting on location in Egypt at the time. Apparently, a scaffolding she was standing on collapsed. Five people died, including Peg. It really threw Lester into a tailspin. He fired most of the staff, shut himself up in his house, and lost interest in life. One of the few people he kept around was Hilda Gettle—and, of course, his brother. I guess Lester and his daughter were pretty close. It was a real tragedy."

Jane hadn't known. "I'm sorry. I didn't realize. What about his wife?" She nodded to the portrait on the wall.

"They were divorced a long time ago. It's just been in the past year or two that Lester seemed to take an interest in life again. I assume that's due to Octavia. Actually, the first time I contacted him about doing a documentary on his film career was in February of 'ninety-eight. He wouldn't even talk about it. But when we tried again this fall, he said yes. He seemed almost eager. I guess that's what love can do."

"You really think it's a love match?"

Again, she shrugged. "Whatever it is, Lester's walking on air, and that means he's been highly cooperative about working with me. We've already done a number of preliminary interviews—all of them tape recorded. And he's given me access to all of his papers."

Maybe that was true, thought Jane, or maybe it wasn't. Whatever the case, she didn't have a key to his files. Perhaps it was just Jane's suspicious nature working overtime, but she felt there might be more here than met the eye.

"My production crew should arrive shortly after Lester and his new bride return from their honeymoon. In the meantime, I've got plenty of work to do." Rising from the edge of the desk, Ellie grabbed her briefcase and crossed to the door.

Once out in the hallway, she pointed to an open door and whispered, "That's the bathroom. There's another one around the corner, on the other end of the house."

"This place is so big, it's confusing."

"You'll figure out your way around tomorrow. If you get seriously lost, I'm staying down at the tack house—it's right next to the stables. Depending on which road you took in from the highway, you might have seen it. It gets kind of lonely down there, so even if you're not lost, I'd enjoy the company."

"Thanks," said Jane. "Night." As she watched Ellie cross to the stairs and start down, she saw a piece of paper flutter to the ground behind her. She took a step toward it, but stopped herself, waiting until Ellie was gone. Only then did she walk over to pick it up. If it was important, she could return it to her in the morning. For now, she felt it might be a good chance to see what the mysterious Ellie Saks was working on.

Once back in her room, Jane slipped on her reading glasses and sat down on the bed. Holding the paper near the lamp, she saw that it was a xeroxed copy of a newspaper article. On the top of the page someone had written, "*Los Angeles Examiner,* July 24, 1957." In bold letters, the headline read:

Hollywood Pays Final Homage to Lew Wallace

On Wednesday afternoon at Santa Monica's Good Shepherd Presbyterian Church, one of Hollywood's true greats was honored at a funeral ceremony attended by hundreds of his friends and loyal fans.

Lew Wallace, 49, star of some seventy movies from the mid-thirties through the early fifties, was laid to his final rest. Among his most notable films were *The Marrying Crowd, For Love or Money, Goodbye, My Love,* and *The Shadow Palace,* also starring his longtime costar and friend, Verna Lange. He won an Oscar in 1947 for his portrayal of Joey Midnight in the movie, *Heat of the Sun.*

Director and longtime friend, Roland Lester, gave the eulogy, calling Wallace, "A man of dignity and rare courage. He was the best man at my wedding, and the best friend I ever had."

The burial took place late Wednesday afternoon during a private ceremony at Forrest Lawn.

Lew Wallace was found shot in his Beverly Hills home on Saturday, July 21st. No further information has been released by the police concerning the details of Mr. Wallace's murder.

"Murder?" whispered Jane, startled by the word. Roland Lester's best friend was murdered?

7

By the time Cordelia made it downstairs the next morning, it was close to eleven. She'd never been an early riser, and couldn't think of a good reason why she should get up with the birds today. Walking through the downstairs like a general surveying the troops, she was surprised to find the entire house engulfed in a cleaning frenzy. Crews of men and women were scrubbing floors, vacuuming drapes, washing, polishing, waxing, and sweeping. Also, several repairmen were touching up some of the worst of the peeling plaster and water damage. The smells of mildew and ancient cigarette smoke were quickly being re-placed by the scents of turpentine and paint, Lysol and lemon wax. The transformation was nothing short of a miracle.

In the midst of it all, halfway between the breakfast room and so-larium, both of which had glorious views of Long Island Sound, Cordelia found her sister conversing with a dapper middle-aged man about the Christmas decorations he and his crew were apparently going to bring out to the house tomorrow. Octavia waved to Cordelia, but continued pointing at various locations and asking for suggestions.

Cordelia strolled around for a few more minutes, mainly looking for Jane, but when she couldn't stand the uproar another minute, she re-treated to the dining room, the only quiet place she could find in the entire house.

Noticing a series of silver chafing dishes on the sideboard, she rubbed her hands together in anticipation of an elegant breakfast. She lifted the cover off the first and found that it was filled with watery-looking scrambled eggs. Dropping the cover with distaste, she moved onto the second. It was brimming with burned sausages and bacon. The third contained hash browns resting in a good quarter inch of oil, and the fourth, toast, thoroughly steamed. If Hilda Gettle was responsible for this catastrophe, thought Cordelia, she should be tied to a chair and forced to eat it—every last ill-prepared morsel. And if that didn't finish her off, Cordelia might just do the job herself.

Pouring herself a cup of coffee and a glass of orange juice, she sat down at the long polished table and saluted the silver candlesticks. "Welcome to Innishannon," she said out loud, emptying her juice glass in several quick gulps. As she pulled the cream and sugar in front of her, a gaunt, stone-faced young man in a white chef's uniform trudged through the pantry doors intent on checking the heat under each dish. "Can I get you anything else?" he asked, after he'd accomplished his mission.

"Under the circumstances, a bowl of gruel might be appropriate."

"Gruel?"

"What about Pop Tarts?"

"Sorry."

"Cold cereal?"

"I think there's a box of cornflakes in the cupboard."

"Fine. Whatever. By the way, who *are* you?"

"The new cook. Just started this morning."

She sat back and looked him over. "What's your name?"

"Leonard."

"Whrere's Mrs. Gettle"

"You mean Hilda? Ms. Thorn gave her the day off. Said that with all the extra work because of the holidays and the wedding, she needed to take it easy."

"Did she now?"

"I heard Ms. Thorn say she'd arranged for a massage and a manicure for her in New Haven this afternoon."

Cordelia wondered what Octavia was up to. Nothing with that sister of hers was ever simple or straightforward. Getting Gettle out of the way today might seem to be a kindness, but if Octavia was about to take over the reigns of the house and force her out, it wasn't quite the deal it appeared to be on the surface. "I wonder if you'd ask my sister to come join me in here for a few minutes."

48

"You mean Hilda? Sorry, but she left right after breakfast."

Cordelia turned to face him. "Do I *look* like Hilda is my sister?"

"Well, no. You look more like—"

"Careful, Lenny."

"I prefer Leonard."

"Finish your sentence."

"All I was going to say was that you looked more like Cher—but . . . well, a Cher that sort of likes her chocolate eclairs, if you know what I mean."

She raised an eyebrow. "F.Y.I., Leonard, Octavia Thorn is my sister. Take your foot out of your mouth and go find her. Tell her she's needed in the dining room."

"Yes, ma'am. Right away, ma'am." He made a quick exit.

"Moron," she muttered, watching him dart out of the room.

When Octavia entered the room a few minutes later, she looked positively flushed with excitement. "What did you do to my new cook, Cordelia? The poor man's stuttering." Pouring herself a cup of coffee, she sat down at the table.

"I can't imagine. I am, as always, the picture of sweetness and light. Are you planning to fire Hilda?"

"Heavens, no. Where did you get that idea?"

"Lurch."

"Excuse me?"

"The guy from the Addams Family. Your new cook—and I use that term loosely. What's next, Octavia? Hilda sitting by the fire, wondering what happened to her job while the Happy Chef is off in the kitchen accidentally sautéing his hat? Before she knows it, she'll be out on the front stoop with her luggage and we'll be starving."

"Why do you always think the worst of me?"

"*I* think the worst of *you*? Ever since we were kids, you told all your friends I was a witch."

"Well, *witchy*, yes. You are." An amused look passed over her face. "Oh, come on. I'm in a good mood today. Don't spoil it."

Stirring a little more cream into her coffee, Cordelia asked, "I don't suppose you know where Jane is this morning."

"She borrowed my car, said something about needing to do some Christmas shopping. I suggested she drive back to Asbury. It has lots of nice boutiques."

Cordelia wished Jane had left her a note. Oh, well. She probably wouldn't be gone long. "Heard anything from your fiancé?"

The good humor in Octavia's face faded instantly. "No. Nothing. But I will. He'll be back today, I'm sure of it."

"Aren't you afraid that when he sees all the money you're spending to spruce up the place, he's going to have a heart attack? Or was that the plan?"

"Stuff the jokes, okay? Can't you see I'm worried about him?"

She did look as if she hadn't slept much, thought Cordelia. "Okay, maybe I am being a little insensitive."

"A little?"

"I'm sorry. He's your boyfriend. I've never even met the man."

Octavia held Cordelia's eyes for a few seconds, then dropped her gaze to her coffee. "I don't know him all that well, either."

"Look, forgive me for asking, but why am I here—really?" Cordelia had just about had it with all the mystery. "You said you wanted to mend fences. You insisted I put our problems aside so that I could be in your wedding. You tantalized me with the notion of meeting the great Roland Lester. You bribed me with the thought of a Broadway show. You hinted at surprises that would blow me away, but refused to be specific. You hemmed, you hawed, you wheedled and begged. You played shamelessly on my curiosity, my generous nature, and virtually every vanity I possess without telling me the one thing I wanted to know. Why the hell did you come to my loft and demand that I come back here with you?"

"I didn't demand."

"Do we have to quibble about words?"

Lowering her voice to Cordelia's natural register, Octavia said, "Cordelia Thorn *does not quibble*."

Cordelia did a double take. "When did you learn to do that? Mimic me?"

"Oh, come on. I've been doing you for years. I used to keep all my friends in stitches."

Cordelia wasn't sure what to say. In a strange way, she was flattered. "You're very good," she said, eying Octavia with newfound respect.

"Thanks."

"But you didn't answer my question."

Glancing furtively around the room, Octavia rose and drew shut the arched double doors separating the dining room from the front foyer. "Want more coffee?" she asked on the way back to the table.

"I want an answer." Cordelia watched Octavia's reflection in the mirror, seeing her stick her tongue out. "You know, Tallulah, if the rest of the world knew how you behaved offstage, I doubt you'd ever be cast in a truly adult role again."

"Ah, I sometimes forget you're a theatrical director now. You probably don't like actors much. You think we're all children. Blah, blah, blah. I've heard it all a million times."

"I wouldn't say all actors were children," said Cordelia, making a bridge of her fingers. "However . . . may I be blunt?"

Octavia waved her hand, motioning for her to continue.

"All actors have hard-ons about themselves. It comes with the territory. You're no different."

"Right. Sure. Whatever you say."

"And you're changing the subject again. You were about to enlighten me?"

Sitting down in her chair, Octavia crossed her legs, then recrossed them, unable to get comfortable. "You're going to think I'm silly."

"Probably."

"But I'm not."

"Just *tell* me. Look, remember when we were kids and you had a problem you wouldn't talk to anyone about, which happened at least once a week. It was always the end of the world. Everything was a cataclysm. You never said anything, but I always knew when you were one step away from total meltdown."

Octavia gave a grudging nod.

"Don't you remember? I can handle anything from attic monsters to how to get Gary Prather to ask you for a date."

"You told *me* to ask *him*."

"There you are. An elegant solution."

Smiling ever so slightly, Octavia said, "I wish you really did have a few good answers."

"I do. I've even added some new ones to my repertoire over the years."

"Well, to be honest . . . I . . . think I may have gotten in way over my head this time and I don't know what to do about it. I needed someone here who's on my side."

"That would be me?"

Octavia shot her sister a disgusted look. "Yes, that would be you."

"And Jane."

"Right. The people in this house are watching me, Cordelia. They aren't my friends. None of them wants me to marry Roland."

"And you know this how?"

"I just know, okay? Call it intuition. And it's getting on my nerves. Sometimes I think they almost hate me, that they'd like me to disappear in a big puff of smoke!" She flung her arms into the air.

"Indulge me for a second. Are you familiar with the term 'paranoia'?"

"I'm telling the truth!"

"Okay, okay. Who hates you? Be specific."

"Well, Hilda for one. She never liked me from the beginning. I had to get her out of here today, otherwise she would have been on my case about everything. Whenever I want to make even the slightest change in the house, she takes it as a personal insult. It's intolerable."

"All right. Who else hates you?"

"Well, Gracie's been okay, I guess. At least she talks to me like a human being. But then there's Christian Wallace. When he arrived, I felt positively invaded. He watches me all the time from behind those tinted glasses of his. Oh, he acts all nice and gentlemanly when he's in a group, but when he knows Roland's not around, he's come on to me like a bull in heat. I find him . . . disgusting. How can I tell Roland what a creep he is? From what Gracie told me, Roland thinks of him as a son. But the worst of it is Roland's brother, Buddy—he's Gracie's grandfather. Roland is devoted to him. Sure, he seems nice enough on the surface, says he wants me to confide in him, think of him as a friend, but it's too much. He presses too hard. Trust me, that man's got so many faces, if we were onstage, I wouldn't know which one to upstage. If anything ever happened to Roland, he'd chase me out of here with a loaded shotgun. Or maybe he'd just shoot me and be done with it."

"You don't think you might be exaggerating . . . just a wee bit?"

"No!"

"Then leave."

"What?"

"Pack your bags and leave. You don't need to stay here. Get married in New York. I'll admit that Innishannon's kind of compelling, in a Daphne Du Maurier sort of way, but find someplace new to live. Someplace the two of you can call home, without all the relatives and friends cluttering up the hallways."

Octavia closed her eyes and looked away. "I can't."

"Why not?"

"Because I made a promise, one I can't break."

"A promise to Lester?"

"Yes . . . partly."

"Why can't you ever give me a straight answer? Do you really need this kind of melodrama in your life?"

"Hey, talk about the pot calling the kettle black."

"Are you comparing me to a *pot?*"

"I'm certainly not comparing you to a summer day."

"Why don't you just tell me what's really going on around here? You and Lester aren't in love. If it's the money—"

"It's not money."

"Then what?"

"I can't tell you! But you've got to promise me you won't leave me here all alone. You remember what you said when I arrived at your loft? You said, 'Little Octavia gets herself in over her head and what does she do? She comes to her big sister to bail her out.' Well, you were right. I know I've done it in the past, and I'm doing it again. The fact is, even with everything that's gone down between us, I don't trust anyone else the way I trust you. That's nuts, isn't it? We haven't spoken in years. We've always been jealous of each other's achievements, jockeyed to be number one in our parents' eyes, but you're the only person I know I can count on when I'm in trouble. And I'm in trouble big time right now, Cordelia."

Carefully folding her napkin and laying it down next to her coffee cup, Cordelia said, "You know, Octavia, the truly bad problems began when you *stopped* talking—to me or anyone else. I wish you'd come to me before Mom died. Maybe I could have helped. Maybe she'd still be alive."

Octavia leaned her head against her hand. "Let's not start in about that again. I can't take it today. You know how sorry I am. If I say it a hundred more times, it won't come out any differently. Okay, so you'll never forgive me. I accept that. But . . . don't leave me now, not when I need you so badly."

There was real desperation in her eyes. "Okay," sighed Cordelia. "You caught me at a weak moment. I seem to be having a lot of them lately. I promise. I won't leave."

"And you'll be my eyes and ears when I'm not around?"

"It would help me if I knew *why* you were marrying that man."

"I'll tell you, I promise. As soon as the wedding's over. I'll be free to tell the whole world in less than a week. And then, as far as I'm concerned, everyone in this house can rot."

8

After an early breakfast at a sunny cafe on the outskirts of Asbury, Jane spent the rest of the morning shopping. The town's main drag was like something out of a picture book. Painted clapboard buildings lined both sides of the narrow street, with quaint wooden signs hanging off metal rods jutting out from just above the front doors. None of the structures were over three stories tall, and most were adorned with pine bows and Christmas decorations.

The town was bustling today with shoppers, so Jane felt lucky to find a parking spot. She pulled Octavia's Volvo up next to an odd, narrow building that served as the town's book shop. She spent a good hour browsing the shelves before turning her attention to the gift shop next door.

Around one, feeling the need for a pick-me-up, she carted her shopping bags back to the car, then looked around for a coffee shop. Halfway down the opposite side of the street, she found a sign that said "The Cyber Grind: Connecticut's First Cyber Coffeetorium." A cold wind was blowing off the water, which made the idea of getting inside a building, any building, even more attractive. When she peeked through the front window she found a surprisingly spacious room filled with people sitting at oil-cloth covered tables. A row of cubicles ran across the back wall, each containing a computer.

After ordering herself a double mocha, she was curious how the computer set-up worked, so she asked a man wiping off the tables how much it cost to use the Internet. He explained that access was six bucks an hour. The time was prorated, so you only got charged for exactly the time you used. Since she had nothing better to do, she thought she'd surf while she sipped.

Once she'd logged on to Netscape, it occurred to her that it might be interesting to see if she could locate some information on the murder of Lew Wallace, Roland's old Hollywood friend. Ellie Saks was obviously researching the story. Jane figured it might be worth a few minutes of her time to check it out. She tried several different search engines. Finally, through Yahoo, she located a rather extensive article written by a man named Arthur Burnside. He'd been a book reviewer for the *Los Angeles Times,* as well as an editor at HarperCollins, San Francisco. And his passion was movie history. The name of the article was "Mayhem in Tinseltown." The piece was divided into nine sections, with the murder of Lew Wallace discussed in section three.

Jane had no idea so many Hollywood actors had died violently or under suspicious circumstances. The chapters read like a Who's Who of Hollywood stardom and included such people as: Marilyn Monroe; the silent screen actor, Ramon Novarro; the fifties bad boy, Sal Mineo; aspiring actress Elizabeth Short, also known as the The Black Dahlia; the Roscoe (Fatty) Arbuckle affair; the director, William Desmond Taylor; actors Gig Young, Nick Adams, Bob Crane, and George Reeves; the infamous Manson Family murder of Sharon Tate; Dorothy Stratten, the subject of Bob Fosse's film; and Rebecca Shaffer, shot to death in 1989 by a deranged fan.

The section on Wallace was the most interesting to Jane, partly because he was such a close friend of Roland Lester's, but mostly because his was one of the murders that had never been solved.

Since his last film, *The Woolcrest Affair,* released in 1952, Lew Wallace had become a recluse. Though he was never officially blacklisted during the late forties and early fifties, several MGM executives later said he'd ruffled enough studio feathers that a campaign of character assassination had been started against him. His early friendship with Charlie Chaplin, as well as his continued friendship with both Howard DeSilva and Ring Lardner, Jr. put him in "suspicious and subversive" company, particularly in a town that was already halfway between paranoia and panic. The House on Un-American Activities

Committee, a group of gung-ho congressmen dedicated to stopping Communist infiltration into the country at large, and the film industry in specific, was in full swing. The fact that Wallace was a decorated war hero made no difference to these purveyors of innuendo.

Wallace, who'd been divorced from his wife for many years and living in the guest house at Roland Lester's Beverly Hills estate, had bought his own home in 1953, the same place where he was later murdered. At the time of the move, Hollywood scuttlebutt insisted that Wallace was romantically involved with several women, young actresses, though he was unwilling to take the marital plunge again. It took many years for the real story to come out.

It seemed that Wallace and Verna Lange, his costar in a number of highly successful films from 1946 through 1951, had been lovers even before Wallace's divorce in '49, but because Lange was still married to her second husband, the two of them had lived together secretly in Lester's guest house. It was an entirely private arrangement, one that was hinted at in the gossip columns but never openly discussed, and one that went on for years. Lange never confirmed the truth of the rumor, although she did admit in a 1997 interview with Connie Chung that she'd once been very much in love with Lew Wallace.

After Wallace moved into his new home, he told friends and family that he planned to start work on a novel. Others insisted it was an autobiography. But everyone agreed that it was a way to save face. For an actor at the peak of his powers, the fact that he was no longer being offered scripts must have cut deeply. Since he didn't seem to be the kind of man who could simply idle away his time, he had to justify his days somehow. It came out later that no one really believed he was actually writing a book, it was just a convenient cover. Many of his closest friends suggested that Wallace had fallen into a black depression. He was rarely seen out socially anymore, and never entertained himself. Jane could only imagine how awful it must have been—losing a prosperous career to innuendo and political smears. More than one friend was quoted as saying that Wallace was one of the most apolitical people in Hollywood. He not only had no interest in politics, he rarely even voted. To suggest that he was a covert Communist was as appalling as it was silly.

57

On the night of July 21st, 1957, the police were called to Lew Wallace's home, a one-story Spanish-style bungalow on Myrtle Drive. They were met at the door by the director, Roland Lester, who was in a state of near hysteria. In an official statement later given to the police, Lester claimed that he and Wallace had made plans earlier in the day to have dinner together that night. When Wallace failed to show up at the restaurant by 8:30, Lester phoned his house thinking that perhaps he'd forgotten. When he didn't reach him, he thought something might be wrong, so he'd driven directly to the bungalow and let himself in by using the extra key Wallace kept under a potted hibiscus on the back patio.

Lester stated that when he got inside, he found the house dark and quiet. He made a quick search and found Wallace in the den, lying face down on the Oriental carpet in front of his desk. When he turned him over, he saw a massive open wound in his chest, a pool of sticky, dark blood underneath. As he was about to feel for a pulse, Wallace's eyes fluttered open. Lester said that he seemed disoriented and terribly weak, but was struggling to say something. Bending down close to his mouth, Lester heard what he thought were the words, "Gideon, dumb sonofabitch. Never had a chance." And then he closed his eyes and stopped breathing. Lester said he immediately felt for a pulse, but knew it was no use. Wallace was gone. He got up and called the police, then took another look around the house to see if he could determine what had happened. Finally, unable to make any sense of the horror, he knelt back down next to his friend's body. He remained there until the police arrived.

The autopsy showed that Lew Wallace had died from a .38 caliber gunshot wound to his chest. The range was close—possibly just a few feet. The bullet missed the heart but hit an artery and he bled to death fairly quickly. The house showed no signs of a struggle or a forced entry, and no weapon was found at the scene. A woman's dress, undergarments, and bathrobe were discovered in one of the bedrooms, but no woman ever came forward to claim them. At the time, forensic evidence couldn't pinpoint the owner.

One of his neighbors said that Wallace had been arguing with a man earlier in the day. Shouts were heard from an open window in the kitchen. Another neighbor said that he'd seen Wallace's son, Christian, leave the house sometime during the late afternoon, but

Christian denied it, insisting he'd spent the entire day at his fiancée's house in Malibu. When his alibi checked out, any suspicion that might have fallen on him was dismissed.

An intriguing piece of evidence the police were never able to follow up on was a statement given by a fourteen-year-old boy, one Sam Robles, who happened to be biking by the house around 9 P.M. on the night in question, shortly before the police arrived at the scene. He said that he stopped next to a tree on the boulevard to check the air in his rear tire when he noticed someone leaving the house by the back door. Since it was getting dark, the boy couldn't give much of a description. He wouldn't even have remembered the incident except that the person was acting so furtively. He or she ducked under an arbor covered in bougainvillea, then tossed what looked like a leather satchel over a low fence. Once on the other side, the person looked around to make sure nobody was watching, then picked up the satchel and took off at a dead run.

For the next few months, over vehement protests from Roland Lester's attorneys, Lester himself became the primary focus of the police investigation. After an intense round of interrogations and a flurry of evidence gathering, it became increasingly clear that Lester could not have fired a gun at such a close range and been so free of blood himself. Since no motive could be established, and no weapon found, the investigation into Lester's involvement was finally dropped. The murder case was never officially closed, but with no more leads to follow, the police eventually had no choice but to move on to more pressing matters.

The article went on to explain that many people over the years had attempted to solve the mystery, but with little success. Wallace did have his share of enemies, as did anyone who'd been in Hollywood for over three decades, but no one person ever stood out as having any particular grudge against him, especially one strong enough to motivate murder. Suspicion for the crime always seemed to come back to three people: Roland Lester, Christian Wallace, and Verna Lange. These three were the closest to Wallace during his last days, and if they weren't involved in the actual homicide, it was a fair guess that they knew more than they were telling.

One of the police officers who'd worked the crime early on

suggested that because Wallace and Lester were about the same size, Lester could have shot him, removed his clothes, washed himself clean in the bathroom or kitchen sink, then put on some of Wallace's clothes and disposed of his own before the police got there. But when no evidence was ever found to corroborate the theory, it was discarded.

The last part of the section on Wallace dealt with speculation on motive and the details of the crime. Conjecture about the actor's last words, "Gideon, dumb sonofabitch. Never had a chance," had become almost a cottage industry in the late fifties. Hundreds of people wrote to the editors of their local newspapers purporting to have the answer. Columnists all over the country took up the challenge, weighing in with their two cents. Articles in magazines appeared, and several books were written about the unsolved homicide. Jane couldn't believe she'd never heard of the case, but then she didn't know anything about the Fatty Arbuckle affair or the murder of William Desmond Taylor either. She imagined that it would be another professional coup if Ellie Saks could get Lester to shed some new light on the old murder.

In the end, the author of "Mayhem in Tinseltown" reported that no one could ever agree on who Gideon was. Some suggested it was Matthew Gideon, a silent screen actor who'd befriended Wallace when he first came to Hollywood. But Matthew Gideon had been dead for years. Others thought Wallace had been referring to Gideon James, a wardrobe designer at Paramount, but James vehemently denied that he'd ever met Wallace. A few people went so far as to suggest that the name Gideon was a direct reference to the Gideon Bible, that with his dying breath, Wallace had attempted to make the point that religion never had a chance in "Sin City." Most rejected this notion out of hand.

The most promising line of speculation, at least according to Arthur Burnside, dealt with the book Wallace may have been writing before his death. If it had been an autobiography, some speculated that he may have been using it to get even, to take his revenge on the person or persons who had started the innuendo campaign against him. Many people talked about the enmity between Wallace and Billy Cannon, an executive at Warner Brothers. Their feud was no secret, but it also didn't seem to be a motive for murder. Some suggested that Wallace may have inadvertently included information in his book that might have been considered libelous, or exposed someone's closely guarded secret. Whatever the case, no copy of the book was ever found.

Roland Lester continued to insist that Wallace never sat down and wrote so much as a single sentence of a novel or an autobiography, and when Verna Lange seconded the opinion, the public at large was left with only two options. Either Lester and Lange were telling the truth, and if so, the book theory was a blind alley, or they were lying. If they were lying, it was a fair guess that they were doing so because they had something to do with the murder. In the end, all the speculation went nowhere. The Wallace homicide was a question without an answer. And the only people who might know the truth weren't talking.

Jane made a few quick notes before she logged off, thinking that Cordelia might be interested in what she'd learned. After all, Octavia was about to marry a man who'd been strongly implicated in a notorious homicide. It hardly seemed likely that a forty-year-old murder would get cleared up just in time for the wedding, so for all practical purposes, Roland was still a suspect, and would remain one, probably forever.

The smell of chocolate chip cookies drew Jane back to the front counter. When she asked to buy one, she was told that if she waited a few minutes, a new batch was about to come out of the oven. She ordered a cup of regular coffee with a shot of espresso and took it over to a table by the window to wait. A cookie would be brought to her as soon as they were ready.

Glancing absently out at the street, she was surprised to find a strange man standing next to Octavia's Volvo. After looking the car over, he bent down and peered into the driver's side window, then tried the door handle. She couldn't see his face very well because he was wearing dark glasses and a hat with a broad brim. He was dressed in a heavy coat and carried a black walking stick with a shiny gold handle. He might not look like a thief, but he had no business messing with Octavia's car. After a few more seconds he turned his back and walked across the street, disappearing into the Heritage Pub. Jane found his interest faintly unsettling.

When she looked in the other direction, she noticed another man striding purposefully toward the pub. For some reason he seemed familiar. He had a certain spring in his walk, though he wasn't young. His hair was sandy, perhaps mixed with a bit of white at the temples, and he was definitely on the heavy side. Suddenly, it dawned on her who he was.

"Hiram Thorn," she whispered, wondering what on earth Cordelia and Octavia's father was doing in Asbury on a Thursday afternoon. His practice was in Boston, hundreds of miles away. Hiram had been the chief of oncology at Boston Central for over fifteen years. So why was he here, passing through the double front doors of the Heritage Pub?

The cookie finally arrived. Jane lingered over it, waiting to see how long Hiram would remain inside. Just as she finished the final bite and took her last sip of coffee, Hiram reappeared. He pushed through the pub's doors, squinting at the bright afternoon sunlight. But this time, he wasn't alone. The man who'd first caught Jane's eye was with him. Neither looked particularly happy. The two men spoke for a few seconds. Finally, the mystery man tapped Hiram on the shoulder with the gold handle of his walking stick. Hiram brushed it away. After a few more words, they parted company. Jane couldn't help but notice that some of the spring in Hiram's step had been lost during his time inside the bar. And his face looked decidedly more pinched and flushed.

"Curiouser and curiouser," whispered Jane, wondering what the ever-meddling Hiram Thorn was up to now.

9

Cocktails at Innishannon were served at six.

Cordelia stood next to the drinks cart in the living room while Christian Wallace mixed her a Bloody Mary, heavy on the Tabasco. She knew it was a morning drink, but in a house where longstanding conventions seemed to rule, bending the rules, even a small one, seemed to appeal. Gracie Lester sat on one of the many loveseats, feet pulled up to her chest, drinking from a can of Coke. Dressed in an oversized flannel shirt and khaki pants, she could have doubled as an ad for The Gap. Cordelia found The Gap tedious and overpriced, and their TV ads moronic and tiresomely energetic. She wasn't sure what she thought of Gracie yet. It would come to her in time.

From what Octavia had told her earlier in the day, cocktail hour was a nightly ritual at the Lester estate. As a young man, Lester had been impressed by all the stories of FDR's cocktail hour at the White House. It sounded so romantic and upper crust that as soon as he had the *shekels* to buy the booze, he indulged in his own "cocktail hour." Cordelia thought the whole idea was pretty dated, but then, when in Rome, etcetera.

Christian was dressed more formally than Gracie. It wouldn't have been hard. He had on an expensive tan sport coat, a black shirt buttoned at the top, no tie, and his jeans looked freshly pressed. With his heavily tinted glasses and his dark tan, he looked like an ad for casual California living. And yet, his skin seemed leather hard, with deep lines in his face, suggesting he'd spent a little too much of his life lying by the

63

pool. He was slim, like his father, with the same quick smile Cordelia remembered from many of Lew Wallace's movies. He had to be in his sixties, so his golden locks were an obvious dye job. A shock of hair fell casually over his forehead, giving him that "I'm still young and with-it" look. Most would probably say that father and son looked alike. Perhaps Lew would have disintegrated in a similar manner, but Cordelia doubted it. There was a strength and a vividness to Lew Wallace's face that Christian's entirely lacked. In many ways, Christian struck her as a poor reproduction, an unfinished portrait. It had probably been hard living in the shadow of a famous father. If Cordelia had been so inclined, she might have pondered it. But she wasn't so inclined. The psycho-babblers had probably already pondered it to death.

"Where's your friend?" asked Christian, pouring himself a glass of mineral water. "What was her name? I'm sorry, I've forgotten."

"Jane."

"That's right. We had a cup of coffee and a short conversation to-gether this morning. You weren't up yet. She's quite charming. Re-minds me of a young Anne Bancroft. Did you ever see *The Miracle Worker?*"

Cordelia nodded, sipping her drink.

"She has wonderful eyes. Very expressive. And blue-violet is such an unusual color."

"Runs in the family." Cordelia couldn't help but notice that she was the only one who'd dressed for dinner. Black silk slacks and a matching top, with a brilliantly colored silk tunic to top it off.

"When it comes to women, Christian has unfailing insight," said Gracie, speaking from her position on the couch.

Cordelia turned to find her lying on her stomach now, flipping through a fashion magazine she'd placed on the floor in front of her. "You two must be pretty good friends."

"Yeah, we are." She turned to the next page. "We've known each other for years. Christian always comes for the holidays—well, ever since his last divorce. How many times have you been married, Chris?"

His smile was indulgent. "You know I've been married twice."

"Like I said, unfailing insight." She closed the magazine and glanced up at him. "But you know what they say. The third time's the charm." Her smile was not only chipper, it was downright seductive.

Was she flirting with him? He was old enough to be her father. Not

64

that it mattered, or that Cordelia cared, but if there was a soap opera playing itself out right before her very eyes, she wanted *details*.

"Ah, here she is," Christian announced, looking up just as Jane came into the room.

"Where've you been?" demanded Cordelia, whirling around to face her friend.

"In Asbury." Jane nodded a quick greeting to everyone, then set her sacks down just inside the door. "I spent the day shopping." She stepped over to the drinks cart and poured herself a brandy.

In a flash, Gracie was off the couch. "I don't think we've met. I'm Gracie Lester, Roland's grandniece." She gave Jane's hand a friendly shake.

"Nice to meet you."

"Likewise."

Cordelia didn't understand why Gracie was scrutinizing Jane so closely, but she was obviously making Jane ill at ease.

"It's nice to have some new people around here for a change," said Gracie, watching Jane sit down. "Not just the usual suspects."

"Hey," said Christian, faking a pout. "What about me? An independent movie producer isn't exactly a nobody. I could cast you in my next picture, make you a star."

"I'm already a star," said Gracie, with a mischievous smirk. Returning her attention to Jane, she asked, "Why don't you come up to my apartment after dinner? I'd love to show you around Gracieland."

Jane's eyes opened a bit wider. "Gracieland?" she repeated.

"Take her up on it," said Christian, sipping his mineral water with an amused grin. "You'll be amazed at what she's done to the third floor."

"Will I?" Jane cleared her throat, then crossed one leg over the other. "I, ah . . . have some plans for later tonight. Maybe we can do it another time."

"Sure. How about tomorrow night? I've got a small kitchen upstairs. I'll make us something. Maybe a frozen pizza. You like pizza?"

Jane gave a less than enthusiastic nod.

"Good. Let's say seven. I've got some work I need to finish first, but I should be done by then."

"Gracie has a graduate degree in computer science from Yale," explained Christian. "She's a real tech whiz. Not as dumb as she looks."

65

"Shut up, asshole."

"I was just kidding."

"Is Roland back yet?" asked Jane.

Gravely, Cordelia shook her head.

Just then, Octavia burst into the room. With a resolute shift of her shoulders, she announced, "I'm not waiting any longer. I phoned the police and demanded that they send someone out here. I promised myself that if Roland wasn't back by dinner tonight, I'd file a missing person's report. For God's sake, he could be lying in a ditch somewhere! Dying, or dead! I've refused to think about it all day, but I can't stand it any longer." Her angry gaze traveled between Christian and Gracie. "And frankly, I don't understand why his family and friends aren't more concerned."

"Please, Octavia, calm down," said Christian, walking over to her. "Look," he continued, putting his arm gently around her back and leading her over to one of the window seats. "Roland does this all the time. He can be gone for days and then, one day, he's back. It's no big deal."

"He's a free spirit," said Gracie. "And he's an adult."

"But where does he *go?*" demanded Octavia. "He's an old man, with a potentially serious heart condition. Don't any of you worry about him?"

From the looks on their faces, Cordelia could tell they didn't.

"What if he forgets to take his medication?"

"Why would he do that?" asked Christian. "There's nothing wrong with his mind."

"Well, if *I've* got anything to say about it," muttered Octavia, "his roaming days are over. He's never going to pull this disappearing act on me again. My nerves can't take it."

Cordelia was never quite sure when her sister was acting. Surely this wasn't one of those times. What would be the point?

"Have you tried calling his brother?" asked Jane.

"Sure. I got him on his cell phone. Unlike Roland, Buddy lives in the twenty-first century. He was in New York, but was driving to New Jersey to spend the night with his son's family. Just like everyone here, he told me to be patient. That Roland will return home shortly."

"Sounds like he knows where he is."

"He insisted he didn't. I don't know what to believe anymore."

"Hey," said Cordelia, her face brightening. "Maybe he's got some rare disease and has to go away periodically for treatments."

"That's *so* helpful," groaned Octavia.

At the sound of a police siren, Christian pulled back one of the heavy drapes. "Looks like the boys in blue are here."

At the same moment, Leonard appeared in the doorway. "Dinner is served," he announced with studied gravity.

"Like hell it is," said Octavia, bolting past him into the hallway, heading straight for the front door.

10

The police stayed for less than an hour. They dutifully took down the information Octavia gave them, but also listened carefully to what Gracie said about her uncle's habits. As the person in the room who'd lived at Innishannon the longest, she explained that Roland often left the estate for short periods—sometimes a few days, sometimes as much as a week. She asked him once where he'd been—she just assumed he went to New York because when he got back, he'd talk about the plays or movies he'd seen—but he'd cut her off, saying that because his life had once been so public, he savored his privacy now. After hearing that, the police had no choice but to inform Octavia that there wasn't much they could do about his disappearance, at least for the moment. They left, asking her to call if she received any new information.

Looking thwarted and deeply worried, Octavia had retreated to her bedroom, leaving the rest of the group to share a quietly strained dinner in the dining room. Jane would have preferred to spend some time alone with Cordelia, but felt she had no choice but to suffer through the small talk, along with a warm and slightly wilted green salad, dry baked chicken, fresh steamed broccoli that was so hard she could barely cut it, and a somewhat puckered baked potato. For dessert, a tiny scoop of lemon sherbet flanked by two burned meringue cookies appeared in front of her. She pushed it away. She'd always resisted the notion that she was a snob about food, but at forty-one, she'd finally decided to accept the title. She loved to eat, loved imaginative cuisine or good simple cooking, so the idea that she had to spend the next week being served this guy's learning experiences, well, it was depressing.

No sooner had dinner ended than Cordelia excused herself to go upstairs and see about her sister. That left Jane free to utilize plan B for the evening. She borrowed a flashlight from the kitchen, slipped on her leather coat, and set off to find the tack house and Ellie Saks.

The night was windy and the sky filled with stars as she hurried along the shoveled path, past the four-stall garage, to the woods beyond. The distant, steady murmur of waves crashing against the rocks made her sorry she hadn't spent any time by the shore earlier in the day. She'd have to remedy that tomorrow.

At dinner, Gracie had mentioned that the stables were a good quarter mile away, down the cobblestone path she was now following. The moon might have provided her with sufficient light, but she was glad for the flashlight, especially when she finally left the headland behind and entered the woods.

As she walked along briskly, glancing occasionally over her shoulder at some barely-perceived sound behind her, she became more and more aware of her growing sense of unease. Perhaps, if her first experience with the stables had been in the daylight, if she knew her destination and felt confident of her way, she wouldn't feel so isolated. Huge, gnarled trees loomed up alongside the walk, their roots like grotesque fingers, rising and twisting in the snow. In spots, they stretched across the path, waiting to trip her. With her left leg still as weak as straw, Jane knew she had to be careful.

She quickened her pace and walked on, attempting to calm herself with the thought that nobody would want to be out here in the dark in the middle of winter. When she finally caught a whiff of wood smoke, she knew she was getting close. As she reached the top of a hill, she could see the path wind toward a stone cottage a few hundred yards in the distance. The wooden stables next to it were dark, but the tack house was ablaze with lamplight.

Feeling as if she'd reached Shangri La, Jane made her way carefully down the hill to a rather formidable-looking oak door. She knocked several times, then waited outside, stuffing her hands into the pockets of her jacket to keep them warm.

A moment later, Ellie appeared, looking surprised but pleased. "Come in," she said, smiling.

"I'm not interrupting?"

"Sure you are, but I'm glad to have the company. I need a break."

They entered through an enclosed hall where Jane imagined the stable hand's coats must have once hung on a series of pegs, with work boots stashed underneath a long, low bench.

Ellie looked just as she had last night—preoccupied but friendly, with her coppery hair tumbling around her broad, freckled face.

Without being asked, Jane was handed a mug of coffee and invited to sit down "anywhere you can find a spot." It was easier said than done.

The main room served as living room, dining room, kitchen, and work room. An open archway led to a second, smaller space, where Jane counted six double bunks. The lower bunk closest to the arch was the only one made up. Cameras and camera equipment were stored in the main room, along the far wall. Two saddles, a bunch of bridles, some horse blankets, a shovel, and a broom were piled in a heap near the refrigerator, remnants of older days. A long oak table served as the primary work surface. A computer and a fax machine dominated the far end, while papers, folders, photographs, books, notebooks, and videotapes were scattered down the length, spilling over onto the chairs. Jane took note of several strange electronic contraptions, figuring they had something to do with documentary making. With the rooms' genial air of disarray, and a wood stove pumping out heat, she felt right at home.

"You had dinner?" asked Ellie, sitting back down at the table.

"More or less. The new cook up at da big house isn't so good." She lifted some papers off of a chair on the other side of the table and made herself comfortable.

Ellie grinned. "I hear you. Even in its current state of disintegration, that place is a little too rich for my blood."

"Don't you ever eat with the grown-ups?"

"Sure, but not when I'm working. It would mess with my concentration." She nodded to the kitchenette. "I'd rather have some fruit and yogurt—and peace and quiet—down here. Of course, when Lester gets back, that will change. I take it he isn't back yet?"

Jane shook her head. Glancing at one of the contraptions in front of Ellie, she asked, "What's that thing?" Printed on the front were the words "**NAGRA**ARES."

"It's a portable audio/digital recorder. I was about to listen to the first interview I did with Lester."

"How long have you been staying at the estate?"

"Three weeks tomorrow." She made a small adjustment on the top of the recorder. "I usually do some preliminary audio interviews just to get the ball rolling. Then I make notes, work on the script—I like to do that on-site as much as possible—and eventually we move on to filmed interviews. It's a long process, but one I enjoy."

"What other documentaries have you done?"

She set her mug down, then leaned back in her chair. "Do you want the long resumé or the short bio?"

"Whatever you feel like giving me."

"Well, I've been doing this for over fifteen years now, so I'm not a novice. Let's see. What am I particularly proud of? I had a chance to tape a long interview with Carl Sagan before he died. He's always been one of my heroes. I worked it into a piece that won a number of awards at various film festivals. More recently, I've produced, directed, and written a few docs for The Discovery Channel, The Learning Channel, and ABC News. When it came to signing the contract with Lester, the fact that I'd won an Academy Award in 1998 for a feature-length documentary I did on Gregg Toland finally tipped the scales."

"Who's Gregg Toland?"

"The famous cameraman? He shot *Citizen Kane* for Orson Welles— a true genius."

"I've seen *Citizen Kane* many times." But she'd never heard of Gregg Toland.

"Lester worked with him a few times. Really admired the guy. This past October, I sent Lester a video of the documentary so he could view it for himself. Two weeks later he signed on the dotted line."

"Congratulations."

"Thanks. My production company is just finishing up an hour-long documentary on another cameraman—Ellery Patrick Strong. He worked mainly in the silent film era, but did make it into the beginning of the talkies. Silent films are one of my major interests. If I do say so myself, it's a remarkable piece." She paused, lighting up a cigarette. "So, what do you do to keep body and soul together?"

"I own a restaurant in Minneapolis."

"No kidding." She blew smoke out of the side of her mouth. "Since I love to eat, I predict we're going to be great friends."

Jane was starting to like this woman. She just wished she knew a good way to broach the subject she really wanted to talk about—without seeming too nosy.

"I hear your friend Cordelia is a theatre director."

Jane nodded, tasting her coffee for the first time. It was so strong, it could have taken the varnish off the table. By the looks of it, maybe it had.

"I met her today. I'd have to say—it was just a brief conversation, you understand—that she and her sister are more alike than either would care to admit."

"You're a good judge of character."

"In my line of work, it comes in handy. You and Cordelia been friends long?"

"Since the eleventh grade."

"Ah. The best kind of friend. Somebody who knew you *when*."

"Right. Before I became a household name."

She laughed. "Exactly."

They spoke in general terms about their lives for a few more minutes, getting to know each other a little better. It became clear to Jane right away that Ellie was more than casually interested in what Cordelia might know about Octavia's forthcoming marriage. She was easy to talk to, which probably made her a good interviewer. When she learned that Cordelia was as much in the dark as everyone else, she changed the subject, asking Jane if she'd like to hear the first interview with Lester, the one she was about to listen to before Jane arrived.

Jane jumped at the chance. "Sure. From what I understand, he's had a fascinating life."

"That's one way to put it." She stood up, stubbed out her cigarette on a plate already filled with cigarette butts, then grabbed a box from under an end table and began riffling through it. She did nothing slowly, though she wasn't careless. Her size and height gave her a definite presence, but she was also graceful, in an athletic sort of way.

"Do you work out much?" asked Jane. "Ski? Do any sports?"

Ellie shuddered. "I'm allergic to exercise. It makes me tired."

Must be genetic.

Everything in the box was labeled clearly. The general disarray was just Ellie's style.

"He's a hard subject," said Ellie, making sure the recorder was set up correctly. "Most Hollywood actors and directors donate their papers and memorabilia to a screen archive when they retire. Lester never did that. Maybe that's part of his allure, but my researchers have had a terrible time finding even the most general information. The only reason this documentary has a chance in hell is because Lester's promised to cooperate. And, of course, I have a signed contract."

"Why do you think he chose to cooperate with you?" asked Jane.

Ellie laughed. "My talent and credentials, of course." Arching an eyebrow, she added, "Also, he's got to have his own reasons. At this point, I'm riding the wave of his current interest. Later on, if he starts pulling his reticent act, I may have my own ways of getting him to open up."

Jane wondered what she meant, but since she'd already switched the recorder on, Jane let it pass. Sitting back, she sipped her battery acid and listened.

LESTER: Is that machine on now? (Clears his throat)
ELLIE: Yes, just speak clearly. I've got a list of questions here. I'll ask them one at a time and you can respond. Don't feel you need to rush. When you're done, I may have a few follow-up questions, or we may move on to another topic. Anytime you want to take a break, just let me know.
LESTER: I will.

Lester had a deep, calm, resonant voice, and his pronunciation, while not British, sounded cultured, not typically American. His voice reminded her of Jeremy Irons. She thought she detected a bit of sarcasm in his last statement. If that was true, it only added to the general aura of sophistication. This was a man who'd been born during the early part of the twentieth century, a man whose roots were closer to the nineteenth century than to the twenty-first. It was probably good to bear that in mind.

ELLIE: Tell me about your early life. Where you were born? What was your family like?

73

LESTER: Well, there's not much to tell really, at least, not much good. My mother was from a poor family in Passaic, New Jersey. Father was, for want of a better term, a drifter. They met in 1916, fell in love, and got married.

ELLIE: What were their names?

LESTER: Emma Selby and Charles Herbert Lesney. After the nuptials, my father made a stab at settling down. He took a job at a dry goods store in Passaic, and I was born nine months later. I believe the actual figure was something less than that, but my mother, in her embarrassment, confused enough people about exact dates that I'm not sure when I actually made my first appearance. I've always celebrated August 24, 1917, but I may be wrong in that. It hardly matters now. Before my brother, Buddy, was born, six years later, father had moved the family to St. Louis. He was certain a fortune could be made in the construction trade there. But, alas, construction required work, and my father was never very good at that. Several months after Buddy arrived on the scene, my father took off for greener pastures. My mother tried to hold the family together as best she could, but she wasn't a strong woman—mentally or physically. I adored her, thought she walked on water, but what does a child know? She eventually left my brother and me on the doorstep of a charity home—an orphanage. It was an immense stone building—at least to my child's eyes—formidable and intensely frightening. And gray. Everything was gray in those days, even the food. But for better or worse, my brother and I were together, and I counted that as a blessing. We always held out hope that our mother would return for us one day, but she never did. I heard later, from a relative, that she died in a car crash in 1928. If Buddy and I had known, we might have stopped hoping. To this day, I don't know if that would have been good or bad. Hope is a powerful emotion. A child, or a man, can live on it for years. But when hope dies, life is no longer worth living. Perhaps it's best to exist with no hopes. My life would have been much happier if I'd concentrated more on reality and less on my own daydreams.

ELLIE: How long did you live at the orphanage?

LESTER: Seven years. I left in August of 1933, the day I turned sixteen.

ELLIE: Didn't anyone try to stop you?

LESTER: You need to understand. It was during the Depression. No one was interested in a sixteen-year-old orphan. For my part, I was only sorry I had to leave my brother. Buddy was nine at the time, almost ten. I know my leaving devastated him, but I couldn't take him with me. I didn't know where I'd end up, or even if I'd make it. I wrote him every week, and he wrote back once I'd found a place to stay. As soon as I made some money and got settled, I sent for him. That took another four years, but he finally came to live with me in Hollywood. I was twenty and he was fourteen. By then, he'd become a very troubled kid. Angry and silent. I worried about him all the time. But as he grew up, he seemed to straighten out. My brother and I have always been close. We help each other, that's the way it is. I know a lot of people look at him and think I've supported him his entire life, that he's never held a real job, but they don't understand. I don't care what other people think. They don't know what our lives were like.

ELLIE: If you could sum up you life in one word, what would it be?

LESTER: (Doesn't hesitate) Lonely.

ELLIE: Perhaps you could explain a bit more. After all, you were an eminent director. Married, with a beautiful wife and daughter. You had friends, family, adoring fans. Why lonely?

LESTER: It's how I felt. Inside. Except for my daughter and my brother, I was never sure of anyone's love, including my wife's. What I truly wanted, I never got.

ELLIE: And what was that?

LESTER: Next question.

ELLIE: (Hesitates) What made you decide to come to Hollywood?

LESTER: During the Depression, I didn't know a single soul who didn't hold on to the movies as if they were a lifeline. Hollywood was glamour. It was excitement. Youth. Hope. Nobody in Hollywood worried about their next meal, or at least, so we thought. I suppose today you'd say it was sex appeal, but to me it was far more than that. Hollywood represented joy itself, in a country that had forgotten how to smile. I wanted the image Hollywood projected—wanted it so badly I would have done anything to achieve it. It was never just the money, but the life that came with it. Of course, when I arrived in 1933 riding on the back of a feed truck, there weren't many jobs for skinny sixteen-year-olds with no skills. Thank goodness I wasn't shy. And I was clever. I didn't know much about myself back then, but I was smart, too. It's a long story, but I finally got myself a job as a caddy at a golf course. It didn't pay much, but I watched the other caddies, decided which were good at their jobs and which weren't. I scrutinized what the good ones did, and I figured out ways to do it better. I spent all my free time learning about golf. I found that I had a natural swing, one people envied, and an aptitude for the game. I'd stay late in the evenings and play until dark. It didn't take long before I knew the course like the back of my hand. I memorized which clubs were used for certain shots and then I'd try them. Sometimes I agreed with the guidebooks, sometimes I found better solutions. Eventually, when the man I was caddying for didn't know which club to use, I'd offer my advice. I quickly gained a reputation as the best caddy at the course. A lot of the big producers and directors at the studios used to come there. They began to ask for me by name, and they tipped well. They even asked my advice on specific shots—how they should gage the roll on a certain green. I struck up a particularly strong friendship with a man named Howard Hawks.

ELLIE: The director?

LESTER: Yes, the director, perhaps America's greatest. He taught me a lot about life, and about films. I don't know why, but we just hit it off. Perhaps he recognized in me some of the same qualities he possessed. I flatter myself by thinking that, I know, but it's an old man's prerogative. I don't quite remember how it happened now, but I started helping him out at the studio, on the set, in his office. Or I washed his car, whatever he needed. He thought I brought him luck. I guess one might say I became his personal gopher. It was an exciting time. If a person can literally eat and drink their surroundings, I did. After years of living in shades of gray, my life burst quite suddenly into Technicolor. I was fascinated by everything I saw, and I learned at the speed of light. I also made friends easily. If I had free time, I'd spend it with the script writers. Or I'd go visit my buddy the voice coach. Most of the actors back in the thirties took voice direction. There was a certain way the studios wanted their actors to sound. Somewhat English, I suppose. I tried it and liked it. I didn't want to sound like a kid from New Jersey by way of Missouri, so I erased all that. Instead of Rolo, I became Roland. Instead of Lesney, I became Lester.

ELLIE: Did you get paid, or were you still working as a caddy?

LESTER: I was still working as a caddy part-time. Just to keep my head above water, I had to work all the time. If not at one thing, then another. But yes, Mr. Hawks did pay me. It wasn't much, but combined with the tips I received from working at the golf course, it was the most money I'd ever had. I lived in a crummy apartment with six other young men. Sometimes it was more than six. None of us were there very much, but it was an address, and that meant Buddy could finally write to me.

ELLIE: So how did you get your big break in movies?

LESTER: Again, a long story. Mr. Hawks was the most relaxed man I'd ever met. On the other hand, you never knew what he was thinking. I was pretty sure he liked me, but I had no idea he was grooming me to be a director. On the set, he was in total command. He had an extraordinary rapport with his actors. He was Cary Grant's favorite director, did you know that? He wasn't much for social consciousness, and his direction wasn't overly artistic. He never won an Oscar—although, they gave him an honorary one a few years before he died. I say, *big deal* to that. Don't get me started on the Academy Awards. You won't like what you hear.

ELLIE: But you won one.

LESTER: Same comment. *Big deal.*

ELLIE: Please. Continue.

LESTER: Think of the movies he made. *Red River. Sergeant York. To Have and Have Not. The Big Sleep. Bringing Up Baby. His Girl Friday.* These are American classics. He tried every genre, and because he understood the essential grandeur in each, he was able to take his personal lifelong theme of human nobility under adversity and blend it into something profound. He once said that for a human being to survive tragedy, the tragedy must be consciously ignored. I agree with him. His voice still rings in my

77

ears. As I said, he started teaching me from the day I walked on the set. He used to say that it's not whether the goal is achieved that finally matters, but rather how well the goal has been sought. That may seem old-fashioned today, but it will always mean something to me.

ELLIE: A thought just occurred to me. If I don't ask you now, I may forget. Did you ever try to find your father?

LESTER: Never. I have no interest in the man.

ELLIE: What about your family on your mother's side?

LESTER: They weren't interested in Buddy and me back in 1926, so why should I care about them? We could have used a few kind relatives back then. Oh, but let me tell you, those vermin came crawling out of the woodwork when I married my wife in 1947. She was a Willingham. Her grandfather was one of the original lumber barons in the Northwest. To say that I married money is an understatement. People I'd never even heard of before started calling me and Buddy up—aunts, uncles, cousins, second cousins, third cousins once removed. I have nothing but contempt for the lot of them. They got what they deserved from me. Nothing.

ELLIE: Getting back to your first years in Hollywood—

LESTER: Right. Well, as I said, I worked with Mr. Hawks for quite a long while. In retrospect, I'd have to say they were the best years of my life. I met people and established relationships that were to last a lifetime. I learned the film business from the bottom up. I tried my hand at just about everything. The harder I worked to help Mr. Hawks, the more indispensable I became. It got to the point that I was always in back of him. People expected to see me there and I was accepted as one of the team. If the script girl got sick, I handled the script for the rest of the day. If Mr. Hawks changed his mind on a scene, decided to reset the camera angle, I lent the gaffers a hand. If the assistant director announced that they were ready for him and he wasn't around, I'd go find him. I even became an unofficial prop man for a while. Worked with the film editors. I listened to what he said—and didn't say. Once he told me, "Always cut on movement and the audience won't notice the cut." I used that advice many times. He even began to allow me to look through the camera. I learned how he visualized scenes. He loved the close-up. So did I. It was sometime in 1936 when I got my first big break. One of the associate producers came on the set and told him that Mr. Meyer had watched some of the rushes and wanted a scene change. Mr. Hawks didn't become upset, as some of the other directors might have, he just grinned and called me over. "Roland," he said, scratching the side of his face, "Arthur here wants a shot of Jack's gun coming out of his pocket. Go make that for him, will you?"

ELLIE: What did you do?

LESTER: I could see the twinkle in his eye. It was his way of telling the guy that the clip was so unimportant, anyone could do it. What did I do? I went to organize the scene. And I did a good job too. Mr. Hawks was a little surprised. After that, he started using me more and more. By 1938, when I made my first film, *End of the Line*, I knew what to do. It was a C movie, so nobody cared. Have you ever seen it?

ELLIE: Yes, many times.

LESTER: It's become what they call a "cult classic." (Laughs) It's not very good, but it helped me get my foot in the door. From there, I was offered other things, and I was on my way. Let me tell you a secret. A good director is a good storyteller, plain and simple. But you've got to pick the *right* story to tell. I've had good luck with my career, but I also made my own luck— especially early on.

ELLIE: Again, I'm curious about something. When did you first meet Lew Wallace?

LESTER: (Long pause) Well, the first time we actually met was after the war. Of course, I'd seen him around town back in the thirties. He was already a big star before the war came along. When he enlisted in the army, I remember some friends at the studio—MGM—gave him a big going away party. He became a war hero, you know. Have you heard *that* story?

ELLIE: I don't believe so.

LESTER: When he came back to Hollywood, he was still recovering from his wounds. The press treated him like a demigod.

ELLIE: Tell me about it.

LESTER: Well, while he was acting as a squad leader of—let me think. I believe it was C Company, Twenty-fourth Infantry near Boulaide, he single-handedly assaulted an enemy machine gun emplacement. There wasn't much cover, so he was in danger the whole time. His company was pinned down by intense gun fire, subjected to a concentrated artillery and mortar barrage. It's amazing to think about it now. I can still hear him recalling the story. Even though he was painfully wounded in the shoulder, he refused to be evacuated and on his own initiative crawled toward the enemy gun. He hurled some grenades, then assaulted the position, destroyed the gun, and with his own rifle he killed two of the Jerries who were attempting to escape. He somehow made it back and rejoined his company. He fought on until their objective was taken and only then did he permit himself to be treated medically. It was incredible heroism. He was awarded the Purple Heart. (Long pause)

ELLIE: If I may ask, what are you thinking about?

LESTER: Just . . . the fact that he was probably the only true hero I've ever known. He really was, you know. In every sense of the word. He went to war to prove something important to himself, and he proved it.

ELLIE: What was that?

LESTER: (Another pause) The usual, I suppose. That he loved his country. And that he was a man. Hollywood welcomed him home with such fanfare in 1944. He got thousands of letters, mostly from women. The studio sent out so many signed photographs they had to set up an entire department just to handle the fan mail. The country adored Lew Wallace back in 'forty-four, but they never really knew him. Nobody did.

ELLIE: Not even you?

LESTER: No, not even me. I can't help but remember that famous quote of F. Scott Fitzgerald's. I used to think about it a lot after Lew's death.

ELLIE: What's the quote?

LESTER: (Pauses briefly) *Show me a hero and I'll show you a tragedy.* It could have been Lew's epitaph.

11

By the time Jane returned to the main house, it was close to eleven. After checking to see if Cordelia was in her bedroom and finding it empty, she came across Christian in a first floor den. His laptop computer was sitting next to him on the couch, open and on, but he was watching *The Tonight Show*. During a commercial he explained that, around nine, Octavia had insisted on driving into Asbury just to get away from the house for a while. Cordelia didn't want her to go alone, so the two of them had left together.

For the next few minutes, Jane sat and watched Jay Leno interview some emaciated actress, a young woman in a glittery tank top, hot pants, fishnet stockings, and cowboy boots. It seemed that blond bimbos were back in style, or perhaps they'd never left. Christian seemed to hang on her every word.

As a commercial came on the screen again, he lit up a Camel. "She's really something, isn't she?"

"Really something," repeated Jane.

"My production company is negotiating with her right now. I optioned a book a few years back. *The Pinterville Process*. Heard of it?"

Jane shook her head.

"Well, it was on the *New York Times* best-seller list for over six months. It's going to make one hell of a mini-major, but we've had some bad luck. Believe it or not, I got a commitment from Paramount, but they eventually put it in turnaround. Miramax passed. Then Fox showed some interest, but they're developing mostly comedies right now. So, I decided to put the package together myself. Director. Actors. Financing. We've got Manfred Price to direct *if* we can capture Isolde for the lead."

Jane didn't understand all the jargon, but decided to ask, "Isolde's the woman on Jay Leno's show tonight?"

"Right. She's incredibly hot right now. She's had the script since early November, but no word yet. If I could just catch a break somewhere. For instance, if I had the director and the financing, I could get the star. Or, if I had the director and the star, I'd have a better shot at the financing. But right now, all I've got are promises. *And* a screenplay that's growing colder by the day." He clenched and unclenched his left fist, holding the cigarette to his lips with the other hand.

Jane noticed that he seemed full of nervous energy tonight. "How long have you been a producer?"

"Too long." He blew smoke high into the air. "But it gets in your blood and you can't get it out. It's a form of gambling, I suppose. Incredibly exciting. Or maybe it's more like a drug. Success is so hard to come by in Hollywood. There are so many variables working against you. And yet the euphoria when you do hit—" He closed his eyes. "It's the best rush in the world. Nothing else even comes close. I must have won and lost at least three fortunes since the early seventies. But," he sighed, tapping some ash into an ashtray, "I figure this is my last chance to hit big. I'm getting too old for the hassle, and yet I can't imagine throwing in the towel. But hey, sometimes, you have to face facts. Eat a reality sandwich. You know what I mean?"

Jane nodded.

"If I don't quit while I'm ahead—assuming this project comes together—I'm going to be spending my golden years in a retirement trailer park. That's not my idea of a stylish exit." He took another drag on the cigarette, then added, "Right now, I'm counting on Roland to back part or all of the project. I made my pitch the day I got here, passed him the screenplay. Now I wait. I loathe limbo. Sometimes I feel like I've spent my whole fucking life there."

"Is something wrong with the screenplay?"

He pinched the bridge of his nose. "It's a long, ugly story. We had Gwyneth Paltrow interested in it for a while. Her people told me that they loved the book, but the adaptation, well, they didn't feel that the main character's psychological journey was developed well enough. It's just an opinion, of course, but now I'm thinking maybe they were right. What we need is a different treatment. On the other hand, it might be easier to slap a new title on it, and new credits. Shop it around again. Scripts get old fast in Hollywood. It's all perception. *The Pinterville Process* is real high concept, you know what I mean?"

"I don't."

"Well, you know. High concept." He said the words more slowly. "I suppose you could say it's *TV Guide*'s influence on the industry. Everybody wants a hot, quick log line. *Pretty Woman* meets *Forrest Gump*. The concept says it all. Understand?"

"I think so."

"Yeah, but it can be a bitch. I had a meeting with Din Russell before I left L.A. You've heard of him, right?"

"Sorry."

He looked over at her as if she were partially brain dead. "He's a big shot in the industry, okay? A major talent agent."

"Oh."

"See, I'm not the kind of guy who gets all hung up on posturing and the personality junk. At that meeting, I took charge. I figured it was my dime. I learned long ago to never go to a meeting without a strategy. A meeting—any meeting—is either won or lost. It's like a war, except nobody gets medals for valor, like my dad did."

"If you win, you just get money and fame."

He seemed to like that. "Yeah. Right."

The instant *The Tonight Show* came back on, Christian's attention returned to the screen.

Jane listened for a few more minutes, but she eventually grew restless. Next to her on the table were a couple of poetry books. After paging through them and deciding they would make good bedtime reading, she told Christian she was tired and was going up to bed.

Without taking his eyes off the TV, he gave a distracted wave and wished her a good night.

She watched him a moment longer, then headed to the living room to pour herself a brandy.

Once back in her room, she found a note from Cordelia placed conspicuously on the center of the bed. Picking it up, she slipped on her reading glasses and switched on the bedside lamp.

Janey:

Where have you been?!!! We need to talk! Octavia is a mess. So what else is new, right? But she's keeping something really big from me. I'm worried for her, and I'm terrified of what she might have already done. This is no marriage made in heaven—more like a bargain struck in hell. And I'm not being melodramatic, so stop shaking your head, or feeling superior, or whatever the hell you do when you think I'm exaggerating. I'm not! Both of my feet are squarely on the ground—well, maybe not at this exact moment due to the fact that I'm sprawled on your bed writing you this missive, but you know what I mean. Cordelia Thorn never exaggerates.

I think maybe I should do something to stop the wedding, but what? Kidnap Octavia? Kidnap Roland? What if somebody already has kidnapped him? Or worse! You have to help me figure this out.

Isn't Christian a putz? Pardon my Yiddish.

And here's the last straw. Dad's coming for Christmas Eve and staying until the wedding. You'd think that idiot sister of mine would have enough class to stop inviting him to these pathetic affairs. I mean really. She's already ruined his life. Now he's supposed to celebrate her happiness? Except, she's miserable. Ha! Sorry, I take that cry of delight back. Octavia and I have called a cease fire until the nuptials are over, so I mustn't gloat—or, at least, you can't tell her that I am.

But what if Roland doesn't show?

Maybe you should kidnap me. Now there's an idea!

We'll talk tomorrow.

For God's sake, don't disappear again!

Later.

Sincerely yours,
Cordelia, the long-suffering.

Jane read through the note a second time, then folded it and put it in the top drawer of the nightstand. Since both Cordelia and Octavia did tend to dramatize their lives unnecessarily, it was hard to gauge what was really going on. Jane wished she could help Octavia in some way, but short of undertaking an all-out search for Roland Lester, she couldn't imagine how. Maybe tomorrow she'd finally get Cordelia to open up and explain what had caused the rift between the two sisters. If nothing else, at least one mystery would be solved.

Sitting down in a comfortably stuffed easy chair with her brandy and one of the poetry books, Jane realized she wasn't particularly tired. In fact, she felt strangely stimulated by all she'd learned today. Human motivation fascinated her. Every life was an intricate puzzle worthy of study, not just by a documentarian trying to shape the elements into a coherent story, but by the person living it. Jane couldn't help but wonder what had happened to Lew Wallace all those years ago, and what part Roland Lester had played in his life, and his death.

Around three in the morning, Jane woke suddenly from a deep sleep. She found that she was still sitting in the chair, the empty brandy glass on the floor next to her, the book still in her hand, reading glasses still perched on her nose. Her back and neck felt stiff and bent, and she was chilled to the bone. As she gazed around the strange room, she wondered what had awakened her. The house was completely silent. Unlike last night, there were no footsteps in the hallway, at least none she consciously remembered. Perhaps it was just the unfamiliar surroundings. All houses had their nightly creeks and groans.

Easing out of the chair, she limped stiffly over to the bedroom door and opened it. She moved into the hallway and listened for a moment, but all was quiet. As she turned to come back inside, she heard movement on the stairs that led up to the third floor. Her room was at the end of the hall, with the stairway in an alcove right next to it. Keeping the door open just a crack, she watched Christian, dressed in his pajamas and a striped silk bathrobe, make his way down the last couple of steps to the second floor landing. As he passed her door heading for his room, he was smiling. Jane didn't like jumping to conclusions, but figured that Gracie and Christian really did know each other well, in the biblical sense of the word.

Once Christian had rounded the corner, silence returned. Except that now, Jane noticed a faint light coming from Roland's study. Christian hadn't noticed it, but then he probably had other things on his mind.

Passing quickly to the other side of the hall, Jane crept down the darkened passage. Standing just to the side of the doorway, she peered cautiously inside. There, sitting behind the desk, head bent next to the glow of the desk lamp, was an old man. White hair. Tweed suit. Thin, David Niven mustache. It had to be Roland Lester. It was just how she'd pictured him. His attention was completely captured by a small framed photograph he held under the light. She didn't have the right to disturb him, but wanted to make sure it really was Lester, and that he planned on staying, not disappearing again into the night.

Clearing her throat, she waited for him to look up. When he didn't, she realized he must be hard of hearing. "Mr. Lester?" she said, a little more loudly.

"Yes?" Adjusting his glasses, he squinted into the darkness. "Who's there?"

She stepped into the room. "I'm sorry to disturb you. My name's Jane. I'm a friend of Cordelia Thorn's, Octavia's sister."

He smiled warmly. "Octavia, yes. You're here for the wedding. It's nice to meet you." He stood and held out his hand.

Jane came forward to shake it.

"Sit down. Please." He motioned her to a chair. "I'm sorry I wasn't here to welcome you. I've been away for a few days, but I'm back now. I'm delighted that Octavia's returned as well, and that you've accompanied her. Say your name again?" He cupped his hand over his ear.

"Jane."

"Thank you. I'm not usually this hard of hearing, but one of my hearing aids needs a new battery and I wasn't able to find one in my desk. I'll have to send out for more in the morning."

He nodded to the book in her hand. "What have you got there?"

Jane realized she was still holding the poetry book. "Just something I found downstairs."

"May I see?"

She handed it to him. "Everyone will be so relieved that you're home."

"Yes, I'm sure," he said, turning the book over in his hand. "This was given to me on my thirty-eighth birthday by my friend, Lew Wallace. See the inscription here?" He held it up, but didn't give it back. Thumbing through the first few pages he continued, "Edwin Arlington Robinson was Lew's favorite poet. Did you like what you read?"

"Very much."

"I was just looking at it the other day. It reminds me so much of Lew. He went around spouting the man's verse all the time. Have you ever seen any of Lew's movies?"

"Sure. Who hasn't?"

He smiled at that. "Yes, he was well known. I was just looking at a picture of him before you came in." With his other hand, he picked up the framed photo and held it under the light again. "There's a young woman staying at my estate right now who's doing a documentary of my life. I'm afraid her questions have stirred up a lot of old memories. Some good, some not so good. It's a hard thing to have your life picked over—explained, defined, reduced. It must be difficult to look into the eyes of another era and come away with any real understanding. But it's important now that there be an official record."

"Why is that?"

He glanced up at her, his face growing serious. "For posterity, my dear. I want the details of my life to be accurate. Accurate about me, about my career, and about all my ups and downs."

Jane wondered if he was finally going to tell what he knew about the Wallace murder. For some reason, she had the feeling he wasn't talking about that. "I understand you and Mr. Wallace were good friends."

He nodded. "You know, forgive an old man for digressing in the middle of the night—I've always been a night person—but Hollywood is such an inherently crass place to live. What was it that comedian used to say? 'Underneath all the phony tinsel lies the real tinsel.' " He laughed, shaking his head. "It's amazing to think I called it home for such a long time. Actually, I believe that in many ways, it's where we made America up."

"That's a rather bold statement."

"But it's true. People think what they see on the screen is real." He scowled, then leaned back in his worn leather chair and threaded his fingers across his chest. "What's a good example?" He thought for a moment, then continued, "Take Clark Gable. I worked with him a couple of times. He was a good actor. Not great, but good. Did you know his leading ladies didn't like to kiss him? He had dentures and he didn't take care of them, so his breath stank. Does that fit the image of the Ladies' Man? That's why you never hear about it. The studios were in charge back then, and I mean in charge of *everything*. The press. The police. If you read widely enough, you may hear a rumor that Gable actually killed someone once in a drunk driving accident. You'll never see that in any newspaper—or police report. The studio covered it up. Golden Boys don't go to jail."

"You sound bitter."

"I suppose I am. I have a right to be. I played the Hollywood game for most of my life—all of my life, really. I still keep the rules. I keep my mouth shut so the illusion can continue. Someone once asked Cary Grant, 'If you could wave a magic wand and be anyone in the world, who it would be?' His answer was 'Cary Grant.' Do you understand? He knew he was nothing like the suave, charming characters he played on screen, but he wanted to be. In reality, the man I knew was a ball of nerves. Very little self-confidence. Overly concerned about his looks. And he was the most miserly human being I've ever met."

"Are you going to make this documentary into an exposé of Hollywood?" asked Jane.

"I haven't decided how far to go. But I'll have to make a decision soon." Again, he picked up the poetry book. Glancing at the table of contents, he asked, "Did you read the poem 'Richard Cory'?"

"I'm not sure," said Jane, trying to recall. "I don't think so."

"Oh, you'd remember if you had. It was Lew's favorite." Closing his eyes, he recited from memory:

> *Whenever Richard Cory went down town*
> *We people on the pavement looked at him:*

He was a gentleman from sole to crown,
Clean favored, and imperially slim.

And he was always quietly arrayed,
And he was always human when he talked;
But still he fluttered pulses when he said,
"Good-morning," and he glittered when he walked.

And he was rich—yes, richer than a king—
And admirably schooled in every grace;
In fine we thought that he was everything
To make us wish that we were in his place.

So on we worked, and waited for the light,
And went without the meat, and cursed the bread;
And Richard Cory, one calm summer night,
Went home and put a bullet through his head.

Very gently, Roland closed the book.

12

Shortly before eight the next morning, Octavia heard a knock on her bedroom door. Throwing on her satin robe and running a brush though her hair, she found Leonard standing outside in the hallway holding a huge bouquet of long-stemmed red roses. When she asked him where they came from, he replied "Hayman's Florists," and told her they'd just been delivered.

After setting the crystal vase down on the dresser, she read the card. The flowers were from Roland. A second later, he appeared in the doorway. She was so glad to see him, she couldn't help herself. She started crying.

"I didn't realize you and your sister would be back so soon," he said. Seeing her distress, he'd hurried toward her, taking her in his arms and gently kissing her hair. "I never meant to worry you. I thought you'd stay in Minneapolis a while longer." Hesitating, he added, "After you left so suddenly, I was worried you'd changed your mind."

"No," she whispered. "I made you a promise. I won't break it."

"I picked the right woman," he said, stepping back, holding her at arm's length. "Not only is she beautiful, but she's got integrity." He smiled. "We've only known each other for a few short months, and yet I've come to care about you quite deeply. I'm glad we've had a chance to spend so much time together. It's meant more to me than you can know."

Seeing him now after being so worried for his safety, after missing him more than she thought possible, Octavia realized she felt the same.

In a strange way, she was a little bit in love with him. At eighty-three, he was still such an intriguing man to be around. Sensitive. Elegant. And he had such a lust for life. His daughter's death had dealt him a hard blow, but he'd recovered.

"Are you feeling all right?" she asked him. "Have you been taking your heart medication?"

"My heart is good for at least another fifty thousand miles."

"Where the hell were you?"

He smiled at her vehemence. "I had to go into New York to see my lawyer. He gave me a copy of the new will."

She moved away from him. "Tell me the truth, Roland. Aren't you worried about your brother's reaction? For all practical purposes, the man's being disinherited."

"No he's not. He's still going to inherit millions."

"A tiny portion of what you're worth. And he has a big family. Not just Gracie, but three grown children and four other grandchildren, all of whom could use a few bucks."

"And they'll get it. From Buddy. Whatever he chooses to leave them in *his* will. Why do you feel I owe him more? Before Peg died, she was my heir. Now you are."

"But for the last seven years, Buddy thought he'd inherit."

"It's not as if he has a birthright. I've taken care of him all my life, quite generously I might add, and I'll take care of him now. He's always complied with my wishes before. He understands my limits. Don't give it another thought."

Octavia felt he was being uncharacteristically obstinate, and yet there wasn't much she could do about it. Roland might trust in Buddy's compliant nature, but she didn't. There was just something about the man that set her teeth on edge. It was partly his fake, saccharin smile. On his particularly obnoxious days he reminded her of Andy Griffith—dumpy, big-toothed, and folksy. He was always so cheerful. So good natured. Then again, maybe it was just her guilt talking. She was a total stranger who'd come along and taken his inheritance away from him. If the shoe was on the other foot, she'd be furious. She was sure that every time Buddy looked at her, he was doing everything in his power to hide the hatred in his eyes. Was she the only one who saw behind the forced smile?

"Besides," continued Roland, walking over and snipping off a small rosebud for his lapel, "I plan to live forever. I'll certainly outlive my brother and the majority of his progeny, the way they all smoke."

"You smoke too."

"Just a few times a year. And only when I'm nervous. You know, I'm going to have to speak to that florist. I asked them to send all buds. These are much too far along."

"I think they're beautiful."

"Good. That's all that matters. And don't give Buddy another thought. Everything will be fine."

He was probably right, thought Octavia. "I'm just glad you're back. But you have to promise me that you'll never disappear again. If you have to go to New York, for whatever reason, you'll tell me so that I won't worry."

"Of course I'll tell you."

Strange, thought Octavia. When he said the words, he didn't look at her. She was probably just being overly sensitive.

As Roland busied himself rearranging the flowers, Octavia fingered the key at her neck. "Roland?"

"Hmm?"

"When . . . exactly . . . do I find out the big secret—what this key unlocks?"

He made a quick adjustment to the bouquet, then moved back to where she was standing and took her hands in his. "Are you saying you're curious?"

"You *know* I am."

"And impatient."

"Roland!"

"You know, it's amazing how serendipitous life can be." Again, he took her in his arms. "I'm more concerned about this part of the inheritance than I am the money. What I have in store for you will make you rich, famous, and immensely powerful in the motion picture industry. You want that, don't you?"

She felt herself shiver with anticipation. "You know I do."

"That's my girl."

"Don't be sexist." She drew back.

He laughed. "To me you *are* still a girl. Life is a matter of perspective."

"You didn't answer my question, Roland. When do I get to use the key?"

His smile grew tender. "We're a lot alike, you and me. What we want, we want passionately."

"The question?" She folded her arms over her chest.

He waited, allowing the tension to build.

"Stop directing this scene in your mind and answer me!"

Now his smile grew playful. "I told you. After our formal wedding on Monday."

"Right after?"

"Well, I think we should attend to our guests first. But by Monday night, you'll have your answer."

"And what will the key unlock? A door? A secret? Pandora's Box?"

"Definitely Pandora's Box," he laughed. "As for the rest, you'll just have to wait and see."

13

Jane was walking down the second floor hall carrying a tray of coffee and pastries to Cordelia's room when she ran into Hilda coming out of Roland's suite. She was carrying her own tray, this one filled with empty breakfast dishes.

"He's back," she whispered as she shut the door softly behind her.

"I know," said Jane.

"He rang down for his pot of tea and toast and I brought it up and set it on the table next to his door around eight, just as I always do."

"I'm sure Octavia's thrilled."

"She's not the only one. Her worrying was contagious. I started thinking something really might be wrong. That woman's going to be the death of me one day." Her tone carried a real sense of threat.

"Why do you say that?"

"You're her friend. I doubt you're interested in my problems."

"No, really. I'd like to know."

She moved a few paces away from the door, keeping her voice low. "Do you realize what that woman did yesterday while I had the day off?" She touched the side of her newly permed gray hair. "She hired a cook! You should have seen my kitchen when I got downstairs this morning. It'll take me weeks to get those burned pans clean. Believe me, when I came to pick up Mr. Lester's breakfast dishes, I informed him what had happened. I've already fired the man. I'm not putting up with it. But you know Mr. Lester. Always the peacemaker. He suggested a compromise. Since we'll be needing more staff over the holidays, what with the wedding and all, he suggested that I send this Leonard person into New Haven to buy himself a butler's uniform. Mr. Lester said he'd call an agency this morning and have some other people sent out. I'm supposed to hire a maid and a cook's assistant. Or another full-time cook. Whatever I want. It's a lot of responsibility, you know, handling all those people. I did it for years, before Mr. Lester let everyone go. But I'm older now, out of practice."

"You'll do a fine job," said Jane reassuringly.

"I hope so. I don't like to let Mr. Lester down. But with that *woman* looking over my shoulder all the time, I'm a nervous wreck. Oh, I'm sorry, Miss Lawless—"

"Jane."

"Jane. Perhaps I've gone too far. As I said, she's your friend."

"In a roundabout way."

Hilda eyed her a moment, then smiled. "Right. I get'cha." Heading toward the stairs, she called over her shoulder, "Next time you see me, I'll be issuing orders like the commander of a battleship. Just call me Captain Queeg." She gave a jaunty wave.

Jane wondered if Hilda remembered that the captain in *The Caine Mutiny* was also mentally deranged. Probably not. As she continued on to Cordelia's room, her mind was occupied briefly by images of a twitchy Humphrey Bogart spooning out strawberry ice cream.

Jane had been up for hours. She'd even hiked down to the shore, sitting on a fallen tree trunk to drink her coffee and watch the waves thunder against the rocks. It was a wonderfully brisk, windy morning. Still, even at 11 A.M., she knew there was a good chance Cordelia was still asleep.

After knocking on the door and getting no response, she turned the handle and entered. Sure enough, Cordelia was lying amidst an abundance of pillows and quilts, snoring softly. The room was dark, but bright sunshine crept in around the edges of the shades, creating enough light for Jane to see that her friend had been perusing a trashy horoscope magazine before falling asleep. The magazine was open to an article on "Scorpio and the Myth of the Vampire." Since Cordelia was a Scorpio, it must have made fascinating bedtime reading.

Jane set the tray down on a low table between two chairs, then drew up one of the shades.

Cordelia stirred, but buried her head under the quilts. "I knew you'd be here at the crack of dawn," she muttered. "I just knew it."

Bouncing several times on the edge of the bed, Jane said, "There's a man downstairs from Transylvania. He wants to talk to all the Scorpios in the house. Something about death and resurrection."

"Very funny. Stop bouncing. I hope you brought food."

"Roland's back."

Cordelia sat bolt upright, yanking off her striped night cap. "He is?"

"Got home last night."

"Is he okay? Where was he?"

"He's fine. And I don't know where he was. But I had a nice chat with him in his study around three."

"In the morning?"

She nodded.

Cordelia eyed the thermal carafe of coffee and the sweet rolls. "And what were you doing up at that hour?"

"Checking the house for the undead?"

"And you found Roland. How ironic." She untangled herself from her covers, yawned, stretched, then slipped into her robe with the dragon on the back, stuffed her feet into her new crocodile slippers, and padded over to the food. "Have you eaten?"

"Yes, all the goodies are for you. All I want is coffee."

"I'll pour." After handing Jane a cup, she sat down, selecting an almond bear claw. "So, pray tell, what did you and Roland talk about?"

"Richard Cory."

"Huh? You mean the poem?"

"And his take on Hollywood. All very interesting."

"For instance?"

"Well, did you know Clark Gable had false teeth? He apparently didn't clean them very well so his breath stank. His leading ladies didn't like to kiss him."

Cordelia turned up her nose. "Yuck. I really needed to hear that at the crack of dawn."

"But there's something else you do need to hear."

"Another piece of repellent Hollywood trivia?"

"No, this is important."

Jane had been thinking all morning about the Internet article she'd read yesterday on Lew Wallace's murder. It was time to tell Cordelia. "All of this started—"

"All of what?"

"Just eat your sweet roll and listen." She began again. "All of this started when I met Ellie Saks, the woman doing the documentary on Lester." She went on to explain about the newspaper clipping Ellie had dropped in the hall, about Lew Wallace's unsolved murder, and that Roland, Verna Lange, and Christian Wallace were, for a time, considered the most likely suspects in the slaying.

"You mean my sister is about to marry a murderer?"

"Can we *please* not jump to unsubstantiated conclusions?"

"But from what you said, it's possible. Even likely!" Cordelia shot out of her chair. "I've got to tell Octavia."

"Tell her what? Nobody knows what really happened."

"But it's information she should have. I doubt Roland ever told her he was a suspect in a homicide. It's not the kind of thing one chucks into the pool of a stagnant dinner conversation."

"Okay, maybe she doesn't know. But after meeting Lester last night, I can't imagine him committing a murder."

"Right. And the boy who lived next door was such a sweet, gentle lad. We can't fathom why he took an assault rifle and blew fifteen people away."

Jane had to admit, appearances could be deceiving. "I doubt we're going to discover the truth at this late date. Unless—"

"Unless what?" Cordelia returned to her chair, pouring herself another cup of coffee. "You've already got an angle, right? Give."

"Well, Ellie had the newspaper clipping, so she must be curious. And since she's the one who's delving into Lester's past, maybe she's trying to unearth new evidence."

"Or already has."

"It's possible. She's in the best position to do it."

"I have to go talk to her," said Cordelia, erupting out of her chair again.

"I wouldn't do that."

"Why?"

"Because if she has discovered something, it's . . . delicate. Think about it. If Roland finds out she's prying into the old homicide, he might refuse to cooperate on the documentary. That would effectively cut off potentially important sources of information—his family and friends. She's hardly going to jeopardize her standing with him by spilling what she knows to you."

Cordelia's entire body seemed to deflate. "But what am I going to tell my sister?"

"All you can do is explain what's in the official record—and that isn't much."

"This is just dandy. And to think, Dad's arriving tomorrow night. A dash of family trauma with the eggnog is always my idea of a good time."

"That reminds me," said Jane, taking a sip of coffee. "I saw your father in Asbury yesterday. I was sitting in a coffeehouse when he came walking down the street. He disappeared into a bar, and when he came out, he seemed to be having an argument with another man."

"Who was the other man?"

Jane shrugged. "He had on a hat and dark glasses. I was sitting across the street, so I never really got a good look at his face. But your father seemed pretty upset. I could tell that much."

Cordelia sat back down, gazing into her cup. "I suppose he could be out this way doing some sort of consultation. But in a bar?" Her thoughtful expression turned quickly to indignation. "After what happened to Mom, I'd think he'd want to stay out of bars."

Jane figured it was time to take a chance. "Look, Cordelia, I know you told me you didn't want to discuss the details of your mother's death—ever. You made me promise never to say Octavia's name again. I've respected your wishes, but . . . I thought that maybe now you might want to tell me about it. I mean, your dad will be here soon. The three of you are going to be together again for the first time since the funeral. If I'm in the dark about what happened, I won't be much help to you. I'm concerned—genuinely. I'm not trying to pry."

Cordelia tossed her napkin on the tray. "Oh, I know that. It's just . . . it's hard for me to even think about, let alone talk about. I'm still so angry at my sister I could—" She turned away, pulling her robe more snugly around her ample curves.

"Maybe this isn't such a good time."

"No. I've wanted to tell you for years. You're my best friend. It's crazy that you don't know. I just . . . couldn't." She cleared her throat, brushing a hand through her hair. "You know me, Janey. I don't like to dwell on the negative. I live in the moment. I always give people the benefit of the doubt, and I am a veritable font of patience, especially where my family is concerned."

Self-delusion, thy name is Cordelia, thought Jane. But she didn't say it out loud.

"But sometimes, even I have . . . difficulties. I tried to help Octavia. I knew she was in trouble as far back as high school. I suppose, with all the problems Dad's had over the years with alcohol, I should have realized Octavia might have the same weakness. But once she'd gone through rehab, I thought she'd licked it."

Jane interrupted her. "I didn't know your sister had been in drug rehab."

"Up in New Hampshire. She admitted herself in the spring of 'eighty-nine. It was mainly for booze and cocaine. She used an alias at the clinic—didn't want anyone to know about it, especially Mom and Dad. I paid for the treatment. She said she'd pay me back, but she never did." Cordelia held up her hand for silence. "Not that I cared. As I said, my saintly credentials remained intact. I just wanted her to get some help." Easing back in her chair, she crossed one leg over the other, then continued, "She stayed clean for several years, but by the early nineties, she started drinking again. She was doing summer stock at the time. Remember, I went to visit her? She tried to hide it from me, but no one keeps secrets from Cordelia Thorn. She insisted it was just a social drink every now and then. No cocaine. No pills. I was heartsick. At the time, Dad's drinking was still sporadic, but getting worse. Mom would call me after he'd passed out at night, asking what she should do. You remember what it was like. I was always talking to her on the phone, listening, encouraging, strategizing. Of course, Dad only drank at home, never out in public. He was a doctor with a reputation to maintain. It was only when Mom put her foot down and said she'd leave him if he didn't get help that he stopped. Thank God he did."

"So, what happened to your mother?" asked Jane.

Cordelia took a deep breath, then let it out slowly. "It was the fall of 'ninety-three. Octavia had just gotten her big break. She'd been offered this amazing part in a Neil Simon comedy, and her first reviews in New Haven were raves. You remember, I showed you all the clippings. Mom and Dad were so proud of her. For her birthday, Dad bought her a 'fifty-six T-Bird convertible, baby blue. Very rare and very expensive. You know how much Dad adores antique cars. Well, the night she took the train up from New York for the birthday party, she'd already been drinking. She drank more when she got there. Dad suggested they all go for a little spin, to test out the car. It was late, around eleven by the time they left the house. Mom got in the passenger side, Dad hopped in the back, and Octavia drove. I have no idea how much she'd had by then, but it was plenty. When they tested her at the scene of the accident, she was way over the legal limit."

"Your mother died in a car accident?" said Jane, feeling confused. "But I thought it was her heart."

"Technically, it was. I'm sorry, Janey. I know it sounds preposterous, but I had to let you think that. I promised Dad to keep what happened a secret. You know how much I adore him. He begged me, literally *begged* me. He didn't want any negative publicity to hurt Octavia. He's very well connected in Boston, has some dear old friends in the police department, and he plays racquetball several times a week with a couple of the judges. Somehow he was able to get the charges pled down, and at the same time, keep everything under wraps. I don't know all the details. In retrospect, it seems incredibly sick, but that's the Thorn family for you. Separately, we're all amazing. Successful. Creative. Admired. But together, we're an Ebola virus waiting to infect a village, an ocean liner ready to sink and kill everyone aboard, a thousand-pound gorilla ready to attack a skyscraper—"

"I get it," said Jane, hoping to stem the tide of analogies.

"The truth is, Octavia ran a stoplight that night. Another driver slammed into the passenger side. Dad, Octavia, and the driver of the other car all walked away from the accident with nothing more than scratches. Mom wasn't so lucky. She lived a couple of days. Dad called me right away and I flew out. But before I left, he made me promise not to tell anyone it was a car accident. I was just supposed to say that mom was in the hospital, seriously ill. You were at the restaurant convention in Denver at the time, remember? I tried to contact you before I left town, tell you my mom was in the hospital, but you were out having dinner. Nobody knew where you were. I left you a message, then took a taxi to the airport and left on the first flight out. By the time I got to Boston, Mom had slipped into a coma. I was never able to speak with her, to say good-bye. She died the next day." Cordelia got up and walked to the window overlooking the ocean. With her back to Jane, she continued, "We buried her three days later. I was in total shock. At first no one told me Octavia had been drinking when the accident happened. But it came out one night over dinner. To her credit, she was the one who finally fessed up. Dad started crying. I started screaming. It was a horrible scene. At the church, I refused to sit with her, so I sat alone on the other side of the aisle. I left from the cemetery, took a cab to the airport, and flew home. I kept the family secret, never told a living soul what had really happened. I just told everyone it was my mother's heart and left it at that. Until Octavia showed up on my doorstep a few days ago, I hadn't seen or spoken to her in years. I had no intention of ever speaking to her again. But . . . she seemed so desperate, Janey. Back in 'ninety-three and 'ninety-four, she'd written me letter after letter telling me how sorry she was, that she'd never take another drink again. She begged for my forgiveness in every way she knew how, but I never wrote back. I couldn't forgive her. I still haven't. I don't know what's going to happen when Dad arrives. I suppose we'll just get through it, like we always do."

"I'm so sorry," whispered Jane, not knowing what else to say. She was stunned.

Cordelia whirled around. "Can you understand *now* why I'm so concerned about *your* drinking?"

Jane felt her face flush. "I'm okay, Cordelia. Really. It's not a problem."

"That's what my sister said. That's what all people who abuse alcohol say. If anything happened to you, I don't know what I'd do."

Getting up, Jane walked over and put her arms around her friend, hugging her tight. She could feel her shivering. "Nothing's going to happen to me."

"Famous last words," said Cordelia, almost laughing, but she held on tight, and she kept holding on.

14

Cordelia and Octavia spent the afternoon in front of the fire in the living room, discussing last-minute wedding details with the caterer, the florist, the minister, the organ soloist, and a steady stream of other necessary participants. Watching from the sidelines, Jane smiled as Cordelia moved into full five-star general mode, checking off various items on a clipboard. Octavia was somewhat less formal, but every bit as concerned that the occasion run smoothly.

In their lighter moments, they reminded Jane of Laurel and Hardy. A little bumbling in their grandiosity, too free with their silly enthusiasm. But when they sank into acerbity, as they both so often did, they became themselves again, the sisters grim. It was sad to watch because, in many ways, they were so much alike. The both laughed at the same things. They were both highly verbal and tended to exaggeration—but exceptionally imaginative exaggeration. What struck Jane as truly odd was the fact that they seemed to have so much fun together, far more fun than they ever had when they were teenagers. But when they became conscious of their laughter and growing camaraderie, they quickly resumed their reserve. Apparently, they felt more comfortable with the status quo.

Jane had no idea whether Cordelia had told her sister about the murder of Lew Wallace, but knowing her old friend as she did, Octavia had received an earful of facts, opinions, and unwanted advice. Whatever had been said, the wedding still appeared to be on.

When the crew arrived from New Haven with the Christmas tree and all the house trimmings, Jane felt it was time to leave the commotion behind in search of quieter ground. Noise had been bothering her lately. She'd even walked out of a couple of movies because they seemed too loud.

On her way back to her room, she passed Roland's study and was surprised to find that Ellie had set up lights and camera equipment inside. Roland was sitting Midas-like behind his desk with Gracie applying makeup to his face. Curious as to what was going on, Jane stood for a moment in the doorway.

"Jane, hi," said Ellie, turning around. "I'm just about to do my first on-camera interview with Mr. Lester."

"You're welcome to join us," said Roland, nodding to an empty chair. "You can be part of the admiring audience."

Jane glanced at Ellie for her thoughts on the matter.

"It's fine with me, as long as you're quiet."

"I'd love to listen in," said Jane, sitting down next to Christian, who was watching Gracie perform her ministrations.

"There," said Gracie, giving Roland's nose a playful tap with the makeup brush. "Handsome as any movie star."

"Right. Raymond Massey in *Arsenic and Old Lace*."

"Oh, Rolo, don't be silly." She gave him a kiss on the cheek.

Jane hadn't seen the two of them together before and was surprised at how affectionate Gracie was with him.

Glancing over her shoulder at Christian, Gracie said, "He looks fabulous, doesn't he?"

"Not a day over seventy-five," said Christian with his usual smirk.

"Let's get started," said Ellie, switching on the lights and stepping behind the camera. "I'll ask the questions, just as we did on the taped interviews."

"Fine," said Roland, smoothing his striped silk tie one last time. Looking over at Jane, he said, "I'm not used to being in front of the camera. I think I prefer directing."

"Okay," said Ellie. "Quiet on the set." She held a small chalkboard in front of the lens.

Jane tipped her head back so that she could read what it said.

Roland Lester, Interview 1, December 23rd.

"We're rolling," said Ellie, standing still for a moment behind the lens. After a few minor adjustments she moved to the side and removed a small notebook from her shirt pocket.

Jane sat back, eyes fixed attentively on Lester.

ELLIE: How many movies have you made during your career?

LESTER: Let's see. Sixty-seven, I think, not including the two I tried to have my name removed from. *The Best Policy* and *Today We Die.* I shot all the retakes for those films, but I never wanted screen credit. They were both romantic weepers. In both cases, the directors had been fired mid-shoot. Other directors were brought in and eventually I was asked to clean up the mess. I could only do so much.

ELLIE: I've always felt that a deeper knowledge of a man allows us a better understanding of his work, that a man's life must figure into the pattern and themes of his art.

LESTER: I suppose that's true. (Waves for the next question)

ELLIE: I've also heard it said that the famous directors didn't really exist off the set.

LESTER: (Smiles) That's not true.

ELLIE: You said in an earlier interview that you first learned about directing from Howard Hawks.

LESTER: (Nods) Mr. Hawks was my mentor, and became a dear friend. But I suppose, beyond the basics, I learned my craft by working. By directing.

ELLIE: At what point did you feel you knew what you were doing?

LESTER: That's an interesting question. (Pauses) Technically, I think I understood what I was after from the very first film—a low budget romantic comedy that nobody expected to go anywhere. When it did, I was as surprised as the next guy. It was called *End of the Line.* The movie was fairly slipshod structurally. But . . . you see, it takes a while to realize what you're doing unconsciously. When you begin to do it purposefully, it makes working much simpler. I'd say, for me, that point came in the mid-forties.

ELLIE: With the first Wallace/Lange movie?

LESTER: That's right.

ELLIE: What about your film technique?

LESTER: That's a rather broad subject. (Pauses) I believe you should never move a camera unless you have to. If you do a lot of fancy footwork, maybe the critics will notice you as the director, but it can hurt the story. I'm always dazzled by discreet camera work. That's not to say I didn't admire directors like Hitchcock. But he was a master, and he always shot it straight unless he had a good reason to do otherwise. If you get too clever, you lose potency. I see so many directors today doing their little dance. Sometimes I actually become physically nauseated by the results. I can't watch *NYPD Blue* on TV. That's not to say I'm against subjective shooting or point of view camera work. On the contrary. That's what film is. Theatre is objective. The Burton/Taylor *Who's Afraid of Virginia Woolf* was a theatre piece. So was *A Lion in Winter* and *Six Degrees of Separation*. Not cinematic in the least—not a true motion picture. Motion pictures are always subjective. I love close-ups, but only when you can get a jolt out of them. I used them for punctuation—and only after the audience had a chance to get to know the character. Then the person's face and what he's thinking means more. Also, it was always important to me to combine artistry and entertainment, without one drowning out the other. I believe firmly that all drama should include comedy. Otherwise, it's hard not to laugh at the solemnity. Drama without some lightness drifts so easily into melodrama. I like to exploit that fine line between comedy and tragedy, and believe me, it takes skill.

ELLIE: Do you have a philosophy about working with actors?

LESTER: Well, I always had a hard time working with anyone I disliked, or was bored by. That's why I made so many movies with Lew Wallace and Verna Lange. We just had a chemistry together. It produced some real magic, if I do say so myself. In general, I think actors are better off when they simply behave—when they don't think overmuch about their motivation. I was happy to talk to any actor if he or she was having a problem with a scene. But I always brought them back to the central story. If they understood that, then I felt they should understand what to do. This may sound funny, but I prefer a blank expression to excess emotion. Melodrama is fake, while real emotion is terribly subtle. Hitchcock once compared a face to a piece of paper. Too much emotion is like scribbling all over the page. Less is more. Blank is sometimes best. That's what made Spencer Tracy so good at what he did. Actually, I didn't know him all that well, but his family problems, and his appalling routine of coffee, dexedrine, booze, and sleeping pills wasn't a secret. Sometimes, when he came on the set, he was just trying to get through his lines without falling down or crashing into the props. He'd have such a hangover. But his face was miraculous. Grudging expressions that were full of subtlety. Watch him sometime. You'll see what I mean. George Cukor directed him in a number of films, and he never gave him one word of actual direction. Tracy liked to do scenes in one take—unlike Hepburn, who could do up to thirty before she felt she got it right. That kind of *emotional* intelligence is what you find in the best film actors.

ELLIE: You loved doing stories about double standards.

LESTER: Early on, I had a very romanticized view of Hollywood, but that changed. I was living in a town where double standards were the rule, not the exception. You're perhaps familiar with the old industry saying, " 'Hello,' he lied."

ELLIE: Yes.

LESTER: It's a piece of mock dialogue, but I think it says it all. Living in a town where lying is as natural as breathing, how could I not be fascinated by it? But you know, I never lost my reverence for beauty. Hollywood is a mecca for the most beautiful people on earth. Sometimes, when an actress would come on the set, I'd have to catch my breath. I still appreciate physical beauty. Perhaps that makes me shallow, but if it does, then so be it.

ELLIE: You worked with a lot of women writers.

LESTER: I did, perhaps a preponderance were female. I was drawn to stories about women who were ahead of their time. When I got a script and I wasn't sure one of the female parts rang true, I'd run it by some of my women friends and writers—just to make sure that I got it right. That was very important to me.

ELLIE: You made a career out of making movies about stories of love and romance.

LESTER: Yes, the Merchant of Venus. I believe Joan Crawford called me that in an interview once. For some reason, it stuck.

Actually, I've made all sorts of movies. Dramas. Comedies. Period pieces. Even some psychological suspense. Suspense is very difficult. I learned early on that true suspense is achieved by giving the audience information, not by withholding it. You must always keep in mind the difference between what's important to the characters and what's important to the audience. They may be two different things. When I was working on *Face the Devil,* with Ray Milland and Susan Hayward, I realized for the first time that I was directing the *audience* far more than I was directing the actors. I've always been fascinated by physiological drama, although I could never buy the idea that, if you discovered the origins of a problem, a fear, a phobia, that it would release you from its grip. That's too facile. I've never been terribly interested in action films or westerns. I think action directors are a dime a dozen, especially today. What I did was more interior, and far more rare. I think human behavior, the human heart, is what makes for a compelling story. I believe relationships interest us more than anything else. After the war, the richness I brought to character detail set my films apart. We'd begun to move away from the artificiality of Hollywood clichés by then, and toward a naturalism more in line with postwar realities. No more "high society" stuff or costume melodrama. We set up shop in the streets, in the living rooms of middle class people. It was perfectly in tune with what I wanted to do. Issues of marriage and sexual equality were on the table for the first time. Sure, there was still a touch of idealism, but none of the Frank Capra kind. His movies still set my teeth on edge.

ELLIE: What did you think of the studio system?

LESTER: I learned very early from Howard Hawks not to hook my star to one studio wagon. Since I'd always been pretty good at the production side of films—putting projects together—I didn't have to rely on long-term studio contracts. I can remember walking up and down the Malibu beach with various producers over the years, negotiating. I loved collaboration. I remember when Dori Sherrie had just purchased the rights to *Hades Following,* the best-seller by Irving Watts. I knew I had to direct it. We had an all-night story conference where I laid out the big setups, the process shots, explained where I thought we should use montage sequences. The train crash could be done on the back lot. But I insisted that certain sets would have to be erected—and I wanted it filmed in Technicolor. I must have sold him on my vision because I got the job.

ELLIE: It was one of your biggest film successes.

LESTER: I fought like hell for that movie. And then I had to fight the producers so that they didn't hack it to pieces. It's a tough game, but I knew how to play it. Not that I always won. Also, because I didn't have a steady contract, projects came and went unpredictably. I remember, it must have been 1945 when I ran into D. W. Griffith. He was floating around Hollywood, out of work, alcoholic, pretty much forgotten. It was a real object lesson for me. Fame is a monster. It eats people alive. (Clears throat) But back to the studio system. Even though it took care of people, making sure they had constant work, it also humiliated them by asking them do idiotic projects. I escaped most of that, until the fifties. Everything changed in the fifties.

ELLIE: Why was that?

LESTER: Several reasons. First, the studio system was just starting to break up, business was depressed. Nothing would ever be the same again. TV had started to take over and dominate people's free time. Some thought it would be the death of the film industry. That's why everything got bigger, more standardized, and from my point of view, far less glamorous. There were no more "small movies." Subtlety was out. Studios were consumed with these grandiose plans to lure people back to the theatres. Things like Cinerama, all-star specials. Believe me when I tell you that the directors of the Golden Age had been spoiled. For most of my early working life, I had an office, a secretary, assistants. Top camera and design people were at my beck and call. Projection rooms were standing at the ready. Sometimes, I'd stay at the studio all night viewing dailies. Budgets were always an issue, but the money was there. But in the fifties, the congressional witch hunts were at their peak. I'm sure a part of it was a reaction to Roosevelt and his policies. The Democrats were finally out of the White House for the first time since 1932 and the term "liberal" took on an ominous meaning. Serious scripts were suspect. Strong women were suspect. Everything was suspect! (Shakes his head)

It was the time of the passive blond. People like Marilyn Monroe. Jayne Mansfield. Doris Day. I hated it, hated the climate of fear that was taking over. Almost overnight, a sizable number of people became unemployable. I don't even know how to explain to you how truly dreadful it all was. The studios reacted by retrenching around old ideas, facile blockbusters, slick packaging. Bible stories became the rage. A lot of contract directors chose that time to retire. When I think about it, by the mid-fifties, Clarence Brown, Robert Leonard, Sam Wood, Mervyn LeRoy, and Victor Fleming were all dead. But I was still a young man. I couldn't just pack my tent and silently steal away. So I took on projects that I wouldn't have even considered earlier in my career. Humdrum sob stories with silly women and oafish men. That was the tenor of the day. I tried to ride it out. So many of the decent films I directed got chopped up in postproduction that I was constantly depressed. During the late fifties some of my best films were the reckless ones—the ones that barely made a buck at the box office. By the mid-sixties, the worst of it seemed to be over, but by then, the entire world had gone crazy. I *hated* the ugliness—the hippies. Culture, style, and beauty were considered passé. I'd always felt that censorship had come along because of bad taste. In my opinion, the 1960's were the pinnacle of bad taste. I made a dozen or so films during the decade. Some I'm proud of, some not. I worked almost full-time until the late seventies. In the eighties, I took on a couple projects, but only ones that really interested me. When I couldn't stand it any longer, I retreated to Innishannon.

ELLIE: I'm curious what your thoughts are on film preservation. Thousands of films have already been lost.

LESTER: Actually, I think less than half of the twenty-one thousand feature-length American films made before 1950 still exist today. It's a travesty. Millions of dollars have already been spent just to restore a few of our more spectacular motion pictures. *Gone with the Wind. Lawrence of Arabia. My Fair Lady.* Only twenty percent of the films from the 1920s have survived. Celluloid, whether cellulose nitrate, which was the primary film used until the 1950s, or acetate-based film, are both easily compromised by heat, light, and improper storage. And, much to my surprise, the

Eastman Color negatives and prints are proving to be an even bigger disaster. Have you seen any lately? They've all turned pink. Can you imagine it?

Ellie glanced down at her clipboard looking for another question when the sound of a crash caused everyone to turn around.

"Oh, gosh, I'm so sorry," said an older man, leaning down to pick up the small table he'd just knocked over. "I'm such a klutz. I was trying to come in quietly, but . . . me and my big feet." He smiled sheepishly, then twirled his finger, directing them to go on. "Don't mind me."

Jane had no idea who the man was. He looked a little younger than Roland, but not by much.

"Buddy, did you want something?" asked Roland, appearing vaguely annoyed.

So this was Roland's brother, thought Jane, glad to finally put a face with the name. She turned all the way around to get a better look at him. He was a good foot taller than his older brother, and at least fifty pounds heavier. Same strong jaw line and thick head of white hair. But the suave quality Roland had worked so hard to achieve over a lifetime was completely lacking in Buddy. In its place Jane found a kind of disarming naturalness. He sat down like any old guy might, his legs spread apart, hands folded in his lap. He didn't pose the way Roland tended to. His hair was a bit shaggy and windblown, not professionally styled and slicked back, like his brother's. Roland's demeanor might be outwardly calm and controlled, but inside, he was clearly a complex man, wound tight by a life in the spotlight. Buddy seemed the antithesis. He wasn't polished, he wasn't in a hurry, and he looked like the kind of guy who wore his feelings on his sleeve. Right now, he seemed ashamed of himself for making such a bumbling entrance.

Before answering Roland's question, Buddy looked curiously from face to face. "I, ah . . . got back a little while ago. You wanted to talk about that . . . stuff . . . this afternoon, Rolo. Remember?"

"Oh, right." said Roland, his expression a mixture of amusement and frustration. "The 'stuff.' Yes." Glancing at Ellie, he said, "I'm afraid my brother's right. We have some business we need to discuss. I'm sorry, but it can't wait."

"Fine with me." Ellie had already turned off the camera. "Maybe we can resume this later."

"Absolutely. By the way, you're all invited to movie night tonight," said Roland, rising from his chair.

"Movie night?" repeated Jane, not sure what he meant.

"When I first moved here, I had a screening room built off the back of the house. It's very comfortable. We can even crank up the old popcorn machine if you like."

"Sounds like fun," said Jane.

"Good. Then it's a date. Nine P.M. We usually watch something from my personal collection. Gracie, maybe you can do the honors tonight. You'll have to pick a film that will keep Christian from falling asleep."

"Is that a comment on my age?" replied Christian testily.

"No, son. Your libido."

On that note, Roland and Buddy left the room.

15

Cordelia and Octavia charged down the hallway, each trying to walk faster than the other without actually running.

"If he's not in his study, then where the hell is he?" demanded Cordelia, sweeping around a corner and nearly taking out a small nest of tables and a rather tacky painted-plaster creche.

"Buddy's here. Since Roland's study is being occupied at the moment by that Saks woman, I'm sure they went somewhere else to find some privacy."

"Like where?"

"Just stick a sock in it and follow me."

As they reached the solarium, Octavia put a finger to her lips. The French doors, curtained in an ancient yellow chintz, were closed, but not all the way.

Through the crack, Cordelia could hear voices. "Are we eavesdropping or taking the pause that refreshes?"

"Shhh!" hissed Octavia.

Cordelia was thoroughly disgusted. They'd come to find Roland to settle their argument. Now they had to cool their heels out in the hall while he talked to his brother.

Cordelia had met Roland earlier in the day and found him utterly charming. During their conversation, he happened to mention that he'd asked Hilda to gather all the press clippings she could find on Cordelia during her tenure as creative director at the Allen Grimby Repertory Theater in St. Paul. He said he was "mightily impressed" with what she'd been able to accomplish—and even further, that she and Octavia had the makings of a creative dynasty, much like the Barrymores. The man had such obvious taste and vision, Cordelia found herself holding her breath at Octavia's good luck. She prided herself on having a sixth sense about people, and Roland Lester was no murderer. He was a prince among men. In this case, it was Octavia who was the frog. "How long do we have to wait out here?" she whispered, narrowing one eye.

"Shhh!"

Never one to shy away from keyholes, Cordelia bent her head to hear more clearly. In her family, eavesdropping was considered light entertainment.

Roland was talking.

"So, everything's all set? You've got the ring?"

"I picked it up at the jeweler's this morning," replied Buddy. "Roland . . . about the will." A pause. "I certainly agree to any and all of your wishes, but Grace is going to be devastated when she finds out she's no longer going to inherit Innishannon."

"Why? All she does is play with her computer and entertain strange, magenta-haired guests. She can do that anywhere. As I told you, I've arranged to transfer the title to the Sante Fe house to her. Upon my death, she'll be the new owner, free and clear, with a million dollars in the bank. What does she need with a big house like this anyway? I've been very generous with her these last seven years, Buddy. She's taken over the entire third floor and I give her complete privacy. I've grown very fond of her, to be sure, but Innishannon will belong to Octavia when I'm gone. That's just how it is."

"You won't reconsider?"

"Why are you pushing me on this?"

"It's just . . . Grace had her heart set on remaining here. I'm not looking forward to breaking the news to her."

"Then I will."

"No, I think it would be better coming from me."

"You almost sound like you're afraid of her."

Buddy didn't reply.

After a few seconds, Roland continued: "One day, I hope Octavia and our children will live here by the shore year-round."

"Your . . . children?"

"Well, *child*. At least one. Octavia and I've talked about it. She wants one as much as I do."

His voice growing anxious, Buddy asked, "Roland, tell me the truth. Is she pregnant?"

Roland laughed. "Buddy, when my bride gets pregnant, you'll be the first to know."

Silence. "I don't understand you. For God's sake, man, you're eighty-three."

"Are you saying I'm too old? Because if you are——"

"No, of course not. If that's what you want. But——" Now he sounded flustered. "When is enough enough?"

"You of all people should appreciate my motives. When I lost Peg, I lost not only my heart and soul, but my future. I have a legacy I want to pass on. I've spent the better part of my life building that legacy."

"And you think Octavia Thorn is a suitable replacement for Peg?"

"That's my business, but yes. I do."

"You really plan to give her everything? I thought, perhaps, I would continue——"

Roland cut him off. "You've worked hard, Buddy. We both have. But a separate document has already been drawn up. Not everyone would appreciate the importance of what we've done, but Octavia will. By the way, did you get everything on the last list I gave you?"

The sound of paper crumpling. "Everything but what I've circled."

"Good man. I'll look at it later. Next question. Have you given Christian his usual Christmas gift?"

"Not yet."

"I'm thinking about backing one of his projects, but don't wait on the gift. I want him happy—and silent."

"I don't like him, Roland. He's nasty, he's self-consumed, and he's greedy."

"And he's Lew's son."

Silence.

"What's wrong, Buddy? Come on, you can talk to me."

"I'm just a little down today, I guess."

"It's not the money, is it? I'll always take care of you. You're still going to inherit millions."

"I don't care about the money, Roland. Money can't buy what's really important. Love. Loyalty. Trust."

"No, I suppose not. Say, before you go, I wanted your opinion on something. An odd thing happened to me the other day. When my limo driver dropped me off in New York, I swear someone was following me, that someone had tailed the limo all the way from Innishannon."

"Are you sure?"

"I saw the man. He was sixtyish. Balding. Driving a green Jeep. I had the limo driver let me off in Times Square, thinking the car would drive off. It didn't. The fellow stopped and waited. I walked for a couple of blocks before getting into a cab, but there he was again, right behind us."

"Did you lose him?"

"Yes, thank God. But it frightened me. I don't like the idea that someone might be prying into my private affairs. Have you noticed anyone following you?"

"Me! No."

"Well, be on your guard. Once Octavia and I are back from our honeymoon, I intend to hire a private investigator and get to the bottom of it."

"Don't be silly! Do it now. If you're in some kind of danger—"

"I doubt that's the case, but . . . maybe you're right. Would you arrange it?"

"Who do you want me to call?"

"The Mitford Agency in New Haven. I understand they're top notch."

"I'll get on it right away. But . . . Roland, maybe you should hire a personal bodyguard, too. Just to be on the safe side."

"No, that feels like an overreaction. Besides, I don't want to upset Octavia."

"Before she arrived, we never had any problems like this," he grumbled.

"You think she's having me followed?"

"No, of course not. But—"

"Because that's ludicrous, Buddy." Roland sounded impatient. "And I don't want you to worry her with this, do you understand me? We'll handle it ourselves."

"Okay, okay. You know what's best."

"I do. Now, will you be joining us for the holidays? You haven't said."

"I'm just back at Innishannon for a few hours. I'm planning to spend Christmas with my sons and their families in New Jersey. It'll be a big group this year. Over twenty people. But, as far as I know, Grace is staying here." He cleared his throat. "I just wish—" His voice trailed off.

"Wish what?"

"Oh, you know. The same old thing. That our families could be closer."

"When are you leaving?"

"Later this afternoon."

"But you'll be back for the wedding."

"Don't worry. Your best man will . . . 'get you to the church on time'." He sang the last few words of the song in his pleasant baritone.

"That was Cukor's movie, not mine. But I appreciate the thought. You are my best man, you know."

"Thanks, Rolo."

Before Buddy could leave, Octavia whipped the door back and burst into the room. "Roland, we need to talk to you. It can't wait."

The two men looked startled. Both stood.

Since Cordelia was part of the "we," she stepped into the room behind her sister. Of course she knew why Octavia had made such a sudden entrance. Roland would never guess now that they'd been listening at the door for the past few minutes. It was a clever ploy, proving once again that her sister was indeed a true Thorn. Machiavellian to the core.

"I was just leaving," said Buddy, offering Octavia a somewhat crumpled smile.

"Not before you meet Cordelia, Octavia's sister," said Roland, his voice proud and hearty.

Cordelia couldn't help but notice that the brothers weren't much alike. Buddy was a taller, portlier version of Roland, although it wasn't his size that set him apart. It was his general dowdiness—even in the expensive clothes. He looked like a sack of potatoes inside Armani burlap. But his eyes were kind and lively. Since Octavia had said such mean things about him, Cordelia was inclined to like him—just for the sake of argument.

"It's very nice to meet you," said Buddy, extending his hand.

"Nice to meet you, too. I guess we're all going to be family soon." Was that grinding teeth she heard?

"Yes." His smile seemed genuine, but a little weary. "Well, I'm afraid I've got to get going. I'm flying out of New Haven later this afternoon and I've got work to do before I go."

"Have a good trip," called Roland.

Buddy waved as he left the room.

Octavia could now focus her full attention on her fiancée. "Roland, Cordelia is being her usual obstinate self. She won't listen to a word I say, so we decided to let you make the final decision."

Smiling indulgently, Roland sat back down and pulled an ottoman under his feet. "What's the problem?"

"I do not *do* puffy sleeves," said Cordelia.

"Pardon me?"

Raising her chin and steeling herself for battle, Cordelia continued, "Puffy sleeves should be outlawed. People should be shot on sight for wearing them. And designers who foist them off on innocent maids of honor should be lynched."

Roland took a moment to absorb her vehemence. "Puffy sleeves?" he repeated, looking confused.

"The dress I bought for her to wear to the wedding," said Octavia. "She doesn't like it. She doesn't like the color either."

"I do not wear *puce*."

"It's not puce," growled Octavia. "It's purple velvet."

"It's puce and it has puffy sleeves and it makes me look like an eggplant."

"Amazing," muttered Octavia. "That's just the look I was going for."

Roland held up his hand for quiet. "Clearly, the dress is unacceptable."

"Thank you," said Cordelia. She knew Roland would be the picture of reason.

"Wait until you hear what she wants to wear," said Octavia, perching on a chair next to a large potted palm.

Cordelia was the only one left standing. She felt the spotlight on her. Thank God she was born for the spotlight. "I've already made my own arrangements for my wedding attire. I'm wearing a tux."

"She's coming in drag," explained Octavia.

"I'm familiar with the concept," said Roland, giving Cordelia an appraising look.

"Well," said Octavia, tapping her foot on the stone tiles. "Tell her she can't. That it's out of the question. I won't have my wedding turned into a circus."

"I refuse to wear that dreary Lady Macbeth rag, not that a woman of her stature would be caught dead in puffy sleeves."

"So what *should* I have bought you?" asked Octavia.

"Well," said Cordelia, thinking it over. "I do gypsy. I do large and sexy. I do some tenth-grade kitsch—when I'm in the mood. I do cowboy. I do Joan Crawford. I do glitter and feather boas on occasion. I do some sixties Earth Mother. I have my 'corporate corporate' look. I have a favorite matador outfit. I've done Randolph Duke and Tommy Hilfiger, when I've had the money. I like fake leopard skin. I like silk and satin. I do lots of retro. I've been known to order from the Victoria Secret catalog, although that wouldn't work for the wedding. I do Dracula. And I do drag. The world is a costume ball and Cordelia Thorn is the queen. But I never—nor will I *ever*—do L. L. Bean, 'country,' or puffy sleeves."

Roland blinked several times. "You certainly know yourself well."

"It's called 'being opinionated,' " said Octavia.

After a few seconds, Roland replied, "Let her wear the tux."

"What? You're joking!" Octavia's face looked like a mirror that had just been shattered by a large rock.

"I'm wearing a morning coat," said Roland. "What sort of tux do you have?"

"Black. Elegant. Just a tad conservative. It should fit in perfectly."

"What do I do with the bridesmaid dress?" demanded Octavia.

"Why don't you wear it at your next cocktail party?" offered Cordelia.

"Me?" she said indignantly. "I wouldn't be caught dead in that monstrosity."

16

Jane wasn't sure why Gracie seemed so intent on inviting her to her third floor apartment for pizza on Friday night, but since she'd agreed to it, she reluctantly headed up the back staircase. It was a couple minutes after seven. In Minnesota, that would be considered fashionably late.

Once up on third floor, Jane was met by a long, carpeted corridor and a series of closed doors, four on each side. Unlike the first and second floor, the woodwork was painted and the doors were smaller. Everything was less opulent, right down to the brass door handles. She assumed this had been the servants' quarters in years past, which would account for the number of rooms and the smaller size. Not sure of where to knock, Jane cleared her throat, hoping it would announce her arrival.

From the far end of the hallway, Gracie poked her head out one of the doors. At the same moment, a small white bichon charged into the hallway, its tail wagging so fast it was almost a blur.

"Busby, *cool* it," called Gracie, her tone annoyed.

The dog raced to where Jane was standing and leaped uninvited into her arms, licking her face and acting insanely excited, as only a dog could. "He's certainly friendly."

"He belongs to my boyfriend. I keep him when he's out of town on business. I hope you like dogs." She took a sip from the beer bottle she was holding.

"I do."

"Uncle Rolo doesn't. That's why I make him stay upstairs. Sometimes he pulls a jail break, but hey, who doesn't?"

Jane carried Busby to the other end of the hall. As she moved past Gracie, she saw that her multicolored dreadlocks had been undone. Tonight she looked like a colorful sheep in need of a good spring sheering. She was wearing worn, light blue overalls—torn in spots—and an oversize white man's shirt, the sleeves rolled up to her elbows.

"I was just about to take the frozen pizza out of the freezer. I hope you're hungry."

Jane wasn't. At least not for what Gracie was preparing. She would have preferred something just as simple, but a little more ambitious. Say, a good cheese or two, some fresh baked bread from a local bakery, pears or apples, and a nice glass of wine.

"Help yourself to a beer. Oh, and sit over there," said Gracie, nodding to a funky-looking brown Naugahyde armchair next to an equally funky-looking floor lamp with an orange paper shade. She busied herself at the counter cutting up the pizza. It had to be small enough to fit into the toaster oven.

Before Jane sat down, Busby jumped out of her arms and scampered away. That allowed her a chance to grab herself a beer from the refrigerator. It was the only major appliance in the room. When she opened it, she found that it was stocked with Coke, Mountain Dew, Samuel Adams Red Lager, milk, and a bottle of ketchup. All the essentials.

Hearing Busby growl, Gracie turned around and shouted, "Stop it, Maurice." Turning to Jane, she added, "I've got three cats. They all like to torment each other."

"You must like animals."

"Of course. They're my co-stars."

Jane didn't understand the reference, but decided not to pursue it. Glancing around, she made herself semicomfortable on the stiff Naugahyde. "You've actually created a loft up here."

The space had been opened up by cutting through the walls separating the rooms and creating broad archways. Behind the closed doors, the apartment was open from one end to the other. The living room, where Jane was now seated, was painted chartreuse and pink and the furniture was mostly blond wood. It was straight out of the fifties, very stylized and cold. The kitchen was merely a stainless steel sink with a white formica counter on either side. On one end sat a toaster oven and a microwave. On the other was a hot plate and a state of the art coffee/espresso maker. Above the counter was some simple open shelving. Gracie seemed to be partial to breakfast cereals, salsa and corn chips, and tea. She didn't have many dishes, but what she did have were expensive, especially the glassware. Jane wasn't positive, but it looked like antique Fostoria.

Beyond the living room was the bedroom, which looked like something out of a romance novel. Everything was done in pastels and feminine fluff. The bed was draped with several satin comforters, and an abundance of pillows covered in flower patterns, paisley, and striped silk were tossed against the headboard. Compared to the starkness of the living room, it looked messy and decadent—but a studied, artful chaos. "What's on the other side of the hall?"

"I haven't renovated that yet. I use one of the rooms for business, the rest for storage. This is the only side that's hooked up."

Jane took a swallow of beer. "What do you mean, 'hooked up'?"

"To my web cams." She nodded to a camera attached to the wall above the doorway.

"What's a web cam?"

"I broadcast my life on the Internet. I call it 'GracielandLive.' You can find it at *gracielandlive.com*."

"I don't get it," said Jane, still confused. "Is the camera on all the time? Can anyone look in?"

"That's the point. It's a continuous webcast. I have five other cameras throughout the loft."

"You mean it really is *live*?"

She nodded.

"People are watching us right now?"

She looked over her shoulder and grinned. "Yup."

"Hearing us?"

"Not yet. In a lot of ways, the technology is still in its infancy, but it won't be long before I begin to use both sound and streaming video on a daily basis. As it is right now, if you went online to check out my site, you'd see us here, but the image would take thirty seconds to refresh. In other words, it would be a still, silent picture that changed every thirty seconds."

"What's 'streaming video'?" Jane took another swallow of beer.

"Moving pictures."

"Like TV?"

"I prefer to think of this as filmmaking. Or, a combination of film-making and documentary art. It's all very new. Very exciting."

"Like *The Truman Show*."

"Actually, that's close. Except, I know I'm being observed. I invite people into my life. All of it." She stressed the last three words, then turned around to see Jane's reaction.

"All of it," repeated Jane. "You mean—"

"I have a camera pointed at the bathtub so people can watch me bathe or take a shower. They can watch me sleep. Eat. Work at my computer. I paint my body sometimes. Entertain guests. Have sex."

Jane glanced up at the camera, then back at Gracie.

"Most of the streaming video sites on the web are total porn. That's not my focus, but since sex is part of my life I don't exclude it. It adds spice. What the hell."

"I see." She turned the beer bottle around in her hand, feeling suddenly self-conscious, as if she were being stared at—which she was.

"Do you?" asked Gracie. Grabbing another bottle of beer from the refrigerator, she twisted off the cap, then returned to the counter and leaned back against it. "I also archive a lot of what I do—my favorite moments. I tinker with my world constantly. I love to try anything new. I live to experience life, to experiment. Across the hall, I've stored tons of costumes, furniture, artwork, junk—anything I come across that I think would be fun to include in GracielandLive. My website is a work of art in progress. A journal of a life. An exploration of what it is to be human in the new millennium. Come on. I'll show you." She plunked a couple of pieces of the cut pizza into the toaster oven, checked the temperature setting, then closed the door.

Jane followed her past the bedroom into a study. Once again, the interior was completely different from the first two rooms. Department store mannequins sat in chairs and stood in groups, making the room seem strangely crowded. Some were nude, but most were dressed in a variety of get-ups. There was a marine in full battle dress, a long black wig sticking out from under his helmet. He seemed to be in deep conversation with a male mannequin wearing a red corset and sheer black stockings. There was a female whose only article of clothing was a pair of sunglasses, a man wearing an old-fashioned double-breasted suit, and a woman in a flapper outfit. A few were wearing mismatched clothes from garage sales. Gracie had even suspended one of the mannequins from the ceiling directly above the computer monitor. It looked as if it were flying.

"It feels like we're interrupting a party," said Jane, noticing a male mannequin impaled on the far wall, a railroad spike protruding from its chest. She couldn't help but grimace.

Gracie's computer was already on. She quickly called up her Internet browser, then moved straight to her site. "Sit in my chair," she said, keeping her hand on the mouse.

Almost in a trance, Jane sat down. For the next few minutes, she was taken on a tour of GracielandLive. An initial montage page gave the general layout of the site. GracielandLive (five webcams). GracielandArt. GracielandZoo. Oracles and Incantations. The GracielandJournal (updated daily). Erotic Graceland. Archives. The Coffin Texts. E-mail GracielandLive. Guests. Membership. Links. Smack in the middle of the page was a picture of Innishannon. Underneath it was the caption, "GracielandLive, the true Magic Kingdom."

"I get it now," whispered Jane. "Co-stars. You said that earlier. You meant your pets."

"I include pictures of all of them. It's the GracielandZoo."

"What does 'Membership' mean?" asked Jane as Gracie continued to click through the site. It was all fascinating, especially the artwork. Something she could spend hours exploring.

"If you want to log on to the complete site at any time, you have to become a member. It's ten dollars a month."

"Do you have many members?"

She removed a large black cat from an overstuffed chair and sat down. "You know, I started doing this in college as a joke for some of my friends. I had one ancient webcam in my crummy apartment. I did a lot of mugging for the camera—that's about it. Back then, I called it Gracie.com. Somehow, it caught on. And it started taking more and more of my time. I barely finished my dissertation because I'd become so fascinated by this whole new world."

Jane couldn't help but notice the excited gleam in her eyes. Gracie truly loved what she was doing.

"The thing is, once I moved to Innishannon and Uncle Rolo told me that the estate would be mine after his death, I started rethinking some of my plans. I've now built the entire site around the notion that this house *is* Gracieland. It's like . . . another realm. A kingdom of magic and wonder. People all over the world recognize Innishannon as Gracieland. If I do say so myself, it's quickly becoming a modern icon. I'm having a poster printed right now. I'll sell it on the site, and I'll make money too." Busby trotted into the room and jumped into her lap. "I'm bursting with ideas. It's all I want to talk about—all I want to do."

"But about your membership numbers—"

"Oh, right. I started out with ten or so. Just friends. In one year it grew to four hundred. Just about everyone hooked up to the web at Yale logged on to the site at one time or another. I guess you could say I became a campus celebrity." She grinned. "Right now, I'm up to almost three thousand, and it's growing every day. It's a very cool community. Doctors. Professors. Tech nerds. Truck drivers. House-wives with a yen for adventure. I have a camcorder I took with me last year to the Sundance Film Festival. I did some mini-interviews that eventually appeared on my site. And I made tons of friends—important friends. I'm going to Cannes this year, as well as the Slamdance Film Festival. That's basically documentary, but I figure I'll learn a lot. I've also been asked to do some Internet radio. Very cutting edge. When Innishannon is finally mine, I'm going to build GracielandLive into something much bigger than the writers of *The Truman Show* ever envisioned. This place is going to be a mecca for the arts—especially, Internet arts. When people tune in, they're going to get an eyeful and an earful. I know it sounds egotistical, but Gracieland is my life. I plan to make it a fascinating one."

Jane found her enthusiasm contagious. She did the math in her head and realized Gracie was pulling in about thirty thousand a month.

As if answering Jane's unspoken question, Gracie added, "I spend a lot of money on equipment. Right now, it seems like as soon as I buy some piece of hardware, it's outdated. And software is like produce—it gets old fast, has to be thrown away. I'm even working on something that will help smooth out the glitches in Internet audio and video technology. The problem is, not everything works on every computer. That will change in time, but I have a hard time waiting—for *anything*."

"Christian said your degree was in computer science."

"My graduate degree, yes. I have an undergraduate degree in communications, with a minor in art, but I also took a lot of undergraduate course work in both American literature and history. I love it all." She leaned back in her chair, stretched her legs out in front of her, and crossed her ankles. "When I first found out I was going to inherit Innishannon—after I got smashed on champagne and Campari with a bunch of my compadres—I did some research on the house. All Rolo knew when he bought the place was that the man who he bought it from purchased it in 1943. But it was built in 1922—during the Roaring Twenties, the time of 'Flaming Youth.' " She laughed. "That feels so right to me, like Gracieland was meant to be here. There are so many parallels between the twenties and now. Just like then, the world is an incredibly scary place. And just like the children of the twenties, I can't do a damn thing to change it. So what *do* I do?" The question was rhetorical. "I live in a sensual microcosm—just like the *The Great Gatsby,* which has always been my favorite book. I'm self-absorbed and feel no guilt about it because my life could end at any moment. All I'm interested in are my own pursuits and my own pleasure. But then, that leaves me feeling restless. My whole damn generation is restless, lonely, and hungry. I'm sick of the system, but it's a monolith. A brick wall. So I ignore it. My uncle and my grandfather figure I'm shallow, but as far as I'm concerned, it's simple survival."

"You've spent a lot of time thinking about all this."

Gracie sipped her beer. "And writing about it. It's all on the site. It's my job to analyze my life as well as live it."

To Jane, Gracie seemed a little obsessed—if one could be a "little" obsessed.

"This house has a fascinating history," continued Gracie, stroking Busby's head. "Did you know someone was actually murdered here? The man who built Innishannon, Alexander Kirk, worked in New York as a Wall Street financier. He was originally from Ireland, and named his house after the place where he grew up. The Connecticut shore must have reminded him of home. Anyway, it seems he had lots of girlfriends, so he stuck his wife and kids up here so he'd be free to play around in New York. She wasn't stupid. She eventually figured out what was happening and threw a fit. What does he do?"

"Divorces her?"

"Can't. He's Catholic."

"Okay. He murders her."

"Bingo. It was poison. The police didn't put it together right away because he was a clever old fart. He used a tea made from jimsonweed. Ever heard of it?"

Jane shook her head.

"It's not hard to find. The police finally figured it out and Alexander Kirk spent the rest of his life in jail. The kids went to live with relatives, and the house was sold. The next guy to live here was a man who produced plays on Broadway. Jeremiah Withers. By the time he moved in, it was 1926. Under his influence, Innishannon became a major gathering place for actors, authors, playwrights, and fine artists who wanted to escape the hot New York summers. Zelda and F. Scott Fitzgerald spent a lot of time here. So did Noel Coward and George Gershwin. Alfred Steiglitz came a few times, as did Orson Welles. Can you imagine it, what this place must have been like back then—and what ghosts are still walking the halls at night? During the second world war, Withers sold it to another man—Allen Darcy. Darcy was an English lord and only used the home when he came over on business, a dozen or so times a year. That's who Rolo bought it from in 1957. My dad grew up here because Gramps and Gram lived here from fifty-seven until Rolo moved in."

"Have you told your uncle and grandfather about the house's history?"

"Oh, sure. As I find stuff out, I pass it on." Gracie sniffed the air, then bolted out of her chair. "Damn!" she shrieked, racing back through the bedroom and living room to the toaster oven.

It was too late. Jane could smell the smoke.

"I burned the damn pizza," she called, slapping open the door and pulling out the charred mess. Sounding dejected, she called, "I guess I'm not much of a cook."

"That's all right," said Jane. "I'm not very hungry."

Her voice brightening, she asked, "How 'bout some chips and salsa?"

To be honest, it sounded better than the pizza. "Fine." She glanced at the mannequins, then down at Busby. He was used to them, but she wasn't. "Why don't we sit in the living room?"

"You read my mind," called Gracie.

As Jane walked back through the bedroom, she saw that Gracie had set a bag of chips and a jar of salsa on the coffee table and was examining the inside of the toaster oven to see if it was completely ruined. When she was done, she opened a bottom cupboard, removed a bottle of tequila and two shot glasses and sat down next to Jane on the living room couch.

For the next hour or so, they ate chips, did a few shots, and talked, mainly about Jane's life back in Minnesota. She felt a little strange, knowing that there was a camera trained on them, but just as Gracie said she would, she forgot about it after a while.

Finally, when there was a lull in the conversation, Gracie got up, turned on some soft music, dimmed the lights, then returned to the couch and sat down, a little closer to Jane this time.

"You have a lot of visitors up here?" asked Jane, downing her fourth shot. She hadn't eaten since lunch, so the buzz from the tequila hit her quickly, making her feel mellow and relaxed. Altogether pleasant.

"I like to keep it interesting for my viewing audience."

"Tell me about your grandfather."

"What do you want to know?"

"Well, are he and Roland close?"

Gracie eased her arm across the back of the couch. "He's always taken care of Gramps—of the whole family, for that matter. Gramps was his personal assistant in Hollywood, and then later, Rolo sent him back here to caretake Innishannon. But . . . close? I don't know if I'd use that word. It's always been my impression that Rolo says 'Jump,' and my grandfather asks 'How high?' Not that he's resentful. I've never noticed that. He's very grateful that his big brother hauled him out of an orphanage when he was still a kid and helped him straighten out his life. See, Gramps isn't much of a go-getter. But he's incredibly loyal. A sweet guy, really, although sometimes he's had to act tough. I may be wrong about this, but if there was ever any dirty work to be done, I think Rolo sent Gramps to do it. That way, my great uncle could continue to be beloved and revered, while Gramps took the fall as the bad guy. It worked out well. Gramps didn't mind. He always looked at what he did for Rolo as a job. All jobs have parts you don't like. My grandfather is a practical man. And he's good with people."

"Are you saying Roland isn't?"

She shrugged. "He's an *important* man. Important men don't always consider the results of their actions, they simply go ahead and do what they want. Rolo isn't imperial or anything. He's just not always Mr. Sensitive."

"And your grandfather is?"

"Usually, yeah." Gracie poured them each another shot.

"What about Christian? You two seem like pretty good friends."

"We are. We've been sleeping together since I was sixteen."

Jane tried not to look surprised, although Gracie's openness had caught her off guard. "Does he ever talk about his father?"

"Sure. All the time. He hated him."

"Really." That was news to Jane.

"Lew Wallace might have been a great father figure on the silver screen, but in real life he was a dud. He was never around because he was always off making a movie. Mary Beth, Christian's mother, wasn't much better. She had a series of disastrous affairs. Christian got dumped a lot so she could go play. Then, after they divorced in 'fifty-one, she remarried—another guy Christian couldn't stand. By the time Christian was a young man, Lew was paying more attention to him, but it was too late. They had way too much negative history behind them." She began playing with the wisps of hair at the back of Jane's neck.

Jane wasn't surprised. She had a feeling this might be point of their get together tonight. "You knew that Lew was murdered."

"Sure. Christian was one of the suspects. But he had an alibi." She started to laugh.

"What's so funny."

"The alibi was a crock. Christian had been over at his dad's house late that afternoon, but he lied about it—got his girlfriend to lie, too. I'm not saying he murdered Lew. I'm sure he didn't. But they'd had a terrible fight that morning. Christian came back for round two later in the day. See, Christian's girlfriend was some snooty tobacco heiress. They'd just gotten engaged. Her parents thought Christian was way cool because he was Lew's son. They didn't know how close the two of them weren't. Anyway, Lew was about to do something that Christian thought would wreck his chances with the girl. So they argued about it."

"Do you know what it was?"

"God, this is all such ancient history. But, yeah. Let me think." She closed her eyes. "I believe his dad had written a book. Something a little too sexy for its day. Christian thought if it ever got published, his girlfriend's parents would pull the plug on the marriage. And since the marriage meant easy street to Christian, he got screaming angry. He

128

blamed his dad for wrecking his childhood, and now he was about to wreck his engagement. All for some porno novel."

"It was a novel?"

"Yeah, that's what he said."

"Sounds like a motive for murder to me."

Gracie looked deeply into Jane's eyes. "You do have an evil mind. I like that."

"Just making a comment."

"Christian wouldn't have the guts to murder someone. For one thing, he's not clever enough to pull it off—at least, not by himself."

"You don't think very highly of him, do you?"

Again, she shrugged.

"Did he ever say who he thought did kill his father?"

Gracie moved even closer to Jane. "He's got a theory. He thinks his father's old girlfriend, Verna Lange, did it."

"Why?"

"She was staying with Lew at the time of the murder. They weren't getting along. The police said a kid saw someone leaving by the back door right around the time of his death. Chris figures it had to be Verna."

"But none of the accounts said anything about Verna staying with him."

Gracie backed up a bit. "Have you been reading about it?"

"My best friend's sister is about to marry Roland Lester. Lester was the central suspect in a homicide. Sure, I'm interested."

"Well, keep what I told you about Verna under your hat." She thought for a moment, then added, "You know, since you're interested, I've got my own theory about Lew Wallace's death."

"I'd love to hear it."

"Well, I figure the novel he was writing was a thinly veiled account of his ten-year affair with Verna. Believe it or not, my grandfather actually walked in on them once, *in flagrante,* as they say. He wouldn't tell me what they were doing, but from the way he made it sound, it was pretty kinky. My guess is, Verna found out about the book and threw a fit. Killed Lew in a murderous rage, then took off with the manuscript. I even said something to my grandfather about it once. He denied there ever was a book. Christian wasn't lying, so I knew I'd struck pay dirt—and I do mean dirt."

129

"Why would your grandfather lie?"

"He was probably just parroting what Rolo'd told him."

"Why would Roland lie?"

"To protect someone."

"Verna?"

"That would be my guess."

"But she'd just killed his best friend."

"Verna and Rolo were tight, too, just as tight as he was with Lew. They were like the three musketeers back then. Always together—at least that's what Gramps told me."

"What did your grandfather think of Lew?"

She hesitated. "I'm not really sure. He's never talked about him much. But I do know Gramps had a major thing for Verna once. You may not believe it, but old Buddy Lester had a real eye for the women back in his younger days. A little like Christian, in that respect."

"But . . . I don't get it. Why would Christian want to protect Verna Lange?"

"This may sound weird to you, but she was really nice to him when he was young. One of the few people who talked to him, liked to spend time with him. What can I say? He cares about her. He loathed his dad. Put it together." The tips of her fingers began stroking the back of Jane's neck.

Jane had just about had it with the seduction scene. "Gracie, come on. Stop."

"Why? You're a dyke. I'm bi. And under these threads I'm a very beautiful woman. Don't tell me you haven't been undressing me with your eyes for the last half hour. I'm not blind."

"Well, I—"

"You knew what I wanted the minute you walked in here. Don't act surprised."

"I'm not surprised. I'm just not interested."

"Sure you are. I bet I could do some stuff to you no one's ever done before."

"And we could provide a few titillating moments for your 'membership.' "

"Would that be so bad?"

"Yeah, I think so." She disengaged herself and got up.

"You're actually leaving?"

"It's about time for Roland's movie."

"But . . . we could make our own movie."

Jane thought it was an incredibly lame line. She wasn't turned on by the voyeuristic possibilities, and she never did like being a foregone conclusion. "Look, Gracie, I just ended a relationship. Or . . . maybe I haven't exactly ended it, but I'm going to. My life is kind of complicated right now." Out of kindness, she couldn't simply walk out.

"I thought we could spend the night together. No strings."

"You're very attractive, but . . . I'm just not up for it tonight."

Gracie looked crestfallen.

On her way to the door, Jane asked, "Should I save you a seat in the screening room?"

Gracie was pouting now. "I'm not coming."

"That's too bad. Thanks for the shots and the chips. I enjoyed the conversation and the tour of Gracieland."

"Right."

"I'll see you later."

Gracie grunted. Jane assumed it was her Gatsbyesque way of saying good-bye.

17

Jane stood at the head of the central stairs, one hand on the banister, breathing in the silence of the old manor house. She couldn't remember ever being at a home quite this grand before. In the daylight, the shabbiness was more apparent, but at night she actually could imagine the ghosts of Orson Welles, Scott and Zelda Fitzgerald, and even the Great Gatsby himself, walking the halls, champagne glasses in hand, jazz playing from an old Victrola, laughter and the smell of the ocean breeze floating in through the open windows. It was summertime—the image dictated it. The image also dictated elegance, high spirits, and inevitable tragedy. For a moment, she wondered if she was sensing the past, or seeing the future. There was something hungry about Innishannon, as if it were waiting, impatiently, for its own rebirth.

As she set off down the broad, carpeted steps, she heard the phone ring. Since no one seemed to be answering it, she assumed that every-one was already down in the screening room. She hurried to the small table just outside the dining room doors and picked up the receiver.

"Hello?" she said, sitting down on a small upholstered bench. She bent to brush a piece of lint off one of her suede boots.

"I'd like to speak to Jane Lawless, please."

It was a woman's voice. "This is Jane." She couldn't imagine who'd be calling her here. Then it struck her. "Julia?" She straightened up.

"Hey, sweetheart. Hi."

"Where are you?"

"I'm still in Paris. I'm calling from my hotel room."

"You sound like you're just down the street."

"The miracle of modern technology."

"What time is it there?"

"It's early." Her voice sounded unusually tense. "Very early. About three in the morning. I couldn't sleep. It's Christmas Eve tonight, Janey. I just had to hear your voice."

It was six hours later in Paris. Jane had done the mental calculation days ago, which probably meant that, once again, she'd been thinking about Julia more than she realized. "How did you find me?"

"I called your house. Your brother answered and said you and Cordelia had gone to Connecticut for the holidays. He gave me the phone number where you were staying. He didn't really say much about why you'd made the trip."

So that's where Peter was. She'd tried calling him yesterday at the lodge, but no one had answered. She was delighted to hear he'd taken her up on her offer to stay at the house. "It's a long story. Cordelia's sister is getting married."

"I didn't know she had a sister."

"That's the long story. We can talk about it another time."

"So . . . how are you feeling? Your leg? Your headaches?"

"I'm better, thanks."

"Really? You're not just saying that?"

"No, Julia. I'm fine."

"Are you still using a cane?"

"I brought one with me, but I haven't needed it."

"Peter said you'd cut your hair."

Of all the things he could have said, why had he told her that? "Yeah, I guess I needed a change."

Silence.

"What about you?" asked Jane. "Are you having a good time?" They'd been talking for all of a minute and already the conversation was strained.

"Actually, I sat next to a very interesting man on the plane coming over. He's Canadian and works with a number of AIDS groups in Africa. I mentioned that I was a doctor and that HIV had been my primary focus for the past few years. Before I knew it, he was asking me if I'd like to help him. He's been working primarily in Botswana, but he wants to expand his focus. He's hoping to help the U.N. mount

133

an education campaign in South Africa. Since I don't need a regular income, and I've got the necessary credentials, he said I'd be perfect for the job."

"What did you say?"

"That I'd think about it. He needs an answer soon." More hesitation. "Janey, I miss you so much." She waited for a response.

Jane didn't know what to say.

"Look, I know I tried once before and you said no, but I'd love it if you could come spend a few weeks with me. It's so beautiful here in Paris. And we need the time together . . . to sort things out."

Of course they needed to talk, thought Jane, but she had no intention of flying to Europe. "I can't, Julia."

"Sure. I understand." Her response came a little too quickly.

Jane's impatience made her feel heartless and selfish. Why couldn't she just tell Julia the truth—that in her mind, their relationship was beyond repair. Except, it seemed like such a cruel thing to do over the phone. "Julia, I—"

"Don't say anything more, Janey. Not now. Not yet. I shouldn't have called."

"No, of course you can call."

"Have a wonderful Christmas."

She felt like a total jerk. "Thanks. You too."

"I love you, Jane. I know you're still angry—"

She heard a knock on the front door. Standing up, she said, "I'm not angry. Not anymore."

"Then . . . try to hold on to the good times. I'm not a bad person, I just got caught up in something I couldn't handle. I never wanted to involve you in my problems. You believe that, don't you?"

"Yes, Julia. I do."

"I'll call. Or I'll write—let you know my plans."

"Okay." Another few raps with the door knocker. "Julia, there's someone here."

"Right, I understand."

Jane wanted to tell her not to be so damned understanding. Maybe if she got mad, it would make things easier—for both of them. "I'm not trying to put you off. Someone really is here and I have to answer the door. If you want to wait—"

"No, I better go. Merry Christmas, Janey. Be well—and be safe."

Before she could respond, Julia hung up.

Slowly, Jane shut her eyes. She was close to tears. She did remember all the good times, and she missed them too. But the trust was gone. Broken into a million pieces. How could two people have a relationship without trust?

Whoever was outside had begun to hammer on the door with the knocker to make themselves heard.

"I'm coming," called Jane, wiping a hand across her eyes.

As she drew the door back, she found a woman standing outside. She was dressed in a loud leopard skin coat, and wearing a wide-brimmed felt hat that, in the darkness, covered the upper portion of her face.

"It's about time," said the woman, sweeping past Jane as if she owned the place. "A person could freeze to death out there. My bags are in the trunk."

"And . . . you're telling me this . . . why?"

"Who are you?"

"Not the butler." Jane had just about had it for today. Perhaps it was time to retreat to her room with a glass of brandy. She watched as the woman removed a package of Virginia Slims from her purse, stuck one into a black and silver cigarette holder, clenched it between her teeth, then used a gold lighter to ignite the tip. "Your name?"

"Jane Lawless."

She sucked in the smoke, then blew it out her nose as she considered the response. "I knew a Berti Lawless once. Set designer at MGM. Any relation?"

"I don't think so."

"No," she said, eying Jane appraisingly. "I don't think so either."

"And you are?"

"Verna Lange."

"Oh!" Jane was surprised, and a little embarrassed that she hadn't recognized her. Then again, Verna had aged a great deal since her days in Hollywood. "I didn't know you were coming. I . . . suppose you're here for the wedding."

Verna removed the cigarette holder from her teeth. "Possibly," she said, stepping over to a mirror and checking her makeup. "Who's getting married?"

"Roland and Octavia Thorn."

Both eyebrows shot upward. "Roland? My *God*." She looked away, absorbing the news, then glanced back at the mirror, touching the tip of her little finger to her lipstick. "Octavia Thorn, the actress? The *young* actress?"

"She's thirty-four."

"Yes, you have a point. Thirty-four *is* the brink of old age in movies. Good thing for her she works mainly on the legitimate stage. She can stay there until they have to wheel her out on a gurney." Continuing to look in the mirror, she removed her hat with a flourish, patting her orange hair back into place. In her day, she'd been one of Hollywood's most ravishing redheads. The hair dye she used now was just short of Day-Glo.

Verna still had her signature full red lips, though the lipstick was painted over the edges to create the same youthful effect. The skin was tight across her cheekbones, undoubtedly due to some expensive cosmetic surgery, but looked fragile and paper thin. And the flesh around her chin and neck was coming unglued. It was probably time for another visit to the doctor. Her figure was still slim. Under the coat, she was wearing a black leotard and pearls. Large, gaudy pearls. Her earrings were also pearl, as was a ring on her right hand. She was a short woman. In high heels, she came up to Jane's nose. For an actress, it was probably an advantage to be short. Jane remembered the tales of the actor Alan Ladd standing on a box to kiss his co-stars. It couldn't have been very good for his male ego.

Verna Lange had to be in her seventies, thought Jane, though she could have passed for sixty-five because of all the construction work.

"Will you do me a favor?" asked Verna, taking off her coat and tossing it and the hat on the bench next to the phone. "Will you be a dear and go tell Roland I'm here?"

"Everyone's in the screening room watching a movie."

"Well," she said, a mischievous glint in her eye. "Why settle for celluloid when you have a real movie legend right in your own living room?"

One thing Jane learned early about Verna Lange: She wasn't shy about her place in Hollywood history.

"God, I can't believe you're really here," said Roland. He was sitting next to her on one of the living room couches, holding her hands in his. "What's it been? Three, four years?"

"You weren't in very good shape the last time I dropped in for a stay." She glanced at Octavia. "I'd say you've recovered."

Everyone had gathered in front of the fire. Jane and Cordelia were sitting together on a love seat. Hilda and Gracie, who seemed to have recovered from her snit, had drawn up two of the tapestry chairs. Octavia sat on a window seat next to Ellie, and Christian stood by the hearth, smoking, his arm resting on the mantle.

Jane was amazed at the transformation in the room. With the extravagantly decorated and lighted Christmas tree by the bay window, the scented candles, the red, green, and gold bows, the fresh eucalyptus bouquet mixed with holly, and all the pine boughs draped here and there, the room smelled like a pine forest inside an expensive department store.

"I'm still living in Atlanta," continued Verna, removing the cigarette holder from her lips and waving it around as she talked. "Still doing my work with UNESCO. My fourth husband, God rest his soul, has been gone for three years now, but I can't seem to make the break and move back to civilization."

"Atlanta is a rather cosmopolitan city," said Ellie.

Verna turned to look at her. "You ever live in the south?"

"No. But I worked in Atlanta a few years ago doing research. I really liked it there."

"Where are you from originally?"

"Southern California."

"The south is a different world, trust me. Thankfully, I have credentials. My mother was born and raised in Charleston." Her smile was sly, but full of good humor. "Believe it or not, I may be flying to Morocco soon. The White House has asked me to chair the U.S. delegation to UNESCO's World Heritage Commission."

Roland looked not only surprised, but impressed. "Congratulations. Talk about a lady who never slows down."

"I'm quite proud of the appointment. I thought I'd come give you the good news in person. My work on the preservation of worldwide national and cultural heritage has finally been rewarded—not that the work isn't reward enough. On the other hand, I've never been one to eschew the limelight. I've even been invited to the White House to lunch with the president and the First Lady."

"When will that happen?" asked Cordelia, hanging on her every word.

"In early January. The press will all be there. I intend to make a real splash, garner as much publicity as I can for the cause."

"I have no doubt the press still adores you," said Roland, squeezing her hand.

"You're right, they do." Glancing at Ellie again, she said, "Southern California, huh? Where in Southern California?"

"Pasadena."

"Ellie is a documentary artist," explained Roland. "She's here because she's doing a documentary on my life."

Verna's large, expressive eyes grew round. "You're joking."

Jane tried to define the look. It fell somewhere between startled disbelief and abject horror.

But Verna recovered quickly. "That's a wonderful idea." She tapped some ash off the tip of her cigarette, keeping her attention focused on the ashtray. "I'm surprised no one's done it before."

"There's been interest," said Roland, leaning forward and cupping his hands around his knees. "But I just wasn't ready."

"I'd love to interview you, Ms. Lange," said Ellie. "You and Mr. Lester are such close friends. I'm sure you could add a lot."

"Ohhhhoho," she laughed, blowing smoke out of the side of her mouth. "You have no idea." When she looked up, her eyes came to rest on Cordelia. "So, you're Octavia's sister."

Jane felt it was an effort to change the subject.

Cordelia nodded. "That's what my parents tell me."

"My father will be arriving tomorrow," said Octavia, stumbling over the last word. She seemed more than a little awed by Verna's presence.

"He's a widower," said Christian with a smirk. "An eminent doctor. Who knows where true love might lie at this point in your life?"

"Thank you for that poignant analysis of old age," said Verna, flashing her eyes at him. "I've missed you, too, dear."

The smirk changed to a smile.

"We're not the Kennedys," sighed Cordelia, fluffing her hair as if the conversation had never left her family. "But the Thorns have a long and proud history in Massachusetts. Actually, our roots go back to the Mayflower."

"They do?" said Jane. It was the first she'd heard of it.

"But . . . somehow, I associate you with the Midwest," said Verna.

"I was an unwilling transplant when I was but a young sapling." Cordelia's look was tragic.

Jane thought she was laying it on a bit thick. But then, with two divas in the room—three, if you counted Octavia—melodrama was bound to be a note that got banged a few times.

"And Grace. You're looking well," said Verna, making the rounds. "A life of leisure must agree with you."

Did they think Gracie did nothing all day but relax, thought Jane. Surely she would correct such an erroneous impression. When she didn't, Jane knew that Gracie's webcast empire wasn't common knowledge. Fascinating.

"My theory is," said Gracie, examining her nails with disinterest, "that once you have a Ph.D., you've proved yourself, so you can coast for a while on your laurels. I'm in my coasting period right now. And yes, it does agree with me, thank you."

"Perhaps I should make us all some coffee," suggested Hilda. "Would anyone like cake?"

"I'm sure Verna is tired from her trip," Roland said before anyone else could respond.

Verna's eyes moved slightly to the side. "Why, yes. I have been up since early this morning."

To Jane, it felt as if the actress was still taking her cues from the director.

"Oh—I was hoping we could talk a little longer," said Octavia, looking disappointed.

"Why don't I show you up to your room?" Roland stood, motioning for Verna to walk in front of him. It was clear he wanted some time alone with her.

"Good night," called Hilda, a little wistfully.

"Sweet dreams," echoed Christian, without the wistfulness.

18

You're sure you don't want to come along?" asked Cordelia, standing by Octavia's Volvo, tossing the end of her red wool scarf impatiently over her shoulder. For the trip into town today, she was wearing her black-and-red plaid hunter's jacket and black designer jeans. It was an outfit that she always wore when she needed to feel strong. Not a propitious sign.

Jane had spent the morning in Asbury doing some additional Christmas shopping. She wanted at least one small present for everyone. She'd promised to have the car back by one. Standing now on the steps to the house, she shook her head, saying, "No thanks. I've got some things I need to do here." The car would already be packed to the gills with Octavia and Roland in the front seat, and Cordelia and Verna in the back. The C70 might be a luxury car, but it wasn't a minivan. Jane wasn't sure where Cordelia thought she would fit. Perhaps in the trunk.

"Okey dokey," said Cordelia, using her best Minnesota accent. "We'll be back by five at the latest." She waved, then wedged herself into the back seat.

They were all headed into St. Albans, twenty minutes away—in the opposite direction from Asbury—for a last minute check of the Presbyterian church where Roland and Octavia would be married on Monday morning. The church was supposed to be small, charming, and terribly historic. Jane assumed she'd have plenty of time to get a good look at it before the ceremony.

Once back up in her room, she spent the next few hours wrapping gifts. She took her time, enjoying the process of making everything look perfect. Apparently Roland liked to open presents on Christmas Eve, so she wanted to be ready.

Last evening, after everyone had gone to bed, Jane and Cordelia had snuck back down to the kitchen, lifted a large jar of herring in wine sauce from the refrigerator and a box of crackers from the cupboard, then returned to Cordelia's room and talked and snacked late into the night. It seemed that Cordelia and her sister had overheard a conversation between Buddy and Roland yesterday afternoon. Cordelia was bursting to tell Jane three big pieces of news.

First, Roland wanted children. Cordelia couldn't fathom it, but when she questioned Octavia about it later, Octavia had said that she'd always wanted a child. If it happened, it was fine with her. Cordelia simply couldn't imagine it—her sister sleeping with an eighty-three-year-old man.

"I know I'm probably being . . . oh, what's the damn word?" she muttered.

"Ageist?" replied Jane.

"There you go, ageist. But mark my words. There's something wrong with this picture. My sister has always been attracted to dark, handsome men in their prime—and I do mean *prime*."

The second point was that Roland was paying Christian for his silence. Cordelia wondered if it had something to do with the death of Lew Wallace. Again, when Cordelia asked Octavia about it, she shrugged it off, making Cordelia even more suspicious, both of Roland *and* of her sister.

Finally, Cordelia said that Roland was being followed. Someone had tailed his limo from Innishannon to New York.

"Does he know who's doing it?" asked Jane.

"Not a clue. His brother wanted him to hire a bodyguard, but Roland refused. Said he didn't want to make a big deal out of it. It might upset Octavia."

"How did she take the news?"

"Silently. That woman is driving me crazy. She's like a human Chinese water torture—drip, drip, drip. Never the whole truth."

Before Jane left to go back to her own bedroom around two, Cordelia mentioned that the evening ritual tonight would be the same as usual. Drinks at six. Dinner at seven. After that, they would all retire to the living room, sit in front of the fire, and try to act like one big happy family as they opened their gifts.

"It all feels so staged, so forced," said Cordelia. "Such a pathetic attempt to trump up something real. I hope you bought me a truly spectacular present, Janey. I need something to brighten my mood."

"I know you'll just *love* the cross-country skis."

"Go to bed." She pushed Jane out the door.

After placing the wrapped presents in two large sacks, Jane stood by the window for a few minutes and watched it snow. According to the weather forecast, four inches were predicted by late evening. Not exactly a blizzard by Minnesota standards, but enough to cover the world with a fresh coating of white.

Around five-thirty, Jane ran a brush through her hair, changed her earrings from silver studs to gold hoops, then took the presents downstairs to place under the tree. Coming through the front foyer, she saw that Hiram Thorn had finally arrived. He was talking to Leonard, who had now donned a butler's uniform.

"Dr. Thorn," she said, setting the sacks down and giving him a warm hug. "I'm glad you made it safely. The roads must be getting kind of messy out there." His hat and coat were covered with large, fluffy snowflakes.

"Is it Jane?" he asked, holding her at arm's length. "My God, I haven't seen you since Lydia and I made that trip back to Minneapolis in 'eighty-six. You look absolutely wonderful. How's that father of yours? Still practicing law?"

"He is."

"We need to sit down and have a long talk. But first . . . where are those two beautiful daughters of mine?" He looked around expectantly.

Leonard took his hat and coat. "In St. Albans, sir. But they should be back any minute."

Hiram cupped his hands together and smiled. "What do you say we go find ourselves a drink?"

Jane led the way to the living room. A fire had been laid in the hearth, and the drinks cart was already stocked with ice, lemon twists, and fresh glasses in anticipation of the evening, but since it was still before six, the room was empty. While Hiram mixed himself a Manhattan, Jane scattered her gifts in with the rest of the presents under the tree. "Did you drive down?"

"I did," he said, taking a hefty swallow before making himself comfortable in one of the wingback chairs. "It's not that far. And I enjoy getting out on the open road."

Jane settled down opposite him, watching him swirl the ice in his glass. He was wearing a suit, matching vest, and tie, but looked completely at ease. As long ago as she could remember, Dr. Thorn had always dressed formally. She'd rarely seen him in anything other than a suit, usually three-piece. She'd met him for the first time after she'd returned from a two-year stay with her aunt and uncle in England. She was sixteen at the time. The Thorns had just moved from Boston to the Twin Cities. Since Jane and Cordelia were both outsiders at school that year, they quickly became friends.

Dr. Thorn always reminded her of a bull. Thick neck. Square face. Ruddy complexion. Heavyset. Not terribly tall. His blond hair had finally turned a yellowish white, and he'd gained weight. But he was still attractive. Cordelia always said he looked liked Albert Finney. When he was a younger man, Jane couldn't see it, but as the two men aged, they could have been brothers.

Dr. Thorn's father was Jewish, born in New York City, his mother French, born in Quebec. He'd grown up in an orthodox Jewish household as a child, but had never practiced his Judaism as an adult. Lydia Thorn, his wife, had been born into a family of Vermont Episcopalians, and that's the religion in which Cordelia and Octavia had been raised, though it had never played a great role in either of their lives.

Cordelia had always been closer to her father, Octavia to her mother. In fact, it wouldn't be stretching it to say that Cordelia was devoted to her dad. Oh, she knew he liked to meddle a bit too much in his children's lives, but to her, it was simple concern. To Jane, however, his motives often seemed a bit more suspect. But then, Cordelia knew him better than she did. Jane was surprised to see him drinking, especially after what Cordelia had told her.

"So," said Hiram, taking another swallow. "This is quite a house. Needs a little work, though. I wouldn't doubt Lester's got some water damage upstairs, judging by the looks of the roof. You'd think he'd take better care of it. Makes me wonder what kind of man he really is."

So there it was. The first indication that Dr. Thorn wasn't completely sold on the idea of his daughter marrying Roland Lester. How could he be in favor of it, unless he was impressed by Lester's fame, or the promise of future wealth for Octavia? Jane doubted either would seriously influence him.

She remembered seeing him a few days ago in Asbury, talking to that man with the gold-handled walking stick. At the time, she'd wondered what he was up to, and now she wondered even more. Did it have something to do with the forthcoming marriage?

"What do you think of the guy?" asked Hiram, crossing his legs and giving her a pointed look.

"Actually, I like him," said Jane. She had to be truthful. Lester had been nothing but kind and gracious to her from the moment they first met. Okay, so maybe she was a little star struck. Who wouldn't be? And she found his history in Hollywood fascinating.

"What does Cordelia think of him?" asked Hiram, finishing his drink in two neat sips.

"I'm not entirely sure. You'd have to ask her."

"Damn right, I will. Between you and me, I think Octavia's lost her mind."

"She seems pretty happy."

"Great. She can smile all the way to a failed career." He thought for a moment. "You think she's really in love with him?"

"I don't know."

He wiped a hand across his mouth.

Hearing a commotion in the front hall, Jane assumed the group had returned. "I think everyone's home."

"Good," said Hiram, standing and setting his empty glass on the liquor cart. "Let's get the introductions over with."

Jane followed him down the hallway, noticing that his mouth was set in a thin, grim line.

She didn't hold out much hope for a pleasant Christmas Eve.

"Dad!" said Cordelia, rushing to him as soon as he appeared. She hugged him tight, then stood back to allow Octavia to do the same.

"My two beauties," he said, putting his arms around both of them and grinning from ear to ear. "God but it's good to see you."

Jane glanced at Roland and Verna. They stood politely to the side, allowing father and daughters to have their moment together. And that's

144

when Jane saw it. The walking stick with the gold handle. The one Roland was holding. She looked up at his face and saw that he was wearing a fedora with a broad brim. Could he have been the man Dr. Thorn had been talking to in Asbury two days ago? It not only seemed plausible, but likely.

"Dad," said Octavia, slipping her arm through his, "I'd like you to meet my fiancé, Roland Lester."

Lester stepped forward to shake his hand. "Nice to finally meet you."

"Likewise."

"I hope you'll call me Roland."

"And you can call me Dr. Thorn."

Everyone laughed.

As Octavia introduced Verna Lange to her father, Jane wondered why the two men acted as though they'd never met before. The more she thought about it, the more sure she was that Lester had been the one she'd seen in town. The hat and the dark glasses had prevented her from getting a good look at his face, but he'd worn a dark topcoat, as he did now, and with that gold-handled stick, it was too much of a coincidence not to be right. Looking more carefully at the cane, Jane saw that the handle had the elongated face of a gargoyle, one of those grotesque fantasy figures that appeared on cathedrals in the Middle Ages. She wondered if it had any particular significance to him.

When she returned her attention to the crowd that was gathering in the foyer, she couldn't help but wonder what the hell was going on. Hiram and Roland were both smiling and acting delighted and enthusiastic. Had Dr. Thorn been meddling in his daughter's life again? From his demeanor the other day, and the comments he'd made earlier this evening, it seemed clear to her that he wasn't about to stand quietly by as the happy father-in-law-to-be. So what was he up to?

Other than the fact that Dr. Thorn drank too much wine, dinner had gone well. Still, Jane felt a sense of unease. She wondered if Cordelia felt it too. Cordelia did seem concerned by the amount of cabernet her father was consuming with his lamb chops and brussel sprouts. Octavia had noticed it as well. There were some veiled looks that passed between the two sisters, and yet neither seemed to want to yank the wine glass out of his hand and make a scene on Christmas Eve.

By nine, everyone had gathered in the living room. Everyone, except for Dr. Thorn. He continued to sit at the dining room table, picking at his pumpkin pie and staring into space.

Cordelia and Octavia whispered for a few minutes near the Christmas tree. Jane watched them out of the corner of her eye as she helped pass out the gifts.

Roland had just opened his first present when the good doctor stumbled suddenly into the room. He was holding his empty wine glass, and looked as if he'd just swallowed a toad.

"Dad," said Cordelia, hurrying over to him. "I think maybe you should head up to bed now. You look beat."

"Sure thing, baby," he said, his eyes fixed firmly on Roland. "But first, a toast."

"We've already had a dozen toasts tonight," said Cordelia. She tried to ease him back through the doorway, but he wouldn't budge.

"This is a new one," he said, his words slurred. "Nobody's gonna make this toast unless I do."

Patiently, Roland stood up. "Octavia, I think you better help your father upstairs."

"I'm not leaving, Lester. So shut up and listen."

"Dad!" said Cordelia, clearly aghast.

"Here's to Roland Lester." He lifted his empty glass.

"Someone go get Leonard," ordered Roland. "Now! I want this man out of here."

Dr. Thorn spread his legs apart, making himself even more immovable. "To Roland Lester," he began again. "A liar. A cheat. Tell them the truth, old man. Tell them who you really are."

"Stop it," cried Octavia. She put her hands over her ears to stop the sound of his voice.

"He's a faggot," sneered Hiram. "Do we all get the picture? Here's to the *faggot* among us." He spit the word at him, then tried to take a drink. "Hey . . . what—" He turned the glass upside down. "Somebody get me more wine."

Cordelia's expression grew resolute as she moved in front of her father to stare him directly in the eyes. "I don't like your language or what you're implying. In case you don't remember, your oldest daughter is a *dyke*."

"I know that," he said, brushing her hand away. "This is only about *him*." He pointed at Roland. "He has no business marrying Octavia! This

146

marriage is a sham. Don't let him use you like this, sweetheart. He'll ruin you, just the way he ruined his first wife. I know. I talked to her!"

"That's absurd," said Roland, looking not only furious but indignant. "The man's drunk, or delusional. He doesn't know what he's talking about."

"I know enough to sink your ship, asshole."

Octavia crumpled onto the couch, tears streaming down her cheeks. "God, someone stop him."

"Dad," said Cordelia, yanking him off balance. "That's enough. We'll talk about this when you've sobered up." She dragged him out through the doorway and down the hall.

"God in heaven," said Roland, sinking down on a chair, a shaky hand held to his forehead. After a tense few seconds, he looked up, his eyes moving from face to face. He couldn't hide the fact that he'd been shaken to the core. Finally, having had enough of the scene, he got up and left the room.

Verna followed him out.

Nobody said a word. The only sound in the room came from Octavia's sobbing.

19

MIDNIGHT, CHRISTMAS EVE

Roland paced back and forth in Verna's room. "I can't sleep," he said, raking a hand through his hair. "I haven't even tried. What's the use after what happened tonight?"

"Have you talked to Octavia?" Verna was dressed in her black leotard and pearls, sitting on the edge of a chair near the window. To someone who didn't know her well, she might have looked calm enough, but Roland could read the tension in her face, see the stiff way she held her hands in her lap, willing herself to be still.

No doubt, she hadn't missed the anxiety in his demeanor either. Roland felt like a firecracker just seconds from going off. "Yes, I spoke with her. Only to reassure her that what her father accused me of was ridiculous."

"Did she believe you?"

"I think so. My heterosexual credentials are impeccable. I spent my life making sure of that."

"You're right. It *was* all about credentials."

"How could anyone who didn't live that life understand? It's a new world today. People announce that they're homosexual all the time and go on with their lives."

"Not everyone, dear. Want me to name the actors and actresses I happen to know who are in the closet?"

"No," he said, looking glum. "It would take too long." He continued to pace, rubbing the back of his neck. "What am I going to do?"

"I guess that's up to you."

"You're certainly a big help."

"All right," she said. Picking up her purse, she retrieved her black and silver cigarette holder, then plucked a Virginia Slim from its package. "Let's talk about it." After lighting up and taking a deep drag, she said, "First, you've got to send that documentary artist packing. If you ask me, biography is a scummy profession."

He hesitated. "I don't know."

"What do you mean, *you don't know?* She's going to jump on Thorn's comment like a jackal picking over a dead carcass."

"That's just it, Verna." He stopped and turned, looking her square in the face. "I'd like to tell her the truth. The whole truth. Put it out there on the table and get it over with, once and for all."

"You're . . . not talking about Lew's death."

"No. Of course not."

She exhaled smoke from her nose. "That's good, because . . . we don't know what really happened."

"No," he said. "We don't."

"Did I ever tell you that you two were the happiest, most devoted married couple I ever knew?"

Roland's smile was sad. "I still think of him every day."

"I do too," said Verna wistfully. "Those were good times. You two were like my older brothers." She stressed the word 'older.' "And, of course, I adored the intrigue."

"More than we did, I'm sure. All that sneaking around . . . it just made me feel shabby."

"How do you suppose Octavia's father found out?"

Roland sat down. "He talked to Sylvia. She had cancer surgery two years ago. He was her physician. I guess it's true what they say— women fall in love with their doctors. She ended up telling him everything."

"Your ex-wife hardly fell in love with the man."

"No, but when you're in a fragile, vulnerable state, you may mention things you wouldn't ordinarily talk about. Sylvia would never consciously do anything to hurt me. She must have trusted Thorn's discretion."

"Never trust a drunk to be discrete."

"I doubt she knew he was a drunk. He's an eminent physician."

"What was it we were saying? So much for credentials?"

Roland leaned forward, clasping his hands between his knees. "The fact is, he called me last week, demanded to talk, but refused to do it over the phone. He drove down from Boston on Thursday and we met at a bar in Asbury. He said he knew for a fact I was gay, and what the hell was I doing, proposing to his daughter?"

"What did you say?"

"I asked him where he got his information. That's when he told me about Sylvia. The first time she and Betsy were in his office, he said he could tell they were a couple. He wanted to put them at ease, so he mentioned in passing that his oldest daughter was gay. That's when they opened up, told him they'd been together since they were in their early twenties. It eventually came out that Sylvia was married to me at one time, and to explain, she told him that a lot of gay people in Hollywood married each other as a way of keeping their sexuality a secret. Of course, she had that insane father of hers to think about too. He would have locked her in a vault and thrown away the key if he'd known she was in love with Betsy."

"What about that business Hiram brought up about you ruining your first wife's life?"

"What do you think? It was just more ravings of a vindictive drunk. He told me last Thursday that Sylvia made it very clear we were still great friends. Good Lord, we had a daughter together. We raised her in a loving home. We didn't even divorce until she was grown. It just wasn't . . . traditional."

"Uncle Lew and Aunt Betsy were always around."

"Exactly. So was Auntie Verna, if I remember correctly."

She watched the ash on her cigarette lengthen and curl. "If I'd been half as good with men as I was with kids, I wouldn't have been married five times. Ah, well. We all have talents and flaws."

Roland leaned back and laced his fingers over his chest. "I have to make a decision, Verna. You've got to help me."

"Would Octavia care if you came clean, told the world you really were a gay man?"

"I doubt it. This isn't a marriage based on love or passion. We have practical reasons for what we're doing. And, since her sister is gay, and Octavia's spent her life in the theatre, my secret would hardly come as a huge blow."

"Then why not tell her now? Tonight."

He shook his head. "It's . . . the same old reticence again. You know what's it's like for me—we've talked about it before. I've never told anyone in my life the truth, except for you, Buddy, and Sylvia. It's not that easy for me to talk about. I get so emotional."

"You don't feel guilt about it anymore, do you?"

"Guilt? This may sound strange, coming as it does from someone so unwilling to talk about his personal life, but I never did feel guilt. I thought my love for Lew was the purest emotion I'd ever experienced. I still do."

She smiled, the cigarette holder clasped in her teeth. "I thought you might say that."

"I'm proud of what we were to each other. What we had."

"Then talk about it. Do it now. Ghosts can't tell the world what it needs to know. Believe me, there are people out there who still think Cesar Romero simply never met the right woman. It's insane." Drawing on her cigarette, she continued, "I heard someone once say that Cesar loved to party so much, he'd attend the opening of a napkin. Actually, he and I went to a few film premieres together. You know the score. The press usually didn't stick around after the feature started, so when the shutters stopped clicking, he went his way and I went mine. Not exactly the fantasy the Hollywood fan magazines tried to push."

Roland laughed, then sighed. "It *is* a story."

"One nobody wants to tell."

"Hiding in plain sight. Think of it. So many people dancing to the wrong tune just to stay employed. It took courage not to play the Hollywood game of arranged marriages and photo-op dates. It was the kind of courage I completely lacked."

"You didn't want your career taken away from you. That's understandable."

"But some people were more open. Men I respected, like Bill Hanes, and George Cukor."

"Cukor wasn't open, dear."

"No, but everybody knew. He mixed so freely with . . . 'a certain type.' Hollywood's gay elite, although no one actually said the words out loud. People just assumed he was homosexual. I never even had the guts to go to one of his parties."

Verna smiled at a memory. "I remember one night I was there when

Edna Ferber and Noel Coward both showed up wearing double-breasted suits. Coward said, 'You almost look like a man.' Ferber replied, 'So do you.' I thought I was going to choke on my martini." She warmed to her subject. "And poor Clifton Webb. There was another gay man who never married. He was so attached to his mother. I guess that's kind of a cliché now, right? Anyway, when Noel heard Clifton's mother had died, and that he was devastated by it, he said, 'It must be tough, being orphaned at seventy-two.' "

Roland's smile was full of fondness. "Those were brilliant people. Funny. Quick. Creative. I miss them all." He sat motionless for a moment, then stretched his legs. "You know, I read things all the time now where people name names—actually *say* who was gay or lesbian back then. People like Cary Grant. I've even heard that his long-time affair with Randolph Scott is finally out in the open. I never thought I'd live long enough to see that day. And Tyrone Power. Of course, I always figured he was bisexual. A lot of the people they're calling gay and lesbian now were really bisexual. He was the most beautiful man I'd ever seen. And one of the nicest men I've ever met." Roland looked down at his hands. "Some of what I read these days are interviews, but mostly they're biographies. People are being outed after they die."

Verna tapped more ash into the ashtray. "I must be reading the same books you are. Barbara Stanwyck. Charles Laughton. Claudette Colbert. Montgomery Clift. I've been pretty amazed at the quality of the truth-telling, too."

"Maybe that's the way it should be. Do it after the person's dead and gone. That way their personal fears can't get in the way."

She glanced over at him. "You really think that's for the best?"

He didn't reply.

"Wouldn't it be better to have the guts to say something while you're still alive? Make sure what's written about you is accurate."

"You don't understand. I've always had this deep, almost over-powering need to be loved—accepted."

"Honey, who hasn't?"

"No, what I'm talking about is different. Take Lew, for instance. He wasn't blacklisted in the fifties because of his friendship with potential Communists. He let his guard down. Got a little too open. People started putting two and two together. I tried to help him, to get him to see what the repercussions of his actions might be. When it finally happened, when he stopped receiving scripts, I think he was stunned. He couldn't believe it because he thought his place in Hollywood was assured. That was Lew's particular blindness. He never understood politics."

"I'm not sure any of us did."

Roland got up again, this time sitting down on the foot of the bed, putting more space between them. "I hate this. Who I chose to love is nobody's business but my own. I mean, who cares? What's the point of talking about it?"

Verna sat up straighter, as if readying herself for a fight. "Well, the fact that you're gay is at least *part* of the point. Certainly, it's not the be all and end all of your life—"

"But that's just it. If I 'come out of the closet,' as they say now, my sexuality becomes the *entire* point. I become 'that gay director.' My life will have an adjective placed next to it on unto eternity. I don't want that. I want my career to be judged on its merits. I don't want to become—in the biographies that will undoubtedly be written— something I never was in my life."

"You mean like . . . open? Honest?"

"No! There was no gay movement when I was a young man. You just were what you were. You may not agree with me, but sometimes I think that was better."

She bit down hard on her cigarette holder. "You know something, Roland, you're one of the most Victorian men I've ever met."

"Look, let's say you have a movie—a love story. Heterosexual love stories are about *individuals*. Stories about homosexual love are stories about homosexuality. I don't want my life to be looked at that way. That's all I'm saying."

Verna mashed the cigarette out in the ashtray as if it were the cause of her frustration. "So, let me get this straight. When you first walked in here, you were just about convinced to tell the world the truth. Now you say that if you tell the world you're gay, that you had a long-term love affair with a famous actor, that it will somehow muddy the waters and prevent the real story from being told."

"Yes. No." He covered his face with his hands. "Oh, God, I don't know what I'm saying anymore."

She rose from her chair and sat down next to him on the end of the bed. Slipping her arm around his waist, she heaved a deep sigh. "You will never be accused of *not* being complex."

He rested his head on her shoulder. "Thanks."

"It wasn't a compliment, dear."

20

CHRISTMAS MORNING

Cordelia rounded a corner in the upstairs hallway and steamed toward her father's bedroom. She wasn't as angry as she'd been last night, she was angrier.

Just as she got to his door, she saw Octavia at the other end of the hall carrying a breakfast tray. As she came closer, Cordelia realized she was bringing the tray to their father. A glass of tomato juice sat next to a bottle of aspirin. Wasn't that just peachy. Enabling the drunk to feel better.

"Morning."

"Morning."

Cordelia knocked on the door. When there was no answer, she barreled inside.

Hiram Thorn snored away peacefully from under a pile of blankets.

Cordelia marched up to the window and let the shade snap all the way to the top.

Hiram kept right on snoring.

"Wake him," ordered Cordelia.

"Me? You wake him."

"You're such a child. You don't want to make Daddy mad."

"Oh, please. I didn't hear you say anything to him at dinner last night about his drinking."

"You didn't either."

"That's because I was trying to keep the peace. The way Dad kept glaring at Roland, I was afraid the evening would escalate into World War Three."

Cordelia gave her sister a withering look. Moving over to the bed, she poked her father in the chest with her index finger.

He snuffled, then resumed his snoring.

"It's your turn," said Cordelia, standing back.

"That wasn't a real attempt."

"Yes it was."

"No it wasn't."

Cordelia pressed her lips together. "Okay. Let's pour the tomato juice over his head."

"You're so . . . so . . . self-righteous sometimes, you know that?"

"Is there something inherently self-righteous about using tomato juice to wake up a sleeping man? I must have missed that page in Emily Post. Would a glass of ice water be better?"

"You're pathetic." Octavia set the tray down, then approached the bed. Shaking her father by the shoulders, she said, "Dad? Wake up."

"Wha—what?"

"It's morning. Time to get up and face the music."

After a few seconds, he opened his eyes, but closed them almost immediately, a shaky hand rising to cover his eyes. "My head."

"It's still there," said Cordelia. "Be grateful."

"I brought you some aspirin," said Octavia, helping him sit up.

"Thanks, sweetheart." He downed two with the juice.

"Good, now that you're feeling better," said Cordelia, looking down at him from her full six-foot height, "I want you to get dressed and apologize to Roland. Or you can apologize and then get dressed. I'm not fussy about the order."

Hiram cleared his throat, giving them a sheepish smile. "You know, girls, I, ah . . . I don't remember much about last night."

Octavia's hands rose to her hips. "Well then, let me refresh your memory. You announced that my fiancé was gay."

"Oh?"

"I don't think I'm ever going to forgive you for what you did, Dad, turning Christmas Eve into another drunken Hiram Thorn moment."

Cordelia narrowed her eyes. "How you could drink after what happened to Mom—"

"I haven't been," he insisted, holding up his hand to protect himself. "Not until last night. I couldn't help myself. And I wasn't lying. Roland Lester is gay. His wife was a patient of mine. She told me the whole story."

"And why would she confide in you?" demanded Octavia.

"I don't know," he said, pulling the covers up to his chest. "People just talk to their doctors. It happens all the time. You know that."

"Roland denies it," she said flatly.

"Then he's lying. Honey, you don't want to marry someone who lies. What am I saying? You *can't* marry a gay, eighty-three-year-old man!"

"It does seem to lack good judgment," offered Cordelia.

"Oh, shut up."

"Girls, please. My head aches. And it hurts me when the two of you fight."

"Well then," said Cordelia, "you must have been in constant pain for the past eight years."

He grimaced.

"Not that what happened to Mom was your fault," she added quickly. She glared at her sister.

"Please!" said Hiram, his voice breaking with emotion. "Stop it!"

Cordelia and Octavia were both startled by his sudden distress.

"Now look what you've done," snapped Octavia. "Why bring up Mother at a time like this?"

Cordelia felt incredibly guilty. "Dad, I'm sorry."

"You wonder why we're not close," continued Octavia. "Well, you can see for yourself. Your oldest daughter's got all the sensitivity of a piece of plywood."

"That's not true," said Cordelia. "Besides, I wouldn't have Mother to bring up if it weren't for you!"

"That's right. I forget sometimes that you're the judgment machine. It's your role in life to represent constant condemnation."

Hiram buried his head in his hands.

"Look at him," said Cordelia. "You've done it again. He stopped drinking, but he started again. Why? You and this idiotic marriage! You tell *me* who the rotten apple in this family is!"

"Please!" cried Hiram.

When Cordelia looked down, she saw that he was in tears.

"It's all my fault," he said.

"Dad, listen," said Octavia, sitting down next to him, taking his hand in hers. "We're done. No more fighting. We promise." She looked up at her sister for support.

Cordelia nodded.

"We just get a little . . . upset with each other sometimes."

He tipped his head back, tears still streaming down his cheeks. "I'm such a failure."

"No you're not," said Cordelia. She'd never seen him like this before.

"My girls hate each other."

"That's not true." Octavia motioned for Cordelia to grab the box of Kleenex on the desk. After handing him a couple of tissues, she waited while he dried his eyes. "Let's just stay with the moment here, okay? Cordelia's right. We need you to apologize to Roland."

He thought about it for a few seconds, then sniffed a couple of times. "I'll apologize for my *behavior,* but I won't take back what I said—or, at least, what I hope I said."

"You called him a faggot, Dad," said Cordelia.

"Did I?" he said weakly.

"He'll never allow you to stay here with something like that left hanging."

"Oh, he's not staying here another minute," said Octavia. "That was never in question."

Cordelia cocked her head. "He's not? Are you planning to pitch a tent for him in the snow?"

"Dad, listen to me." She waited as he blew his nose. "I've made a reservation for you at a very nice hotel in New Haven. I called the Hanford Inn as soon as I got up. Luckily, they had a cancellation. Once you're done talking to Roland, I'm driving you there myself. In fact, we can spend the rest of the day together. If Cordelia wants to come along, that's fine with me."

"You're not spending Christmas with your fiancé?" asked Cordelia.

Octavia shot her a look that said, essentially, *Up yours.* "No, I'm spending the day with my father. You're very important to me, Dad. I want you to understand some things about Roland. We need to talk."

Hiram reached out his hand to Cordelia. "Will you come too?"

Cordelia felt so incredibly frustrated she could have spit nails. "Not unless you promise that you'll get some help for your drinking. Talk to a counselor—a therapist."

"Sweetheart, I haven't had a drink since your mother died, and I promise, I won't do it again. Last night was just . . . I couldn't face what I had to say without a little help. It was wrong, I know that now. Alcohol doesn't help anything. I'll apologize to Roland and then we can all be off." Glancing up at Octavia, he asked, "Even though I don't approve—even though I hope you'll change your mind—I'm not being banished from your wedding, am I?"

"No, of course not. If you weren't there, who'd give me away?"

Cordelia turned to the window. Under her breath, she whispered, "I would. In a heartbeat."

21

Jane sat on a fallen tree trunk on the empty beach, staring silently at the water. Long Island Sound looked like a sea of gray slate today, very remote and calm. Its peaceful appearance was in sharp contrast to her own inner turmoil. The fog had risen a few hours ago, lifting first to the tops of the trees, then disappearing into the air. She'd stood for a while drinking a cup of coffee on the flagstone terrace, but grew restless, feeling the need to be closer to the water. Her mood had grown increasingly somber as she watched a heavy blanket of clouds move across the horizon. With all the snow, the trek to the beach had been treacherous. That's why she'd brought her cane with her today. It was the first time she'd used it since she'd come to Innishannon, and the mere sight of it made her spirits plummet. When would she finally be rid of the damn thing? It spoke so eloquently of limitation and vulnerability, two things she'd been wrestling with for the past several months. In reality, perhaps the struggle had gone on much longer than that.

Closing her eyes, Jane remembered a similar beach, this one on the southwestern coast of England, where she and her mother had once sat and talked. She couldn't have been much more than nine at the time. And yet, the words her mother spoke had burned themselves into her memory. Taking her hand, her mother had said, "The world will always be a better place because you're in it, Janey. You and I, we're so much alike. Sometimes it worries me that I've passed on my flaws to you, but then, I've also passed on my strength." She went on to say that she didn't worry about Jane the way she worried about her brother. She said Jane would grow up to be a good woman who'd never be afraid to use her intelligence. "You're going to have a wonderful life, sweetheart, because of your inner strength, and because you've got a big heart. You know how important it is to help others."

At the time, Jane didn't know her mother would be gone in four short years. When she did die, those words came back to her, not just as a benediction, but as an edict, a prophecy. If she wasn't strong, it was somehow a betrayal of her mother. She may not have defined it quite so clearly, but deep inside, she'd absorbed the message.

So, what did she do the summer after her mother died? She ran. She asked her dad if she could go back to England to stay with her Aunt Beryl and Uncle Jimmy for a while. Her mother had been English. Jane had spent the first nine years of her life living in England. For many reasons, not the least of which was the fact that she felt closer to the memory of her mother there than she did in Minnesota, she had to go. She didn't think of it as weakness, she thought of it as necessary. Her father assumed she'd stay a few weeks and then come home. Instead, she ended up living with her aunt and uncle for two years. It had caused a rift in the family that had taken the better part of her adult life to heal.

It was funny how self-delusion worked. Jane never thought of that time as running away, not until recently—not until she'd been attacked in her home, sending her to the same hospital where her mother had died. Jane could have died as well. Brain injuries, she'd been told, especially the kind that put you in a coma, were never simple. And yet she'd survived, proving once again that she was still the same strong old Jane. Except, her health—always taken for granted—had been severely compromised. Her inner confidence, once a given, had also been altered. She should have seen the truth years ago, but for whatever reason, she'd maintained the fantasy until it was simply impossible *not* to see reality. The fact was, she wasn't anything like the strong woman her mother had envisioned.

And now, she had to wrestle with the idea that she might never regain full use of her left leg. The doctors assured her she would, but at the same time, they always hedged their bets. There might be some residual pain and weakness. For how long, they couldn't say. Weakness in her leg somehow translated into weakness in her soul. She knew it made no rational sense. The worst part was, nobody had prepared her for how the injury would change her inside. Nobody warned her about the nightmares, the sleeplessness, the constant nervous stomach. Was that going to last forever too?

Jane hadn't really confided to anyone about how she was feeling, what she was thinking. It was odd, but voicing her thoughts out loud made them seem more dangerous somehow. Cordelia knew something was wrong, but she always put everything down to ill-fated love and loss. Jane found that explanation tedious. What she was dealing with had nothing to do with love, but it did have a lot to do with fear. For the first time in her life, she felt tired, middle-aged, and afraid.

She sat for a long while with her elbows on her knees, her hands buried in her hair. Brooding was best done away from the eyes of friends. The rocks and the sand wouldn't try to "help," or "make it all better." Cordelia had recently perfected a "terribly worried" expression that drove Jane crazy. It was best to keep her thoughts to herself. When she returned to the house, she'd move back into "people" mode—put the mask back on.

Hearing the snow crunch behind her, she whirled around.

"Hey, it's only me," called Ellie. She was almost to the beach. "Can I join the party?"

Jane was startled, and her face must have shown it. There it was again. Another overreaction. Why was she so damn jittery?

Ellie made her way around the fallen tree. She was wearing a down parka, lined Gore-Tex mountain pants, arctic boots, and a wool hat and matching mittens. By contrast, Jane had on a flannel shirt, an insulated vest, jeans, and hiking boots. So much for Southern California vs. Minnesota's idea of winter gear. For a moment, Jane felt very strong indeed. "Sure, pull up a tree trunk and sit down."

"You okay?" asked Ellie as she made herself semicomfortable, her feet resting on a rock.

"Don't I look okay?"

"I usually read people pretty well. I'm not trying to pry or anything, but you seem kind of on edge."

"Well, yeah . . . I haven't been sleeping well lately."

"Since you arrived here?"

"No, it started before that." She forced a smile. "I'm just a little tired today."

"I suppose you're upset about what happened last night with Dr. Thorn."

Jane had to laugh. "He's the least of my worries. But, now that you mention it, it was quite a scene. Cordelia and Octavia drove him into New Haven this morning after brunch—after we finished opening the presents we never got to open last night. They're spending the afternoon with him, and then he's going to stay at a hotel for the night."

"Probably for the best."

"Yes, I think so, too. So, how's the documentary coming? You're in pre-production now, right?"

"Hey, very good. You're learning the jargon."

"I'm a quick study."

Ellie tried to restuff all of her curly copper hair under her hat. She was clearly fighting a losing battle. "For your lesson today, let's discuss the term 'documentary.' Lots of people don't like that word anymore. They think it's outdated. Actually, in my humble opinion, defining any genre can be difficult."

"Putting limits on where it begins and ends."

"Exactly. A lot of audiences don't like the idea that the film they're about to watch is going to teach them something. They just want to be entertained. That's why you'll see the terms 'nonfiction film' or 'reality-based narrative,' or dozens of other ways to say documentary without actually saying it. Personally, I'd like to redefine the word, not do away with it. A good documentary should be both entertaining *and* enlightening." She clapped her mittens together to keep her hands warm. "I've been sitting in that tack room all morning, swilling down coffee and working on the script for the Lester doc. Thought it might be a good idea to get a little fresh air." She gazed out at the sound, then looked up at the sky. "Good thing I brought some warm clothes."

Jane tried to hide her amusement. "Yeah, good thing. Say, that was quite a camera you were using the other day to shoot Roland's interview."

"The Arriflex? It's a real workhorse."

"How much would something like that cost?"

"New, around twenty-five thousand. I usually travel with a digital betacam too. That's a video format. The Arriflex SR is sixteen milimeter. I finally convinced Lester to shoot the wedding with the betacam. It's a better way to capture an event like that—I can shoot the guests talking, get individual comments and good wishes. If he wants to transfer it to film later, he can. Oh, and good news. I received a video print yesterday of the piece I just finished on my grandfather."

"I didn't know you were doing something on your grandfather."

"Sure, I mentioned it to you the other night. His name was Ellery Patrick Strong."

"He's the cameraman you were talking about?"

"Among other things, yes. He was the black sheep in the family. Committed suicide when he was still a young man and left my grandmother with three kids to raise all by herself. I knew my family had covered up some important facts about him. Not that my grandmother didn't love him. She used to say that, with his Irish charm and bright blue eyes, he'd swept her off her feet. He proposed to her between takes on one of his many movies. I've always romanticized the guy, thought of him as a free spirit. Turns out he was unfaithful to my grandmother, alcoholic, and probably fathered a child with another woman. But he was also a dreamer, straining against the bonds of his Irish Catholic upbringing. Since I'm kind of a dreamer myself, I still identify with him.

"When I was working on my graduate degree in Documentary Film and Video at Stanford, I kept a small picture of him in my wallet. The young Paddy Strong, standing behind his camera, cigarette dangling from his lips, a mischievous grin on his ruddy Irish face. I couldn't help but wonder what had caused a man so full of high spirits to commit suicide at such a young age. I knew the Depression hit him hard, but by 'thirty-eight, the film industry was back on its feet. Paddy should have been too. The mystery of his life—and early death—always haunted me. I found some of his old films in my grandmother's attic about five years ago. That's what started me on the path I'm on today. I solved the mystery of his death—at least partially. It's all in the documentary. Hollywood killed my grandfather, Jane. And in a strange way, it's still paying the price."

"That sounds intriguing."

"It is. My grandfather was many things, some of them unsavory, but he was also a genius. Now that Roland has agreed to cooperate with me, it's only a matter of time before I put it all together. I'm planning to combine the documentary of my grandfather with the piece I do on Lester."

"Did Roland know your grandfather?"

"To my knowledge, they never met."

"Then . . . what—"

"That's all I can say for now."

"But . . . does Roland know that you have your own agenda?"

She shook her head. "If he did, I'd be out on my ear. I watched my grandfather's doc last night after our Christmas Eve extravaganza. The mixdown had its share of problems, but all in all, it went incredibly well."

"Mixdown?"

"More jargon, sorry. It's the final editing, when you put all the tracks together—music, narration, etc.—building it into the finished product. I couldn't be more pleased. I'm also pretty happy that Verna Lange just happened to drop in when she did. I talked to her before dinner last night and she's agreed to sit for an interview before she leaves. That's a real stroke of good luck. You never know who's going to be cooperative and who isn't."

When Ellie picked up a small rock and pitched it into the water, Jane noticed for the first time that she was wearing a wedding ring. How had she missed that before? Nodding to it, she said, "I didn't realize you were married."

"Neither did anyone else around here. Has Christian hit on you yet?"

"Christian? No."

"Well, give him time. You're good looking and you're at least twenty years younger than him—two prerequisites as far as I can tell. I wasn't that surprised when he made his move, but when Gracie invited me up to her lair and proceeded to ply me with wine and then nibble on my ear, I thought I better dig out the damn ring. It doesn't guarantee anything, but it usually gives people at least a moment's pause, and me an excuse."

"Is your husband a documentary artist too?"

Her eyes rose to a bird about to land in one of the winter-bare birch trees behind them. "God, no. I think I've pretty much soured the guy on documentaries for the rest of his life. We're separated. Have been for the last thirteen years."

"I'm sorry to hear that."

"It was my fault. David thought he was marrying a fun-loving young woman who liked to party, liked fast cars and expensive clothes, worked in an office as a secretary, and would continue to work there on unto eternity. When the film school bug bit me, he was tolerant. We didn't have any children and didn't really intend to, and since he made a good salary, money wasn't an issue. Six years later, he was growing a bit weary with the school thing, but knew it would be over soon. Problem was, after I got my degree, I immediately signed on with a production company that took me all over the world. It was the kind of job opportunity that didn't come along every day."

"They must have considered you a good catch."

"I was still green when it came to the real world of documentary filmmaking, but yeah, I was always at the top of my class. For the next few years, I was gone more than I was home. And then, as I started becoming successful in my own right, working on my own projects, even when I was home I was so busy we hardly saw each other. Like I said, it was all my fault. Neither one of us has ever wanted to remarry, so we never went ahead with the divorce. I still see him occasionally. I still love him. He's been living with the same woman for three years now. They seem happy, and I'm glad he's finally found someone who'll stick around and share his life with him. For me, I don't think a long-term relationship is in the cards."

Jane eased her left leg out in front of her. She'd been sitting in a bent position so long, it ached all the way from her thigh down to her ankle. "What did you think of Dr. Thorn's revelation last night?" She hoped that by asking the question in an animated fashion, she could cover the fact that she was in pain. "About Lester being gay."

"Oh, there was never any doubt in my mind about that. I was wondering if he was ever going to bring it up. I'd decided not to say anything right away because I didn't want to antagonize him when we were just getting started." She glanced over at Jane, then added, "He and Lew Wallace were lovers for years. I guess he's still not willing to talk about it."

"I had no idea."

"Not many people do. Like I said, Lester is a very secretive man."

"How did you find out?"

"Research, as well as some good, old-fashioned snooping."

Jane wondered if Ellie might not be the one having Roland followed. In the light of what she'd just said, she appeared to be the most likely candidate.

"I didn't just use the official channels. I tapped into the Hollywood grapevine. That's always more accurate than what's put out by publicists or studios. Actually, if it hadn't been for Wallace, Lester might have remained in the closet forever."

"Meaning what?"

"Toward the end of his life, Wallace got careless. He let a few things slip to the wrong people. It got around."

"You know," said Jane, hoping Ellie would level with her, "you dropped a photocopy of a piece of newsprint when you left Roland's study the other night. I picked it up. It was all about the murder of Lew Wallace."

Ellie searched Jane's face for a long moment, then gave a grudging nod. "Yes, that's one part of the story."

"Tell me the truth. Do you think Roland had anything to do with his murder?"

She hesitated. "It's possible." Picking up another small rock, she tossed it between her hands. "It's also possible that if he was responsible, he had someone else do the dirty deed for him. That would be consistent with the way he ran the rest of his life."

"Like who?"

"His brother."

Jane was stunned. "Buddy? But he seems like such a sweet man."

"Looks can be deceiving."

"Okay. Point taken. But . . . what was Roland's motive?"

"The obvious one was to shut Wallace up."

Jane shook her head. "I don't want to believe that."

"Another reason could have been the book Wallace had just finished writing."

Now she really had Jane's attention. "All the accounts I've read said that this book theory could never be proved. And Roland denies there ever was one."

"God, I wish I'd brought my cigarettes." Ellie felt inside in the pockets of her parka. Giving up, she said, "There definitely was a book. It was called *In the Belly of the Beast*—an autobiography of Wallace's life in Hollywood. A friend of mine at Little, Brown, a guy who's been in publishing forever, did some checking around New York. Turns out, Wallace actually sent it to a Random House editor back in the late fifties. That was another piece of luck tossed in my dog dish. The

Random House editor sent it back posthaste, wouldn't touch it with a ten-foot pole. It was all about Wallace's gay affairs, mostly in the thirties and forties, but later as well. He actually named names. Gave dates and places."

"He must have kept quite a diary."

"Or had quite the memory along with a little black book full of phone numbers and addresses. The thing is, monogamy was never part of Wallace's lifestyle, but constancy was. Roland Lester was definitely the love of his life for over ten years. Even so, he had a varied sex life, both before he met Lester, and afterwards."

"And Roland didn't want the book to be published because of what it might reveal about him?"

"That's one theory. Actually, I talked to the Random House editor personally. His name was Byron Vance. He died a couple of years back, but he remembered the manuscript like it was yesterday. He told me that before he returned it to Lew, he even copied portions of it for his own files—typed it himself."

"Was that legal?"

"Probably not. He was pretty young at the time. Maybe twenty-five. In the closet himself, and low on the totem pole at the publishing house. Wallace knew him socially, that's why he sent the manuscript to him."

Jane simply couldn't imagine it. "You're saying that Roland either murdered or had someone else murder the love of his life to keep their love a secret?"

"Sure. Why not? I just don't happen to think that's what happened."

Now she was confused. "Lester murdered him for another reason?"

"Yes, I think so." Ellie's expression grew increasingly intense. "You see, it all had to do with a card game the two of them played back in the late forties. It was all in Wallace's book, and now it's in the documentary I made on my grandfather. Wallace lost. Lester won."

"A card game? I don't understand. Won what? Money?"

"No, something far more important. When I finally get my hands on the proof I'm looking for, it will blow the lid off a Hollywood scandal the likes of which no one ever dreamed possible."

"But . . . proof of what?"

She shook her head.

"You can't just stop there."

"I've already said too much."

"You must think Lester is the key, otherwise you wouldn't be here."

"He is." She looked up with a faint trace of mischief in her eyes. "Don't you just love a good mystery?"

"No, I like a good mystery *solved*."

"Patience. I'll get there. One way or another."

Jane held her eyes for a moment, then said, "This means a lot to you, doesn't it?"

"It means equally as much to Lester. That's why I've got to be careful. God, I've got such a big mouth sometimes. I *can* trust you, can't I? You won't go repeating our conversation to him?"

"Roland Lester seems like a nice enough guy, but I know how to keep a confidence."

"Good." Ellie squeezed Jane's arm. "Oh, and while we're on the subject, will you do me a favor?"

"What?"

"The more I think about what's at stake here, the more concerned I am about Octavia's safety. I can't come right out and say anything to her directly. I'd have to offer an explanation, and for obvious reasons, I can't do that. Let's just say I'm sure there are others who know about the secret of the poker game. If Lester plans to share *everything* with his new wife, there are those who might want to prevent the wedding."

That sounded ominous. "Like who?"

"Who were the main suspects in the Wallace homicide?"

"Roland, Verna, and Christian."

"Add Buddy to the list and—enough said."

As Jane mulled it over, Ellie continued, "I've been curious about Christian ever since I got here. I mean, he has no real reason to be here, and yet here he is. Apparently, he comes every Christmas. I don't buy this touchy-feely, 'he's part of the family' malarkey. Except for Gracie, nobody even talks to the guy. Not that anyone would want too—willingly, I mean."

"You don't find him charming?"

"God save us from charming men, right?" She elbowed Jane in the ribs.

Jane didn't carry a sign around her neck, but she thought Ellie knew she was gay. It didn't seem fair that others knew and Ellie was in the dark, especially since they seemed to be working on the beginnings of a real friendship. "I don't worry much about charming men. I'm gay."

Ellie backed up and looked at Jane with surprised eyes. "You are?"

"Any problems with that?"

"Not unless you want my body."

Jane grinned. "I have good impulse control."

"Good." She returned the grin.

Out of the corner of her eye, Jane spotted Christian walking along the shore in a short-sleeved polo shirt, a sheepskin jacket slung over one shoulder. She glanced at Ellie's parka and then back to Christian's polo shirt. They each seemed to lack a certain weather sense. Christian was talking on his cell phone, the picture of the harried Hollywood producer. When he saw them, he waved, talked for a few more seconds, and then flipped the phone shut and slipped it into his pocket.

"Speak of the devil," whispered Ellie, watching him approach.

"Afternoon, ladies," he called, an over-confident smile on his face. Brushing his dyed-blond hair off his forehead, he added, "Or, I should say, Merry Christmas?"

"Afternoon," said Ellie, her voice something less than welcoming.

"Since Roland's barricaded himself in his study, and everyone else is gone, I thought I'd go for a walk. I should have left my cell phone back at the house. Problems and more problems."

"With your movie?" asked Jane.

"If I don't get the financing soon, I'm going to lose the director. I just found out he's been offered another film. He's chomping at the bit to get something finalized with Isolde. I can't get her without solid backing. I keep chasing tails, but I can never grab the dog."

"Where's Gracie?" asked Ellie, clearly disinterested in his plight.

"In town, I suppose. Although, everything would be closed today, wouldn't it?" He shrugged. "She took her car and left right after breakfast. Maybe she went to see one of her many boyfriends. I can't keep track of them, so I call them all 'Jason.' "

"That's friendly," said Ellie. She stared at him. "Aren't you cold?"

"Not really. Are you?"

"No, I always dress like I'm about to climb the Himalayas."

He smiled. "Well, I'll let you two get back to your conversation." He started to leave, but stopped himself. Turning around, he said, "I should tell you that Roland has scheduled another movie for tonight. It's supposed to replace the one that never happened when Verna arrived. A silent film classic, I'm told. Should be entertaining."

"What time?" asked Ellie.

"Nine sharp. You know Roland. He means nine on the dot."

"I'll be there," said Jane.

"Me too," said Ellie.

"Say, maybe afterwards, the three of us can have a few shots of vodka together. I put a bottle of Stolichnaya in the freezer yesterday—for a special occasion."

Both women smiled pleasantly but noncommittally.

"Great, then I'll see you tonight."

As soon as he was out of earshot, Ellie said, "Once the film's over, I have a feeling I'm simply going to *have* to wash my hair." Her eyes still fixed on his back as he drifted down the beach, she added, "That man makes my skin crawl."

22

Roland bent over the desk in his study, finishing a note to Ellie. With the exception of the light from a small desk lamp, the room was deep in shadow. Outside, the gray afternoon had faded to night, but Roland had paid no attention. He'd put in seven hours of hard work today, and he was finally done.

Ever since Octavia and her family had left, he'd been reading sections of his handwritten journal notes into a tape recorder. He realized that his enthusiasm for the project, now that he'd made the decision to reveal the full truth of his life, bordered on obsession. He couldn't just hand over this highly personal material to Ellie, but he did want her to have access to sections of it. A tape recording seemed the quickest way.

Once started, the words he'd written became so vivid in his memory that he could hardly stop reading long enough to decide what to record. He hadn't spent much time writing in his journal in years, not since Lew died. After he was gone, the old desire to capture and preserve his world on paper dwindled. Oh, he'd written some about his daughter, Peg, but as much as he loved her, he'd merely recorded events, leaving out the more personal thoughts and emotions. A large part of his heart had died the moment Lew's stopped beating. It sounded like a line from one of his less successful movies, but in this case, it was accurate.

Hearing a knock on the door, Roland called "Yes?" He didn't look up from his writing.

Christian opened the door wide enough to stick his head into the room. "It's eight-thirty. Are you going to set up the movie in the screening room?"

With great deliberation, Roland pulled off his reading glasses and slowly raised his eyes. "Come in a moment."

Christian did as he was told, but stayed near the door, his hand remaining on the knob.

Roland wondered what the younger man had read in his face to make him behave so cautiously. "Chris, this will be the last year I give you the usual Christmas money. I no longer require your silence."

Christian's expression sobered.

"You can stay for the wedding tomorrow if you like, but pack your bags and be out of the house by tomorrow night. Oh, and don't come back. The bank is closed—for good."

"I don't understand." Christian seemed shaken. "All my life, you've been like a father to me. I could always count on you."

"You mean you could always count on my money. You disgust me, son, just as you probably disgusted Lew."

Christian looked as if he'd been slapped. "What about the financing for my movie?"

"Get out."

Squaring his shoulders, he glared ineffectually, looked as if he was trying to think of something to say, but finally left.

Well, though Roland, tossing his glasses on the desktop, at least he didn't put up a fight, or try to whine or charm his way around the inevitable. Maybe Lew had played a part in creating the man his son had become, but Roland was sick of carrying around his lover's baggage. He'd paid enough.

As he dropped the finished tapes and the note into a manila envelope, quickly writing Ellie's name on the front, Verna appeared in the open doorway looking concerned. "What's wrong with Christian? He walked right past me in the hall without even acknowledging my presence."

"Probably has a touch of indigestion."

She folded her arms over her chest and leaned against the door frame. "Right. What did you say to him? I saw him come out of here."

"Nothing important. Listen, Verna . . . you know what we were talking about last night?"

She nodded.

"Well, I've made a decision. I'm going to tell Ellie the truth. I want

173

my relationship with Lew to be included in the documentary. It's about time, don't you think?" He expected her to be happy. Instead, her expression clouded over.

"Are you sure that's wise?" She moved into the room and shut the door behind her. "I've been thinking about it too."

"And?"

"If you announce to the world that you and Lew were lovers, it's bound to stir up interest in his death. There's no statue of limitations on murder, Roland. Believe me, you don't want to open that can of worms again. None of us do."

Amazingly, he'd never thought of that. He'd been so fixated on what people would think of *him,* how the revelation would affect the way his career would be viewed, that he'd missed an important ramification. Feeling suddenly flattened, he said, "I just told Christian that I wasn't paying for his silence any longer."

She lowered herself into a chair. "Okay." She thought for a moment. "Look, it's perfectly simple. Just tell him it was a joke. You have a sadistic streak. You didn't mean it."

"He wouldn't believe me. I didn't just tell him no more money, I told him to go to hell."

"Oh." Her chin sank to her chest.

Glancing down at the floor, Roland saw his journals lying open around his desk. "God," he whispered, feeling incredibly thwarted.

"What are you going to do?"

"I have absolutely no idea."

"All we've got left is damage control, Roland."

"Meaning?"

"Let me think about it."

The fact was, Roland was sick to death of thinking, and of hiding. He'd always been a public figure, and yet the public had no idea who he really was. It had never bothered him before, but it did now. He wanted to be judged—and valued—on his own terms. If the movie-going public couldn't do that, to hell with them. He wasn't a man who made snap decisions, but this time it felt right. "Verna, listen to me. I'm not changing my mind about what I'm going to tell Ellie. We don't know what happened to Lew. I could never hurt him. Neither could you. Maybe it was Christian after all. If that's the case, what do I care if the truth comes out?"

She flashed her eyes at him. "Am I talking to a wall here? Do you really want to dredge all that up again, have the police poking into your private affairs? I know I certainly don't. Especially now. I've got worlds to conquer, Roland. I refuse to let the past destroy my present."

"But you can't be sure it would."

"You're so damn naive sometimes. And what about the book? What if we didn't destroy all the copies? What if there's another one out there somewhere?"

"There isn't."

She gave him a long, hard look. "You know, Roland, you inherited Lew's estate. That means if a copy of that autobiography ever surfaced and people decided to sue, dozens of different families could come against you. It could mean financial ruin."

"You *are* the bearer of good tidings tonight." He smiled at her affectionately. "Don't worry. Lew promised me he'd burned his copy of the manuscript."

"What if he didn't? Or what if he had more than one?"

Roland shook his head. "Even if someone has a copy, it wouldn't matter."

"Of course it would."

"Just take a deep breathe, Verna. If your scenario is true, then why haven't these same families come against the people who write the tell-all biographies? People's sexual preference is becoming almost common knowledge today. Old actors and actresses are being 'outed' all the time. The fact is, their families know there's too much information out there supporting the truth, so they leave it alone."

"Nobody knows who slept with who unless they were *there*. Everything we know is hearsay. Anecdotes."

"Okay, you've got a point. But it isn't *just* hearsay, you know that. The truth leaks out, no matter how hard one tries to cover it up."

She shook her head. "God, I don't know why he ever wrote the damn thing."

Roland gathered up his journals and locked them away in the filing cabinet next to his desk. He wanted to give Verna a few seconds to clam down. Once he was done, he turned to her and said, "I've recorded parts of my journals for Ellie." He handed her the envelope. "I'd like you to give this to her tomorrow after the wedding. Octavia and I will be gone for a few days. I want Ellie to have this information right away."

She glanced at the envelope, then back at Roland. "You're really going through with this?"

"I am. No looking back. No second guessing myself. Don't worry about the murder investigation. I would never let anything hurt you. Do you understand what I'm saying, Verna?" He paused, watching her face. "Do you?"

She seemed at a loss for words. "I . . . think so."

"After fifty years, let's stop the pretense. We both know what happened to Lew."

They stared at each other for a few seconds, neither speaking.

Finally, Roland walked around the front of the desk and took hold of her hands. "I've got to run downstairs and set up that movie. Are you coming?"

She still seemed a bit dazed. "What's playing?"

"Something very special."

"What? Tell me now, Roland. At least I'll have *something* to look forward to."

Bending down close to her hear, he whispered, *"A Daughter of the Gods."*

She pushed him away. "Don't be ridiculous."

"No, really. I've got the reels all ready to go."

"Are we talking about the same movie? Brenon's silent film classic? The one he shot in Jamaica in 1916?"

"The very same."

She snorted. "You've been hitting the bottle, right?"

He drew her up out of the chair. "What can I say? I'm a man of many surprises."

"Or an alchemist."

His smile was full of mischief. "Let's go find out."

23

On Monday morning, Cordelia peered through the velvet curtains at the droves of sartorially splendid filing into the church. The wedding party, sans Roland and Buddy who were still back at the house primping, had arrived at First Presbyterian in St. Albans shortly after nine. The ceremony was to begin at ten-thirty. Cordelia thought the building, sitting on a square in the center of town, looked like something out of a Currier and Ives lithograph—charm that had decayed into picturesque smarm. Quaint had never been her idiom.

"This town makes me feel as if I should recite the Pledge of Allegiance until I drop exhausted to my knees," muttered Cordelia, looking over her shoulder at her sister. Octavia was sitting on a stool in the center of the dressing room, a man in a brown tweed suit going over every inch of her to make sure she was perfect. The wedding dress Octavia had chosen was truly breathtaking, almost as breathtaking as Cordelia's Raffinati tux. Both of them had done their hair in a classic chignon, but it was too late to change that now. People could snicker if they wanted. At least Cordelia had chosen a different lipstick color, the bright red matching the rosebud in her lapel.

Returning her attention to the sanctuary, her eyes nearly popped out of her head. "Is that Nathan Lane out there?"

Octavia winced as the tweed suit plucked a tiny eyebrow hair. "Probably. I invited him."

"And Rosie O'Donnell?"

"I do live in New York, Cordelia. And I hardly hide my light under a bushel."

She couldn't believe her eyes when Regis and Joy Philbin walked in next, followed by Betty Buckley. Cordelia wished now that she'd looked at the guest list. "And you were going to deck me in puce and puffy sleeves!" In an instant, she saw her entire life pass before her eyes. It was as close to a near-death experience as she ever wanted to come.

"Be a dear and fetch me a glass of water."

Cordelia shot her sister a cautionary look. "If I were you, I wouldn't trust me near a glass of water right now. It might end up in your cleavage." Watching the crowd a few seconds longer, she added, "Do you know *anyone* who isn't famous?"

"Well . . . you."

Cordelia turned, saw the smirk, and glared.

"If you're going to give me an opening like that, you should expect me to use it."

"I *expect* you to remain civil until this is over. You were the one who insisted I come. The least you can do is not insult me."

Octavia's expression turned suddenly sad. "I'd hoped that, by now, we would have resolved our differences. You know how much I want us to work on healing old wounds."

"Then don't add new ones to the heap."

"I was just joking. Really, Cordelia. We always joke like that. I'm sorry if I hurt you."

Cordelia lifted her chin, trying to project an air of wounded nobility. "Just because I don't work in New York doesn't mean I am unknown."

"Of course you're right."

"I realize I'm a big fish in a small Minnesota puddle, but I've done remarkable work in the time I've been at the Allen Grimby. I could make a case that regional theatre is at least as important as the Broadway stage, perhaps more important." She knew she was protesting too much. And now she felt like a fool. Yanking on her cufflinks, she turned back to the crowd, watching the press jockey for the best positions in the room.

"Has Roland arrived yet?"

"No." Cordelia could see her father sitting with Jane and Hilda in the front pew. "Hilda's wearing black. Don't you find that a bit strange?"

"She has no fashion sense."

Their father seemed to be in a remarkably cheerful mood today. Perhaps his blowout on Christmas Eve had been cathartic in some way. Jane had picked him up in New Haven before breakfast and brought him back to Innishannon. He'd cooled his heels in the living room while the rest of the household settled into its pre-wedding uproar. Cordelia thought she could smell alcohol on his breath when he'd first come in the door and kissed her hello, but she couldn't imagine that he'd had a drink at eight in the morning. It had to be his aftershave.

Gracie and Christian huddled together in one of the rear pews, while Verna sat between Susan Lucci and Donald Trump, talking animatedly. Cordelia didn't much care for her sister's selection of organ music. Organ music in general seemed a little "bargain basement" for such a star-studded affair, but then Octavia had a tedious traditional streak that tended to manifest itself at the oddest moments.

Ellie Saks had set up a tripod near the front, but was walking around with the camera on her shoulder, filming the pregame show. She seemed to be in her element, zooming in on people's faces, trying to catch the rich and famous in an unguarded sneeze.

"I wonder where Roland could be?" said Octavia. "He's going to be late."

"He'll be here."

"Where's my cell phone?"

"I left it in the car. Did you want to carry it up the aisle? I know you're a trendsetter, but it seemed a little much."

"What if they've had an accident?"

"He's fine, Octavia. He's just not here yet."

Ten minutes later, they were still waiting. The New York royalty was growing restless.

"There he is," said Cordelia, flapping her arms energetically as Roland and Buddy entered the sanctuary from the back. They walked up the center aisle, nodding and smiling at various friends. "Buddy's talking to Reverend Mulcaster now." She paused. "Now he's motioning to the organist."

"And?"

"It's show time."

Octavia climbed down off the stool, allowing her designer one last appraising look.

"Buddy just nodded for Dad to come get you. I think we're ready." She turned to find that her sister had suddenly burst into a veritable conflagration of nerves. It was oddly affecting in some strange, familial way. Cordelia was always terribly sentimental when it came to commitment ceremonies of any kind. This was hardly the end of a fairy tale where the prince marries the princess and everyone lives happily ever after. It was more like the princess marrying the prince's great-grandfather. Even so, she felt tears well up in her eyes. Her sister had been married three times before, and this was the first time she'd ever attended one of the weddings. Of course, knowing Octavia, there would be many more opportunities in the future. "You look truly beautiful."

Octavia seemed touched. "Thanks." As she struggled to get her jitters under control, the tweed suit placed a bouquet of light pink roses in her arms. "Thanks, Ron."

"We're all set," called Hiram, sweeping through the side door. He stopped when he saw Octavia in her wedding gown. "You're a vision, sweetheart."

Octavia blushed.

Cordelia wiped a tear from her eye. God, she was such a sap.

Hiram offered his daughters his arms and together, the bride, the bridesmaid, and the father-of-the-bride hustled to the back door of the church.

The moment had finally come. The wedding march began.

Approaching the front of the sanctuary, Hiram handed Octavia off to Roland, then stood to the side with Cordelia and Buddy.

Reverend Mulcaster began his speech.

"Dearly beloved, we are assembled here in the presence of God, to join Roland Lester and Octavia Thorn in holy matrimony; which is instituted of God, regulated by his commandments, blessed by our Lord Jesus Christ, and to be held in honor among all mankind."

As Cordelia listened, she noticed that Roland was sweating, wiping at his brow over and over again with a handkerchief. Octavia seemed oblivious to anything but the minister's words. Wouldn't it be amazing, thought Cordelia, if the groom picked this moment to call off the ceremony? It looked to her like he was having an attack of cold feet.

The minister continued: ". . . instructed those who enter into this relationship to cherish a mutual esteem and love; to bear with each other's infirmities and weaknesses; and to comfort each other in sickness, trouble and sorrow. . . ."

Roland lurched forward, grabbing Reverend Mulcaster's arm to prevent himself from falling.

The crowd gasped.

"I'm all right," said Roland, waving off the help that was already rushing toward him. "Please, everyone sit down. Let's just continue."

Octavia looked stricken. She put her arm around his back and whispered something into his ear. He smiled at her tenderly, then nodded to the minister.

Mulcaster returned to his notes, trying to find his place. "Ah . . . in honesty and industry to provide for each other, and for their household, in temporal things; to pray for and encourage each other in things which pertain to God; and to live together as the heirs of the grace of life." He looked up, raising his hands. "Let us pray. Dear Father in heaven, we ask that you—"

This time Roland stumbled backward, falling awkwardly against one of the pews. As he slid helplessly to the floor, Octavia tried to hold onto him, but he was too heavy and slipped out of her grasp. She tossed her flowers away and knelt down next to him. "Roland, what's wrong?"

Cordelia stood back as at least a dozen men and women rushed to his side. Someone finally called, "Get an ambulance! Now!"

In an instant, everyone in the room was up and milling about, some hurrying out to find a phone, but most just looking concerned, pushing their way toward the front to get a better view of what was happening.

"Give him some air," called Buddy. "Please. If everyone could just stand back."

Cordelia saw the look of horror on her sister's face. Roland's eyes were closed, but he was asking for water. She took it as a good sign.

After that, it was all a blur. The ambulance came. Roland was wheeled out. Octavia and Buddy rode in the ambulance, while Cordelia and her father took Octavia's car, and Jane drove Buddy's. The nearest hospital was in New Haven, a good fifteen miles away.

When Cordelia and her dad finally burst through the hospital doors, they found Octavia sitting in the waiting room just outside the emergency room. Her dress was in shambles, and she was red-faced and crying.

"How is he?" asked Cordelia, sitting down next to her. Her father sat on the other side, putting his arms around her for support. Jane was already there too, standing off to the side, hands in the pockets of her slacks.

"I don't know, but it's bad. I could tell that much from what happened in the ambulance. Roland just kept asking for water. He said his head ached. By the time we got to the hospital, he was so weak, he couldn't talk. I'm not even sure if he was conscious. They took him into the emergency room as soon as we arrived, but they wouldn't let me come with him. The nurse said a doctor would be out to talk to me as soon as they know anything."

"Where's Buddy?" asked Cordelia.

Octavia seemed to be in a daze. "Buddy? Oh, he went to find the chapel. I guess he wanted to pray. He's blaming himself for the whole thing. Said he should have seen how sick his brother was before he collapsed. Really, he was terribly upset. I think the paramedics wanted to sedate him right there in the ambulance, but he refused. He said he had to be there if Roland needed him."

"You have absolutely no idea what's wrong with him?" asked Cordelia.

She twisted part of her dress. "It could be his heart. He's been on different medications for years. The paramedics asked me what he was taking now, but I didn't know. I *should* have." Her face puckered and she started to cry again. "He's eighty-three years old. What if he dies? I don't want him to die. Not yet." Her tears were suddenly mixed with anger. "He can't leave me alone! That wasn't our deal."

"What deal?" asked Cordelia. "What are you talking about?"

Octavia buried her head against her father's shoulder. She clearly didn't want to talk about it.

A few minutes later, a woman in green-garbed doctor drag entered the room. "Octavia Thorn?" she asked, searching their faces. Her sober expression encouraged none of them.

"Yes?" said Octavia, rising from her chair.

"I'm Dr. Diaz. Is Mr. Lester's brother here too?"

"He's in the chapel."

"I see. Perhaps one of you would go get him."

Octavia blanched, sagging slightly against her father.

"Would you do it?" asked Cordelia, nodding to Jane.

She quickly hurried out.

"How is he?" asked Octavia.

"I'm afraid my news isn't good. Mr. Lester died a short while ago. We did everything we could. I'm very sorry. Any questions you've got, I'll try to answer."

Octavia was squeezing Cordelia's arm so hard, under other circumstances, she would have cried out in pain. Instead, she asked, "It was his heart then?"

"We're not sure," said the doctor. "That is to say, I'm not. The reason he died was because his heart stopped. But I'm not positive what caused it to stop, or what caused the convulsions."

"Convulsions?" repeated Octavia, looking horrified.

"He was in and out of consciousness, but at one point he indicated that his skin felt as if it were on fire. And he had significant thirst. None of that is consistent with heart problems." Taking hold of the stethoscope around her neck, she added. "We'll need to do an autopsy. I can give you more specifics when that's completed."

"Oh, God," said Octavia, sinking down into her chair.

"Is that really necessary?" asked Cordelia.

"I'm afraid it is. We'll need authorization. Since you're his wife—"

"The marriage never took place," said Hiram, interrupting her before she could continue.

"Well, then the next of kin would be his brother?"

"I suppose so," conceded Cordelia.

"Then I need to talk to him right away. Have the woman at the desk page me when he gets back." Before leaving, she glanced down at Octavia. "I'm very sorry for your loss, Ms. Thorn."

Octavia didn't look up, but managed a nod.

"Thank you, Doctor," said Hiram.

"I wish I could have done more."

24

As the sun set behind the mansion, Jane walked across a stretch of snow to the bronze statue of Venus. She'd seen the frozen fountain from her bedroom window, but so far hadn't taken the time to give it a closer look. Inside the house, everyone had gathered in the living room to wait for Buddy's return from the hospital. He'd stayed on to sign papers and make arrangements for Roland's body to be transferred to a funeral home in New Haven once the autopsy was completed.

Jane felt every bit as overwhelmed by Roland's sudden death as everyone else, but she'd also grown intensely claustrophobic inside the gloomy atmosphere of the mansion. Octavia couldn't seem to stop crying. Verna couldn't stop smoking. And Hiram wouldn't stop drinking, even though Cordelia let him know, in no uncertain terms, that his behavior was unacceptable. Everyone else just sat around being grim and silent. Under other circumstances, Jane might have poured herself a glass of brandy to mellow out, but Hiram's behavior disgusted her. Fresh air was better.

The statue that stood before her was a copy of the Venus de Milo—the famous Greek sculpture that depicted a beautiful half-clothed woman, thought to be the likeness of Venus, goddess of love and beauty. If Jane remembered her college art history correctly, the statue had been discovered on the island of Milos sometime in the 1800s. It was complete serendipity that a man with some knowledge of Greek sculpture happened to be walking past a lime kiln just as the owner of the sculpture was about to chop it up and toss it into the flames. The statue, now in the Louvre, had been damaged over time and was missing both arms. Jane remembered reading that art historians liked to debate what the woman might have been doing with those arms. Some thought she was holding a battle shield, resting it on her knee, while others thought she might be holding a spear, or gazing at her reflection in a mirror.

According to Hilda, Roland had commissioned the reproduction shortly after moving to Innishannon. There was a plaque near the base. In the fading twilight, Jane could just make out the words, "From the heart of this fountain of delights wells up a bitter taste to choke us, even amid the flowers." The words belonged to a first-century Roman, Titus Lucretius Carus. It was a harsh quote to place on something so lovely, but Roland must have had his reasons.

As she walked around the fountain to view the sculpture from a different angle, she saw Buddy's car approaching the house at warp speed. After pulling into the circular drive, he cut the engine and got out. Jane waved, hoping to have a word with him before he went inside. Buddy waved back, but seemed so intent on his own mission that he didn't stop.

"Buddy, could I talk to you for a second?" she called. He was already halfway up the steps. She wanted him to know that the brake light on his Lexus had come on—and then gone off—while she was driving it from the church to the hospital. It wasn't smart to ignore a warning light, even at a time like this.

When he turned around Jane saw that the anguish he'd displayed so fervently at the hospital was completely gone. It had been replaced by worry, perhaps even a little anger. "Not now. Is Grace inside?"

"She's in the living room."

He turned and charged up the last few steps, disappearing into the house.

Jane followed, but just as she reached the door, she heard another car approach. Glancing over her shoulder, she saw that a squad car was just pulling in, followed closely by a second.

She waited as four men, three in police blues and one in a suit and heavy raincoat got out. Each of them took a quick look at the house and the grounds before hurrying up the steps to the front door.

"Do you live here?" asked the cop wearing the suit. He was middle-aged and tall, at least six-five, and had the body of a football player a few years past his prime.

Jane shook her head. "I'm a guest. But Mr. Lester's brother just got back. He's the next of kin."

"Can you take us to him?" His accent was pure New York. The friendly smile took her by surprise. "John Toscano." He shook her hand. "I'm a detective with the New Haven P.D.'s major crimes unit."

Major crimes? "Jane Lawless," she said, smiling back at him. It felt wrong to be so cheerful after witnessing something so tragic, but for a police officer who dealt with life and death on a daily basis, it was probably routine. "I came for the wedding. Except it didn't—"

"Yes, we know."

She nodded. "I'll show you the way."

Once inside, she led them down the hall to the living room. She could hear Buddy's voice explaining that his brother didn't believe in funerals. He wanted to be cremated and his ashes scattered in Long Island Sound. A small private ceremony was all he'd allow. Everything was in his will, something Buddy seemed to be on intimate terms with.

As Jane and the police entered, she assumed that Buddy hadn't had a chance to talk to Gracie yet because he'd been waylaid by a room full of anxious faces.

"Which one of you is Buddy Lester?" asked the detective, removing some papers from the inside pocket of his coat.

Buddy stiffened when he saw all the blue uniforms. "Can I help you?"

"Are you Mr. Lester?"

"Yes."

"I'm Detective John Toscano, New Haven P.D. I have a warrant here to search the house."

"A warrant," repeated Verna, standing up. "What for? What's going on?"

He stared at her a moment. "Say, aren't you—"

"Yes. Verna Lange."

"My God, I'm such a fan of yours." He seemed at a loss for words.

"I'm sure I'll be a fan of yours too, John, just as soon as you explain to me why you're here."

Jane wondered what effect her celebrity was having on him.

"Come on, John." Her famous eyes implored. "Roland Lester was one of my dearest friends."

"Well," said Toscano, straightening his tie, "I'm sorry, Miss Lange, but we have evidence that Mr. Lester's death was a homicide."

Octavia gasped.

"The doctor who treated him worked for several years with a poison control unit in Richmond, Virginia. She was pretty sure she'd seen his symptoms, before, so she ordered a blood test. Before the results came back, he passed away."

"Can I assume she's seen the results now?" asked Verna.

"Yes, and she notified the New Haven P.D. immediately. We were able to get a warrant from a judge before he left for the day."

"Let me get this straight," said Buddy, steadying himself against the mantle by holding out a trembling hand. "You're saying my brother was *murdered?*"

"That's what we suspect." He nodded to his men and they quickly disbursed throughout the house.

"But how?" asked Octavia. She was standing now, too. "What sort of poison?"

"And you are?"

"Octavia Thorn. His . . . fiancée."

"My condolences, ma'am. From what I was told, it's called James-town weed, or more commonly, jimsonweed. It's usually administered as a tea. Takes a couple of hours to become fatal."

The mention of jimsonweed struck a bell in the back of Jane's mind. "Excuse me," she said, waiting until she had Toscano's attention. "This may have nothing to do with anything, but I believe the man who built this house, Alexander Kirk, used a tea made from jimsonweed to poison his wife."

His face stayed blank, eyes steady. "How do you know that?"

"I told her," said Gracie, raising a finger. She'd been sitting on one of the window seats, looking out through the curtains.

"Your name?"

"Gracie Lester. Roland's grandniece." She tossed back her frizz of multicolored hair.

He walked a few paces closer. "How did you hear about the poisoning?"

"I did some research on the house when I first moved in."

"When was that?"

"About six years ago."

"Do you always do research on the houses you live in?"

"I've never lived in an eighty-year-old mansion before. It was just curiosity."

"Did you tell anyone besides Ms. Lawless what you learned?"

"Sure. I told everyone. In case you're interested, Kirk ended up in jail." She returned her attention to the window.

It was Hiram Thorn's turn to speak. "I demand to know if you're suggesting one of us had something to do with Mr. Lester's death." In his drunken state, he'd blundered right to the point.

"I'm not suggesting anything, Mr.—"

"*Dr.* Thorn. Dr. Hiram Thorn. Father of the bride."

"There *was* no marriage," said Buddy, looking at Hiram with complete disdain.

While Toscano asked a few more questions, Jane tried to fit her mind around the fact that Roland's death had been a murder. If it was true, who had a motive? Octavia and Hilda were certainly off the hook. Neither would have any reason to harm him. Jane couldn't imagine that Ellie would want to hurt him either. She had important information she needed Roland to confirm. He could hardly do that if he was dead. And Dr. Thorn might not have wanted his daughter to marry Roland, but it hardly seemed likely that he would kill the groom to prevent it. Jane also couldn't imagine why Gracie would want to hurt her great-uncle. On the other hand, Buddy, Christian, and Verna all had potential ties to a long ago homicide. Jane felt that piece of information might be crucial, and it also might be overlooked by the police unless someone told them about it.

"Until we receive the final autopsy results and know for certain what happened to Mr. Lester, I have to ask all of you all remain in the area." His gaze traveled around the living room. "Most of you are staying here, right?"

"I'm not," said Hiram.

"You might as well move back in," said Octavia. She glanced at Cordelia.

"Were you all here last night?" asked Toscano.

"Everyone stayed on the grounds except for my father," said Octavia. "He was at a hotel in New Haven."

"But he was here this morning," said Christian, his arms draped casually over the back of a loveseat. It was the first time he'd spoken. "Just trying to be helpful," he said, attempting an innocent look.

"I'll need to get statements from all of you before I leave," said Toscano. "But first, I have to make some phone calls. While we're searching the premises, I'd like to ask that each of you remain in this room."

"What about going outside?" asked Christian. "Can't we at least get some fresh air if we need it?"

"All right. Just keep out of our way." He nodded politely to Jane as he left the room.

Jane sat and talked quietly to Cordelia for a few minutes, then closed her eyes and tried to rest. After listening to Dr. Thorn snore for a good half hour, she couldn't stand it another minute. She grabbed her coat and headed for the front door. It was pitch dark out now. The refreshingly crisp afternoon had turned icy. She wished she could have changed into more comfortable shoes before hitting the path that led into the woods, but it wasn't possible. For now, she simply wanted to spend some time getting everything straight in her mind about the Wallace murder. Toscano could find out more specific information from the Los Angeles police department, it was simply a matter of pointing him in the right direction. When she gave her the information, she wanted the presentation to be clear and to the point.

The crescent moon was her only light as she made her way toward the tack house. Since Ellie was in the living room back at the mansion, there would be no cup of strong black coffee waiting for her at the end of her trek. Tonight it would have been an unnecessary distraction because what she needed most was time alone to think.

She walked at a leisurely pace, struggling to assemble the details of the story in logical progression. Ellie would be a good source of information about Roland Lester's life in Hollywood. Jane decided to leave out the part about Ellie's grandfather and her Hollywood scandal theory: the card game, the illusive proof she'd come to Innishannon to unearth, Lester being the key. Ellie had been so cryptic about it

189

yesterday, Jane wasn't even sure she understood what she was talking about. Best to stick with the facts and let Toscano work from there.

Before she knew it, she'd reached her destination. In the distance, she could see the tack house sitting dark and silent, bathed in weak moonlight. The stables next to it were also dark. As she approached the buildings, she was surprised to hear a low murmur of voices coming from inside the stables. She darted behind a metal barrel next to the stable door and listened.

Speaking from the darkness, Gracie said: "I don't care what that detective says, I want them all out of here. Now! It's my house. I make the decisions now."

"I won't allow it!" It was Buddy, and he sounded furious.

"How are you going to stop me?"

"Grace, don't push me. I'm not a nice man when I'm pushed."

"Oh, come on. That hard-boiled crap might have worked for you a long time ago, but it doesn't cut it with me. I'm not afraid of you, or anyone else, for that matter."

"Gracie, shut up!"

"You shut up."

"Don't talk to me that way!" He was aghast. "I'm your grandfather."

"And I'm your grand*daughter*. Don't I deserve some respect too?"

"Of course you do. Just . . . lower your voice. People could take your words the wrong way."

"You mean Toscano might think I poisoned Roland? Is that what *you* think?"

"No!"

"That I'm impulsive. I don't think before I act."

"Sometimes you don't."

"So you do believe I poisoned him. In your eyes, I've already been convicted and sentenced."

"I never said you poisoned my brother!"

"I was mad enough to."

"But you didn't."

Silence. "How could Rolo do that to me? Give Innishannon to Octavia?"

"I told you I felt terrible about it, but there was nothing I could do."

"Unless *you* offed the old guy yourself."

"Grace!"

"I'm sorry. I'm just . . . upset."

"You don't kid about something like that. That's what I'm trying to impress upon you."

"Oh, lighten up."

"I've never seen you behave so . . . so coldly before."

"I'm still mad at him, okay? We were friends. But if he had to die, I'm glad it happened before he married Ms. Broadway. That's all I'm saying. Nothing more."

"Oh, Gracie," said Buddy, and sighed. "What am I going to do with you? You've got to stop talking like that. I absolutely insist! The police are here. They'll want a statement. You've got to use your head."

More silence. "Why are you digging in your heels about throwing all these idiots out?"

"Because it looks bad. Do I need to draw you a picture? You thought you were going to inherit a multimillion-dollar estate. Then Roland decides to marry. In his new will, the property goes to someone else. Except if he dies before Octavia becomes his wife, the house would still be yours."

"All right, all right. I get it."

"Then stop acting like a spoiled brat. You don't officially own Innishannon—not yet."

"Then we'll call the lawyer tomorrow, get it all settled."

Jane could hear wood creaking, as if someone were sitting down.

"Listen," said Buddy, sounding tired, "Octavia's been living here since September. She just lost her fiancé."

"Boo hoo. Like it was the romance of the century."

"I don't understand it either, but she must have had some feelings for my brother. It's not right, just tossing her out. She needs time to grieve. If she wants to do it here, let her. If she wants to leave, she can. But you can't be cruel, Grace. I won't allow it."

"Maybe she did it—maybe she murdered him."

"She had no reason to."

"Then who did?"

"I don't know. I just want you to be smart." He hesitated. "I'm glad we had a chance to talk."

"So you could make sure I didn't feed him the tea."

Silence.

The next sound Jane heard was a door slamming on the other side of the stables. A second later, Gracie appeared, sprinting toward the road. It took almost a minute before Buddy came out. He might have wanted to go after her, but his old body wouldn't move that fast anymore. He raised his head slowly and looked up at the moon, then pushed his hands into the pockets of his coat and started back through the woods.

When Jane got back to the house, she knew she was supposed to return immediately to the living room, but instead she followed the smell of fresh coffee to the dining room. Toscano was sitting at the long polished table, a notebook sitting open in front of him, talking on his cell phone. Looking up, he motioned her inside.

She saw that the coffee urn had been filled and cream and sugar set out. Pouring herself a cup, she sat down at the table and waited for him to finish his conversation. He seemed to be talking to someone about the autopsy. From what she could gather, it would be a while before the full results came back, though the preliminary outcomes sounded as if they bore out the emergency room doctor's conclusions.

"So," he said, flipping shut the phone, "let's talk." He pulled his coffee cup in front of him, then leaned over it. "I called back to the station and had a short background check done on you."

"You did?"

"Once we figured out you were from Minneapolis, an associate of mine called a buddy of his in the Minneapolis P.D. He got quite an earful." He studied her a moment, then went on. "You own a restaurant. Your credit rating is excellent. You've never been married. You drive a Trooper—"

"Maybe you found out what's wrong with the engine. It's been idling kind of rough lately."

He grinned. "Your father is a well-respected defense attorney, and your brother is a cameraman for a local TV station."

"That's my entire life. Now you know everything."

He sat back in his chair and folded his arms over his chest. "You've also helped solve a couple of major homicides. Impressive, for a novice. And a strange . . . avocation."

She shrugged.

"You're also a friend of the bride."

"Octavia is my best friend's sister."

"Yes, Cordelia Thorn. The large woman in the tuxedo sitting next to Octavia."

She nodded.

"So, tell me, Ms. Lawless, what do you think's going on here? It occurs to me that you've got an opinion I should hear."

It was the opening she'd been looking for. For the next few minutes, she discussed the Lew Wallace murder case. After giving him all the facts, they sat and talked over the potential ramifications. She mentioned that she had a file upstairs in her room. If he wanted to take it with him, he could. Toscano seemed not only surprised by the amount of research she'd done, but by her critical analysis. He agreed, the old murder did open up a whole new range of possibilities.

"You ever thought of joining the police force?"

She glanced at him over the rim of her coffee cup. "I like running a restaurant, thank you."

"But you like doing this too. Don't lie to a cop."

She smiled, then gave another shrug.

Glancing back at his notebook, he said, "Of course, I appreciate the tip about Wallace, but we also have to consider that Mr. Lester could have been murdered for something more immediate, more tangible."

"Like money." She thought of Gracie, but didn't say anything.

"Money. Revenge. Jealousy. We'll check out his will, see if it provides us with a motive or two." Folding his arms over his chest, he added, "I don't suppose you came across a copy during your . . . investigation."

She shook her head.

"No. Well, I guess I'll have to rely on official police sources for that."

"Oh, one other thing. Before Roland died, he thought he was being followed."

"By who?"

"He didn't know. His brother, Buddy, could fill you in on the details."

"Hey, John," said one of the officers. He was standing in the doorway, holding a small plastic sack carefully by the edge. "I think we got it."

Toscano shot to his feet. "Where?"

"The brother's room."

Jane turned to look.

"Go get him. I want to talk to him ASAP. And tell Reilly to bag the teapot and cup and get it to the lab tonight." Toscano turned to Jane. "Sorry, but I—"

"I'm leaving."

"I'd like to talk to you again."

"Tonight?"

"No, but . . . later this week. Maybe we could have a cup of coffee together in New Haven."

"Can I assume I'm no longer a suspect?"

The smile returned. "You never were."

25

Come into my office," said Cordelia, dragging Jane out the front door, across the drive, and over to the crumbling stone fountain. She still had on her tux, but had thrown a heavy wool Hudson Bay blanket over her shoulders to keep warm.

Thankfully, Jane had already put on a jacket and was about to head outside again herself.

"There are way too many prying ears inside that house," said Cordelia, tugging the blanket more snugly around shoulders.

"I believe the term is, 'prying eyes.' "

"Eyes. Ears. Elbows. Knees. I didn't hustle you out here to talk about anatomy." She paced anxiously through the snow. "Boy, this is amazing, isn't it? Buddy poisoning his brother? At least it lets Octavia off the hook, and that's all I care about."

"You never thought your sister—"

"Of course not," she said flatly. "But Octavia's been so damn closed-mouthed ever since we got here. I can't put my finger on what it is, but I know when she's keeping something from me. At least now I know she wasn't hatching some plot to off her fiancé."

Jane hadn't considered Octavia a suspect. She was surprised to find that Cordelia had.

"Wouldn't it be amazing if Roland's death had something to do with that stuff you dug up on Lew Wallace?"

Ever since Jane had heard the patrolman announce he'd found a substance in Buddy's bedroom that looked like jimsonweed, she'd been

195

trying to imagine what was going on. Sure, she had suspicions that Roland's death might be connected to that long ago murder—she'd spent a good half hour trying to convince a detective of its relevance—but the more she thought about the whole situation, the more she wondered why the murderer had picked *this* moment to get rid of Roland, on the day of his marriage. Given the timing, it seemed more likely that the motive had to do with the marriage itself—even with Octavia.

Cordelia continued to pace farther and farther away from the fountain. "I wish that Toscano person hadn't insisted on closing the dining room doors and then posting that Jesse Ventura look-alike outside."

"I guess he was worried about prying ears too." Jane waited a moment, then said, "You know, if you don't get back over here, all the people with prying ears in the next county will be able to hear our conversation."

"Oh, all right." Fixing Jane with a disgruntled look, she stomped back.

"Answer this," said Jane, leaning back against the fountain and looking up at the stars. "Let's say the murderer really was Buddy."

"You doubt it?"

"Just stay with me here. If he did poison his brother, why leave the evidence in his own room? Why not hide it in someone else's?"

Cordelia patted Jane's arm as if she were a slow child. "He did it to throw suspicion off himself."

"Excuse me?"

"Oh, Janey, don't you ever watch A&E? The murderer always stashes the poison in his own room, then protests that he wouldn't do something that dumb. He'll typically say something like, 'If I was the killer, I'd have thrown it away, flushed it down the toilet, or planted it in someone else's room, but I would never just leave it lying around my *own* room, ready to incriminate me.' " She turned her palms face up, as if it were self-evident. "It's simple misdirection. Colin Dexter would never allow something so elemental to fool Morse."

"Let me get this straight. You're saying that Buddy left the poison in his bedroom to point suspicion *away* from himself?"

"Now you're getting the hang of it."

Jane wasn't sure she was getting anything—except a headache.

"But . . . what if, just in this one atypical case, someone actually did plant the poison in Buddy's room to make it look as if he were guilty?"

"It's amateur thinking," sniffed Cordelia. "Poor plotting. And besides, it's way too obvious. Criminals never do obvious, stupid things. They're clever. Devious."

"I don't think that's always true."

"You've got to reason like Agatha Christie, dearheart." She elbowed Jane in the ribs. "Buddy's as guilty as he is clever. I'm just glad this is getting sorted out sooner rather than later. I have no interest in hanging around here a moment longer than I have to. Except—" She looked off toward the woods.

"Your father?"

"What am I going to do, Janey? He's a mess. He was doing so well after Mom died, but now with Octavia's latest fiasco, he's fallen off the wagon. He needs help. Both of us talked to him about it yesterday. He said he was okay, that he was going to stop drinking, but then right away this morning, he shows up at the house with liquor on his breath. The signs are all there. I've got to stop ignoring them. I also can't imagine how he could go back to Boston and resume his position at the hospital without being fired, or being sued for malpractice because of some hideous mistake. My father is falling apart right before my very eyes and, so far, I haven't been able to do a thing to stop it. That's why . . . I mean, I'd feel so guilty just leaving him now, the same way I left him when—" Again, she abandoned the end of the sentence.

"You had good reasons for leaving the way you did after your mother died."

"Yeah. That's what I keep telling myself. But I should have phoned him more. Checked in to see how he was doing. He probably felt that I blamed *him* for what happened to Mom almost as much as I blamed Octavia."

"Did you?"

She squeezed her eyes shut. "Yeah, in a way, I did. I still do. He should never have let her drive in the state she was in. He wasn't drunk. He should have seen a disaster in the making. We've only talked a couple times a year since Mom's been gone, and we always keep it light. I used to be able to talk to my dad about anything. You know how close we were. Remember that story I told you about the time I joined that gymnastics team?"

197

"And your father announced to everyone you'd be in the Olympics one day."

"He was always behind me, one hundred percent. Thought I could do anything I set my mind to. His love gave me such confidence."

"Yeah, he's always been proud of you."

"And then there was the time I was sure I was destined to be the next Isadora Duncan. I adored my pink tutu, and my little ballet slippers. I used to fly across the practice room, leap into the air. Of course, I knocked down a lot of chairs and some of the other students, but I was just learning."

"Sure you were."

"My dad would come watch me dance every chance he got."

"Until one day the teacher told your mother that you seemed way more interested in the cookie you got at the end of class than the dancing."

"I tire easily."

"And she pulled you out."

"It was for the best. My future in a microcosm. Mom was a realist. Dad was the one who told me to reach for the stars. Now . . . it's like we're strangers." She turned on Jane with a fierce look. "I feel like Octavia not only took my mother from me, but my father too. And now she wants me to forgive and forget?"

Jane slipped an arm across Cordelia's shoulders and together they stood looking back at the mansion.

After a couple silent minutes, Cordelia sighed. "What really bothers me is that Dad's drinking has actually become worse. He never used to drink in public. Now he thinks nothing of it. Alcoholism is a progressive disease, Janey. I know it's tough. I know it's one day at a time. But he's not even trying anymore, all because of this damn marriage. The stress pushed him right over the edge. And now, how do we get him back?"

Jane could hear the despair in her voice. "Maybe you and Octavia should arrange an intervention. You know, like the one you did with that actress friend of yours in Wisconsin. Dianna Stanwood. It helped her."

"Yeah, I suppose it's a thought."

Jane dropped her gaze from the high gables to the front of the house, where the door had just opened and two of the police officers had walked out. Buddy Lester stood between them, his head bowed.

"That was awfully fast," murmured Jane, noticing Toscano come out next, followed by the last officer.

As Toscano conferred briefly with one of his men, Jane turned to Cordelia, "Stay here. I'll see what I can find out."

"Why should I stay here?" asked Cordelia indignantly.

Jane glanced back at her, holding a finger to her lips.

When Toscano saw Jane approach, he waved and then walked around the back of the car to meet her. "Looks like we've got our man," he said, massaging the muscles in his neck.

The only thing Jane could imagine was that Buddy had confessed. "Did he actually admit to it?" she asked, stopping a few feet away.

"Not exactly."

"Are you just taking him in for further questioning then?"

"Between you and me, he made it clear that he didn't want to talk to us until his lawyer was present. He phoned the guy and got him to agree to meet us at the station in forty-five minutes. My expectation, based on what he did say, is that yes, Buddy Lester poisoned his brother. I think he wants to see if he can cut some sort of deal before he gives a full statement. I've already sent the evidence to the lab, told them to push it through right away. We can start building our case as soon as the report comes back. All in all, I'd say it was a good night's work."

"I guess congratulations are in order."

He reacted with a slow grin. "But who knows, the information you gave me on the Wallace murder may still figure into it somehow."

Jane still didn't get it. "But . . . I mean, is that usual? For someone to just cave in and say they're guilty?"

"I've seen it happen before. I think we're just lucky that the emergency room doctor was so heads up. With a man Roland Lester's age, the death could easily have been blamed on heart problems, which I'm told, he had. I think that's what Buddy was counting on. Frankly, it might have worked. Leads grow cold fast."

"So . . . that's it, I guess."

"I hope so." He turned as the squad car Buddy was riding in drove past heading back to the highway. Glancing at his watch, he returned his gaze to Jane. "How much longer will you be staying here?"

"I don't know. A few more days."

"I'll give you a call, let you know what's happening."

Jane was a little amazed at how nice he was being. "Thanks. I appreciate it. So will the Thorn family."

She waited as he got into his car. After starting the engine, he rolled down the window and looked at her again with his quietly amused eyes. "At least you won't be sleeping in the same house with a murderer tonight."

If the comment was meant to calm her nerves, it didn't.

"I'll talk to you soon." He studied her a moment longer, then drove away.

She was probably way off base, but she had a vague sense that he was interested in her. It was a complication she didn't need. She shrugged it off, knowing that in all probability he wouldn't call and she'd never see him again.

Slipping her hands into her pockets, she drifted back to where Cordelia was standing. "Looks like you were right. Buddy didn't quite confess, but Toscano thinks it's only a matter of time."

"I knew it! What did I tell you? I swear by those A&E mysteries." Her good humor faded when she looked over at the front door. "Now what?"

Octavia had just burst into the cold night air, exhaling steam—or was it smoke?—as she charged straight for them. Making her way across the snow-packed ground in her high heels and wedding gown, she stumbled again and again, looking like a drunken sailor walking across a swaying poop deck.

Cordelia started to laugh.

"What's so funny?" snarled Octavia, realizing the moment she reached them that one of her heels had broken off. "Damn," she snapped, almost in tears.

"What's wrong?" said Jane, seeing that her distress went far beyond the state of her footware.

"Everything."

"Here it comes," said Cordelia, eyes rising to the heavens. "Poor me. The world conspires to ruin my life."

"It does."

"I am an innocent victim of the cosmos."

"Oh, shut up." She was in no mood for Cordelia's blather. She batted at her cheeks, refusing to let her sister know the true state of her emotions.

The only way Cordelia seemed to be able to interact with her sister was by keeping her at arm's length through barbs, humor, and taunts. Sometimes it reminded Jane of their teenage interactions, when sarcasm generally ruled, but Cordelia's tone held more of an edge now. It was sad to watch. "Come on," said Jane gently. "This has been a horrible day for you. You've lost someone you—" She wasn't sure if "love" was the right word, so she finally settled on, "—your fiancé. You have a right to cry."

"It's not just that," said Octavia, "I'm . . . frantic. Desperate!" Just like Cordelia, she would have started to pace, but her shoes prevented it.

"And what are you frantic and desperate about?" asked Cordelia, the picture of reasoned calm.

"Our wedding night."

"Oh, I see. We're talking about Roland again."

"Who else would I be talking about?"

"I thought you might be angry at Dad for allowing your crazy mixed-up life to stress him to the point that he needed a drink."

Octavia shot her a ferocious look.

"I'm just trying to get your desperation sorted out. Don't get mad at *me*."

"What about your wedding night?" asked Jane, trying to head off a major blow-up.

Octavia flicked her eyes to the bronze sculpture of Venus, as if the statue might be eavesdropping. "That's when Roland was going to tell me about . . . this." Her hand brushed at her throat, then tugged a small gold chain away from her neck until she'd lifted a key from under the lacy folds of her gown.

"What's that?" asked Cordelia, standing up straight, hands rising to her hips.

"A key."

"It's a skeleton key," said Jane. "Did Roland give it to you?"

She nodded.

"I *knew* you were keeping something important from me!" squawked Cordelia, twisting around. Flinging her arms wide, she added, "I knew it. I knew it. I knew it!"

"What's it open?" asked Jane.

"That's just it. I don't know. Roland said he'd show me after the ceremony today. He promised me riches beyond my wildest dreams—and power."

"Well, come on, girl," said Cordelia, grabbing her sister by the hand. "Let's go find it."

"Not so fast," said Octavia, standing her ground. "I've tried it in a few of the locks inside the house, but you're right, I haven't done a systematic search. That's what has to happen next, but I just don't feel like I can handle it alone anymore. I need help, from both of you."

"You've got it," said Jane.

Octavia cocked her head to one side, then smiled gratefully. "I think Cordelia's a lucky woman to have a friend like you."

Jane didn't know what to say.

"Look," said Cordelia, the wheels turning inside her mind, "we can't just go barging back in there looking for old locks. We have to do it when nobody else is around."

"After everyone's gone to bed," said Jane.

"Right," said Octavia slowly, thinking it over. "That's a good plan. We'll wait until everyone's asleep."

"Let's synchronize our watches," whispered Cordelia.

Jane thought it was a bit silly, but glanced at her watch anyway.

"It's nine-twenty-seven," whispered Cordelia. "Let's say we all meet in my room at three A.M."

"Check," whispered Octavia.

Jane almost did a double take. Once again, Octavia proved that she and Cordelia were two peas in a very preposterous pod.

26

On the way up to her bedroom to change into something more comfortable, Jane decided she'd take another look at the notes she'd copied off the Internet the other day, just in case she'd missed something. She might even add a few lines on the possible motive for Roland Lester's murder.

For instance, if the wedding had gone off without a hitch, Gracie would have lost Innishannon to Octavia. There were those who might not appreciate what a big deal it would be to Gracie, but after the evening she'd spent in Gracieland, Jane did. She couldn't help but wonder if Buddy had somehow resolved to sacrifice himself on the altar of the justice system to end all further investigation into his impulsive granddaughter's potential role in the affair. It seemed like a stretch, but then, anything was possible, especially if Buddy felt Gracie was guilty and that her impatience and bad judgment would eventually give her away.

Next, there was the little matter of the money Roland had been giving Christian Wallace for his silence. At first, just like Cordelia, Jane figured it had something to do with Lew Wallace's murder. But now, after learning that Lester had been in the closet all of his adult life, she was beginning to think that the money had been offered to keep Christian silent about the true nature of the relationship between Lew and Roland—assuming Christian knew about it. That being the case, how did the wedding change anything? As far as Jane knew, Christian was still receiving the hush money. Wouldn't it be in his best interests to keep Roland alive and writing checks? And what about the money he was hoping to get from Roland for his latest project? Time was running out for Christian. He'd come to the point in his life where he had to make a killing at the box office to assure he'd have enough money to see him comfortably through his old age. Why murder the person who held the key to his potential success? Unless? Had Roland refused to back him? Innishannon, even in its current dilapidated state, was worth multiple millions of dollars. What if Christian and Gracie had teamed up? Perhaps it sounded crazy, but it *was* possible. It was to Gracie's obvious advantage for Roland to die before the marriage took place, and if Christian had cut a deal with her for money in return for his help, his current financial problems could be over. And yet, were either of them so cold and ruthless—or desperate—that they'd resort to murder to get what they wanted?

And then there was Verna. It did seem odd that she'd show up on the eve of Roland and Octavia's wedding, not a clue in the world that it was about to take place. Or had that been the actress playing a scene? What part had she played in the Wallace homicide? To Jane, Verna was a big question mark.

And yet, in the end, if Buddy did turn out to be guilty, all Jane's theories and questions were moot. There was still the matter of the key Roland had given to Octavia. Also, the dirt on Roland that Ellie had come to Innishannon to unearth. But in the end, it was possible that none of that had anything to do with the murder.

Ellie! Jane hadn't considered it until this very moment, but Roland's death would have a major impact on her documentary. Would Gracie allow her to stay in the tack house and dig through her great-uncle's life now that he was gone? Surely Ellie had a contract that would allow for such an unforeseen event. Not that Gracie couldn't make her life—and her research—difficult if Ellie tried to go against her wishes. On the other hand, Gracie might welcome the publicity the documentary would generate.

Jane hoped that all would be made clear after Buddy gave his statement to the police, although she wouldn't feel entirely comfortable that a murderer had been caught until Toscano tied up all the loose ends.

After tucking her black turtleneck into a pair of gray cords, Jane stepped up to a small mirror to remove her fancy silver filigree earrings and replace them with small crystal studs. Once finished, she found the file and sat down on the bed, switching the light on over her head. As she slipped on her reading glasses, she began to worry that she might fall asleep while she was reading. Best to set the alarm. Synchronizing the clock with her watch—and feeling stupid doing so—she picked up the file and began to contemplate what an old murder might have to do with a new one.

When the alarm suddenly went off at a quarter of three, Jane came awake in a flash of absolute terror. It took her a minute to realize where she was and that she wasn't in any danger. Reaching out to switch off the alarm, she lay back against the pillows, her heart pounding so hard she almost thought she was having a heart attack.

It was the same dream again, the one that had been destroying her sleep for over a month. She was at home in Minneapolis, a dark presence lurking somewhere inside the house. She would fall or stumble and then try to get up, but her body felt like lead. She was an iron filing and the floor was a magnet. She'd crawl desperately toward the front door, but it was like trying to move with huge weights strapped to her arms and legs. Sometimes she almost seemed aware of the fact that she was dreaming, but it didn't make the nightmarish world go away. Neither did the fact that she knew what the dream was about. She was reliving the attack she'd experienced in her home in late October. Since she had nothing to fear from that person any longer, why did her mind keep replaying the same scenario, again and again?

After prying herself off the bed, Jane ran a brush through her short hair, then headed to the bathroom to splash cold water into her face. She made it to Cordelia's room a few minutes after three.

"Get in here," whispered Cordelia, yanking her inside.

Only one faint light burned, but it was enough for Jane to see that both Cordelia and Octavia had blackened their faces and hands.

"Here," said Cordelia, handing Jane a piece of charred log from the fireplace.

"Don't you think that's a bit much?"

"No," whispered Cordelia, her eyes bulging emphatically. She scrutinized Jane's clothes. "At least you dressed in something dark."

Both sisters were wearing black from head to toe.

"Have you considered how it will look if we get caught?" asked Jane. "I mean, could we *be* more obvious? Why don't we each get a sheet, poke two holes in it—"

Cordelia held up her hand for silence. "If you're coming on this mission with us, you do as you're told."

"Mission?"

Octavia nodded.

In a room with more heat than light, Jane was outnumbered. She smeared the charcoal on her face and then stood at attention. She didn't have the energy to salute.

"All right," said Octavia. "Here's what I propose. We have no way to search the third floor, but it doesn't seem logical to me that Roland wanted us to spend our wedding night in Gracie's apartment. I got the distinct feeling he planned to make it a very special evening, the key being the denouement."

"Ah, the rules of dramatic structure," said Cordelia reverently.

"But . . . here in the house?" asked Jane. "With everybody watching?"

"If the key doesn't open a door or a cabinet in this house," said Octavia, hands rising to her hips, "I'm sunk. I can hardly search the entire world."

"I think she's right," said Cordelia. "I vote that the key fits an Innishannon lock."

Jane could have pointed out that what the key unlocked would hardly be decided by the democratic process, but it seemed pointless. Besides, Innishannon was the best place to start, and so far, the only idea they had.

"Now," continued Octavia, keeping her voice low, "I've already searched Roland's study."

"Doesn't surprise me," said Cordelia. "That's just like you. You were always pawing through the presents under the tree *days* before Christmas Eve, making little tears in the paper, rattling the boxes until the contents shattered."

Octavia looked down her nose at her sister. "Bite me."

"Don't think I won't. And I have *very* sharp teeth."

"Like all good rodents."

Cordelia's eyes bugged out.

"Stop it," whispered Jane. "If you two get into a fight, you're going to wake the entire house."

Octavia narrowed her eyes at her sister for a moment before going on. "There are nine bedrooms on this floor. Roland's is connected to mine, so I've checked that too, but the rest need to be searched."

"How are we going to do that?" demanded Cordelia. "People are sleeping in them."

"Well, obviously, we can't do it tonight. But what we can do is search all the rooms on the first floor and look around the basement."

"I don't *do* basements," said Cordelia flatly.

"You're such a delicate flower."

"I'll search the basement," offered Jane, hoping to head off another tiff. "And what about the screening room?"

Octavia sighed. "I suppose we should look in there too. But let's do it last."

"Shouldn't we synchronize our watches again?" asked Jane.

Catching the sarcasm, Cordelia gave her a half-lidded glance, then proceeded to the door. Pressing a finger to her lips, she led the way out into the hall and down the stairs. Jane was a little surprised that Octavia didn't object to Cordelia leading the pack, but then the older sister *was* the older sister. Some entitlements never changed.

For the next hour, the three women made a painstaking search of the first floor, including the living room, dining room, library, solarium, TV room, billiard room, breakfast room, the butler's pantry, the food pantry, and finally the kitchen. While Octavia and Cordelia busied themselves examining the cupboards, Jane took a look around the surprisingly small basement. Virtually nothing had a lock on it, with the exception of an old wooden box in the furnace room. Thankfully, it was open and empty.

Returning to the kitchen, Jane whispered, "There's nothing in the basement."

"There's nothing in here either," said Cordelia dispiritedly. She climbed down off a chair.

"I guess we better head down to the screening room," said Octavia, sounding as depressed as her sister. "And then I can go to bed and spend the rest of the night looking for locked doors in my dreams."

It sounded like more fun than Jane was having.

Using their flashlights to guide them, the three women entered the back passage that led to the screening room. They crept down a half-flight of stairs and passed silently into the sixteen-seat auditorium. Roland had built the addition onto the west side of the house sometime in the early eighties. Outside, the lower half of the wall was brick with the top half matching the rest of the Tudor structure—white stucco and dark brown half-timbering. Inside, floor-to-ceiling dark green curtains covered the side walls, with the screen running the entire length and breadth of the front. It wasn't large enough for Cinerama, but it was perfect for the old black-and-whites—Roland's favorites. The matching dark green seats were large and plush, and reclined for easy viewing.

"Can we turn on a light?" asked Octavia, sinking onto a bench right underneath the projector opening. "I'm sick of using these flashlights. Everybody's asleep. The search would go much faster if we could see."

Jane didn't think it was a good idea, particularly with their faces painted to look like they were about to make a nighttime raid on the Watergate. But before she could register her protest, Cordelia hit the dimmer switch on the wall next to the door and turned the recessed ceiling lights on full blast.

"I'm not sure that was smart," said Jane.

Cordelia was already beginning her circuit of the room.

Octavia just sat where she was, her head tipped back, gazing up at the screen. "This is a wild goose chase."

"Are you giving up?" asked Cordelia, examining the bottoms of the chair seats.

"No. I'm just struggling with my ennui."

"Bag the ennui. Get up and help us."

Jane watched Cordelia for a few seconds, then walked over to the projection room. A padlock hung from a hinged ring, preventing her from opening the door. "Damn," she muttered, giving it a frustrated tug. "What the—?" She bent down to get a closer look. "Hey, look at this. Someone cut through this lock with a bolt cutter, then tried to glue it back together. It didn't work."

Octavia finally got up off the bench. "Why would someone do that?"

"To get on the other side," said Cordelia, wiggling her eyebrows like Groucho Marx.

Jane removed the padlock and opened the door. Cautiously, she crept inside, followed closely by the two Marx sisters.

"Is there a light in here?" asked Cordelia, bumping into Octavia and nearly sending her crashing into the projector.

"It's right here," said Jane, pulling a cord.

For a few seconds, they all just stood and stared. Nothing seemed out of place. Nothing looked damaged or broken. The booth was small and completely enclosed, padded with soundproofing material to keep the projector noise at a minimum.

"I don't get it," said Cordelia, scratching her head.

Octavia moved over to a floor-to-ceiling cupboard that covered the back wall. As she opened it, Jane noticed that one of the movie canisters was standing upright, leaning against the other canisters, which were all lying flat. Since it was the only thing that seemed even remotely out of order, she pulled it off the shelf and removed the cover.

"Hey, the reel's missing." She examined the canister to find the name of the film. "It's the one we saw the other night. *A Daughter of the Gods.*" When she turned around, she saw that Cordelia was frowning. "Something wrong?"

"I'm . . . not sure."

"Look on the projector," suggested Octavia. "Maybe Roland never put it away."

"There's nothing on the projector," said Cordelia, continuing to act as if she'd just swallowed a bad oyster.

"But why take the reel and not the canister?" asked Octavia.

"Whoever did it was probably hoping nobody would notice it was empty. Shhh," said Jane, stepping back to the door.

"What?" asked Octavia impatiently.

Jane closed her eyes. "I thought I heard something."

Cordelia marched out of the booth and looked around. "No one's here. No one cares. We haven't found anything because there's nothing *to* find."

Octavia's shoulders sagged under the weight of her disappointment. "No riches. No power. This whole night has been one big fat dead end."

But Jane wasn't done examining the cupboard just yet. After pulling out all the canisters and reading the titles, she felt around the inside walls. Under the lowest shelf, she discovered a small button. "I wonder what this does?" she said, pushing it. Jane and Cordelia stood still as the cabinet disappeared slowly into the side of the wall.

Octavia retreated toward the projector, her mouth gaping open.

When the cupboard had disappeared completely, they could see now that there was a locked metal vault behind it.

"Try your key," said Cordelia.

"It doesn't take a key," said Jane. "It's a combination lock." She'd no sooner said the words than the lights in the main room flickered and then went off.

"Hey, what's going on?" said Cordelia, lunging for the cord to turn off the light in the projection booth.

Jane *had* heard someone, but her feeling of vindication was short-lived. "Just stay calm," she whispered, not feeling particularly calm herself. At least this wasn't her nightmare. No matter who was outside, they were flesh and blood, not the menacing presence in her dreams.

"I can't see a thing," muttered Cordelia. "I can't even see my hand in front of my face."

"Good. Just be quiet," whispered Jane. Feeling in her back pocket for her flashlight, an idea struck her. "Stay down—and stay here."

"What are you going to do?" whispered Octavia.

She didn't answer. Easing out of the booth, she reviewed her mental image of the room. She knew there were two rows of four seats on either side of a wide aisle. A raised walkway ran in back of the seats and led to the exit. Whoever'd shut off the lights must have been standing by the door. Right now, they couldn't see any better than she could. She needed to get a fix on where they were.

Slipping the flashlight out of her pocket, she flattened herself against the edge of the projection booth, feeling a warning twinge of weakness in her left leg. She assumed, rightly or wrongly, that whoever had turned out the light might also have cut the lock. Switching on the flashlight, she skittered it across the floor. She hoped it would illuminate the room without giving her position away. If the intruder had a weapon, they didn't have a chance. If not, it was three against one.

It turned out to be a lucky throw. The flashlight wedged itself between two of the seats, the light pointing to the left of the door. Jane saw a figure jerk to the side, then turn and race back up the narrow hall. Her better judgment gave way to her adrenalin. Pushing away from the booth, she rushed toward the door. Halfway there her left leg buckled and she hit the concrete floor with a hard thud.

In an instant, Cordelia was out of the booth and hurrying toward her. "Janey, are you okay?"

She'd landed on her left side, and in the process, twisted her knee.

"Speak to me, Jane! Speak to me!"

"I'm okay, Cordelia."

"Nothing's broken?"

"I think I hurt my knee." She took a moment to assess the damage, glad that Cordelia couldn't hear her heart pounding. "God, I'm such a klutz." She'd probably bruised her shoulder too, but that wouldn't prevent her from walking. "Could you help me up?" She wanted to see how much it hurt.

"Are we safe?" asked Octavia, peeking her head out from inside the booth.

Leaning on Cordelia for support, Jane was finally able to stand. "Yes, I think we're safe."

"Could you see who it was?"

"No. There wasn't enough time."

"Are you in pain, Janey?" asked Cordelia.

"A bit. I've got a knee brace in my room. You'll have to help me upstairs."

"I've got some prescription painkillers," offered Octavia. At Cordelia's scornful look, she added, "I was in a boating accident last fall. I dislocated a finger. You can check my medical records if you want. I only took a few pills. I never even got a refill."

"Thanks for the offer," said Jane, her arm around Cordelia's waist. "I might take one." She tried a few tentative steps.

"What are we going to do about the safe?" asked Octavia.

"Push that button again and make sure the cupboard rolls back against it," said Jane. "We'll deal with it tomorrow."

"But what if the person comes back?"

"If they had the combination, the contents are already gone. We'll just have to wait and see."

"I'm so sorry you fell," said Cordelia, holding Jane tight against her. "Was it your bad leg, or did you slip?"

"I slipped," said Jane, lying. "Don't worry. I'll be fine in the morning."

27

With the help of her cane, Jane limped downstairs late the next morning. Octavia's painkillers seemed to have done the trick. Her sleep had been deep and mercifully dreamless. She woke around ten, showered and dressed, all the while wondering what the new day would bring. After yesterday, she had the feeling that anything was possible. Her knee was stiff and sore, her left leg a little more tentative than it had been for the past few weeks, and her shoulder would probably turn black and blue, but she could walk, and for that, she was grateful.

The first person to greet her was Cordelia. She was hurrying down the central hallway, stuffing the last bite of an apple into her mouth.

"Where's the fire?" asked Jane, hoping there was some coffee left.

"Ellie's setting up her equipment in the library. She's interviewing Verna this morning."

"So it's *Verna,* now?" Cordelia had been referring to her as "Miss Lange" ever since she'd arrived.

"We had a simply *wonderful* talk at breakfast. We're both late risers, you know. Verna said all creative types were."

"Sounds like you two bonded."

"We did." Lowering her chin and speaking more confidentially, Cordelia added, "She's deeply broken up about Roland. Christian was trying his best to comfort her."

"How thoughtful of him."

"And, of course, I was too. Everyone's horribly shaken. Hilda was in tears when she brought out the food. Poor woman. She probably

212

loved Roland just as much as anyone else who lives in this house. How's the knee?"

"Sore."

"Maybe you should see a doctor."

"I'd rather have some coffee. How's your father?"

She gave Jane a pained look. "Still in bed."

"He probably has a bad hangover."

"One would hope."

"Or he's hiding."

"That's fine too. When you're done in the dining room, come to the library. Everyone's gathering in there."

"Any word about Buddy?"

She shook her head. "I haven't seen Gracie this morning. She might know more."

Jane nodded to the library. "What's the hurry with the interview?"

"Verna's planning to leave late this afternoon. She's taking a limo into New York around five, staying the night in a hotel, then flying back to Atlanta tomorrow morning."

"Doesn't she have to get permission from Toscano first?"

"I can't imagine why. Buddy's in the slammer. What do they need her for?"

Good question, thought Jane. After pouring herself a cup of coffee, she limped her way back down the hall. Her knee continued to feel sore, but the stiffness was going away.

Ellie was busy making adjustments to her camera when Jane walked in. Verna stood near a bay of tall windows, waving her cigarette around energetically as she chatted with Christian, Octavia, and Cordelia. The room already had enough smoke in it to set off an alarm.

Before Jane could sit down, Ellie motioned her over.

"What's up with your leg?" she asked, pushing a pencil behind her ear.

"I twisted it. It'll be fine in a couple of days."

"Are you in much pain?"

"Not really."

"Because——" She hesitated, glancing at the lighting equipment leaning against one of the bookshelves.

"Is there a problem?"

"Well . . . I've still got so much to set up, and I don't want to keep Verna waiting. Except . . . the thing is, I forgot one of my power cords."

"You want me to go get it for you?"

"Could you? My van's right outside. You wouldn't have to walk."

"Just tell me where it is."

"You're a lifesaver." Fishing for her keys in the pocket of her jeans, she said, "You'll find the cord under the far end of the long work table. It's bright orange with a red and black bungie cord holding it together. You can't miss it."

"No problem," said Jane. "I'll be back in a flash."

Grabbing her coat from the front closet, she headed outside.

The morning was damp, the temperature mild. Back in Minnesota, weather like this could easily herald the end of winter. In Connecticut, it was probably a different story. A light mist was falling, making Innishannon's grounds look gloomy, out of focus, and at the same time almost romantic. The woods beyond were shrouded in fog. Not wanting to waste time, Jane unlocked the van's door, slipped into the seat and started the engine.

Entering the tack house a few minutes later, she was surprised to find that it was in a much worse state of disarray than it had been last Thursday night. Ellie probably had a system, but with papers, files, correspondence, video tapes, cigarette butts, and half-eaten plates of food everywhere, Jane couldn't imagine what it was.

She found the cord right where Ellie said it would be, except that it was under a heavy plastic tarp and at least half a dozen East Coast telephone directories. A brown plastic sack of what looked like paper garbage was stuffed down next to it. Jane had to remove it all to get at the cord.

She felt an attack of conscience coming on. This was such an incredible opportunity to do a bit of snooping, she simply couldn't resist. She didn't want to upset any of Ellie's "order," so the garbage sack seemed a logical choice.

Removing the twist tie, Jane sorted quickly through the contents. Much of it appeared to be drafts of the script Ellie was writing on Roland Lester. Near the center of the sack, she found at least a dozen faxes that had been scrunched up together into a ball. Smoothing them out, she skimmed the contents. Most were from Ellie's production company back in L.A. appraising her of certain technical problems they were having on the EPS video. Jane didn't understand the reference, but the next to the last fax caught her attention.

It was from a man named Salvador Barros, and it was dated this morning. The body of the note said:

Dear Ms. Saks: I'd be delighted to talk to you about the card game. I am an old man now, but my memory is still alive and kicking, and that night remains vivid in my recollection. For many years, I counted myself a good friend of both Roland's and Lew's. Yes, I worked with Roland on a number of films. I was a set manager for 30 years. I never turn down a chance to talk about those days. It won't be long before all of us who lived in Holly-wood's Golden Age are gone. I am 92 and live with my daughter. Call me whenever you like at 555-998-9832. I shall look forward to talking to you. Salvador

Jane realized immediately that finding this fax was an incredible stroke of luck. Ellie believed Roland had murdered Lew Wallace, not because of the book he was writing about his life in Hollywood, but because of some long-ago card game. Ellie had also said that if she ever found the proof she was looking for, it would blow the lid off a major Hollywood scandal. In the end, it seemed her documentary was nothing more than a piece of investigative journalism.

On her way to the door, Jane passed by a new addition to the room. Ellie had brought in a small TV and a VCR and set them up next to the picture window. Jane glanced at the tape on top of the machine, curious what she'd been watching. *Silent Film/Silent Life: The Story of Ellery Patrick Strong, Hollywood's Greatest Hero.*

So this was it. The video copy of the documentary Ellie had done on her grandfather. It seemed like a rather bold title, but then Ellie had called him a genius. She'd also refused to be any more specific, which left Jane wondering what he'd done to warrant the title. She had to fight the urge to sit down, switch on the TV, and watch the video. Unfortunately, since she'd promised to get the power cord back to Ellie on the double, she couldn't. She'd already taken extra time out to sort through the garbage sack. Perhaps, later in the day, she could approach Ellie, mention that she'd love to see her newest documentary, and then hope like hell that Ellie would let her see it.

Because . . . one way or the other, Jane intended to watch that tape.

28

Ellie checked the hookup on the studio lights, then moved behind the camera to make a few last minute adjustments. Everyone else in the room sat quietly, waiting for the interview to begin. Once again, Jane was amazed at the amount of equipment Ellie had to haul around just to shoot a short interview. No wonder she was looking forward to her crew arriving after New Year's.

"Okay," said Ellie finally. "Let's get started. Quiet on the set." She held a small chalkboard in front of the lens.

VERNA LANGE, INTERVIEW 1, DECEMBER 27th

"We're rolling."

Verna took a moment to light a fresh cigarette, then settled back into her chair, making sure the ashtray was close at hand. Giving the back of her bright orange hair a quick pat, she nodded her assent.

"As I said before, we can handle this anyway you like, but just to get started, I thought I'd ask a couple of general questions." Ellie sat down in a chair and picked up a clipboard.

Verna lifted her eyes, heavy with mascara, to the camera. Her expression came suddenly alive, the elegantly penciled eyebrows rising to welcome her unseen audience.

ELLIE: I have a copy of a filmography here that lists all seventy-nine of your films. That's quite an achievement.

216

Verna: Have you read any of the biographies they've done of me?

Ellie: I've read them all.

Verna: (Taps ash into ashtray) Then you've done your homework. Good girl.

Ellie: You did twelve films with Roland Lester. In five of them you starred with Lew Wallace.

Verna: We were box office gold back then, an unbeatable team.

Ellie: Let's get a little background. You were born in—

Verna: (Warningly) Next question.

Ellie: Your name, before Hollywood changed it, was Delma Klarner.

Verna: (Laughs) Can't you just see that on a theatre marquee?

Ellie: You grew up in Zanesville, Ohio, the daughter of a banker and a homemaker. You have an older sister, Letha, and a younger brother, Warren.

Verna: I went to school, learned my ABC's, and grew up. Let's move on.

Ellie: You came to Hollywood in 1940.

Verna: I was just a child, but I knew what I wanted.

Ellie: And that was?

Verna: To be a star like Garbo, like . . . Harlow. I wanted to be kissed passionately by men like Clark Gable, Tyrone Power, Douglas Fairbanks, and Lew Wallace. I wanted fame, fortune, glamour, everything Hollywood had to offer.

Ellie: And did you find it?

Verna: (Slightly defensive) Of course. But life never proceeds in a straight line, and accomplishment is never easy. I learned many things along the way, my dear. But we can talk about that some other time. (Puffs languidly at her cigarette) Why don't we get down to business. You're doing a docu-mythography on Roland Lester. Let's talk about him.

Ellie: I want to tell the truth, Ms. Lange. Please don't doubt that.

Verna: Everyone wants to tell the truth, dear, but when it comes to human beings, that's easier said than done. I hope you know that.

Ellie: I do. Was Roland a good director?

Verna: For me, the best. He gave me my first big break by ordering screen tests and then insisting that the studio cast me in a major supporting role in the film, *Under His Spell* with William Powell and Loretta Young.

Ellie: That was 1942.

Verna: We didn't work on another film together until he started directing again after he came back from his service in the Army Air Corps.

Ellie: That was 1944?

Verna: (Nods) Roland was ill for nearly a year. He enlisted in the summer of 'forty-two and worked for a while with Howard Hawks setting up schools all over the country to teach people aerial gunnery. While he was somewhere in the South, he came down with meningitis and became terribly sick—high fevers, severe headaches, and convulsions. He was sent back to Hollywood to recover. By the time we did another film together, I'd moved up in the world. I was cast as the lead opposite Claude Raines, a man I adored.

Ellie: Do you mind if I ask you about specific actors?

Verna: Go ahead. If there's something I don't want to answer, I won't.

Ellie: What did you think of William Powell?

Verna: A skirt chaser. Next question.

Ellie: Loretta Young?

Verna: Quite pretty—that, not her talent, got her cast in film after film. You know the story about Gable and Loretta, don't you? No? They fell in love while working on a movie together. She got pregnant and a few months later took off for Europe on a vacation. It was all very hush hush. Well, of course, she had the baby, stayed gone long enough to get her figure back, and then returned. A year or two later she adopted a child, which was very unusual at the time. She wasn't married. Of course, it was *her* baby. Everyone knew the truth by then, but nobody talked about it. Perhaps the studio insisted on handling it like that, or maybe it was her idea, who knows? Whatever the case, it always struck me as ironic that one of Hollywood's most insufferable goodie-two-shoes did something so dishonest. She was terribly religious, one might almost say fanatical. When she was shooting a movie, she insisted on putting a "swear box" on the set. If she caught someone swearing, she'd try to shame them into putting a nickel or a dime into the coffer. I was told that Barbara Stanwyck used the word "damn" in front of her once. Knowing that Loretta was about to pounce, Stanwyck simply walked over to the box and said, "Here's five bucks. Why don't you go fuck yourself?" (Roars with laughter)

ELLIE: Were you friends with Barbara Stanwyck?

VERNA: No, but I admired her as an actress.

ELLIE: If I could just name a few other actors and actresses you worked with?

VERNA: Sure, and I'll give you the first word that comes to mind. Sort of like a Hollywood Rorschach test.

ELLIE: Bette Davis.

VERNA: Gutsy. She never did any cheesecake, and I admired her for that.

ELLIE: Tyrone Power.

VERNA: Beautiful. A sweet man.

ELLIE: Montgomery Clift.

VERNA: Smart. Lots of personality. Never got to know him, but I enjoyed working with him enormously. It was his eyes, I think. Amazing eyes.

ELLIE: Fred MacMurray.

VERNA: No comment.

ELLIE: Laurence Olivier.

VERNA: Overrated.

ELLIE: Robert Preston.

VERNA: I had a terrible crush on him. Did you ever see him on Broadway? He had a voice like golden thunder.

ELLIE: John Wayne.

VERNA: Couldn't abide his politics. He certainly didn't publicize it later in life, but back in the fifties he was one of the biggest Hollywood supporters—financially—of the Ku Klux Klan. (Shudders)

ELLIE: Doris Day

VERNA: I know she's not in vogue any longer, but I liked her. Did you know they offered the part of Mrs. Robinson in *The Graduate* to her before they asked Ann Bancroft?

ELLIE: (Horrified) I hadn't heard that. Ricardo Montalban.

VERNA: Wooden. As John Cassavetes so aptly put it, Ricardo is to improvisational acting what Mount Rushmore is to animation.

ELLIE: Stewart Granger.

VERNA: (Shrugs) Not my type.

ELLIE: Vivian Leigh.

VERNA: Beautiful woman. Beautiful soul.

ELLIE: Robert Mitchum.

VERNA: Great sense of humor. I adored him.

ELLIE: Clark Gable.

VERNA: (Bites down hard on her cigarette holder) I had such a crush on him when I first came to Hollywood. I remember the first time I saw him in person—it was at a premiere of one of his movies. I thought I was going to faint. There's a lesson in that, my dear. People idolize without knowing who or what they're worshiping.

ELLIE: You didn't like him?

VERNA: (Irritably) No.

ELLIE: You knew him personally?

VERNA: Socially, that was enough.

ELLIE: Could you elaborate?

VERNA: I probably shouldn't. (Flicks ash into ashtray) But what the hell. Let me tell you a little story. Lew was on the set of *Gone with the Wind* the day George Cukor was driven off. The truth has rarely been told. It wasn't even covered on that documentary the Turner Network did a few years back. I had such high hopes for it too, but they apparently considered the information—even though they knew it was factual—too distasteful. Hollywood likes to keep its dirty little secrets away from the general public. Image is everything.

ELLIE: What happened?

VERNA: Well, you need to understand some background first. In the twenties, Gable had been an extra in one of Billy Haines's silent movies. Billy was a huge star. Handsome, funny—and gay. I've heard different versions, but it always came down to the same thing. Apparently Gable and Billy had a short . . . tryst. It was a one-time event. Gable was nobody in Hollywood at the time, and he was drunk, as he so often was. Billy was box office, and it just happened. Now, if you know anything about the history of *Gone with the Wind,* you know Gable wasn't looking forward to playing Rhett Butler. George Cukor had been working with him for weeks on his southern accent, but when the time came to shoot the first scene, Gable refused to use it. There were other actors who had been considered for the part, but the one thing I think we can all agree on is that Clark Gable *was* Rhett Butler— accent or no accent. One other point. A few weeks before the filming began, one of George's close friends, Andy Lawler, announced at a rather well-attended party that George was directing one of Billy's old tricks. Well, the comment flew around Hollywood at the speed of light and of course it got back to Gable. As you can imagine, for a man who'd been nurturing his macho image most of his adult life, he was livid. He went to Billy and told him if he ever heard such a thing again, he'd beat him within an inch of his life. During the early negotiations for *Gone with the Wind,* Gable had been lobbying for his director buddy, Victor Fleming, to direct the movie. George was known as a "woman's director," but he was a good friend of Selznick's so he got the nod. He didn't shoot the burning of Atlanta, which was the first scene that got done—I believe Bill Menzies did it—but he took over from there. And with all the attention George was giving to Vivian and Olivia, Gable's worst fears were realized almost immediately. He assumed George was going to throw the movie to the women. You have to understand, Fleming and Gable had a lot in common. They both considered themselves manly men, both liked motorcycling and hunting. And they both shared the same prejudices. Behind the scenes, they always referred to David Selznick, the producer, as "that Jewboy up there," and they called George "that fag." Everybody'd heard it at one time or another— it was part of their tough image. Shortly after the Lawler incident, George was on the set, preparing things for Gable's next take. Selznick was there too. So was Lew, but he was just standing around waiting for Franchot Tone to get done. He'd promised him a ride someplace. Anyway, all of a sudden, Gable started muttering. "I can't do this . . . I can't do this scene." Then he exploded. "I won't be directed by a fairy! I have to work with a *real man!*" I guess the set grew so quiet you could hear a pin drop.

Lew said all he could hear was George's footsteps as he walked off the sound stage and left the building. The next day, Gable didn't show up for work. A short time later Fleming replaced Cukor. The official whitewash from the press office said something like, "Due to disagreements over individual scenes, a mutual decision was reached. A new director will be selected." George's version was reported by Louella Parsons, something like, "Cukor felt the script was inadequate." That was true, it was a mess, but it wasn't the reason he was fired. The worst part was, nobody ever challenged Gable on his hatred of homosexuals and Jews. He could be a bastard to the last, but everybody protected him. They still do. I don't know about you, but I've had my fill of it.

ELLIE: That's a fascinating story.

VERNA: A true story. Now, let's move on.

ELLIE: (Consults notes) I understand that you were the maid of honor at Roland Lester's wedding in 1947. How well did you know his wife?

VERNA: (Grumbles inaudibly)

ELLIE: Excuse me?

VERNA: This is going to take forever. Our walk down memory lane has been fun, Ms. Saks, but since we've already broached the subject, why don't we just cut to the chase? I've got something I want to say. (Removes cigarette holder from her mouth) If Roland were here, I'm sure he'd do a much better job than me, but he isn't. The only thing I can do is give you my take on . . . the situation.

ELLIE: What situation?

VERNA: (Sits forward in her chair) Two nights ago, Hiram Thorn told a room full of people that Roland Lester was a homosexual. Roland denied it, of course. Quite honestly, the issue has rarely been raised, but when it has, he could always point to his wife and child and shut people's mouths with his heterosexual credentials. People in this country are naive. Even today. They think if someone is married, that's the end of the story. It isn't *now,* and it wasn't *then.* For a homosexual in Hollywood, at least during our reign, marriage was a must. (Thoughtful pause) The night before Roland's wedding to Octavia, he and I talked upstairs in his study. He gave me two audio tapes he'd prepared from sections of his personal diaries and he asked me to give them to you yesterday, while he and Octavia were off on their honeymoon. Unfortunately, none of that happened. I've been thinking about our conversation ever since and I feel that it's up to me to set the record straight—no pun intended. It's what Roland wanted. In many ways, I take it as his last request. But before I go on, you must understand that I loved Roland Lester like a brother. (Tears slightly) He was one of the finest men I've ever known. We didn't keep in contact as much after we both left our careers behind, but we've managed to stay connected. Every time we get together, it's as if the years just melt away. For a long time, I believe I was Roland's only real confidante so it makes a certain sense that I try to explain this part of his life to you. At least, I want to try.

ELLIE: Were he and Lew Wallace lovers?

VERNA: They were much more than that. For eleven years they were completely devoted to each other. It took Lew's death to end their relationship. I believe they'd still be together today if Lew had lived.

ELLIE: Openly together?

VERNA: The concept of "openly gay" had no meaning back then. The term hadn't even been invented. All I can say is that Roland reached an important decision before he died. He wanted the world to finally understand who he was.

ELLIE: Why now?

VERNA: (Shakes head) I've asked myself the same question. The fact is, I don't know.

ELLIE: Could it have been his age?

VERNA: (Dourly) Well, none of us are going to live forever. All I know is, he must have had his reasons. I *can* say that he loved his wife, Sylvia, but as a friend, nothing more. They both wanted a child. Peg was the light of their lives. Sylvia was the daughter of a wealthy Washington industrialist. The family money was in lumbering, I believe. Sylvia's female lover, Betty Engles, was hired to answer Roland's correspondence, essentially so that she could be around the house without anybody wondering why. Mainly, she just delegated things to others. It worked out well. When there's a mutual motive, matters can be . . . properly arranged.

223

ELLIE: So, both Roland and his wife were gay.

VERNA: Yes.

ELLIE: Just out of curiosity, can you name other gay/lesbian Hollywood marriages?

VERNA: (Stubs out her cigarette) Rod La Rocque and Vilma Banky, for one. You probably don't even remember their names. Charles Laughton and Elsa Lanchester. Then again, maybe Elsa was just . . . unusual. Hard to say. Robert Taylor and Barbara Stanwyck. I remember Billy Haines said to me once that at parties, Stanwyck reminded him of a young man in desperate need of a good finishing school. (Smiles) Then there was Cedric Gibbons— he designed the Academy Award statue—and Dolores Del Rio— one of Garbo's lovers. Laurence Oliver and Jill Esmond. Larry was involved with Danny Kaye for years. All London knew. Their wives knew. America is always the last to know—or to believe. Oh, and Bob Cummings told me once that Janet Gaynor's husband might be Adrian, the MGM fashion designer, but her wife was Mary Martin, the stage actress. Of course, there were many studio-arranged marriages where only one of the partners was Sapphic or homosexual. Or sometimes an actor or actress was what they called "double gated"—liked both men and women— and found that marriage offered them something they truly wanted. Some would marry again and again, others only once. A few may have actually been trying to change who they were. I'm thinking of Cary Grant now. I never had the sense that he was a very happy man. He was married a few times, but I learned early in the game that an address meant nothing. The studios felt strongly that if someone was going to carry the burden of the public's sex fantasies, they had to get married. End of story. But returning to Sylvia and Roland. Sylvia wanted to escape the scrutiny of her family as much as Roland wanted to escape the prying eyes of Louella Parsons and Hedda Hopper.

ELLIE: The gossip columnists.

VERNA: (Nods stoically) Everyone was on their stink-list at some point or other, but you didn't want to cross them, or give them an inch. Back then, public opinion was terribly important. It was absurd, really. We're talking about the same naive yet judgmental public that was fed nothing but lies and studio hype in the movie magazines, and believed it as if it were gospel. Hedda and Lolly convinced people that they were the guardians of our national morality. (Snorts) In reality, they were snooty, voyeuristic parasites who lived off Hollywood scandal. Oh, they could help build a career, but they could take it away just as easily. The studio bosses hated them, but considered them a necessary evil. It was just the way things worked. I tried to keep my head down and avoid the gruesome twosome as much as possible, but they eventually had a heyday with all their little blind items about Lew and me shacking up together in Roland's guest house. Unbeknownst to them, they were working for us that time, not against us.

ELLIE: How did it work?

VERNA: What? You mean Lew and I?

ELLIE: And Roland.

VERNA: Well, you have to understand. When Roland arrived in Hollywood in the mid-thirties, he saw all the . . . what's the word? (Thinks) *Cruising* going on around him. The Hayes office was doing its worst to push the production code on everyone, and the Depression made people scared, but still, life went on. There was a sort of innocent winking at Sapphic women and "sophisticated" men. Of course, Roland had heard about Bill Haines's arrest on morals charges, even though the studio got the charges dropped. And then when George Cukor was arrested while he was filming *Camille*—well, let me tell you, it put the fear of God into Roland. Not that anyone ever heard about George's arrest. MGM squelched it. Nobody could prove it after the fact, but it happened. What it did was make Roland into one of the most circumspect homosexuals in Hollywood. That man was wound so tight by the front he had to maintain, sometimes I thought he would explode. Frankly, I felt his marriage was good for him. Lew was good for him, too. Lew was a lot more easygoing than Roland. But sometimes he took silly chances.

ELLIE: Like what?

VERNA: Oh, he'd say things at parties—be a little too open. If Roland was there, he'd be over in the corner grinding his teeth. When I first knew Roland, before he explained that he was sexually . . . uncommon, as he put it, he was scathing in his condemnation of homosexuals. He used to make fun of them, call them "the girls." When he finally told me the truth, I realized that, even more than George, he epitomized circumspection. You see, there were these pockets in the movie business where homosexuality thrived—sketch and design, decoration and sets, costume and makeup. But the only first-rank director who people talked about as actually being "one" was George. Roland always stayed away from his famous "Cukor Sundays." He was intensely curious, but he wouldn't allow himself to go. Actually, George and Cole Porter were often referred to as the "rival queens of Hollywood." They each threw wonderful parties. There was some mingling of the groups—I know because I went to parties at both houses—but in general people tended to connect with one set of friends or the other.

ELLIE: But back to Roland, you, and Lew—

VERNA: (Shifts in her chair, then pauses to light another cigarette) Lew and I had such incredible screen chemistry together, don't you think?

ELLIE: (Nods)

VERNA: Yes, well, as soon as our first movie, *Lost and Found,* was released, the gossip started. Lew was still married at the time—1948—and so was I—but that just made the whole thing more titillating, I suppose. I will say, that man really knew how to kiss. (Laughs heartily, then coughs) Actually, Lew's wife had committed *the* unpardonable sin in Hollywood, so she was completely out of favor with the fan rags.

ELLIE: And what was that?

VERNA: She got fat. People would actually come up to Lew on the street and urge him to give her the boot.

ELLIE: That's disgusting.

VERNA: That's Tinseltown. But I digress. (Appraising pause) When Roland first came to Hollywood in the mid-thirties, Lew was already a big star. There was a twelve-year difference in their ages. Lew had been more discrete about his personal life than other actors of his day, but there'd been talk. The studio had been pressuring him for years to get married, so in 'thirty-eight, he took the plunge. The fan magazines had a heyday. "Confirmed Bachelor Weds Woman of His Dreams"—stuff like that. Lew's new bride just ate it up. She wasn't an actress so she'd never had any experience with a Hollywood studio's publicity machine moving into high gear. When he left to go to war in 'forty-two, she did a lot of interviews on what it was like to have "your man" at the front. To me, it was always apparent that she liked who Lew *was* far more than she liked Lew. Anyway, when he came back a hero, all the talk about him being "temperamental" or "sophisticated" stopped.

ELLIE: How did Roland and Lew first meet?

VERNA: (Takes a long drag on her cigarette) They'd known each other socially for a number of years. It was on the set of *Candlewick* that they really became friends. Lew had been cast as the male lead opposite Bette Davis. (Laughs suddenly) Years later I remember him saying that, working with Ms. Davis for the first time, he'd never been so scared in his life—and he'd been in the war! (Another laugh) Anyway, I don't think Lew and Roland became lovers until later, after Roland and Sylvia were married. And even then, they were never obvious. Still, I could tell Roland had never been so happy. He seemed far more calm, more in command, less distracted somehow. And then, when we had such a big hit on our hands with *Lost and Found,* the studio just kept finding vehicles for us to do it again and again. All the while, the fan magazines kept up this patter about Lew and me being star-crossed lovers. When Lew divorced, in 'fifty-one, he moved into Roland's guest house.

ELLIE: I'm curious. What was Buddy Lester doing while his brother was becoming a famous director?

VERNA: Well, the first house Roland owned was a two-bedroom craftsman-style bungalow on Orangewood Drive. His brother and his brother's wife lived with him then. Roland got Buddy jobs around the lots, but Buddy was never very careful with his money. He'd overspend, then he'd have to hit Roland up for a loan. Eventually, Roland just hired him to be his personal assistant. When Roland moved into the new house, he bought Buddy a small place in the San Fernando Valley. By then, Buddy and his wife had a child and another on the way. To be honest, I never had the sense that Buddy was jealous of Roland's good fortune. On the contrary, I think he was proud of him. Buddy wasn't ambitious. He liked being given tasks to perform, and he loved being a dad. He also had a rather roving eye, if you know what I mean, but I don't think his wife ever found out. If she had, well, let's just say it would have been the end of his marriage.

ELLIE: I'm sorry I interrupted your story. You were saying that Lew Wallace moved into Roland's guest house in 'fifty-one.

VERNA: (Elaborately exhales a puff of smoke) Yes, but now we're talking about his estate in Beverly Hills. It was a Spanish-style home, with a private courtyard full of oleander, magnolias, petunias, and roses, and a red-tiled roof covered in bougainvillea. Against the blue, Southern California sky, the colors were simply extraordinary. I remember lying by the pool in the late afternoons, sipping something cold and feeling my skin so incredibly alive. I really believe the world was more vivid back then. (Contemplates the mental image)

ELLIE: You moved into the guest house too at some point, right?

VERNA: (Nods) I got the divorce from my second husband in 'fifty-two and moved into the guest house almost immediately. That really set off rockets in the gossip columns. Roland's wife was always off in Europe with her girlfriend, so that gave us the chance to act like the teenagers we so clearly still were. The stories I could tell you! Most of the time, Lew lived up at the main house with Roland and I had the guest house all to myself. We were a conspicuous threesome all over town. Everybody thought Roland's presence was just a ploy—to cover Lew's and my relationship. Nobody ever guessed the truth. Until—(A slight down turning of the lips)

ELLIE: (Coaxing) Until what?

VERNA: (Slow frown) I'm sure you know about the House on UnAmerican Activities Commission. The blacklists. The graylists. The fifties witch hunts in the film industry.

ELLIE: Yes, and I know Lew Wallace was a target.

VERNA: Lew's last film, *The Woolcrest Affair,* came out in 1952. He received very few scripts that year. By 'fifty-three, the year he moved into his own house in Beverly Hills, he'd stopped receiving scripts entirely. You have to understand, this came at the pinnacle of his career. Sure, he'd been box office in the thirties, but he'd never been as popular as he was in the late forties and early fifties. He was a major film star, and he disappeared almost overnight.

The blacklists, in my opinion, were simply the product of a studio mentality acting from primal economic fear. The executives figured that the industry would lose a huge part of their audience if they didn't appear to cooperate with the congressional investigating committees. They didn't give a hoot in hell about politics or art, all they cared about was money—and survival. In many ways, I understood, especially at a time when TV was growing in popularity, eating into the industry's bottom line. But understanding it didn't make it any easier to live with when I saw a friend being attacked. The investigations had been going on since 'forty-seven. By 1950, most people connected to the film industry were scared to death, or at the very least, they'd become self-censoring. Not Lew. He felt his position—because of his war record and his popularity—was unassailable. In 'fifty-one, he did something incredibly stupid. He wrote a letter to the editor of the *LA Times*. I didn't know Lew as a young man, but after the war, people said he'd changed. He was more confident, less self-depricating. He'd always projected this amazingly virile image on screen, but I believe he'd proved something to himself in Europe. Unlike Roland, I don't think he felt much guilt about being a homosexual. He wasn't religious. He just thought loving a man was another way to live your life, and that society would eventually figure it out. Given that background, and the fact that he was a liberal to the core, hated all prejudice, you can understand why he did what he did. (Holds her cigarette out in front of her and studies the tip) Remember what I told you about the day George Cukor walked off the set of *Gone with the Wind*?

ELLIE: (Nods)

VERNA: Well, that story had been festering inside Lew for years. I don't know what set him off, but in the summer of 'fifty-one, he composed a letter to the editor of the L.A. paper in which he detailed those events, including all the pertinent background information. He stressed the racism inherent in the situation, as well as the outright hatred of homosexuals, and he labeled both evil. He even drew parallels to Hitler and the Nazis. It was a reckless, foolish thing to do, I suppose, but it was also terribly brave. Roland and I had no knowledge of the letter until I happened to see a response lying open on Lew's desk. It was from one of the top executives at MGM. Apparently the paper had passed the piece on to him. The executive, who shall remain nameless, was doing verbal handsprings he was so angry! How could Lew pass such obvious garbage off as the truth? The man threatened Lew with legal action if he tried to take his "spurious" story elsewhere. That was the beginning of the end for Lew. A whispering campaign began. Oh, nobody called him a Jew-lover or a faggot around me, but I knew what was going on. The moment he mailed that letter to the editor, Lew's fate was sealed. The only one who didn't seem to know was Lew. Since work in the film industry is always unpredictable, he didn't get the message until the scripts completely stopped coming in 'fifty-three. By then, it was too late.

ELLIE: I've heard of the blacklist, but what was the graylist?

VERNA: (Smoking now in quick jabs) The blacklist was fairly straightforward. People who went before the committee in Washington would name names. Those names were printed in the daily newspaper. From there, they went on the blacklist and no Hollywood studio would hire that individual unless they'd gone through the process of clearing themselves. Sometimes people refused to name names, and that meant their name would automatically be put on the blacklist. The graylist was far more complex and fiendish, much more a product of right-wing opportunism, revenge, sometimes even mistaken identity. Lists like "Red Channels" started appearing. They weren't official, but they might as well have been. The problem was, sometimes a person didn't know until years after the fact that his name was on one of these unofficial lists. That's what happened to Lew. By 'fifty-four he'd figured it out, although he never actually found out where it was printed. The way it worked was, he was supposed to submit to a clearance procedure, usually something like a letter detailing what he'd done and an apology for all his subversive acts and memberships. But since that wasn't why Lew had been graylisted in the first place, he could hardly answer the charge. In fact, there was no charge, just his name on some under-the-table list. If he addressed the innuendo, he'd have to deny that he was a homosexual. That would open up his entire life to the jackals in Washington. It was an impossible situation. I watched the daily toll it took on him, and on his relationship with Roland. (Pauses to stub out her cigarette, then remove the butt from the holder) Three years later he was dead.

ELLIE: That brings me to some questions I was hoping to ask.

VERNA: About his murder.

ELLIE: Yes, that, and about the book Lew was writing before he died.

VERNA: There was no book. That was just a rumor that got started because people wanted to know how Lew was spending his free time. Who knows? Maybe Lew started the rumor himself.

ELLIE: You're positive there was not book?

VERNA: Absolutely. (Looks disgusted) This is exactly what I told Roland would happen. If he opened up his life, if he told the truth about his relationship with Lew, it would only serve to resurrect interest in that old murder case. I'd prefer to let sleeping dogs lie.

ELLIE: Why is that?

VERNA: Because it's ancient history.

ELLIE: But the murder was never solved.

VERNA: (Waves the empty cigarette holder dismissively) I've made my peace with it. So had Roland. What else could we do? And now, what could possibly be served by dredging up that horrible time? No. I won't participate in it. (Looks suddenly over at the door) What the hell are you doing here?

29

Buddy stood in the doorway, looking as if he'd spent the night sleeping under a drain spout. His clothes were wet and wrinkled, his hat actually dripping water.

"What's going on in here?" he demanded.

"Mr. Lester!" cried Hilda, rushing to his side and helping him off with his soggy coat.

"We're doing an interview," said Ellie, rising from her chair.

Jane joined everyone as they stood. She figured the weather had taken a turn for the worse—the drizzle had turned, not to snow or sleet, but to rain.

"Answer my question," demanded Verna. "We all thought you'd . . . I mean . . . when you left with the police last night, we all assumed—"

"What? That I'd poisoned my brother?"

"Didn't you?" asked Cordelia weakly.

Buddy removed his hat and shook the water out, then handed it to Hilda. "Apparently the police don't think so."

"How did you get home?" asked Octavia.

"I called Grace. She and Christian drove in to New Haven to pick me up." He stared at the camera. "Is that thing still on?"

"I'll turn it off," said Ellie. She quickly switched off the studio lighting, then stopped the recording.

A night in an interrogation room hadn't done Buddy's general mood any good. Jane wondered what had happened. Toscano had been so sure he was about to confess.

"I'm going up to bed. I'm exhausted."

"But we deserve more explanation than that," said Verna.

"It's all you're going to get."

"But what happened to Roland?" asked Octavia. "We need answers."

"The police are gathering their evidence. I'm sure they'll make an arrest soon."

"If the police didn't arrest you," said Verna, her gaze drifting toward the windows, "that means I'm stuck here. I'll have to cancel my flight back to Atlanta."

"Why are you in such a rush to leave?" asked Buddy.

"I'm not in a rush," she said indignantly.

"Could have fooled me. I would think you'd want to stick around at least long enough to attend my brother's—your *dear* friend's—memorial service."

"When will the memorial be?" asked Verna.

"As soon as we get his ashes back. Probably later in the week." His eyes were bloodshot and his hands shook. Interestingly, with his hair wet and pulled back from his face, he looked far more like Roland now. He also looked every day of his seventy-five years.

"Can't you give us *any* more information?" pleaded Octavia.

"Let the man go," said Hilda testily. "He's about to catch his death."

Buddy seemed unsteady but resolute as he turned and walked off down the hall.

"You should all be ashamed of yourselves," said Hilda, tossing his coat over her arm with disgust. "Suggesting Mr. Lester had anything to do with his brother's death. I won't have that kind of talk in my house." She turned on her heel and marched out.

Your house, thought Jane. That was an odd way to put it.

"Don't mind her," sighed Verna, smoothing her lipstick with the tip of her little finger. "She's been in love with the Lester boys for years."

"In love?" repeated Jane.

"Isn't it obvious?" Verna gave the door a sideways glance, then rolled her eyes to the heavens.

Octavia sank down in her chair. "What am I going to do?" she whispered.

"Do about what?" asked Cordelia.

Verna checked her watch. "One of us should find out if they're planning to feed us lunch. All this reminiscing has made me ravenous."

She bustled out of the room, muttering, "And I've got to call my travel agent. I'll be on the phone with that insipid man all afternoon."

Cordelia didn't want to be disturbed—or overheard—so she took her cell phone into the billiard room and closed the door. As far as she could tell, nobody used the room during the day. If she kept her voice down, nobody would hear.

Punching in the number of a friend in San Francisco, she thought about the movie Roland had shown them two nights ago, *A Daughter of the Gods*—the one that was now missing a reel. She also recalled the promise Roland had made to Octavia. "Riches and power beyond your wildest dreams." Putting those two things together, Cordelia felt she knew what Roland planned to give Octavia on their wedding night. If she was right, it was a whopper of a gift.

Her body felt suddenly electrified as the line was picked up.

"Hello?"

"Stella?"

"Yeah?"

"It's Cordelia."

"Hey, babe! How's everything in the Minneapple?"

"I'm in Connecticut."

"Why?"

"My sister."

"She OD or something?"

"No. Listen, you're my authority on silent movies. What would you say if I told you I just viewed the film *A Daughter of the Gods*?"

Laughter. "I'd say *you're* the one who's on something."

"I'm not kidding. I saw it. Two nights ago."

"A video copy?"

"No, the actual film."

"Where?"

"I can't say."

"Honey, if somebody has a reasonably decent—even a *terrible*—copy of that film, we're talking . . . amazing! It's the movie Martin Scorsese has been searching for forever. Believe me, if there was a copy out there, he'd have found it. Maybe what you saw was a joke."

"It's no joke. Tell me, how much would something like that go for?"

"You mean in money?"

"No, in balloons."

"Well, it would be worth whatever you could get for it—whatever someone would be willing to pay. Fifty thousand, maybe. Maybe more."

"A lot more?"

Sighs. "Look, silent movies are an important part of our history, but they're not exactly in huge demand. When you find them, they're never in great condition."

"What if you had a lot of them? Rare movies, films people thought were lost?"

"You're talking money again?"

"Stella!"

"Okay, okay. I'm guessing, but . . . maybe a million?"

Hardly *riches and power beyond your wildest dreams.* "Are you absolutely positive? It seems to me that something that rare should be worth more."

"Well, okay, if you found, say, *Greed,* Erich Von Stroheim's ten-hour masterpiece, you could add another million. I mean, that's the Holy Grail of the silent film era. Everybody's looked for it, but it's never been found. And then if you had, say, *Purity,* or Theda Bara's *Cleopatra,* you'd have an incredible collection. But we're not talking high tech stock here."

"Oh." Cordelia felt her entire body deflate.

"You sound disappointed."

"I am."

"Look, I could be wrong. Maybe those films are priceless—worth ten, twenty, thirty times what I suggested."

At least it was a glimmer of hope. "Do you think that's possible?"

"Anything's possible, Cordelia. Now, if you want to talk actors, directors, studios, equipment, restoration, preservation, I can give you facts and figures. But . . . putting a price on material I'm fairly certain doesn't exist isn't something I can do. I'm sorry."

"So, you're saying, you really don't know."

"Right. I'm giving you my best guess."

To Cordelia, the operative word there was *guess.* "Thanks, Stella."

"No problem. Sorry I couldn't tell you what you wanted to hear. Hey, try calling the American Film Institute. Someone there might have a better idea." She repeated the number by heart.

"You're incredible."

"I'm just a simple department store clerk, but I do keep my Super-woman costume and cape in the closet, just in case."

"Gotta run."

"Later, doll."

"You know, Stella, every time I call, you sound more and more like Humphrey Bogart."

"Hey, thanks!"

"We'll always have Paris."

"In our case, it was Anaheim."

"Was it a Motel Six?"

"A Super Eight."

"Ah, those were the days. Poor but impetuous youth. Bye."

After turning off the phone, Cordelia slipped it into her pocket. She wasn't exactly back to square one, but she hadn't hit the jackpot either. Glancing at the billiard table, she decided there was no better way to get her intellectual juices going than by playing a quick game. She grabbed herself a cue from the rack on the wall, then racked up the balls. The billiard table was so ornate, it looked like something from a sixteenth-century Spanish galleon. Just as she was cuing up for the break shot, the door burst open.

"There you are. I've been looking all over the house for you."

Cordelia glanced wanly at her sister, then returned her attention to the ball. "Maybe you should install loudspeakers. Oh, I forgot. The house doesn't belong to you anymore."

"That's what I want to talk to you about."

"Is Dad up yet?"

"He's in the dining room having lunch."

"Has he had a drink?"

"No. I don't know. I don't think so." She closed the door, then leaned against it, watching Cordelia make the shot.

Once the balls had all come to a stop, Cordelia scrutinized the table, looking for her next shot. "We've got to do something about him. I'm not even sure he should drive back to Boston alone."

"I know. And we'll talk about him, I promise we will, but right now I've got something I need to tell you."

"Another news flash, like the key?"

Octavia hesitated as Cordelia pocketed a ball. "Yes."

"Yes, what?" She bent over the table, only half listening to her sister.

"It's another news flash, like the key."

Her head jerked up. "Tell me I didn't hear what you just said."

"Will you stop judging me long enough to hear me out?"

"I've heard you out. Do we have to do this every day?" For the first time, Cordelia actually looked at her sister. Octavia seemed jumpy and nervous, and her eyes were puffy, as if she'd been crying. "What's wrong?"

"It's all coming apart." She began to drift uneasily around the room. "I thought, if Buddy confessed to the murder, the police wouldn't need to investigate any further. They'd have what they needed and they'd leave me alone. That's why I didn't tell you last night. It wasn't the right time. It had to be the right moment, otherwise you'd get angry all over again."

"Just speak to me in plain English, Octavia."

"I didn't tell you everything before. I couldn't. Roland made me promise I'd keep everything a secret until after the wedding yesterday."

"There was no wedding, Octavia. So tell me now."

She took a deep breath, as if readying herself for battle. "Roland and I were married three weeks ago. The church business yesterday was just for the sake of the family and the press, but we were already . . . legally . . . husband and wife."

Cordelia was stunned. Aghast. Agape. "You mean . . . you dragged me all this way for a farce? You put Dad through God knows what kind of stress for a *charade?*"

"I wanted to share my happiness with you!"

"And just exactly *what* are you happy about?"

Octavia threw herself into a chair, looking everywhere but at her sister's face. "I'm Roland's rightful heir."

"Yippy skippy!"

"Don't you get it? That's a problem now."

Cordelia was totally confused. "Maybe you better draw me a map. Your life seems to require one."

"*Motive,* Cordelia. The fact that I didn't tell the police we were already married is going to make it look like I was trying to hide something."

"You were!"

"But it wasn't about Roland's murder. I wasn't trying to get rid of him so that I could get my hands on his money. I would never hurt him, you know that."

"Because you needed him to tell you what the key was for."

"No, not *only* that. I cared about him."

"Right, as any new wife would care about her great-grandfather."

"It's always the same. You twist *everything* I say."

"Honey, nobody needs to twist what you say. It already comes out of your mouth that way."

"Do you hate me that much?"

"Trust me, Octavia. You don't want to ask me that question right now."

"But . . . how can I explain it to the police? I can't tell them about the key, they'd never believe me. And besides," she added, biting her thumbnail, "I don't want anyone to know about it."

"A lot of good that key's going to do you in prison."

Both women jumped as the door opened.

"What are you two shouting about?" asked Hiram, looking concerned. "I could hear you all the way down the hall."

"Dad," said Octavia, plastering a light-hearted smile on her face. "Are you done with lunch?"

"I was done a long time ago. I went out for a walk. The rain's pretty much stopped."

"Are you feeling better?"

Wasn't that just like her sister, thought Cordelia acidly. Enabling the drunk. Making nice to Daddy.

"I'm feeling fine. That aspirin really helped."

For several seconds, no one spoke.

Finally, Hiram said, "You two weren't arguing about me again, were you?"

"No, of course not," said Octavia, a little too quickly. "We just have loud voices. Theatre people, you know." She tittered, as if her explanation covered everything from the fall of Communism to the price of gas.

Hiram seemed to buy it. "What do you say I take my two beautiful daughters out to dinner tonight? Christian was telling me about a wonderful seafood restaurant in New Haven. It would be good for you, Octavia. I know you want to stay here until all this nastiness has been settled, but you need to get away from the house."

"Sure, that would be great," said Octavia. "Wouldn't it, Cordelia?" She smiled at her sister with clenched teeth.

"Yeah, great."

"Something wrong, sweetheart?" Hiram cocked his head at his oldest daughter.

"No," said Cordelia, feeling as if she'd just refought the Battle of Britain—and lost. "Everything's just dandy, Dad. Just dandy."

30

Before Ellie left the house with all her camera gear, Jane spent a few minutes with her in the library, asking if she had any free time later in the day. Somehow, she hoped to talk Ellie into allowing her to see the documentary she'd made on her grandfather. Jane felt it might answer some important questions, but Ellie put her off, saying she had errands to run in New Haven, and when she returned to the tack house, she needed to get back to work. Perhaps tonight she'd have some free time. If she did, she'd call.

Feeling thwarted, but hoping to get together later, Jane limped down to the dining room and had lunch. As she was finishing her Cobb salad, she asked Christian if she could use his laptop computer for a few minutes. He told her he'd left it in the solarium. She could use it for as long as she liked.

Jane found the computer all set up and sitting on a small writing desk. After connecting to the web, she typed in "www.gracielandlive.com," curious to spend a few more minutes checking out the site.

When the homepage finally popped up, she found herself staring again at a low, aerial view of Innishannon—The Magic Kingdom in Gracie's online world. The photo must have been taken many years ago because the building itself, and the grounds surrounding it, were perfectly maintained. Sitting as it did on the edge of the headland, Innishannon presented a striking image. Behind the house, the lawn sloped from the flagstone terrace to the stony beach, where waves hurled themselves against the rocks, sending spray high into the air. No wonder Gracie loved this house. It had a real sense of majesty.

Below the photo were two links: Members and Guests. Jane clicked on the guest icon and was taken immediately to another page that explained the terms of membership. Scrolling down to the bottom, she found an icon that said, "Take a free tour of GracielandLive." She clicked on this and eight boxes appeared. Gracie had divided the site into eight main rooms. The other night, Jane had only looked briefly at four or five of them. Now was her chance to see it all:

GracielandLive (5 webcams)
GracielandArt
GracielandZoo
Oracles and Incantations
GracielandJournal
EroticGracieland
Archives
The Coffin Texts

Each of these titles were also links. Jane started at the top and worked her way down.

The webcam shots showed five views of an empty apartment. Gracie wasn't around. Finding the images of little interest, Jane quickly moved on.

Opening up GracielandArt, Jane was given nine different buttons. Clicking on them one at a time, she found both scanned drawings and art created on the computer—all highly imaginative, wildly colorful, even childish in a self-conscious, adult-mimicking-a-child sort of way. Gracie clearly wasn't attempting to produce great art, but what she did express was a great deal of attitude—jazzy, funky, even a little down and dirty hip-hop-inner-city cool. Nothing was approached seriously. Instead, playfulness seemed to be the order of the day. Jane found the art oddly affecting.

Next came GracielandZoo—pictures of Gracie's cats. Her "Co-stars."

The fourth room was called Oracles and Incantations. The background was a kaleidoscope of images. Many were taken from tarot cards, others from the Aztecs, the Incas, and from ancient Egypt. Inserted into the mix were short sayings. A few from India. Several from the Gnostic Gospels. Quotes from P. T. Barnum. Mick Jagger. The Apostle Paul. Bertolt Brecht. Billy Bob Thornton. This was probably just a small taste of what the entire room was like, sort of wisdom on acid. At the bottom of the page, Gracie had included what she called, "Blessings and Curses." One generic blessing and one generic curse had been included, available for downloading to whomever might be interested.

Jane skipped the next door, GracielandJournal, because she wanted to come back to it at the end.

EroticGracieland was a page of body shots of Gracie. Most were fairly artfully done. Some were pure, steamy porn. Christian was included in one of the shots, so Gracie hadn't been lying about their relationship.

Next came Archives. These were mostly art shots of the apartment— one platform shoe taken with a fish-eye lens at an odd angle. Bottom-lit photos of Gracie's face. A broken teapot. Still lifes of cats, of hats with ostrich feathers, mannequins in kinky positions—anything and everything Gracie saw with her digital camera that interested her.

The last room, The Coffin Texts, was unavailable to guests. Gracie wrote a short note explaining that this was the title of a novel of enlightenment she'd been working on for several years. Her words weren't meant for those uninitiated in the ways of GracielandLive. It sounded silly, but it was probably a smart marketing move—holding something back, tantalizing a potential member with the promise of revelation, even if it was just a tongue-in-cheek revelation. Jane assumed the whole thing was a joke. If it wasn't, she had some serious doubts about Gracie's mental health.

Returning to the GracielandJournal, Jane clicked on the icon and was taken to five days' worth of Gracie's personal journal notes. The young woman wasn't only a physical exhibitionist, but an emotional one as well. Beginning with last Thursday's entry, she wrote about a boyfriend named Michael. It sounded like an ongoing saga, one she'd written about at great length many times before. She talked about their "issues"—his brutal streak and fear of intimacy, her refusal to give him the time and attention he wanted. She also included a laundry list of everything she'd just bought at the store. She'd visited a Target in New Haven, picking up such things as a furry pair of winter boots, two scented candles, some KavaKava ("'cause I'm way too whacked out nervous sometimes"). She ranted for a while about not needing her mother to approve of her life, and then described a new bra she planned to buy. Jane skimmed the passage, then moved on.

On Friday, Gracie wrote at some length about a book she was reading. She didn't give the title, but it was a history of God, a discussion of Judaism, Christianity, and Islam. She was intrigued by the religious experience but impatient with belief systems—dogma, doctrine, anything that smacked of limitation. She said she wanted to do more research into the mystics, especially "the dark night of the soul," something that fascinated her. She quoted Augustine. "Yearning makes the heart deep." She ended the day's entry by saying that Verna Lange had just arrived at the doors of the Magic Kingdom, and told her readers to stay tuned.

Saturday's entry was brief.

Christmas Eve, one A.M.
It's finally come. I've always wondered how I would face it, how I would react to my own dark night of the soul.

First came the conversation with my grandfather. He called from New Jersey to tell me my life, as I've known it, is over.

Then came the panic, the horror. An insect was crawling around inside my chest and I couldn't get it it out. I coughed until my voice was hoarse, beat my lungs with my fists, but nothing helped. I felt like I was going mad.

I have to understand this myself before I can tell you more. All I know for sure is that hatred is like an insect. It's tiny and ugly, and can bite you before you even know it's there.

Once again, she signed off by saying, "Stay tuned."

It was all pretty cryptic—except for the part about the conversation with her grandfather. Buddy must have called her on Christmas Eve to tell her about Roland's new will, that Roland was leaving Innishannon to Octavia. As soon as the marriage took place, Grace's future tie to the estate would be dissolved.

Jane read on.

Sunday's entry was longer. Gracie mused about fate, about Michael, about Gregorian chants and the aging of rock 'n roll—Geezer Rock, she called it—and how glad she'd be when all the Boomers had finally been blasted into oblivion. She included her top ten list of "Bad Ass" records of all time. She even gave a recipe for the perfect soft-boiled egg, her favorite breakfast. She seemed chipper, alternating between philosophic and superficial, but she said nothing more about her conversation with her grandfather. At the end of the day's entry she put an addendum.

It's nearly three A.M. I couldn't sleep, so I went downstairs a few minutes ago to raid the refrigerator in the main kitchen. I drifted around the house for a while eating a sandwich. You know how much I like it when it's all dark and quiet. I love creepy.

As I passed the living room arch, I saw a pinprick of light. I stopped and watched it. It would grow bright and then go out. Grow bright again, then fade. I realized after a few seconds that what I was seeing was the tip of a cigarette. Someone was in there, sitting in the back of the room, smoking. I couldn't see who it was, any more than they could see me. I waited a second, wondering if I should say something. I thought it might be my grandfather. Roland is getting married in the morning, and I knew Gramps wasn't happy about it. Me, on the other hand, I'm thrilled. (That's sarcasm, in case you got confused.)

As I stood there, wondering what to do, I heard someone begin to sob. It got louder and louder until I realized it had to be Roland. I heard him say, "I'm so sorry. God, I'm so sorry." Then the small lamp next to him went on. I backed into the shadows, watching as he picked up a picture frame off the end table. There are bunches of pictures of Lew Wallace, Verna Lange, and Roland's daughter all over the house, but I knew this one was a studio shot of Lew. Roland just kept crying, begging for forgiveness. It made me feel sort of squirmy inside. I wanted him to stop.

Finally, he seemed to calm down. He lit up another cigarette, then held up the picture. He actually asked it what to do. He said he was scared. He sounded scared. His voice was all quivery. He said he wasn't sure he should go through with it. He meant the marriage, I'm sure. I wanted to scream, "Yeah, right. Screw that f–king marriage." But I didn't. He seemed kinda fragile. Kinda strung out. It reminded me of that one scene in the Bible— Gethsemane. You know the story. Or you can look it up. In his own way, I figure Roland was asking for the cup to be taken from him. I almost felt sorry for him. But, as they say, the moment passed.

The last entry included in Gracie's guest journal was on Monday. It was very simple and to the point.

Roland Lester died today. Stay tuned.

So that was it. Jane's tour of GracielandLive was over. She wasn't sure what she'd learned, but it was all food for thought. After shutting off the computer, she spent the rest of the afternoon reading in the library. She wanted to stay off her injured knee as much as possible, and Roland's book collection turned out to be a wealth of information on film and the film industry. She'd already skimmed a biography of Lew Wallace and was about to skim one on Verna Lange when she heard a heavy knock on the front door. Curious who it might be, she set the book down and grabbed her cane.

After sitting so long—it was nearly four o'clock—her knee was stiff and sore, and her leg wobbled ominously as she put weight on it. Damn, she thought, steadying herself against the wall. She closed her eyes and marshaled her resolve, then started again. This time, her leg seemed to hold.

Halfway down the hall, she saw Leonard rush into the foyer. She assumed real butlers never rushed, not that she'd had much experience with them. This guy had about as much class as a hubcap.

She could hear a male voice say, "We're here to see . . . ah, Octavia Thorn."

"About what?" asked Leonard, removing a toothpick from his mouth.

Jane finally reached the door. Standing outside were two men in gray coveralls. Behind them she could see a van parked in the drive.

The words HIGGINS SAFE AND LOCK were written in bold black letters on the side.

"Just tell her the locksmith's here."

"Sure thing." Leonard turned around, then looked up.

Jane did the same, seeing Octavia coming, or more accurately, slinking down the central stairs. She was buffed and polished and incredibly gorgeous, completely changed from the more casual way she usually dressed. For the first time, Octavia seemed every inch the glamorous—even luminous—stage star that she was. She'd done her hair and makeup, draped herself in gold jewelry, and put on an off-the-shoulder black dress with a deep slit up the side. It wasn't the kind of thing one would wear into the boss's office to ask for a raise. Or maybe Octavia would. The fabric and design were sleek and silky, and as tight fitting as an oilskin across a snare drum. No more innocent bride stuff. The current queen of Broadway was a knockout and she knew it.

"I'm Octavia Thorn," she said, motioning for the men to come inside.

Jane smiled at their obvious discomfort. They weren't sure where to look, or how deeply to inhale the scent of her perfume.

"Leonard, will you show them to the screening room. The vault is in the projection booth, along the back wall. I'm sure you can get along without me for a few seconds."

The head locksmith nodded. Both men quickly followed the butler out of the room.

"What's the occasion?" asked Jane.

"When I'm feeling as low as I am today, looking good always helps my mood."

"It'll probably do wonders for everyone's mood," said Jane.

"You think so?" She moved a bit closer, looking deeply into Jane's eyes. Jane couldn't help herself. She started to laugh.

"Do I amuse you?" she asked in a deep, throaty voice.

She was being such an obvious vamp, Jane could hardly take her seriously. "No, Octavia. You're breathtaking. And you better get downstairs before they drill a hole in one of the seats by mistake."

"I suppose you're right. You *are* made of flesh and blood though, aren't you?"

"I've known you since you were eleven."

"So?"

"You really want to get a rise out of me?"

"No," she sighed. "I'd rather get a rise out of the detective who was here last night."

"Toscano?"

"He reminded me of Rock Hudson."

"He did?" Jane didn't see it. "Well . . . maybe a Rock Hudson with less hair and forty pounds heavier."

"Yeah, he was a hunk, all right, but I'll bet it was mostly muscle."

"Maybe you'll have a chance to find out."

A hand rose to her hip. She'd dropped the vamp act altogether now. "If only my womanly wiles could keep me out of the clink."

"Why would someone put you in the clink?"

"It's a long story. For the full script, consult my sister." Glancing toward the back of the house, she said, "Are you coming?"

Jane nodded to her cane. "Don't wait for me. I'll be along in a few minutes."

By the time Jane finally made it to the screening room, the drilling had already begun. During a momentary lull, she asked Octavia how long they thought it would take.

"Five minutes maybe," she said, her attention riveted to the safe. "Maybe less."

As soon as the drilling began again, Jane found a folding chair and sat down to wait. The noise acted like a beacon, drawing everyone down from their lairs. Christian and Verna arrived first, followed by Hilda, Cordelia, and her father. The last one to come through the door was Buddy.

"What are you doing?" he demanded, stomping angrily up to Octavia. He had to shout to be heard.

"I'm having the safe drilled open."

"What safe?"

"The one behind the wall in the projection booth."

His eyes narrowed. He was obviously surprised, but Jane could read something else in his face too. She couldn't define what it was.

"This isn't your house," he shouted. "You can't just take it upon yourself to do something like that without consulting my granddaughter."

"It is my house."

"What?" He cupped his hand over his ear.

"I said, it *is* my house." On the last word, the drilling stopped.

Buddy's unblinking eyes met hers. Very slowly, he replied, "Say that again."

"Honey, the house belongs to Gracie," said Hiram. He was leaning against the back of one of the screening room seats, directly next to Christian.

Touching the strand of gold at her neck, Octavia turned to face the assembled crowd. "Look, you're all going to find out sooner or later. The fact is, Roland and I were married three weeks ago in a private ceremony. The wedding yesterday was just for show—for the press and for family."

"What?" said Buddy, the impact of her words causing him to back up.

Everyone in the room was startled into silence.

Before anyone could speak, the drilling started again.

Jane glanced at Cordelia, hoping to catch her eye, but saw that she was watching her father, trying to gage his reaction to this newest twist in Octavia's convoluted life.

When the drilling finally stopped, one of the men emerged from the projection booth. "It's open now, Ms. Thorn. You can go in."

Octavia beat Buddy inside, but only by a few seconds. Cordelia followed close behind, but had to content herself with standing in the projector room doorway.

"This is like watching Geraldo Rivera about to open Al Capone's vault," said Christian. His good humor, as always, was tinged with sarcasm.

"Shhh," said Verna, clearly not amused.

While everyone waited silently for word from inside, Jane felt a tap on her shoulder. Glancing up, she saw that Ellie had come up behind her.

"Could I talk to you for a second?" she whispered. She retreated a few steps, signaling for Jane to follow.

Jane limped to the far end of the room. "What's up?" she asked, noticing Ellie's worried look.

"Remember when I asked you to get that electrical cord for me this morning?" she said, her voice barely audible. "I gave you the key to the tack room and you went down there to find it."

Jane nodded.

"You didn't . . . I mean . . . there was a video on top of the VCR."

"The one you did on your grandfather. Sure, I saw it as I was leaving."

"You didn't by any chance take it, did you?"

"Me? No. I'd never do something like that without asking you first."

The worried look deepened.

"What's wrong?"

"It's not there. I got back from New Haven a few minutes ago and the video was gone."

"Are you sure? Maybe you knocked it off the VCR when you were bringing your gear inside."

She shook her head. "My equipment's still in my van."

"I hope you don't think—"

"No, I believe you. I never really thought you'd taken it."

Jane felt a moment of intense guilt for snooping through Ellie's sack of paper garbage. "Do you think someone broke in?"

"No. There's no sign of that."

"Then how—"

"A key. Roland had one. So does Buddy. And there's an extra set to the garage and the tack room on a hook in the kitchen. It's in plain view. It's even labeled."

"So you think someone staying *here* took it."

"Who else?"

"Is it the only copy you've got?"

"Of course not, but that's not the point."

Jane rubbed the side of her jeans. "But how would anybody even know the tape existed?"

"They wouldn't. Unless the person who got into the tack house was just looking around, seeing what there was to see."

"Why?"

"Because they wanted to know if I was on to something."

"About Roland? The scandal?"

"Exactly."

"But who?"

Before Ellie could answer, a voice called, "Ms. Lawless, there's a guy on the phone who wants to talk to you."

Jane looked up to see Leonard standing in the screening room doorway. Ever the class act, he was eating a doughnut. "I'll be right there."

"You go," said Ellie. "We can talk later."

"But . . . answer my question first. Who do you think was in the tack house?"

"I don't know, Jane. But I intend to find out."

On her way to the door, Jane shot a quick look over at the projection booth. The two workmen had been banished from the inner sanctum and Cordelia had disappeared inside. It wouldn't be long now. Jane didn't want to miss the unveiling, but she had to take the call.

"Hello?" she said, sitting down on the couch in the TV room. She lifted her bad leg up on a footstool.

"Jane? Toscano here."

"Hey, hi. I was hoping we'd hear from you today. I guess Buddy wasn't your man."

"He made it home, I take it."

"Around noon."

"Frankly, I don't know what's going on with that guy. But we didn't have enough evidence to make an arrest. We're still working the case."

"Then, he's still a suspect?"

"We haven't eliminated anyone. Well, except for you and your friend Cordelia."

"And Cordelia's father."

Silence. "What do you say we have lunch tomorrow?"

"Where?"

"Ming's. In St. Albans. It's on High Street, a few blocks down from the church where Mr. Lester and Ms. Thorn got married—or didn't get married, I guess. Think you can find it again?"

"What time?"

"How does noon sound?"

"I'll be there."

"In case you've forgotten what I look like, I'll be the one with the rose clenched in my teeth."

"You must make quite an impression on your men."

"Oh, I'm the department misfit. A kid who grew up dirt poor in

250

the Bronx, escaped his roots and graduated with honors from Yale, only to sign on as a grunt the following year with the New Haven P.D. I mean, what's wrong with this picture?"

"Probably nothing."

"Hey, good answer. See you tomorrow."

31

Dinner that night was a study in tension. Buddy sat silently with his glasses perched on the end of his nose, reading the legal papers Octavia had given him covering the details of her marriage to Roland. He'd already called his lawyer, and was planning to meet with him first thing in the morning. The rest of the diners picked at their food.

Almost as soon as the safe was opened, Cordelia and Octavia had ejected everyone from the screening room, including Jane, saying they needed time to take inventory. If Buddy had seen what was behind the metal door, he wasn't talking. Around six, the sisters had sent written word up to their father saying they were sorry, but they wouldn't be able to have dinner with him in St. Albans tonight—oh, and could he see to it that two roast beef sandwiches on rye—extra pickle, no mustard—were sent down to them so they could eat while they worked.

Dr. Thorn seemed to take the news in stride. Of anyone at the dinner table, he was the most animated. Jane wondered at his sanguine mood. Apparently, Octavia's marriage to Roland was okay as long as the bridegroom was deceased. Not a drop of alcohol passed his lips all during dinner.

Once the gloomy meal was over, Christian and Dr. Thorn broke out the chessboard, setting it up on the unused end of the long dining room table, while Buddy and Verna retired to the TV room. Gracie hadn't been seen or heard from since she'd dropped Christian and Buddy back at the house around noon. Jane could tell Buddy was concerned about her, and wanted to catch her as soon as she came home.

The TV room had a clear view of the front door, so, like a good soldier, he took up his position and waited. He no doubt wanted to break the news about Innishannon to her gently, not that there was a good way to tell Gracie that she'd just lost Gracieland. An explosion was imminent, and no one knew that more keenly than Buddy. Jane felt sorry for him as she limped past the room, catching a glimpse of him staring blankly at the TV screen, knowing that his mind was a million miles away. All in all, it hadn't been a banner day for Buddy Lester.

Entering the living room a few minutes later, Jane found Hilda sitting in one of the wing chairs by the fire, knitting. It was such an inviting scene, and yet as Jane walked to the drinks cart to pour herself a brandy, she saw that the older woman was crying. "I'm sorry," she said, feeling like an unwelcome intruder. "I'll just fix myself a drink and leave."

Hilda removed a handkerchief from her apron and wiped her eyes. "No, stay. I'd enjoy the company."

For the first time it struck Jane that Roland's house manager no longer kept to the nether regions of the mansion, as she had when he was alive. It was a curious transformation. And although others in the household were surely dealing with their sorrow, Hilda was the only one to openly show her grief.

"You have some beautiful yarn," said Jane, easing down onto the other wing chair.

"I found it at a little store in Asbury," she said wistfully. "Mr. Lester had his driver take me in for the day."

"His driver? He didn't own his own car?"

"Not for years. When he needed to go somewhere, he'd always call the same service. I believe he even dealt with the same man. A Mr. Yablonski."

As Hilda resumed her knitting, Jane sipped her brandy and watched the fire. After a few minutes, she roused herself and said, "From what Gracie told the police, I understand that Mr. Lester must have spent a good deal of time in New York."

"Oh, yes. He had himself driven there at least twice a month, although I couldn't swear that was his destination. I guess I just assumed. When he came home, he'd talk about the Broadway plays he'd seen and the films . . . always the films."

"How long would he be gone?"

"Well, it varied. Sometimes it was as short as three days. Other times as long as a week. Now, Mr. Lester's *brother*, he's the one who's gone for weeks at a time. He flies all over the world, you know."

"Doing what?"

"Oh, he just loves to travel. He gives me his itinerary so I always know where he can be reached—just in case Mr. Roland wanted to talk to him. I do envy him. He's got the time and the money now, so he takes off whenever he's in the mood. Comes back to Innishannon when he's tired. He goes to Europe mostly, but he's also been to Asia a few times, to Australia and South Africa, and to the Middle East."

That was interesting, thought Jane. Why did she have a feeling there was more to it than simple wanderlust?

Hilda sighed, then clicked her needles sharply. "But I never knew when Mr. Roland was leaving, or when he would return. I guess I got used to his erratic schedule over the years. If I'd been the worrying kind, I would have pulled out all my hair long ago, but I trusted that he was a man of the world. He had things to do, and when he was done, he'd come home."

"What if there was a family emergency and you needed to reach him?"

"I couldn't. If he was gone for more than a few nights, he'd phone sometimes. But he never gave me a number where he could be reached."

"Do you remember the name of the limousine service?"

"Crown Coaches. Mr. Lester once said it was a Hartford company with a branch in New Haven."

"And he used the New Haven branch?"

She nodded.

Jane continued to sip her brandy, feeling it warm and soothe her nerves. She knew Cordelia would give her an argument, but after a couple of drinks, she felt more in control. The tension coiled inside her body retreated, if only for a little while. "Okay, so the limo would arrive and he'd leave with his luggage."

"Just one piece. A large old beat-up suitcase. I didn't understand it. I mean, he had beautiful, expensive luggage stored upstairs, but he never used it. The driver would come into the house and carry it out to the limousine."

"Was it heavy?"

"Oh, yes, very."

"Would Mr. Lester always take it—even if he was only planning to be gone for a few days?"

"Always," she said, switching the empty needle to her right hand.

"Did Mr. Lester have any friends in New York?"

"None that I'm aware of. Of course, he was a very well-known man in his day. I'm sure he has friends all over. Although, he's lived at Innishannon for almost twenty years. A lot of his old pals have died." She teared up again, her hands falling to her lap. "I just can't believe he's gone. I'm sorry to say this, but I rue the day Octavia Thorn ever set foot in this house. She's been a bad penny from the very beginning."

"In what way?"

"Oh, don't get me started."

"No, really. I'd like to know."

She wiped her nose with her hanky, then resumed her knitting. "Well, she had to have all this special food brought in because she's always on a diet, and then her special bottled water. She needed 'space,' as she called it, even if Mr. Lester wanted to spend time with her. Sometimes she wouldn't come down for meals for days. Everything had to be sent up to her room, which meant I had to do it. And she was forever down in the mouth, griping about this or that. Nothing was good enough for her high standards. The house wasn't clean. The air smelled of mildew. The bedding was old. Mr. Lester would take her into town for shopping trips. He'd buy her beautiful new things, but when they came home, she'd retreat to her room and not show her face for the rest of the day. Her ingratitude was appalling. She is by far the worst house guest we've ever had. I never understood why she moved in here. And I wish to God she'd leave before something else happens."

"Are you saying you think she had something to do with Mr. Lester's death?"

Her dour look and the click of needles jabbing each other was the only answer Jane would get. "I'm sorry if I've upset you. If you didn't want to know my feelings on the matter, you shouldn't have asked. I'm from Missouri, Jane. I don't mince words."

"Have you lived in Connecticut long?"

"Since Mr. Lester moved here. I worked as a hairstylist in Hollywood for many years. That's where I met Mr. Lester. We hit it off right away—we were always laughing or joking about something. When he moved into his new house in Beverly Hills, he asked me to come work for him. I've been his house manager ever since."

"Ms. Lawless!" called a man's voice.

Glancing behind her, Jane saw Leonard steaming down the hallway toward the living room.

Hilda turned too. "Leonard, what have I told you? No running in the house. And enter the room before you call someone's name. We do *not* raise our voices."

"Yes, ma'am." He leaned into the door frame with both arms, stretching a leg out behind him as if he were about to go for a run. "Ms. Lawless, Cordelia and Octavia would like you to come down to the screening room."

"Now?"

"Right away."

Jane got up immediately.

"Be sure to come back and let me know what they found," said Hilda.

"I will," said Jane. "If I'm allowed to." She quickly finished her drink and handed the empty glass to Leonard on the way out the door.

"So, what do you think?" asked Cordelia, standing proudly amidst stacks of film canisters. "We've made a list of every film inside the vault."

"There were twenty-two," said Octavia, running her finger down the clipboard. "Mostly Lew Wallace's but some others as well. Old films. Even some newsreels."

"What do you think it means?" asked Jane, poking the top of a box open with her cane.

"Seems pretty obvious to me," replied Cordelia, settling her weight on her right hip. "The temperature and humidity in the vault were electronically controlled. Roland was collecting old films, preserving them as best he could. This is just a handful of them. I'm sure he's got a warehouse somewhere—maybe two or three. I'll bet, when you add everything up, you're looking at millions of dollars worth of old movies."

"That was his secret," said Octavia. "My wedding present. The key must fit some old lock on a warehouse door."

"And it's up to us to figure out the location," said Cordelia eagerly. "I told my sister you're a whiz at stuff like that."

"Buddy's name is on all the boxes," said Jane. "Why not ask him?"

"First," said Octavia, "if he did know what my key unlocks, he'd never tell me. But I don't think he does. See, Roland told me once that nobody knew where the secret was."

"Those were his exact words?"

Octavia thought for a minute. "Yes, I think so. Remember, Buddy didn't know about this vault. It was a complete surprise to him."

"It's obvious what was going on," said Cordelia, looking impatient. "Roland used his brother to find the films, and then took it from there."

"I think she's right," said Octavia. "Buddy may assume a warehouse exists, but he has no idea where it is."

"Warehouses," said Cordelia, correcting her. "Maybe there are five or six, or even more." Her eyes glowed with possibilities.

Jane had a million questions. She started with the most obvious. "Does it seem logical to you that a warehouse, especially one that housed precious material, would have such a poor security system that a skeleton key could unlock the door?"

Cordelia waved the question away. "All right, all right. So we haven't thought everything through to the last, final, totally defined detail. Maybe the key is symbolic, or it opens a box that contains a record of the movies Roland owns—with a corresponding list of warehouse addresses."

"Fine, but what about copyright? Roland might have copies of the films, but wouldn't the studios still own the rights to them, and therefore, any profit?"

"A lot of those studios aren't even in business today," replied Octavia.

"But some are," said Jane.

"Well, I'm sure Roland must have looked into the legalities," snapped Cordelia. "Why are you trying to ruin the moment for us? This is a huge discovery!"

"I agree, it is," said Jane, knowing if she voiced any more reservations, Cordelia would drop kick her through a window. Thankfully, there were none in the screening room, otherwise she might already be outside.

"Will you help us?" asked Octavia, looking a little desperate.

Jane could hardly say no. "Sure, I'll do what I can. But you might want to hire a private investigator. I'm afraid, as much as we might want to help, Cordelia and I can't stay here forever. We've got jobs back in Minnesota, and a search like that will take time. Also, if this has anything to do with Roland's murder, you should probably talk to the police. Tell them what you found, and what you suspect."

"And have the entire world searching for those films?" shrieked Cordelia, puckering her face in horror. "*No way*. And you won't say one word to Toscano either, got it?"

It was a command, not a suggestion—and a bit too *Mein Kampf* for Jane's taste. She hated being backed into a corner, but this time she felt she had no choice but to cooperate. "I got it."

"Good. Now, you need to see what else was in the vault." Cordelia led Jane into the booth where three more boxes were stacked next to the projector.

"What are they?"

"Personal papers."

"Really? Now you've got my attention."

"I thought you'd be interested. Here's the deal. We're each going to take one and go through it tonight. Whatever we find that turns out to be relevant, we'll discuss it tomorrow morning. Privately. We'll all meet in my room at ten."

"Awfully early for you, isn't it?"

"Yes, but we have to make sacrifices in life, Jane."

"You'll have to carry my box up for me." She nodded to her cane.

"No problem. Why don't you wait down here while Octavia and I put everything back in the vault? We had the safe crackers install a new lock before they left."

"That was smart."

"Always thinking," said Cordelia, tapping her forehead. "Always thinking."

Once Jane started digging through the papers, she couldn't have stopped for an earthquake or a tornado. Hours ticked away as she sat in the middle of her bed, reading. To begin with, she'd divided everything into two stacks. She had no idea what straw Cordelia and Octavia had drawn, but she'd gotten the box that was at least half-filled with old studio contracts.

As she sipped from the bottle of brandy she'd bought several days ago while she was shopping in Asbury, she found it fascinating to discover what Roland had been paid—or more often, hadn't been paid—for his direction. There was a note attached to one of the documents that led her to believe it was the norm for studios to hold on to the final contracts themselves. Because Roland so often worked independently, not under the auspices of any one studio, he was able to demand a signed copy of the contract for his own files. In many ways, Jane was learning that Roland had been considered quite the maverick in Hollywood.

Every contract Jane looked at contained an interesting clause: "If the artist shall conduct himself in his private life in such a manner as to commit an offense involving moral turpitude under federal, state, or local laws or ordinances, or shall conduct himself in such a manner that shall offend against decency, morality, or social proprieties, or in a manner that shall cause him to be held in public ridicule, scorn, or contempt, or in a manner that shall cause public scandal, then the producer may at its option and upon one week's notice to the artist terminate this contract."

To Jane, such a clause seemed not only draconian, but having sat at the same dinner table with her lawyer father for most of her young life, she knew the language was full of inexactitude, which gave the owners of the contract almost carte blanche to do whatever they wanted. A clause like that could cast a very real pall on a young gay man or woman's life. At the very least, it would generate a climate of suspicion and a constant need for denial—whether spoken or implied. No wonder people guarded their privacy with such vigor. One blind item in a newspaper could end a career.

The second stack contained Roland's real estate purchases. Jane already knew that he hadn't become a multimillionaire from directing, or through any inheritance from his heiress ex-wife. But he had made some smart investments all along the way. Early on, he started buying land in Los Angeles and Palm Springs. The land was eventually sold at a huge profit. Roland then moved on to houses, mainly in Beverly Hills, but also two hotels in Palm Springs. From there, he branched out, buying up vacant lots in Culver City, Brentwood, and Malibu. Only one name was on the deeds—his—so Jane assumed his wife had nothing to do with it. Apart from directing, Roland had been an extraordinary businessman.

By one A.M., Jane was beginning to feel the effects of the brandy and the late hour, but since she only had a small stack of papers left to cover, she kept on reading. Leaning back against the pillows, she skimmed the correspondence between Roland and his real estate agent, Dan Fanlow. A few of the letters were actually quite funny. Or maybe it was just the booze. When she finally finished, she removed her glasses, rubbed her eyes, and glanced at the clock. The numbers swam so disconcertingly she closed her eyes again. She needed to rest for a minute before she got up to change into her pajamas. There wasn't any hurry. She knew she'd had too much to drink, but the dizziness was a small price to pay for the feeling of relaxation.

When the knock came on the door, she barely heard it.

"What?" she said, opening her eyes and staring up into Cordelia's angry face. "It's not morning yet, is it?"

Cordelia picked up the bottle. "How much of this did you drink tonight?"

"Not much. I'm just tired. And my leg ached. You know the brandy helps." She watched Cordelia scrutinize the papers on the bed.

"Did you finish going through the box?"

"Every last page."

"How about dinner? Did you eat any?"

"Not much. I'm not a masochist."

"You know, Jane, I came in here because I discovered something important in my box. I thought you'd want to know right away."

"I do," she said, closing her eyes again. The urge to sleep was irresistible. "I do," she insisted. A few seconds later—or an hour later, she wouldn't have known the difference—a quilt was pulled up to her shoulders and the light was switched off.

32

By nine the next morning, Jane had showered, dressed, and taken two aspirin. She felt a little shaky, but her knee didn't ache quite as much, and she'd had seven hours of solid, dreamless sleep. She grabbed herself some breakfast in the dining room, then poured a second cup of coffee and headed up to Cordelia's bedroom.

Octavia was already there. Both sisters were still in bathrobes and slippers, groaning like it was the middle of the night.

"You're looking chipper, Janey," said Cordelia, her Rubenesque form draped languorously over a chair. Octavia was sitting across from her, paging through some papers.

"I'm fine," said Jane. She hoped that would put an end to any conversation about last night. "So, who wants to do the first report?"

"I will," said Octavia, stifling a yawn. "Okay, my box was mostly old scripts and Roland's directorial notes. I will say it was all fascinating. I brought some of it to read, but there's really no point. It's nothing we can use. Who's next?"

"I'll go," said Jane, sitting down on the bed. She quickly explained what had been in her box, ending with a few comments on the morals clause. She'd brought along one of the contracts so she could read it to them verbatim. Everyone thought it was a fascinating piece of movie history, but it didn't move them any closer to their goal of finding the lock Octavia's key fit.

"So, Roland made his money in real estate," said Octavia, looking reflective as she tapped her fingernails on the arm of her chair.

"You didn't know that?" asked Jane.

She shrugged. "I've had my lawyer go over his new will. I know his bottom line. I know what I've inherited. And I'm aware of his bequests. How he made his money was never really at issue." Nodding to her sister, she said, "You're next."

Cordelia glanced at the chaos of papers on the table next to her. "Well, my box was mostly correspondence. Letters from friends. Letters from business associates. Letters from charities. Letters about awards. Letters from fans. Letters from universities wanting him to come and talk. Letters from his daughter. Letters from his wife. Letters from Lew when he was on location."

"Mushy letters?" asked Octavia.

"The early ones were. I'm sure it's all stuff Ellie Saks would kill to get her hands on."

"Will you give it to her?" asked Jane, hoping the answer was yes.

"Absolutely," said Octavia, clasping her hands behind her head. "I want that documentary to be first rate in every way."

"Can I tell her that?" said Jane. "She'll be thrilled."

"Sure, why not? Say, do my eyes deceive me, or did you two really hit it off?"

Cordelia raised an eyebrow. "Did I miss something?"

"We're friends," said Jane. "I like her. I'm interested in what she does for a living."

"That's all?" asked Cordelia.

Octavia stifled another yawn. "When we're done here, I'm going back to bed."

"Then, can I borrow your car?" asked Jane. She had no intention of answering Cordelia's last question. "I'd like to drive into St. Albans."

"Any specific reason?" asked Cordelia, innocence incarnate.

Jane didn't want to tell them she was having lunch with Toscano. She assumed they would consider it fraternizing with the enemy. "My leg's a bit better. I need to get out and do some walking, preferably on a level sidewalk. Hey, you want to join me? We could do three or four miles together and then have lunch." With that itinerary, she felt confident Cordelia wouldn't take her up on the offer.

"Heavens, no." Cordelia made a sour face. "My sister has the right idea. A few more hours of beauty sleep. And then . . . a long soak in a hot tub."

"Hey . . . we've got to get started looking for those warehouses," said Octavia, sitting up straight. "This is no time for an extended tub. Jane, you must have some idea what to do next."

"I do. Use the yellow pages. Hire yourself a private investigator."

"But—"

"I'm not saying I won't help, but you've got to be practical. You don't have to tell them *everything*. Just the basics. Let them take it from there. Actually, with your money, hire five investigators." Jane could see the sisters were both adrift in a sea of indecision. "Look, here's your assignment. When you get up—"

"After we have lunch," said Cordelia, peevishly.

"After you have lunch," repeated Jane, "find the yellow pages, either New Haven or better still, New York, and make a list of ten investigation services. Then, each of you call five. Take notes. Select the best five from the lot and hire them. By then, I'll be home. We can work on our own game plan." That seemed to satisfy them. They each sat back in their chairs looking as pleased as if they'd thought of it themselves.

"If that's everything," said Jane, getting up, "I need to go."

"Not so fast," said Cordelia, searching for a paper on the table in front of her. "Here, this answers one of our questions about Lew Wallace. I don't know why it was included in Roland's correspondence, but we shouldn't look a gift horse in the mouth." Massaging her temples, she read:

March 17, 1957

Dear Lew:

Thanks so much for sending the manuscript. I got it on Friday and spent the weekend reading it. Let me assure you, In the Belly of the Beast *is beautifully written and observed. And while it is an amazing piece of heretofore unrecorded history—and a story I couldn't put down—I'm sorry to say that the material, though obviously true, is unpublishable.*

As you may well understand, I would dearly love to see your autobiography in print. Your life is a fascinating one and will undoubtedly be written about by others in the future with far less accuracy and intimate detail. However, the book, as it stands now, would never make it past our legal department. You, of all people, will surely understand that the men named and discussed as well as the studios who employ them would shriek libel to the high heavens if we even considered publishing this volume. The legal fallout would be devastating.

Should you care to rewrite the manuscript—leaving out the homosexuality—I would certainly consider passing it on to a more senior editor. In fact, I encourage you to do just that.

One word of caution. If you seek out and find another, less reputable house who is willing to take your book on, please think hard before going ahead with it. Though I know the words you write are true, I believe strongly that the world is not ready for such honesty. You would only do yourself harm—irreparable harm, I am afraid. Please believe that I am your friend and that I pass on this advice knowing you will receive it in the spirit in which it was intended.

I wish you the very best with your future writing and film projects. Please call me if you have any questions.

Sincerely yours,
Byron H. Vance
Associate Editor
Random House

"So," said Cordelia. "What do you think of that?"

Octavia rose from her chair, retying her satin bathrobe. "It's interesting, but it's got nothing to do with our search."

Jane wasn't so sure, but she wasn't going to argue the point, at least right now.

"It might have something to do with Roland's murder," said Cordelia sternly.

"I hope it does. Then everyone will leave me alone."

Jane and Cordelia exchanged glances.

"I'm going back to bed. Why don't you follow me to my room, Jane, and I'll give you my car keys. Later, Cordelia. Enjoy your beauty sleep. At your age, you need it."

Ming's on High Street was nothing like Jane had imagined. For starters, it was a Jewish deli. Next, it was more of a lunchroom than a restaurant. The floor was covered with cracked red linoleum and the tables were the chrome and formica variety popular in the fifties. But Ming's wasn't attempting to be trendy, it was just being its old, outdated self. The food was displayed behind a long deli counter. Corned beef. Chopped liver. Lox. A crock of homemade dill pickles. Cole slaw. Potato salad. Against the back wall were racks of fresh baked breads. Onion rolls. Bagels. Rye breads and challah. Jane figured there had to be a story behind the name.

She found Toscano waiting for her at a back table, sipping from a can of Mountain Dew and looking at a menu.

"Where's the rose?" she asked, pulling out a chair and sitting down opposite him. She stuffed her cane under the table, hoping he hadn't noticed it.

Toscano looked over at her with his amused brown eyes. "What rose?"

"The one you said you'd be wearing in your teeth."

"Oh, that one." He scratched his cheek, then checked his watch. "You're five minutes late. I ate it. What can I say? Hungry cop on the go."

"So, you're telling me you don't have much discrimination when it comes to dining out?"

He grinned. "*Au contraire,* madam." His New York accent murdered the French. "This place has the best hot pastrami sandwiches in the state, maybe even in the universe. That's why I suggested it. You're in for a real treat, assuming you like hot pastrami."

"I do."

"Then let me suggest for madam, a hot pastrami on rye, slathered with Stugel's. It's a local mustard, a cross between ballpark and dark German. Cole slaw *du jour.* A kosher dill. And for dessert—"

"I'm not sure I'll get that far."

"The chocolate cake/is—" He touched his fingers to his lips. *"C'est magnifique."*

"Are you trying to impress me with your international style?"

"Is it working?"

"No."

"Hey, can't fault a guy for trying." He pushed away from the table. "Just sit right there and I'll be back with the grub in a flash. Oh, what do you want to drink?"

"Coffee, black."

"Coming right up."

During lunch, they talked about the original owner of Ming's—a Chinese American restaurateur who kept the place going from the fifties to the early eighties. Toscano said the food was passable, but nothing to write home about—his words. But when Irving Greenberg, an old high school buddy of his, moved up here from the Bronx in '87, he turned the place—almost overnight—into the best Jewish deli this side of Tel Aviv. Again, his words: "Irv has an odd sense of humor. He wanted to keep the old name. Said it would be a real talking point— great for local publicity. Turns out, he was right. He does a huge business in Ming's Matza Ball Soup. Ming's Cheese and Blueberry Blintzes. Ming's Bagels. Who knows, he may even take it national one day. It's great food, right?"

She had to agree. The sandwich was wonderful, nothing like the bland fare served at Innishannon. She was about to answer in the affir- mative when the sound of a crash nearly caused her to jump out of her chair.

"Hey," said Toscano, reaching for her hand. "It was just some dishes."

Realizing her reaction had been way out of proportion, she tried to cover with a smile. "Sorry. I've been . . . kind of jumpy lately."

"I noticed."

"It's nothing."

He nodded to the cane on the floor. "What's all that about?"

"I tripped two nights ago. Banged up my knee."

"Yeah, but you were limping on Monday night, too."

She shrugged. "My left leg is weak. I was . . . hurt a few months ago."

"Hurt how?"

He wasn't going to let it drop. She decided to tell him the truth. There was no real reason not to. "Someone attacked me in my home. Hit me over the head. I was taken to the hospital in a coma. When I finally woke up, I had some paralysis on my left side."

"*Some* paralysis? You like to minimize things, don't you, Jane?"

"I'm better now. I'd even stopped using the cane . . . until I tripped."

"But your nerves aren't better."

Again, she shrugged.

"You having trouble sleeping?"

"Sometimes," she conceded.

"Ever replay the attack in your mind? Or . . . have you had flashbacks? Do you just snap and feel like you're back there—at the moment of the attack?"

"You must be a good interrogator," she laughed, starting to feel uneasy. "You fire questions faster than I can think of answers."

"I'm concerned."

"Well, you don't need to be."

"Just one more comment and then I'll quit." He added a packet of sugar to his coffee, stirring for a second. "Ever heard of Post Traumatic Stress Disorder?"

"Sure. It's what happened to G.I.'s who were in the Vietnam war."

"It can happen to anyone, Jane. They taught us about it at the Police Academy. All it is is a natural emotional reaction to a trauma. In other words, it's a *normal* reaction to an abnormal situation. It happens to a lot of cops, guys who take a bullet, or witness something they can't handle. Cops have this peculiar notion that they're made of steel. They're not. I'm not. Sometimes, when a guy won't deal with it, post traumatic stress can end a career."

"You think that's what I have?"

"Maybe."

"Well, I don't."

"Because you're too tough?"

"No, of course not. I'll admit, I was hurt, scared, and I don't like feeling helpless, but I'm getting better all the time. Stronger. This knee thing was just a minor setback."

"Okay, okay." He smiled. "Just . . . take care of yourself. Now, how about that piece of cake?" As he wiped his mouth on a paper napkin, the digital pager on his belt went off. He immediately pulled it free and checked the number and the message.

"Do you have to go?"

"And miss the cake and a few more minutes of your company? Not on your life. You want a piece?"

"I think I'll pass." She hadn't even finished her sandwich yet.

"You'll be sorry. But that's okay. I don't mind sharing if you change your mind." He was a man who obviously loved to eat. Actually, except for the pep talk on the general state of her mental health, Jane had enjoyed the conversation. But now, she wanted her questions answered. She didn't know how much time they had before he had to leave.

When he returned from the front counter, he was carrying his cake, an extra-large piece, and the coffee carafe. "They pretty much let me do what I like around here. Sometimes I even come down on weekends to help Irv in the kitchen. I find it relaxing." He filled her cup, then his, and finally handed the pot to a waitress who was passing by.

"Now, let's get down to business."

Jane cocked her head.

"What do you want to know?"

"You mean . . . about your investigation?"

"Come on. The only reason you agreed to meet me today was to pump me for information, right? I know I'm irresistible, but I doubt I'm your type."

The comment made her pause. Had he been flirting with her all this time? Cordelia always said she didn't know how to flirt—and that if someone was flirting with her, they just about had to hit her over the head to get her to notice. God, what had she gotten herself into this time?

"Look, Jane. I think you're great, and I'd love to get to know you better—even pursue a relationship with you, if that's where it led— but I'm a realist."

"Meaning?"

He held up his hand. "You don't have to explain. Don't you remember? I did that background check on you the other night. I told you all about it."

"You told me about my credit rating."

"Well, my source also mentioned that you give a lot of money to gay charities. And that you lived with a woman for ten years. I'm not stupid. But hell, I like to flirt. And I like you. I didn't figure there was anything wrong having lunch today. And if you stick around long enough, I might even invite you to dinner. I know this *great* Italian place in New Haven. The best tagliatelle primavera you'll ever eat." Again, he held up his hand. "No strings. Just friendship. Believe it or not, I have lots of gay friends. It's just . . . sometimes when I meet someone attractive and bright like you, I wish things could be different."

Jane couldn't help but smile. "You're a rare cop."

"We're not all Neanderthals. Now," he said, digging into his cake, "ask away. I'll tell you what I can."

She was relieved to be off the hook when it came to his expectations. It made her like him all the more, and wish they had the chance to become better friends. "Okay, first, why did you let Buddy go? I thought he'd confessed, or was about to. Did his lawyer prevent it?"

"Lawyers are a pain in the ass." He stopped suddenly and looked up from his cake. "Oops. Didn't I hear that your father was a lawyer?"

"A defense attorney."

"My favorite kind."

"It's all right. My dad would probably agree with you about lawyers, at least part of the time."

Swallowing the piece of cake, he continued, "No, Buddy didn't let his lawyer call the shots. But he did want to cut a deal. Like I said, he was pretty anxious to get it over with."

"The confession."

He nodded.

"So what happened?"

"He told us he put the jimsonweed in the tea."

"Really." Jane leaned forward, arching her fingers over her coffee cup. "I know Hilda always took a tray of tea and toast up to Roland's room around eight, set it on the table right outside his door. I suppose that's when he did it."

"That's what he said." Toscano took a quick sip of coffee.

"You don't believe him?"

"I don't know what to think. Whoever did put the poison in the tea packed it into one of those metal tea bags—the type you use for loose tea. They probably just walked by, dropped it into the pot, and let it steep with the two paper tea bags until Roland came and got it. It took just a few seconds. Anyone in the house could have done it."

"But Buddy admitted to it. He must have given you a reason."

"Yeah, he said he hated his brother because he'd stolen his inheritance from him. We've seen the new will. Buddy gets six million dollars, but maybe that wasn't enough for him. Roland's new bride gets the rest. It's a sizable chunk of money."

"Do you know about—" She hesitated.

"Octavia and Roland? That they were already married? Yeah, we found out. I wish she'd told us the other night. The fact that she didn't makes me wonder if she's got something to hide. Does she?" He fired the question at her point blank.

Jane was a little startled. "I don't know. I don't think so."

"Well, if she does, we'll figure it out. But back to Buddy. Who knows? Maybe he got more in the previous will. But it's all moot. What's important is what Buddy *thought*. If he figured his brother was trying to cheat him, that's plenty strong enough motive for murder. Anyway, while we were talking to him, I got a report back from the lab. The plastic sack we found in his room, the one with the jimsonweed in it, had one perfect print on it. The only problem was, it didn't belong to Buddy. We wondered how he'd explain that. So we asked him."

"Whose print was it?" Jane had to know. But then, when he didn't answer right away, she wondered if she'd crossed a line.

"It belonged to Christian Wallace. We had his prints on file because of the police investigation of his dad's murder. I'm not positive, but I think Buddy's attorney overheard a couple of my officers talking about it in the hallway."

"Why do you say that?"

"Because when the lawyer returned to the interrogation room after stepping out to get a drink of water, he asked for a private conference with his client. When we resumed questioning, Buddy seemed different somehow. We asked him why there were none of his fingerprints on the plastic sack. He said he used gloves. We asked him where the gloves were. He said he'd thrown them away. We asked him where. He said in a dumpster behind the church. We checked behind the church."

"No gloves?"

"No dumpster. Then he told us he flushed the contents of the teapot down the toilet before he and Roland left for the church, including the tea bags. But we found the two regular tea bags in the bathroom garbage. So we asked him about that. He said he got confused. He meant to say that he'd only thrown out the contents of the teapot. We asked him what he'd done with the little metal tea ball. He said he cleaned it and put it back in the kitchen drawer with the rest of them. We asked which drawer. He said the one next to the silverware drawer. He was right about that. But we only found one metal ball, and it was rusted shut, like it hadn't been used in years. He said the 'rest of them,' like there were a bunch there. We called him on it. He said there were usually at least two, but maybe one had gotten lost. He couldn't remember. How was he supposed to remember details like that? He was in a hurry.

"Then we wanted to know where he got the jimsonweed. He said he bought it at a store in New York City. He knew it was poison because of what his granddaughter had told him about the man who built Innishannon. He said he went to the library and studied up on the weed. But he couldn't recall the name of the business where he bought it *or* the location. He was a old man and his memory wasn't what it used to be. As far as I was concerned, it was all sounding fishier and fishier. I couldn't take that story to the D.A. and tell her to make a case out of it. She'd laugh me right out of her office."

"Did you ever ask him about Christian? About his fingerprint?"

"No, we didn't want to tip him off—just in case I was wrong about him already knowing." He pushed the cake toward her. "At least take a taste. You'll be sorry if you don't."

She picked up her fork and cut off a good-sized bite. "Hey, it's wonderful. Really."

"The secret is ground hazelnuts and espresso. And the chocolate frosting is a buttercream with something else in it—can't remember. Must be my age." He grinned.

She took another bite.

"See," he said, beaming. "Would I give a restaurateur bad food advice?"

"Not if you know what's good for you."

"We did ask Buddy some general questions about Christian. He doesn't like the guy, that came through loud and clear. He said he'd been on Roland's payroll for years. Seems Roland wanted to keep Christian quiet about his relationship with Christian's father—Lew Wallace. They were lovers. We asked how much he paid. Buddy said that the usual Christmas check was for something like one hundred thousand dollars. This year, he got an extra one hundred thou."

"Have you called Christian in to talk to him?"

He shook his head, pushing the empty plate away and pulling his coffee cup in front of him. "We wanted to do some checking first. Seems the guy's a producer—not a real steady profession, but a lucrative one, on and off. From what we could find out, Christian experienced some bad luck with his last two movies. He's dead broke."

"He told me he'd asked Roland to back his latest film project. He sounded pretty hungry, like he was really counting on it."

Toscano seemed interested. "Buddy told us that Roland pulled the plug on Christian the night before the wedding. Told him to get out of the house and never come back. No more money. In my book, that's another strong motive."

"Does he inherit anything in the new will?"

"You really should think about going into police work, Jane. Yes, he gets two million in cash and some miscellaneous stock worth, maybe, another couple hundred thousand."

"Did he know he would inherit?"

"A guy like him? I'd be surprised if he didn't."

"But then, if Buddy wasn't guilty, why would he confess?"

Toscano shook his head. "First, I'm not sure he isn't guilty. But, for the sake of argument, let's say he isn't. The first thing that comes to my mind is that he was trying to protect someone."

"Who?"

"His granddaughter? I don't suppose you'd have any idea why he might do that?"

"Actually—" She hesitated.

"Come on, Jane. Let's have a little give and take. If you know something, tell me."

"Well, in the earlier will, Grace got Innishannon. In the new will, Octavia got it."

"But Grace inherited one million in the new will and no cash in the old. And she got some huge, fancy house in Sante Fe. She might take a financial hit, but she still comes out way ahead."

"You don't know the whole story." Jane filled him in on the evening she spent in Gracieland, as well as the conversation she'd overheard between Buddy and Gracie in the stables. She also mentioned her website, told him to check it out.

"Well, there you have it," said Toscano, leaning back in his chair. "Buddy threw himself to the dogs in place of his granddaughter. But all that means is Buddy *thinks* she's guilty. It doesn't mean she really is."

Jane waited as a waitress warmed Toscano's coffee and then hers. "So, you don't think Roland's death had anything to do with Lew Wallace's murder?"

"No," he said, stirring more sugar into his coffee. "I don't. Not that what you discovered isn't interesting. I had the L.A.P.D. fax me what they had on the old murder case. You covered all the basic points the other night. Who knows? Maybe someday, someone will solve it. I hope they do. But I've got to spend my time where it counts, and that won't be digging through Hollywood history. I'll leave that to you." His pager went off again. "Damn," he said, picking it up and glaring at it. He digested the information, then said, "This time I've got to go. I'm sorry."

Jane smiled at him. "This has been fun—and instructive."

"Good. Then, when I invite you to dinner, will you come?"

"As long as it isn't tomorrow night. Cordelia and I have theater tickets for a Broadway show."

"Which one?"

"A Moon for the Misbegotten."

"The Eugene O'Neill revival. I hear it's supposed to be fabulous." As he rose from his chair, he tossed some cash on the table. "Oh, I should tell you. I sent one of my men out to Innishannon this morning. I wanted to make sure everyone's going to stick around for a few more days."

"I think Cordelia's father wants to drive back up to Boston tomorrow morning. But you don't need him, do you?"

His expression sobered.

"What? You can't possibly think he had anything to do with Roland's murder."

"Look, Jane, I know Cordelia is a good friend of yours. But, yes, her father is a suspect."

"But—"

"If I tell you something, can you keep it under your hat? I'm taking a chance here, so you've got to promise me."

"Sure, I promise."

"We talked to a bunch of his associates at Boston Central. The week before the wedding, he told a friend—another doctor—that he'd rather see Roland dead than married to his daughter."

"But . . . that's just something people say when they're upset."

"Maybe. Then again, who would have a better working knowledge of poison than a doctor?"

Jane was dumbstruck. She thought back to the meeting between Hiram and Roland in Asbury, several days before the wedding. She wondered for a second if she shouldn't say something to Toscano. There was obviously bad blood between them, but . . . murder? "I can't believe Hiram Thorn could . . . could kill someone."

"For your sake, I hope he didn't." He tipped his head toward the door. "Can I walk you out?"

"No, I think I'll stay and finish my coffee." It was probably just vanity, but she couldn't stand that thought of him watching her limp outside to her car.

"When are you and Cordelia leaving?"

"The way it looks now, we'll probably be here through New Year's. After that, I've got to get home, even if Cordelia decides to stay."

"I'll call you."

"Okay." She smiled. "Thanks for lunch."

33

After, lunch, Jane drove to New Haven. Crown Coaches was located on Spaulding Avenue, just north of I-95. Before leaving the house, she'd called to ask if it would be possible to talk with Mr. Yablonski today, Roland Lester's limousine driver. The woman who answered said he had a morning run, but should be back at the lot sometime around two. If Jane didn't mind waiting a few minutes, she was sure he'd be able to see her. She also mentioned that he was the manager now. He only went out on runs when it was an old, valued customer like Mr. Lester, one who asked for him personally.

Jane pulled up to the curb across the street from the lot at a few minutes after two. Five limousines of various sizes—two white and three black—were parked next to a small, one-story building. There were spaces for eight other limos, suggesting to Jane that it was a thriving business.

As she was about to lock up the car, she noticed Octavia's cell phone lying on the passenger seat. Thinking that it should be hidden from view, she picked it up and was about to slide it under the seat when she changed her mind and slipped it into the pocket of her leather jacket. She never carried a cell phone back home in Minneapolis, but in a strange town, it seemed like a good idea.

Once inside the building, Jane approached the secretary. There were three offices behind the main counter. One of them had the name "Dave Yablonski" on it, the other two just said "Office."

"Can I help you?" asked the woman, her eyes dropping to Jane's cane.

"I called earlier. My name's Jane Lawless."

"Oh, right, Mr. Lester's friend." She tapped a pencil against the side of her head, giving Jane the once-over. "You wanted to talk to Dave. He's here. Let me just see if he's available." Pushing a button on her console, she announced Jane's arrival. "Go right in," she said, poking her thumb at the partially open door.

Jane found Mr. Yablonski seated behind a desk, his attention riveted to a computer screen. He was past middle age, with receding brown hair, dark circles under his eyes, and a thin, wiry body. He had on a white shirt and tie, a black chauffeur's coat and cap hanging on a rack in the corner. She stood in front of him for a few seconds while he finished typing.

"Ms. Lawless," he said finally, looking up and smiling expansively. "Please, have a seat. I understand you wanted to talk to me about Mr. Lester. First——" The smile dimmed. "——let me say that I was so sorry to hear of his recent death. He was one of our oldest and most valued customers."

Jane made herself comfortable. "And an old friend of mine."

"Of course," he said, studying her for a second. "I understand he was . . . poisoned?"

"That's what the police think."

"Awful. Simply horrible. But then, when big money is involved——"

"That's what I think, too," she said in a confidential tone. She was trying to play him. By bringing the conversation down to a more intimate level, she hoped he'd respond in kind.

"Do the police have a suspect?"

She paused dramatically, then lowered her voice for emphasis. "Just between you and me, they found a fingerprint on the murder weapon."

"Really." He leaned forward. "I hear it was tea. Poison tea. They must have found something on the teapot."

Another nod. "An arrest is imminent."

"Do you know who?"

"Someone you'd never suspect. I can't say any more."

"Wow." His voice was almost a whisper. "How do you know Mr. Lester?"

"Oh, I've known Roland since I was a child. My father was a set designer at Fox. They worked together on a whole bunch of movies."

"No kidding." Again, he scrutinized her face. "And you were here for the wedding, I suppose."

"I was. As I told your secretary, I'm staying out at Innishannon. I have a couple of questions I hoped you could answer. That's why I'm here today."

"Sure, anything I can do, just ask."

She smiled. "I'm a writer by trade, mostly fiction, but I'm thinking of doing a biography of Roland. The last, oh, fifteen, twenty years of his life are rather blank. I understand you drove him into New York regularly."

"I've been his driver since 1987."

Jane took out a pen and a notebook, flipping to the first open page. "How often did he go to New York?"

"A couple times a month. Sometimes less, occasionally more."

"I understand he always took a heavy piece of luggage with him."

"Well, it was heavy when he left, but it was empty when he returned."

That was interesting. "Did he ever comment on it? What was inside?"

"Never. Mr. Lester was a very private man."

That would be his epitaph, thought Jane, unless Ellie used her documentary to open up his life, to reveal his secrets and explain why he had to remain silent about so many things. "Did he have an apartment in New York?"

"Actually, he always had me drop him off at the post office in Times Square. I'd carry that suitcase into the building and get him set up in line so he could push the luggage along with his foot instead of having to pick it up."

"Are you saying he mailed the contents of the suitcase somewhere?"

"I don't know anything for a fact, but that would be my guess."

Musing out loud, Jane said, "I wonder if he stayed at some hotel."

Yablonski folded his hands on the desk top. Whatever he was thinking made him grow increasingly uncomfortable. Finally, he said, "No, I don't think so."

"Why's that?"

"Well—" He hesitated. "I don't usually pry into my customers' lives,

277

you understand, but in Mr. Lester's case, I had my reasons. I wanted to see where he went after I dropped him off." Again, he paused.

"I'm all ears," said Jane, prompting him.

"Well, when he was done at the post office, he hailed a cab. It took him to the Upper West Side."

"Do you have an exact address?"

"Sure. I used to drop another customer of mine off a few doors down. It's One-sixteen West Eighty-Sixth."

Jane wrote it down.

"A brownstone. Mr. Lester paid the cabby, then carried the suitcase up the steps and used his key to go inside. I had another run in New York that afternoon, but I went back later that night after dark, just to make sure it really was his place."

"And?"

"There was another man's name on the mailbox."

"Do you remember what it was?"

"Sorry. I figured Mr. Lester probably stayed with a friend when he was in town. Made sense to me."

"But . . . didn't you pick him up at that address when he was ready to come home?"

"No, he was always standing right outside the post office in Times Square. Rain or shine, sleet or snow. Like I said, he didn't want anybody knowing his business."

Jane made a few more notes. Looking up, she saw him watching her. He must wonder what he's getting himself into, she thought. "I can't tell you how glad I am that you followed Roland, Mr. Yablonski."

"Dave."

Again, she smiled. "Dave. Your name will never appear in print—unless you'd like it too, of course—but that was a stroke of genius."

"It was?"

"It's given me a window into Roland's life, one I could never have gotten any other way."

"Well, gee . . . thanks. I was just using my natural instincts."

"You should have been a private detective, Mr.—I mean, Dave. Like Spencer up in Boston."

"Or Magnum P.I. That guy was the best."

"Tell me, what made you decide to follow Mr. Lester in the first place?"

"Simple. About a year ago, I'd taken him into New York on a

278

Monday. It was wintertime. He told me to come back for him the following Thursday. I said, fine. I'd be there. I stayed in New York that night, did some short runs, then drove a client up to New Haven the next morning. That was a Tuesday. After dropping her off at the AmeriSuites in Shelton, I got a hankering for a bowl of chili at the Clockwork Grill in Wister." At Jane's questioning look, he added, "It's all part of the Greater New Haven area. Anyway, I'd just come out of the cafe when I saw this man on the other side of the street. He was coming out of a convenience store carrying a sack of groceries. He didn't look like Lester—I mean, he had a dark beard and dark hair, so he had to be a lot younger, but something about the way he walked reminded me of the old guy. I watched him for a couple more seconds, and that's when I saw it."

"Saw what?"

"His walking stick. The one with the gold handle. The crazy-looking head. He always took it with him when he went out. You've probably seen it lots of times. Anyway, how many guys do you see walking around with a cane like that?" He waited for her answer.

"Not many."

"The answer is, *none*. It had to be Lester. The beard, the hair, all fake. So I called out to him. Hey, Mr. Lester. Why the get-up?"

"What did he say?"

"Nothing. He looked a little startled, then he turned his back to me and walked away as fast as he could, which wasn't very fast. And that led me to believe he was the old man."

"Did you follow him?"

"Not then. But it got me to wondering. I'd dropped him off in Manhattan on Monday. If I was right about spotting him, he was in Wister on Tuesday afternoon. And when I went to pick him up on Thursday, there he was, big as life, standing right in front of the post office in Times Square. So I figured the guy was up to something kind of hinky, you know what I mean? If he wasn't, why the disguise?"

"Did he say anything about it when he got into the limo that Thursday?"

"Not a blessed word. Acted like it never happened. But it did. And it bugged the hell out of me. That's why I followed him in New York the next time I drove him down. Near as I can figure, he must stay at the brownstone for the night, then take the train—Metro North—up to New Haven, and a cab or whatever to Wister. Then, a day or two later, he reverses it. He takes Metro North south to Grand Central. Maybe he stays another night at the brownstone, and then he meets me at the appointed place at the appointed time. That way, nobody knows what he's up to."

"And what was he up to?"

"Beats the hell out of me."

Jane had to admit, it beat the hell out of her too. "But, doesn't it seem like a lot of trouble to go to, just to hide your destination?" Roland saw lots of plays and films while he was in New York, so he couldn't have spent all his time in Wister. And what on earth was in Wister anyway? Something didn't gel.

"Hey, I'm just telling you what I saw."

"And I appreciate it," said Jane. "One last question. The last time Mr. Lester went to New York was a week or so ago."

"Right."

"He told his brother that he thought someone had followed the limo. Do you know anything about it?"

"Sure. It was a green Jeep Cherokee. Lester was pretty upset. He got out of the limo where he normally does, but left the luggage in the trunk. Asked me to take it back to Innishannon."

"Did you?"

"Sure. But not before I nailed the guy's license plate, just in case Mr. Lester wanted it later. Problem was, I never saw Lester again. He made it home that time without my help. And then . . . next I hear, he's dead."

Jane's pulse quickened. "I don't suppose you remember the plate number."

He pulled some slips of paper out of the top drawer of his desk. Finding the one he wanted, he said, "YTM nine seven three. Connecticut plates."

She wrote it down. Rising from her chair, she held out her hand to thank him for his time. "You've been a huge help, Dave."

"Just make sure you spell my name right in the book you're writing."

"It's a promise."

34

On the drive back to Innishannon, Jane got to thinking about the fax she'd found yesterday in the tack house. She wanted to call this Salvador Barros herself and ask him what he knew about the 1940's card game, the one Ellie thought might hold the key to a scandal that would rock Hollywood to its very foundations. The problem was, if Jane talked to him and he said something to Ellie about it, how would she explain where she got his name and phone number? No, she had to wait. She decided right then and there to pay a visit to Ellie. Cordelia and Octavia were no doubt squabbling about private investigators, arguing over various ins and outs, hiring themselves up a storm. If she allowed herself to be sucked back into their clutches, Jane was afraid she wouldn't be able to get away from the Sisters of the Unholy Obsession for the rest of the day—well, at least, not without a gun and a silk stocking.

Before that happened, she wanted to tell Ellie the good news about the three boxes of personal files Octavia was planning to give her. In return, Jane hoped she could get Ellie to talk more openly about the video that had been stolen from the tack house yesterday afternoon, and that openness might lead back to the fax. Jane finally had some leverage, not just because of the boxes, but because she'd discovered information Ellie didn't have. She would only part with it in return for Ellie's cooperation.

Jane felt certain she was on the trail of something big, something Roland had spent the last twenty years of his life—perhaps even longer—trying to keep secret. Octavia and Cordelia could search for warehouses until hell froze over. As far as Jane was concerned, she had more important avenues to pursue. She reasoned that it was all connected: Lew's murder, Roland's murder, the scandal, the old films Roland and Buddy were amassing, Ellie's documentary of her grandfather, and her interest in Roland's past.

Parking Octavia's Volvo in front of the stables, Jane limped up to the tack house door and knocked. Ellie's van was outside, which meant she was home. Jane's luck was holding. She'd put some important pieces of the puzzle together today, and she was about to add a few more. When there was no answer, she knocked again. Finally, in frustration, she shouted, "Ellie, are you in there?" She banged on the door with her fist.

Using her cane to help maneuver her through a patch of ice and snow-covered brush, she edged up to the front window and squinted through a crack in the curtains. She assumed it was a little unusual for the curtains to be closed on such a bright, sunny day, but maybe Ellie was editing film or watching TV, or whatever she did when she wasn't conducting an interview.

Cupping her hands against the glass, Jane made a quick scan of the front room. Maybe Ellie was sleeping in her bunk. Or maybe she'd gone out for a walk. All Jane knew was that every explanation she came up with only made the knot in her stomach twist harder.

Walking around to the side of the house, she looked through a second window. This time she saw her. Ellie was lying face down on the braided wool rug—and she wasn't moving. Seized by panic, Jane rushed back to the front door and tried to break it down. She flung her shoulder at the door with all her might, but it was no use. It wouldn't budge. As she scanned the outside of the cottage, looking for something to help her get inside, she spied a metal trash can. She tossed her cane away, picked it up and heaved it through the front window. Then, taking the wool scarf from around her neck and winding it around her hand, she knocked the rest of the glass away from the frame. An instant later, she was inside.

The rush of adrenaline that hit her system was so powerful, she forgot about the pain in her knee and the weakness in her leg. All she could think about was Ellie—reaching her, helping her. But when she saw the heavy iron shovel leaning against the refrigerator door and the back of Ellie's head crushed by a brutal blow, her mind short-circuited. Time and place got mixed up. Instead of the tack house, she was back home in Minneapolis. It was night. She was alone. She'd just heard a strange sound coming from the study. Now she was sprawled across the desk, terrified by the pain inside her head, sinking, slipping, falling to the floor, trying to focus her eyes on a face, but she couldn't. She couldn't even keep her eyes open. The world was going dark. She had to get up, get away!

Rushing to the door, Jane threw back the bolt, bursting into the sunshine. Inside her mind, it was the dead of night. She lunged into the woods behind the stables, bare branches tearing at her clothes. She fell, slipping on the ice, tripping over rocks, but kept moving, crawling away, have to get away, running as fast as she could, the brush scraping her face, running until she couldn't run a foot farther.

Her left leg finally collapsed and she collapsed with it. Covering her head with her arms, she lay motionless, cringing in terror, gasping for air. She was crying, shivering, craven. This was the end. It had to be. Any second now he'd find her. She was helpless, so tired she couldn't move. It was her dream. And there was Ellie, lying on the floor. The gash in her head. The blood. The coffee pot still on. Two mugs on the counter. The smell of stale smoke. And the glass from the window all over the floor. He must have gotten in through the window. Sure. But—

Jane closed her eyes and fought to concentrate. Hadn't she broken the glass? She was standing outside looking in, and then she was inside, trying to get out. Everything was all screwed up.

As her breathing became more regular and her heart rate slowed, she lowered her arms and looked around. It was as if someone had turned on a light switch. All of a sudden, it was daytime again, and she was . . . lying in a puddle of freezing water in the middle of nowhere. She sat up, running a hand through her hair and trying to get her bearings. What the hell had happened? Every muscle in her body ached. Her knee was on fire, and at the same time she was both sweating and freezing cold. And her cane? Where was her cane?

The truth of what had just happened began to seep slowly into her consciousness. She must have freaked out when she saw Ellie. It was like a repeat performance of what had happened to her.

And then . . . the reality of the situation descended.

Ellie was still on the floor of the tack house.

Jane had to get back to her. Wait, she thought, trying desperately to keep her nerves from short-circuiting again. Calm down. Breathe. With a wound like that, there was very little chance she was alive. But Jane couldn't be sure until she checked.

Remembering the cell phone in her pocket, she ripped it free from the wet, tangled mess that had become her jacket and punched in 911. Her voice shook as she explained to the dispatcher what little she knew. She gave him the address and then said she'd meet the police outside the stables. She had every intention of keeping her promise, that is, if she could find her way back, and if her legs would carry her that far. At this moment, those felt like two big "if"s."

One thing Jane knew for sure. She'd never tell a living soul what happened—how she'd found Ellie and then run off like some scared, cowardly dog. She was embarrassed and frightened by her crazy behavior. She was coming apart, having some sort of breakdown. She had to get her mind off her emotions, had to focus on the here and now. Pull it together. Get back to the stables. Deal with the police. And in the process, she needed to think up a good excuse for why she looked the way she did.

Jane didn't return to the main house until after dark. The police had been busy at the tack house for hours, taking pictures, gathering evidence, and getting statements from the mansion's inhabitants who'd all rushed down to the stables as soon as they'd heard the sirens.

Ellie's body had been covered with a sheet, but wouldn't be removed until later. Toscano, who'd arrived shortly after the paramedics, said that he and his men would probably be around most of the night. He encouraged Jane to leave. Get out of her wet clothes and get some dinner. When she finally did go, she saw that virtually everyone was still standing outside in the cold, waiting for the smallest crumb of information.

Cordelia cornered her by Octavia's car.

"Are you okay?"

"Yeah. I'm just a little shaken up."

"Then what happened to you?" She touched Jane's face.

The thought of going through the entire story again was too much, but she had to say something. "When I found Ellie, I thought I heard something outside, behind the stables. So I went around back to see what it was. That's when I thought I saw movement in the woods."

"So you took off after her killer?" Cordelia's eyes bulged with horror.

"No, Cordelia. Nobody was there. I just slipped on the ice and fell in a puddle."

"Chasing the murderer!"

"Will you please lower your voice." They were getting looks from the crowd. "Listen to me. Ellie's been dead for hours, probably since this morning. Just ask Toscano if you don't believe me. I didn't risk anything."

"Nothing but your life!" She crushed Jane against her, then held her at arm's length. "Are you sure you're okay?"

"I'm freezing to death, but other than that, I'm fine. I'm going to drive Octavia's car back to the main house."

"Take a hot tub. Good. Use my bubble bath. It's in my room on the dresser. Lilac or Lilly of the Valley. Whatever appeals to you."

As if bubble bath could help. "And then I'm going to bed. We'll talk in the morning."

"Right. I'll fill you in on the private investigators we hired."

Jane couldn't wait.

Back at the house, she peeled off her wet clothes in the bathroom and then stepped into the shower. The hot water felt good as it flowed down her body, over every curve, every raw nerve. She turned her face up to the spray, letting it wash through her hair and down her back. The intensity of the past few hours had left her physically and emotionally exhausted. But a welcome numbness was creeping inside her now. If she stood motionless, waited just a little while longer, she hoped it would take over completely.

Half an hour later, she'd put on a white terrycloth robe and was lying in the center of her bed, listening to the clock tick. She wanted to sleep. The hot water had relaxed her muscles, but had done nothing for the lump of tension in her stomach. In fact, now, she had something new to keep her awake. Every few minutes she felt a tiny adrenaline rush. It was a strange sensation, as if someone were touching her with an exposed electrical wire. But there was no stimulus, nothing frightening. Her body was on automatic. She'd never experienced anything like it before, and she prayed it would go away. At the same time, she was afraid it wouldn't.

After staring at the ceiling for a few more minutes, she got up and dressed. She didn't know what else to do. As she came down the stairs, she saw that the house was still quiet. The kitchen was also deserted, so she scrambled herself a couple of eggs, made some toast, and ate in the dining room alone. If at all possible, she didn't want to talk to anyone for the rest of the night. But the idea of spending what was left of the evening cooped up in her bedroom was too depressing.

She finally decided to take a chance on the billiard room. It was in the back of the house, and she assumed nobody was going to be playing games tonight. Also, it was the only room on the main floor, other than the living room, that had a working fireplace. After pouring herself a triple cognac from the decanter on the drinks cart, she limped down the hall to the billiard room and busied herself building a fire. Her knee ached when she put too much weight on it, but after the workout she'd put it through today, it could have been much worse.

When she was all done, she turned off the lights and sat down on the old leather couch. Analysis could wait. All she wanted was to sit and sip her drink—if possible, achieve a certain degree of oblivion, one that would allow her a few hours of sleep.

Her glass was almost empty when she heard footsteps in the hallway. Turning toward the door, she willed it to remain closed, but her psychic efforts were useless. As the door moved inward, the dark silhouette of a man came slowly into view.

"Oh," said Christian, stopping just inside the room. He squinted toward the fireplace. The fire had burned down to glowing embers, but it was still visible. "Is someone here?"

"It's Jane."

He switched on the top light. "Great minds think alike. Are you hiding?"

"That was the idea."

"Mind if I throw another log on and join you?"

Before she could think of a polite way to say "get the hell out of here," he was searching through the wood box for a suitable log. "Birch will catch the fastest. Here's one." He carried it to the hearth, gave the embers a good stoke, then tossed it on. When the log finally ignited, he swiveled around and rubbed his hands together expectantly. At the same time, his gaze dropped to Jane's glass. "I think I'll join you."

Moving over to a small mahogany chest, he flipped open the top, revealing a set of crystal decanters and glass tumblers. "Back in the days

286

of yore, when the men would retire to the billiard room after dinner with their cigars and brandy, this mini-bar was used all the time. I understand it's left over from Innishannon's original owner." He poured himself a Scotch, then nodded to the decanters. "Would you like another?"

If she had to put up with his presence, she might as well. "Sure. Why not."

"What are you drinking?"

"Courvoisier."

Once the liquor had been poured, and the lights turned back off, he settled himself into a chair next to the couch. "Awful business down at the stables."

It was just the opening she'd dreaded, and it was enough to shatter her fragile calm.

"Must have been a terrible shock, finding her like you did. I understand you're quite the hero, chasing the killer into the woods."

Jane took a larger than normal swallow of cognac. She was already well past caring how much she'd had to drink. "Just to set the record straight, it wasn't the killer. It was probably a deer."

"You're too modest." He reflected a moment as he watched the fire, then continued, "It seemed to me that you and Ellie were becoming pretty good friends. You were together on the beach the other day. And I've seen you talking together several times."

"I liked her," said Jane. Tears burned her eyes. She had to change the subject, either that or she had to leave. "Is everyone back from the stables?"

"Just about. They've all gathered in the living room. I couldn't take it. It's like a wake without the body or the priest. But poor Verna." He sighed.

Jane slowly turned to him. "What's wrong with Verna?"

"She's still down there. That police detective—Toscano—is questioning her. Seems they found two of her cigarette butts in an ashtray."

Jane didn't understand. "What does that prove?"

"Don't ask me, I'm not the expert. It was Toscano who seemed to think it was a *vital* clue. Especially after what happened last night."

"And what was that?"

"Well—" He seemed to relish knowing something she didn't. "I don't believe you were around much last evening, but a police officer rang the front doorbell around nine. He'd come to check on Roland's study. I assumed he wanted to see if anyone had tampered with the police tape they'd stretched across the door. He was here for a few minutes, and then left. The same man came back shortly after one today, ostensibly we were told, to remove the tape. But when he got upstairs he discovered one of Roland's filing cabinets had been broken into. I assume it must have happened in the night."

"What was taken?"

"I have no idea. But . . . this is just speculation now, you understand." He paused to take a sip of his drink. "I think Verna did it."

"Why do you say that?"

"Just the way she's been acting all day. She gets all feisty and defensive when she thinks someone's about to challenge her actions. Verna always knows best. It's her cross."

"Have the police talked to you about Roland's murder yet?"

He seemed startled. "You mean besides the other night? No. Why should they?"

"No reason, I was just curious." Even in the darkness, she could feel him studying her face. "Tell me, Christian, when you were growing up, did you know that your father was gay?"

He shrugged irritably.

Jane figured if he didn't like her questions, he could leave. She hoped he would.

After a few seconds, he said, "Sure, I knew what he was. My mother called him a filthy faggot every chance she got. I didn't understand what she meant at first, I just knew it was bad. Eventually, I learned all the terms. She was a foul-mouthed old hag, and I hated her guts, but I hated my father even more. It's hard for a man to admit something like this, but my father never loved me. He was far too busy being a movie star to spend time with his son. Not that I cared. I was ashamed of what he was. I didn't even want to be around him. On those rare occasions when he did come by the house to take me to the park or the zoo, I'd refuse to go. People always said to me, 'Wow, Christian, it must be great having Lew Wallace for a father.' I'd just smile. I learned early on to keep my mouth shut. But I was never—ever—going to be like him. How could he do that to me? I needed a father, not a fairy!"

"You must have really hated Roland."

He was about to respond, when he realized he'd crossed a line and said too much. "Why, no," he said after a few well-considered seconds. "Roland was always nice to me. In fact, I didn't know about his relationship with my father until I was quite a bit older, although I'd known Roland since I was seven or eight. When I was a teenager, I remember fantasizing that there'd been a mistake at the hospital. Roland was my real dad and Verna was my mom. She was so much fun. And Roland—God, the way he doted on his daughter, Peg. I freely admit I was jealous."

"Then, you don't hate all faggots?"

He turned to look her square in the eyes. "No, Jane. Just the ones who pretend to be fathers."

Before he could say more, the door to the billiard room opened again.

"Christian?" It was Gracie. "I need to talk to you." She sounded upset.

Instantly, he rose from his chair. "What's wrong?"

"Can you come now?"

He glanced down at Jane. "I'm sorry, but we'll have to finish our conversation another time."

Even in the darkness, she could see the relief in his eyes. He didn't want to talk about his childhood any more than she wanted to discuss her heroism. "I'll look forward to it."

Moments later they were gone.

Finding her cane pushed halfway under the couch, she got up and threw a couple more logs on the fire. When she sat back down, a wave of exhaustion hit her so hard she could barely lift her legs up to lie down. She knew she should probably go upstairs to her bedroom, but to do that would require her to pass the living room. She couldn't risk it. What if someone stopped her? Wanted to talk? The fire had taken the chill off the room. And the leather couch was reasonably comfortable. Snatching a pillow from the other end, she stretched out. It felt so good just to give in.

Before she drifted off to sleep, she concluded that beds were oppressive inventions. They held such promise for the weary, exhausted soul, but at the same time, their expectations were too high. If you didn't get down to business and fall asleep right away, you became a disappointment. Couches were better. All they ever expected of you was a nap.

Jane woke shortly before three, shivering cold and miserable. The fire had gone out long ago, and she felt as if she'd been lying on a field of lopsided footballs. Rubbing the small of her back, she located her cane and got up. Thankfully, the curtains were open, so the moonlight guided her to the door.

As she trudged up the central staircase, she thought she heard the faint sound of crying. The closer she got to her room, the louder the sobs became. She realized it had to be Gracie. Of course, she'd been upset earlier. But that was hours ago.

Walking beyond her room to the servants' stairs, Jane listened for a moment. She could hear a male voice talking now. But it wasn't Christian. She closed her eyes and bent her head in concentration.

She finally realized it was Buddy. He was speaking gently, softly. She couldn't make out his words, but she could tell that whatever he was saying, it wasn't working. Gracie continued to cry, her words garbled by her sobs. And she sounded angry. Jane assumed that she was still upset about losing Innishannon to Octavia. Christian must not have been able to help, so she'd turned to her grandfather.

Poor Buddy, thought Jane, walking wearily back to her room. When it came to his granddaughter, he had his hands full.

35

I don't want to talk about it anymore," said Jane. Her patience was just about exhausted. "It's over and done with. I'm fine. I wish I could say the same for Ellie."

"But . . . why do you *do* such foolish, dangerous things?" Cordelia sat behind the wheel of her father's Lincoln, gesturing so broadly that if they'd been in a smaller car, she would have smacked Jane in the face.

Since noon, they'd been speeding down I-95 heading for New York City. Jane's Christmas present to Cordelia had been two Broadway theatre tickets. With Ellie's death still so fresh in her mind, she felt intensely guilty about leaving Innishannon, even for one night, but since she had a pressing reason for wanting to visit New York, she felt she had to go. And anyway, Cordelia would have been terribly disappointed if they'd missed the O'Neill revival. She needed some time to relax and unwind too, except that she was unwinding all over Jane.

First it was Octavia. She looked awful. She wasn't eating. She was being contentious, obnoxious, furtive. Calling private investigators yesterday had been nothing but an exercise in futility. Octavia had played it so close to the chest, she wouldn't give the poor saps more than a shred of information to help them find the warehouse. And still, she expected miracles. Miracles! She wouldn't listen to the voice of reason—a.k.a., Cordelia. And this morning, she refused to come out of the bathroom to say good-bye. Octavia was scheming, or she was depressed, or self-consumed, or deluded, but whatever it was, it was driving Cordelia up the wall!

And then there was their father. Dr. Thorn had gotten stinking drunk again last night. Cordelia and Octavia had to pour him into bed. He'd been on his best behavior for one night, but after the discovery of Ellie's body in the tack house, he'd had a good dozen vodkas with lime. It was disgusting, but at least he wasn't bitching anymore about going back to Boston. He'd agreed to stay on at Innishannon through New Year's, which gave the two sisters a little more time to figure out how to handle the situation. Cordelia insisted that he needed to get into drug rehab ASAP, but Octavia kept waffling. She didn't want to confront him about his drinking—not yet. Couldn't Cordelia see he still hadn't gotten over their mother's death? Cordelia insisted that was the point. Octavia's own guilt was preventing her from seeing how desperately he needed help. "It's almost as if she's trying to protect him from me. As if," she snapped. *"As if."*

"As if what?" asked Jane, leaning her head back against the headrest and closing her eyes.

"As if I wanted to hurt him."

"Maybe she thinks he'll hurt you."

"How could he hurt me?"

"Okay, maybe she's protecting herself."

"Of course she is! At Dad's expense. That woman drives me wild!" Cordelia turned down the car's heater. For the moment, she was providing her own. "He's right on the edge, Janey. He's not even acting like himself anymore. For instance, in the past couple days, when we're talking, just shooting the breeze, he tears up. For no reason. Yesterday we were discussing the rug color in the hallway. A really passion-filled topic, right? I might be able to work up some genuine emotion about it—mainly horror—but my father could care less. But when I turned around, there he was, batting a tear away from his cheek. Oh, he tries to hide it, but his face gets all mottled and puffy. Remember how I always thought he looked like Albert Finney? Well, he's looking more and more like W. C. Fields to me all the time. And with his little snarling asides, he's about as subtle. He gets angry at the drop of a hat, and then the next minute, he's telling me how much he loves me—or Octavia, or Mom. His emotions are all over the place. I know it's the booze, and his own guilt over Mom's death. But, I mean . . . really! All that blustering on Christmas Eve about Roland being a faggot. In *my* presence. The man's lost touch with reality. He's a born meddler, Jane. Thank God I never inherited that failing."

Jane recalled what Toscano had told her yesterday. Hiram Thorn had actually made a threat against Roland's life. Sure, it could be explained away. It was just a passing remark, the sort of thing people often say when they're upset. But the man Cordelia had just described to her was no longer in control of himself. Anything was possible.

"And then yesterday," continued Cordelia, munching on some corn chips, "I find out you've been chasing down murderers in the woods. I asked you to come to Connecticut to help me, not give me a heart attack."

"Let's drop the subject, okay?"

Cordelia harumphed. "At least tell me why we had to leave so early today. We can't check into our hotel until three. Knowing you, I doubt you want to spend the afternoon shopping. Not that I'd mind. A little mindless consumption sounds good to me right about now."

After a bad night's sleep, Jane was tired. She'd hoped to take a short nap before they hit Manhattan. But first, she had to fill Cordelia in on what she'd learned about Roland—his trips to New York with the old suitcase, the Times Square post office, his limo driver spotting him in Wister, the disguise, and the brownstone in the West Eighties. Jane didn't know what it all meant, but she intended to find out.

After stopping for a quick lunch in Stamford, they arrived at the brownstone just after two. Cordelia performed an incredible piece of curbside surgery, parking the car with only millimeters to spare between a Saab and a BMW. The traffic in Manhattan had been typically congested. They would have made better time, but in order to circumvent a traffic accident, Cordelia hung a right, zooming up behind a slow-moving garbage truck. Two years later, the truck turned. Out of frustration, Cordelia turned in the opposite direction and they found themselves on a one-way heading straight for Central Park.

Easing out of the front seat of the Lincoln, they stood for a moment gazing at the brownstone.

"Very posh." whispered Cordelia, her eyes traveling up four flights to the top of the building.

"I hope someone's home," Jane whispered back.

"You're sure the place doesn't belong to Roland?"

"For all I know, Alfred Hitchcock could greet us at the door."

"Let's hope not. He's been dead for over twenty years."

As they walked up the steep stone steps, Cordelia fluffed her hair and inspected her clothes. At Jane's questioning glance, she said, "Just in case it's someone a little more contemporary. Like Steven Spielberg. Look," she whispered, frowning thoughtfully as Jane rang the bell. "The name on the mailbox says 'Gorham.' "

A moment later, the door drew slowly inward. Standing before them was a tall, elegantly thin, elderly man who could have easily been a butler—he'd played many—but was instead one of Britain's greatest living actors. He wore the same sardonic smile that had made him world famous. "May I help you?"

"My God," rasped Cordelia, unable to move or even blink. "Sir Jefferey Gorham."

Since Jane was every bit as tongue-tied as Cordelia, Sir Jefferey finally said, "Thank you, my dear. At my age, it's good to have these little reminders. But may I assume you're here for another reason?" He rubbed his index finger against his thumb, waiting.

Recovering first, Jane said, "I'm Jane Lawless. This is Cordelia Thorn."

Still transfixed, or perhaps transported to another place and time, Cordelia gave a deep curtsy.

"Ms. Thorn is Octavia Thorn's older sister," added Jane.

"*Older?*" said Sir Jefferey, smiling his wry smile. "Surely not."

Cordelia face reddened.

Jane continued, "We're sorry to bother you. I assume you know about Mr. Lester's recent marriage."

"Indeed, I do. And of his death." The smile faded.

"I know this may seem like an intrusion, but . . . we were hoping to ask you a couple of questions. It's important. We've come a long distance."

He pondered the issue for several, weighty seconds, then seemed to reach a decision. "I assumed someone would arrive on my doorstep one of these days. But I thought it would be the police."

"I don't think the police know about you. Mr. Lester kept his personal life quite private."

"Ah yes, there's the rub. One's personal life. Please. Won't you come in?" He led the way through a narrow hallway to a small parlor overlooking a back garden. Waving for them to sit, he resumed his place on a silk-covered loveseat, one that was strewn with newspapers. A cup of tea rested on a small round table next to him.

The room was beautifully appointed. The rug was an Oriental Saruk, the walls paneled in oak and studded with oil paintings, mainly Impressionist, but a few more modern pieces. All the furniture was antique. "Where are my manners? May I get you something to drink? Tea? Coffee?" He smiled almost affectionately, like an uncle or an old friend, relaxed and attentive.

"Nothing for me, thanks," said Jane. She glanced at Cordelia.

"No," she squeaked. Clearing her throat, she tried again. "No, thank you," she said, her voice a good two octaves lower.

Over the years, Jane had heard rumors that Sir Jefferey was gay. Recently, she'd read an article in an entertainment magazine that said he'd danced with Rupert Everett at a gala in London, a benefit for some charity. There were even pictures. It was all in good fun, but the article said quite plainly that not only was Mr. Everett gay, as everyone already knew, but so was the eminent octogenarian.

Sir Jefferey caught Cordelia staring at a stuffed woodchuck standing on a pedestal directly next to the arched doorway. "Ah, I see you've discovered Bob."

"Bob?" she replied, looking guilty, as if she'd been caught doing something naughty.

"I believe Americans would call him 'road kill.' A dear friend of mine from Alabama sent him to me many years ago. He found him in an antique 'barn,' as he called it, just as you see him now."

Bob was dressed in a blue choir robe. And he was grasping a cigarette in his tiny right paw.

"Since my friend in Alabama often comes to visit, I felt I couldn't just slough the poor thing off into the attic, as one might want, so I gave him a place of honor in my home, if not in my heart. The pedestal was my idea, based on the theory that if you can't hide it, flaunt it. Bob and I have had many a long, disturbing conversation over the years. He is a cynic, I'm sad to say. Hard to have around, but then we make do in this life, even with our whimsy."

Jane couldn't help but smile. He was as delightful off the screen as he was on.

"But to get back to your reason for being here. You say you have . . . questions?"

His voice was so cultured, his pace so slow, the interior of the house so utterly still that Jane felt a moment of compassion for the bull in the china shop. Her thoughts were racing a mile a minute, but she had to take it easy, slow it down. By comparison to Sir Jefferey's innate calm, she felt incredibly agitated and on edge. "I wonder," she began, forcing herself to take her time, "would you mind telling us how long you've known Roland Lester?"

He raised his chin and thought for a moment. "We first met in Hollywood in 1959. We did a film together in 'sixty-seven, though it was hardly a high point in either of our careers." He picked up the teacup and held it in his hand. The look in his eyes grew amused. "Ever since that picture, I suppose you could call Roland my 'main squeeze.' Isn't that how you young people put it?"

"You were lovers?" asked Jane.

"For over thirty years. I'm afraid his death has hit me rather hard. Many of my friends didn't know about us, but of course my best chums did. The parlor has been filled with flowers for days. I had them all removed this morning. At my age, with so many of my contemporaries gone or on the verge of going, it seems silly to make such a fuss. But then, Roland was special. Such a dear, dear man. I shall miss him keenly for the rest of my life, however long the good Lord grants me."

It was a sad speech, and a heartfelt one. Jane knew she and Cordelia were intruding on his private grief, and yet she'd come for a reason. She couldn't just leave.

"Did you ever visit Innishannon?"

"Once. Many years ago. It is a magnificent house. But we decided quite early on to keep our personal lives separate. The world has changed a great deal since Roland and I were young men. Unfortunately, I don't believe some of us have the temperament to change with it."

"How often did Roland stay with you at your brownstone?"

"When I'm here, it was usually at least four times a month. For many years now I've divided my time between New York and London, and occasionally my work still takes me on location. We always kept in contact by phone. When we were both in New York, we'd often stay in, spend a quiet day together. We're both avid readers. Both like to cook. And then other times, we'd go out on the town to a movie, or a new stage play. When I was gone, Roland would stay here by himself. Business occasionally brought him into the city."

"Do you know what kind of business?"

He took a sip of tea. "Roland had been amassing a private film archive for years, so I assume he came fairly often to look at movie reels, see if they were worth purchasing. Occasionally, I'd put him onto something. So many of the old films are gone now, or in such a sad state, they'll never be repaired. I know this grieved him. We all have our social concerns. The environment. Nuclear weapons. The ozone layer. The disappearance of this or that flora or fauna. I suppose film preservation isn't high on the list of significant threats to mankind, but it moved us. We were both rather enamored of Hollywood's Golden Age. Actually, that's what drew us to Ms. Thorn." He turned his attention to Cordelia. "Your sister is not only a wonderful actress, she has true star quality. You may think this just the babbling of an old man, but she has an aura around her on stage. It's palpable, at least it is to me. I haven't seen anything like your sister in decades."

"Really," said Cordelia, a little dazed. "I'll tell her you said so."

"Yes, do. How is she feeling?"

"Not very well. Roland's death was a real blow."

He nodded. "Especially now. This must be such a trying time for her. In case you didn't know, I helped Roland select her."

Jane and Cordelia exchanged glances.

"Select? You mean as a potential wife?" asked Cordelia.

"Well yes, that. But Octavia knew their marriage was nothing more than a legality."

"What else is there?"

He studied Cordelia's face, then set the cup down. "You know, of course, that your sister is pregnant with Roland's child."

"What?" Cordelia shot out of her chair.

"Pregnant?" repeated Jane.

"But . . . that was the entire point of the marriage. I can't believe she hasn't informed you."

"Believe it," said Cordelia, her expression growing steely.

"Oh dear. Perhaps I'm telling tales out of school."

"No, you don't. You can't just leave it at that. My sister may have an aura around her, but from my standpoint it's more miasmal than it is celestial."

"Could you please explain?" asked Jane.

"Well—" His gaze drifted off. "After Roland's daughter, Peg, died, he was desolate, inconsolable. She was to inherit all his archival work. She understood the importance of film preservation. She'd been raised in a motion picture family and had gone on to produce movies herself. When she died, it was as if Roland had lost not only his daughter, but his claim on the future."

"What about his brother Buddy's family?" asked Jane.

Sir Jefferey waved the idea away. "Not one of them is the least bit interested in motion pictures. Oh, I believe they were truly enchanted by the thought of Roland's fortune, but his directorial legacy meant nothing to them. I don't believe he ever told them about his private archive. There was no point. In fact, I believe, other than his brother, I'm the only one who knows. He wasn't even going to tell Octavia until the wedding night."

"Do you know where the films are stored?" asked Jane.

"Out of the country, somewhere. Switzerland, perhaps? I really don't know."

Cordelia cleared her throat. "Getting back to my sister's pregnancy—" She finally sat down. Or, more precisely, she dropped down in her chair like a two-hundred-pound sack of flour.

"That was why he invited her to dinner last fall. He wanted to tell her a story—about Peg. What she'd meant to him. How deeply affected he'd been by her loss. And how he'd found a solution to his pain. He wanted to have another child. But not just any child. He wanted to have a child with Octavia. He desired beauty and an inborn affinity for the arts. He wanted a woman who understood that films are *the* art form of the twentieth century. I realized Octavia's only made five movies herself, that her career has been primarily on the legitimate stage, but to my mind that is simply an oversight. Many a night we sat in bed and watched her films. She was luminous. The night she came to Innishannon, Roland made her an offer. He knew her stage play had just ended it's run, so she had some free time on her hands. He said that if she'd stay at Innishannon for six months—"

"They slept together?"

"Heavens, no. Nothing like that. Many years ago, Roland had his sperm frozen. Don't ask me why. But if Octavia would submit herself to being artificially inseminated, and if she succeeded in getting pregnant, Roland promised to marry her. She would inherit the bulk of his estate—which I believe is worth multimillions of dollars—and full custody of the child. On one condition. The child must reside at Innishannon until Roland's death. He felt he had many vital years left to give him or her. You have to understand, the curse of old age is not that we are old, it's that we are still young. He was so full of love for this unborn child. He had so many dreams of what they would do together. Octavia could spend as much or as little time at Innishannon as she wanted. She could pursue her theatre career full-time or part-time. If she liked, Roland would see to it that she received movie scripts. Even at his age, he still had markers he could call in. Octavia would never want for anything. I believe that the second insemination attempt was the charm. Of course, Roland knew Octavia didn't much care for being cooped up at Innishannon. She was used to a more active, free, even flamboyant, lifestyle. And yet, on the night of their marriage, she told Roland that she had wanted a child for years. She never expected it to happen, but she was glad now that it had. She knew that Roland would make a wonderful father, and she pledged to him that she would love their child with all her heart for the rest of her life. It was a touching scene."

"You were there?" said Cordelia.

"The ceremony took place in this very room. I had it decorated for the occasion. Roland told me your sister's favorite flowers were white tulips, so I had several dozen flown over from Holland."

"You mean my sister knew you and Roland were lovers?"

He seemed shocked. "My dear, you couldn't have known Roland Lester. He would never have hurt or embarrassed Octavia so crudely. She knew we were friends. And she knew I was happy for her. Perhaps she suspected more, but she never said anything to either of us. You must understand, the ceremony here at the brownstone was just a formality. Octavia had demanded a real wedding—one to which she could invite her family and friends. Roland was against the idea at first. He said if she remained adamant, she would have to wait for her wedding gift."

"He'd given her a key," said Cordelia, almost in a trance. "On their wedding night, he was supposed to show her what it unlocked. But he died before he could tell her."

"I don't suppose you know anything about it," said Jane.

He shook his head. "Roland was my friend, my lover, my mate, but in many ways my career forced us to lead separate lives. I'm sorry I can't help you more. When someone dies, I find there are always these questions left behind. Mysteries of one sort or another. The most intriguing mystery of all, of course, has to do with the essential Roland Lester. We think we know our friends and lovers, but we don't. Not really. We know parts of them. We know how they make us feel about ourselves. But loving someone gives you no special window into a soul. Ask a hundred people who knew Roland what he was like, and I suspect you'll receive a hundred varying opinions. If I had hated him, I would have very different thoughts to bring to the table, but would it be any less valid?"

Jane found his musings fascinating, but since she and Cordelia might be deposited on the front doorstep at any moment, she had to press on. "Did Roland ever wear a disguise when he came to visit you?"

Sir Jefferey tipped his head back and laughed heartily. "A disguise? No. Never. Neither of us were ever *that* careful."

"Do you ever remember him wearing one in public?"

"Heavens, no. Why would he do that?"

"When he came to visit you, he always carried a large suitcase. Did you ever see him unpack?"

He looked down at his teacup. "Now that you mention it, no. There really was no need to bring anything. He has a full closet of clothes upstairs. And as to other travel necessities, we have everything here, or we could send out for it."

"Did Roland always arrive by taxi?"

He nodded. "Always."

"Do you suppose he flew down from New Haven?"

"He loathed planes. If he had to travel, he always took a limousine or the train. I imagine he took the Metro North from New Haven, and then a cab from Grand Central."

"I don't mean to change the subject so abruptly, but I know you're a busy man. Did Roland ever speak to you about his friend, Lew Wallace?"

"Yes, many times."

"Did you know, for instance, that Roland was a suspect in his murder?"

He gave a guarded nod. "But the murderer was never found. And Roland assured me he had nothing to do with it."

"I'm sure he didn't. Did he ever mention a card game he and Lew played, oh, sometime in the late forties?"

"A card game? Not that I recall."

Not only was Sir Jefferey staring at her now, but so was Cordelia.

"What card game?" she asked.

"It may not be important."

Sir Jefferey glanced at his watch.

Jane needed to squeeze in one last question. "Did Roland ever speak about a Hollywood scandal? Something he might have been a part of?"

"What an odd thing to suggest. Where are you getting these ideas, Ms. Lawless?"

He deserved an answer. "Actually, a friend of mine was doing a documentary on Mr. Lester. She's been staying at Innishannon for several weeks."

"Yes, I know all about her. Ellie Saks."

"It was her theory that Roland had a central role in a major Hollywood scandal, one that up until now has remained a secret. Unfortunately, before she could prove her theory, she died."

"Died?"

"Yesterday. She was murdered."

His face suddenly paled. "How dreadful."

"I think she died because of what she knew, or what she suspected."

"Hey," said Cordelia, looking hurt. "How come you never told me any of this?"

"I just told you now."

Sir Jefferey glanced at his watch again.

"We've stayed too long," said Jane, rising from her chair.

"No, not at all," he said, smiling at them once more, this time, a little more sadly. "I do, however, have a late afternoon appointment and I mustn't be late. The doctor," he added, making a sour face.

"Of course," said Jane. "You've been very helpful."

"I think not."

He walked a bit more slowly as he led them back to the front door. "I'm feeling very old these days. Sometimes I don't know what to make

301

of this cruel world of ours, but then I don't want to leave it either. It's a dilemma."

"Thank you, Sir Jefferey," said Jane, extending her hand.

He shook it firmly, and then shook Cordelia's. "Please, promise me you'll let me know if you learn anything. If I were a younger man, I'd insist on going with you, giving you every assistance I could. Alas—" He tapped his heart.

"We'll keep you informed," Cordelia assured him.

As he held the door open, he smiled his wry smile one last time. "Good luck."

36

Jane sat at the hotel bar, gazing at a half-filled cup of coffee and waiting for Cordelia to join her. Since they'd checked into their suite at the Ambassador Midtown with Cordelia's monster suitcase and Jane's small overnight bag, Cordelia had changed her clothes at least three times, all the while sputtering about her sister, the secret pregnancy, how she'd been lied to again and again and was just about at the end of her rope. She wondered how her father would take the news, and how on earth someone as innately self-consumed as Octavia could even consider giving birth.

Jane tried to calm her down. Why spoil the entire evening being furious when she had the rest of her life to rant about her sister? Cordelia must have agreed, because by the time she'd put on her third costume, her mood had improved. Apparently, there was a certain look she was struggling to achieve for her night on old Broadway, but she kept changing her mind on what it was.

First, she'd tried on a slinky black number. Jane approved, but Cordelia thought it was a little too Morticia. Off it went. Next came a more boxy, Joan Crawford look, complete with slightly squashed hat and veil. Cordelia vamped around the room in that for a few minutes, then retreated to her bedroom again, looking dejected. About ten minutes later she emerged in a sequined fire-engine-red evening gown, one that emphasized her ample cleavage. She called it her *homage* to Ethel Merman. While gazing at herself in the mirror, she sang a rousing few lines of "There's NO Business Like SHOW Business."

Jane laughed and clapped. "*A Moon for the Misbegotten* will have to go some distance to be more entertaining than you. What else did you bring in that suitcase?"

"Well, I can do a sort of blousey Jean Harlow. I dress all in white and wear my platinum blond wig. That's for when I'm feeling particularly alluring. Oh, and before we left home, I found this marvelously dumpy tweed coat and matching skirt in a secondhand store. I already had those clunky black old lady shoes. I call it my Margaret Rutherford look. But——" She wrinkled her nose. "——I don't think New York's ready for that yet."

She was contemplating a fourth change of attire when Jane said she needed a breath of air and that she'd meet her downstairs. The curtain wouldn't rise for another forty-five minutes, so they were in no danger of being late.

Jane took the elevator downstairs and quickly located the bar. Pulling out a stool, she ordered herself a coffee. What she really wanted was a few minutes alone to think. The conversation with Sir Jefferey Gorham had cleared up some of her questions, but again, not all of them. It came as no surprise that Roland and his brother had been collecting old films for years. That's why Roland had installed a secret vault behind the projector room. But, if Buddy didn't know about the vault, what else didn't he know?

Jane assumed the luggage Roland carried to New York two or three times a month contained film canisters. She also assumed they were packed and ready to mail to his private stash, which she now knew was somewhere out of the country. But, if it was that simple, why carry them to New York personally, as if it were some top secret piece of governmental espionage? Why not just have UPS pick up the canisters at the mansion? And what had Roland been doing in Wister wearing a disguise, buying groceries at a little neighborhood store? Had the limousine driver been wrong about that?

Something Hilda said to her the other night kept popping into her mind. Roland was usually gone from Innishannon once or twice a month. But Sir Jefferey said that he was at the brownstone a good four times a month. If the figures they'd given her were accurate, something didn't add up.

Jane leaned her elbow on the bar, then rested her head against her hand and closed her eyes to think it through. What if Roland came to

New York, sent off his films, took a cab from Times Square to the brownstone and stayed for a night or two with Sir Jefferey, then took the train up to Wister, stayed there for a day or two, came back to New York to the brownstone for another night or two, and then took a cab to the post office in Times Square where he was picked up by Mr. Yablonski and driven back to Innishannon? That would account for it. He would be at the brownstone two times for every one time he was away from his estate. But if that scenario was true, what drew him to Wister? And where did he stay? Part of the puzzle was missing.

Thinking she had several potentially important leads she still hadn't tracked down, Jane left her coffee cup on the bar, took her cane and walked out into the lobby. She found a bank of pay phones around the corner from the reservation desk. Retrieving her billfold from her back pocket, she slipped out the piece of paper on which she'd written Salvador Barros's phone number. It wouldn't matter now if she called him. Ellie wasn't around to find out. The sad truth was, if Jane hadn't rifled through Ellie's garbage, an important link to Roland's past might have been lost forever.

Picking up the receiver, Jane pushed her card into the slot, then tapped in the number. She waited, drumming her fingers on the top of a phone book until the line was picked up.

"Hello?" said a woman's voice.

In the background, Jane could hear children laughing. "May I speak with Salvador Barros?"

"He's resting right now. What's this about?"

"Well, my name is Jane Lawless. I'm a friend of Ellie Saks. Ellie is . . . was, I mean, is a documentary artist. She's doing a—"

"Oh, sure. The piece on Roland Lester. My father's been looking forward to talking to her. Or you, whatever. Give me a second, and I'll go get him. My grandchildren are here right now, so it may take a minute."

"That's fine. I'll wait." Her gaze swung back to the lobby. She hoped Cordelia would continue to be indecisive for a few more minutes.

Finally, Salvador Barros came on the line. "Hi, this is Sal."

"My name's Jane. I'm delighted to talk to you."

They exchanged pleasantries for a few minutes. All the while, Jane kept working her way toward the question she wanted to ask. "Actually, Mr. Barros, the reason for my call is—"

"Yes, yes. The card game. Ellie seemed very interested in it, though I'm not sure why. I suppose because it was such a colorful situation."

"Colorful?"

"Sure. You gotta understand. It was a long time ago—back in the late forties. Lew and Roland were doing okay, financially I mean, and so was I, pretty much, but the other three guys were just getting started. Marty Mulloy, Nick Trisko, and Ira Sloan. None of them had a pot to piss in, if you know what I mean. We were all working together on a film right then. Can't remember the name. But hey, the bunch of us always had a great time together. Lew provided his living room, and Roland provided the booze. If Roland's brother Buddy was around, sometimes he'd join us."

"Was he there that night?"

"Nah. It was just the six of us."

"But, if you played together a lot, what made this one night special?"

"Didn't Ellie tell you? It was the stakes. We were all broke." He laughed. "Well, except for Roland. But he wasn't going to float every-body in the room a loan."

"Lew was broke too?"

"Well, no, but he didn't have much cash on him. He was the one who started it. See, he wanted to raise the ante, so he asked Roland for five bucks. Roland said something like, 'Why the hell should I give you money so you can turn around and take the pot?' We all figured Lew was holding a winning hand. So, what does he do?" Salvador paused dramatically. "He takes off his shoe and dumps it in the center of the table. 'There,' he says, 'That should be worth five bucks.' We all laugh. Mulloy's next. Instead of using his last dollar, he pulls off his tie and throws it down on the table. 'I'm in,' he says. We all roar. Then it's Ira's turn. You've gotta get the picture here. Ira was a real skinny guy. Had this old belt that held up his pants. Well, he gets up, unhooks it and pulls it off, and of course, his pants fall down. Everybody's dying. He throws the belt on the table and says, 'I'm in, too.' I was next. I think I tossed in a package of Chicklets and a bag of jelly beans. I've always had a sweet tooth. Trisko puts in a picture of his mother-in-law. Don't ask me why he had it on him. At this point, Roland pours everyone more whisky. It's his turn now, so he thinks a minute, then takes off his shirt, bunches it into a ball, and it goes on top of everything else. He sits at the table in his undershirt, smoking a cigar, proud as a lord. Then it's Lew's turn again. He jumps up and runs out of the room. He's gone two, maybe three minutes. When he gets back, he's waving this piece of paper over his head. 'I bought this for two hundred bucks from a guy who said it would revolutionize the film industry.' Everybody laughs."

"What was it?" asked Jane.

"Some formula a guy named Stern or Storm . . . I know it started with an S . . . tried to sell MGM back in the thirties. I'm not sure why Lew even kept it. It was all a hoax. Lew worked with this Stern on a few films. The guy was a cameraman. Also thought of himself as an inventor. But he was down on his luck. Lew told us the whole sad story, how Storm had just been thrown out of the studio chief's office and was sitting outside on the curb. Lew ran into him on his way to lunch. I guess the guy was crying. Two hundred dollars was a lot of money back then too, especially for something as worthless as his formula, but Lew was always a soft touch. He said he felt sorry for the guy."

"But, how do you know the formula was worthless?"

"Lew said MGM tested it. It was a flop."

"What was it supposed to do?"

"It was a chemical process. The liquid was supposed to bond with the cellulose nitrate and turn it into a kind of plastic that wouldn't burn or deteriorate. I mean, if somebody ever did discover something like that, not only would he be a billionaire, he'd probably get a medal. But back to my story. Lew drops the formula on the table, tells the sad, sad tale about where he got it and how valuable it is, and after everybody has a good laugh, it's Mulloy's turn again. Nobody figures he can top Lew."

"But he did?"

Sal let out a belly laugh, then started to cough. When he'd recovered, he continued, "Mulloy thinks for a minute. The guy was a real card. Always kept us laughing on the set. Anyway, after a couple of seconds he rips off his toupee, flips it onto the table, and says, 'I see you and call.' I mean, we all roared—fell off our chairs. Maybe we were kinda drunk, but God it was funny."

As Sal continued to cackle, Jane asked, "Who won the pot?" She already knew, but needed him to confirm it.

"Roland won," he said, coughing a couple more times. "Don't quote me, but I think he had a full house. He was kind enough to give Mulloy back his hairpiece and Ira back his belt, but he kept Lew's shoe and the formula. It was all in good fun. You can see now why I never forgot that game."

"I do," said Jane, feeling the flesh on her arms begin to pebble. This was it. It had to be. In her entire life, she'd never had such an urge to yell "Eureka!" before. Out of the corner of her eye, she saw Cordelia flouncing toward the phones. Her *homage* to Ethel Merman had won the coin toss. "Thanks so much, Mr. Barros. If I need to call you again, just to confirm a few points, I hope you don't mind."

"Call anytime," he said, his voice hearty and full of good humor. "I got a million other stories I know you'd love."

37

Over breakfast the next morning, Jane and Cordelia went step by step through everything they'd learned since arriving at Innishannon. Jane had a working theory now that she was determined to prove, one that centered on the formula Ellery Patrick Strong, Ellie's grandfather, had developed over seventy years ago.

As Cordelia poured more maple syrup on her pancakes, she shook her head and said, "You know, Janey, my sister would really be up the creek without a paddle if we weren't here. If I do say so myself, we are truly amazing. We should hire ourselves out to the C.I.A."

"Right. The two crackpots from Minnesota." She took a bite of her Eggs Benedict. "We're not there yet, you know, but we're close."

"Okay, so you believe this formula was the reason Roland was murdered, right?"

"I'd like to. It would simplify everything. But at this point, I'm not one hundred percent convinced. There are a lot of potential motives out there, most of which have nothing to do with the formula. Think about it. As far as we know, only two people were aware of the fact that Roland was collecting old films."

"Buddy and Sir Jefferey."

"Right. Now, knowledge of the film archive means nothing. It's only when you put it together with the formula that you have a motive for murder. I think we can agree that Sir Jefferey is off the hook. That leaves Buddy. It would be easy to point the finger at him, say he's behind everything. It makes a certain sense. He had motive and opportunity. He was the closest to Roland, and responsible for most of the film gathering. But we can't rule out the idea that someone else knew about the film archive, too. It's hard to keep a secret for such a long time without any slips. But that also goes for the formula. At the very least, whoever took Ellie's video documentary of her grandfather knew about it."

"What do you think was on the documentary?"

"Besides the general story of her grandfather's life? I figure it must have contained Ellie's theory about the formula, that's why she called him 'Hollywood's greatest hero' in the title. When we were talking about him a few days ago, she called him a genius. Now I know why. On the other hand, if she'd had all the proof she needed—and a copy of the actual formula—she never would have come to Innishannon. So, in a sense, the theft of that video provided the motive for her murder. Someone wanted to keep her quiet until they had the formula safely tucked away for their own use. But the theft happened *after* Roland died. That muddies the waters. Was his murder tied to the formula or wasn't? We simply have to follow where the yellow brick road leads us."

"This is so frustrating."

"I agree."

"Buddy, Christian, or Verna. I always come back to them."

Jane gazed at Cordelia over the rim of her coffee cup. "So do I."

"What about Gracie?"

"She could have murdered Roland out of rage at losing Innishannon, or a sense of betrayal. She was certainly angry enough."

"And Verna?"

Jane shrugged. "She might have had a reason we know nothing about, or she might have been afraid that, with Roland's current obsession for truth telling, he might decide to spill the beans about the Lew Wallace murder."

"Meaning, she was responsible."

"Self-preservation can cause people to do some terrible things."

"And Christian?"

"He could have poisoned Roland to get his hands on his inheritance. It's an old story, but it's still a powerful one. Christian needs money right now—badly."

"Maybe he stole the documentary."

"Maybe he did." Jane took a sip of coffee, then set the cup down. "I just wish I knew more about film preservation."

"You obviously think Strong's formula worked."

"You bet I do. I don't know the details of what happened at MGM, but I'd say the lab that tested it got something wrong. Roland must have retested it, just out of curiosity. From that point on, I'd say he started collecting old movies like crazy. Reprocessing them."

"But . . . why didn't he tell anyone? How could he just sit on something so monumentally important?"

Jane had the same questions. "Well, the only thing I can figure is that, back in the forties, film preservation wasn't a very important issue. Sure, I suppose people felt bad that some of the old silent films were gone, but it wasn't like it is today. Nobody really thought of motion pictures as significant art. Being a good businessman, Roland probably figured it would be worth more money if he sat on it for a while. He probably started collecting out a desire to see his films—and Lew's—kept in the best possible condition for posterity, or maybe he did it just for his own enjoyment. And since he grew up during the silent film era, he no doubt had some favorites there too. From then on, it just took off. By the time he realized how truly important the formula was, he may have had other reasons for keeping it a secret."

"Like what?"

"Well, after what happened to Lew, I'll bet Roland grew to hate Hollywood—hate the studios and the system. And yet he probably still loved the films. We may never know the full story, but whatever happened, he had his reasons for keeping the formula a secret. We do know he planned to pass it all on to his daughter, but when she died, he was left without a curator, so to speak, without someone to shepherd his legacy into the twenty-first century."

"And that's where my sister comes in. Octavia and her little bun in the oven."

Jane nodded. "He probably thought his brother was too old to take on the job. And apparently he didn't think anybody in Buddy's family was up to the task either. Roland was going to tell Octavia about the formula on their wedding night, maybe even show her where he kept it, how it worked."

"You think he had the reels processed somewhere near Innishannon?"

"I do, yes. Here's how I think it worked. It was Buddy's primary job to locate the old prints or negatives. He no doubt placed adds in newspapers or trade journals all over the world. Hilda said he traveled a lot. That would explain it. Roland occasionally came to New York to look at a film, but I assume Buddy was the primary buyer. Let's say Buddy brought the films he found to Innishannon. Roland's part was to see to it that they were processed, then sent to the warehouse."

"Division of labor. Makes sense."

"It also meant Buddy was nothing but a glorified gopher. Roland used him to find the films, but kept him out of the full loop."

"Which—if he found out about—he probably didn't like. Hey, that sounds like another pretty strong motive."

"Yes, but only if Buddy knew about the formula and gained access to it before Roland died. He couldn't risk getting rid of Roland unless he had the formula in his hot little hand. Nobody could. That's why, if Roland's death was linked to the formula, someone had to know of its existence *before* his death."

"In which case, Ellie's documentary only confirmed what the killer already knew."

"Right. I'm just afraid, by the time her documentary finally sees the light of day, the formula will be long gone."

Cordelia gave an involuntary shudder.

"We know that somebody was having Roland followed before he died. That means someone was attempting to piece together his movements, just like we're doing."

"Trying to find the formula?"

Jane eased her left leg out from under the chair and stretched it partway into the aisle. "That would be my guess."

"Maybe Ellie was having him followed."

"Yes, I'd thought of that. It's certainly possible. I think Roland was processing the films himself. He was so secretive about everything else in his life, it hardly seems likely he'd hand the formula over to a professional lab."

Cordelia stabbed at a small piece of breakfast sausage with her fork. "Okay, so if he wasn't doing it at Innishannon, where?"

"Like I said, we have to follow the yellow brick road."

"To the Emerald City?"

Jane waved at the waitress for the check. "No, Cordelia. To Wister, Connecticut."

Just like Derby, Orange, Ansonia, Hamden, and Woodbridge, Wister was part of the greater New Haven area. Like so many other small towns in New England, it had a church on the village green, a main street dotted with small shops, and also boasted a few local attractions. In Wister's case it was the Cleridge Rose Gardens and Heritage House, one of the oldest clock museums in the country.

The Clockwork Grill was located a good fifteen blocks south of the center of town on a street that was primarily residential. It was a well-maintained, middle class neighborhood. Most of the houses were wood frame or stucco. Some had garages. Some didn't. And just as the limo driver had said, across from the restaurant was a small convenience store.

Yesterday morning, before Jane had left Innishannon, she'd taken a couple of the newspaper announcements of Roland's death from the stack Hilda had gathered together in the library. In each one, a photo had been included.

Sitting in the car across from the store, Jane took out a black felt-tip pen.

"What's that for?" asked Cordelia.

Retrieving the newspapers from under the seat, she found the photos and quickly drew a dark beard, dark glasses, and a hat on the head shots.

"Hey, not bad. Very mysterious."

Handing one to Cordelia, she said, "Rip it off the page. We don't want to give anyone more information than they need."

"We're going to show these around town, right?"

"Starting with Gary's Dairy over there."

As they headed for the front door, Jane said, "Let me do the talking. Just play along."

"Play along with what?"

She held a finger to her lips. Approaching the cash register and the woman standing behind it, she smiled. "Hi. I'm wondering if you could help us. Have you ever seen this man in here?"

Adjusting her glasses, the woman took a closer look. "Sure. He comes in every now and then. Who wants to know?"

Jane's expression turned eager. "I told you, Cordelia. He's here."

"Who is he?" asked the woman, clearly curious.

"Our father," said Jane. "It's a long story. He wandered away many years ago from——"

"Our farm," said Cordelia.

Jane grimaced. Why couldn't she just keep her mouth shut?

"Where's the farm?" asked the woman.

Jane had no idea.

"Boston," said Cordelia, looking pleased with herself.

"Boston?" repeated the woman, looking skeptical.

Jane gave Cordelia's back a friendly pat, then eased her hand up to the back of her neck and squeezed hard.

"Ouch!"

"Actually, it's in Cambridge. It's part of the Harvard Agricultural school. Our father maintained the, ah . . . the experimental farm."

"It was the pesticides," said Cordelia, looking grieved. "They went to his brain. Made him do strange things. One day, he just wandered off. Poof. Gone. Left Mom and my sister and I all alone. We were churning butter at the time. I'll never forget it."

"Your whole family lived there?"

"Sure," said Cordelia, elbowing Jane's hand away from her back. "We helped raise the pigs and the ostriches."

"Ostriches?"

"They're all the rage now, didn't you know? They're absolutely delicious served with a nice beurre blanc sauce. A good chardonnay. We planted the corn and oats. Tilled the soil with our ox and the sweat of our brows."

Now the woman looked really confused. "Harvard has an experimental program that uses oxen to till the soil?"

Jane knew she should have left Cordelia in the car. "We got rid of the ox. We use a John Deere tractor now. It's much better."

"We do?" said Cordelia, looking shocked. "What happened to the ox? I loved that ox!"

"We ate it," said Jane. "Anyway, back to our father. You don't happen to know where he lives, do you? We're pretty sure it's somewhere around here."

The woman had grown suspicious. "He always pays cash."

"Oh." It was the last thing Jane wanted to hear. "What about friends? Does he ever come in with anyone?"

314

"No, always alone."

"Did you ever see him get into a car."

"I never looked."

"Well, then, did he buy a lot of groceries? More than he could carry?"

"Nope, just the one sack." She stood back, crossing her arms over her chest and narrowing her eyes. "Aren't you two kind of old to be living on a farm with your father and mother?"

"Oh, we've all got our Ph.D.'s," said Cordelia, picking up a shrink-wrapped stick of beef jerky and reading the label. "Mine's in farm machinery. My sister's is in . . . seeds. You know. How they grow. Sprout. How much water to give them. She did her dissertation on potting soil."

"Come on," said Jane, giving Cordelia's arm a warning tug.

But the proprietor wasn't done. "I think *you're* the two who wandered away from the farm. The *funny* farm."

Cordelia stood her ground. "Look, lady, with all the problems facing the family farm today, I would think you could show a little more compassion."

"Thanks for you time," said Jane, yanking Cordelia away from the counter and out the door.

Once they were back at the car, Cordelia said, "The nerve of some people. What did she think? That we were lying to her?"

"We were."

"Yeah, well, but . . . still."

Jane spent a few moments surveying the street. "Here's what we're going to do. I want to split up. You take the odd-numbered houses. I'll take the even. We'll keep going for a few blocks, then if we don't find anything, we'll turn and come back this way on the next street over. We've got to canvas the entire area before we drive back to Innishannon." She glanced at her watch. "It's just after one. I'll meet you back here at two. We can compare notes on where we went. If we haven't found anything, we keep going. Deal?"

"Deal," said Cordelia.

"And be sensible. Just tell people Roland's a friend of the family, that he's been missing for years. Someone said they saw him in town and you're just checking."

"I can make up my own story," said Cordelia, a pout forming. "I am a nationally known creative director. That means I have a modicum of creative ability."

"Okay, okay. Just . . . don't get into any trouble."

By three, they still hadn't come up with a lead.

"My feet are killing me," complained Cordelia, sitting on the hood of the car. "And I'm starving." She gazed at the Clockwork Grill longingly.

An entire section of town still remained. The houses in that area were pretty run-down. Jane had left it for last because her instinct told her that Roland would purchase something with a better resale value. He was, after all, a good businessman who'd made millions in real estate. But perhaps, in this instance, he'd been after something else. "Look, why don't you go in, get yourself a bite to eat while I do a little more canvassing."

Her face brightened. "I'll ask inside the restaurant if anybody knows him."

"Fine. If I don't find anything, I'll join you. But give me a good hour. You can occupy yourself for that long, right?"

"No problemo." Cordelia hopped down off the hood and waved over her shoulder as she dashed across to the cafe.

Jane made sure she still had the newsprint photo of Roland in the pocket of her coat, then started up the street. She wasn't setting any speed records today because of her leg. Then again, she'd realized as soon as she'd approached her first house that a cane and a limp lent a certain credibility to her image. In other words, nobody who looked like her was going to be out doing something illegal or malicious.

When she reached the top of the hill, she turned to her right. A long block stretched in front of her. The houses weren't exactly ramshackle, but if a real estate agent had been asked to sell one of them, it would definitely be advertised as a "handyman special," or a "real fixer-upper."

Jane knocked on the door of the first house. She waited, glancing at a bent snow shovel sitting next to a rusted screen. When nobody answered, she knocked again, then leaned down to read the name on the mailbox. "Newton," she whispered. It didn't ring any bells. She peeked in the narrow window next to the door, but finally gave up.

The next house was a little Cape Cod style bungalow. White with blue trim. One story. Standing under the portico, Jane pushed the doorbell. She couldn't hear a corresponding ring inside, so she figured it wasn't working. She knocked on the door a couple of times, but it seemed pretty clear nobody was around. "Strike two," she whispered, walking back down the sidewalk. Glancing up at the sky, she realized it was starting to snow. The temperature had been hovering around the freezing mark all day, which meant the roads could be a mess on the way home. Not a welcome prospect.

As she was on her way up to the next house, she heard a voice calling, or more accurately, shrieking, "Jane! Wait! Jane!" Turning around, she saw Cordelia rounding the corner and racing straight for her, out of breath, but with the trill of victory in her eyes.

"Jane, I've got it." She screeched to a halt, bent her head to catch her breath, then stuffed the last bite of a grilled cheese sandwich into her mouth.

"What have you got?"

"My waitress," she said, still breathing hard. "She'd never seen Roland before, but she took the picture around to everyone in the restaurant. The guests. The manager. The cooks. The other waitresses. This one woman, her name was Mickey Freeman, said that he lived next door to a friend of hers. Carla Roebling. Mickey's seen him a whole bunch of times. Said his name was Lesney."

Of course! Why hadn't Jane thought of that? He'd used his real name. She should have checked a phone book before they started going house to house.

"I looked it up in the Wister white pages back at the restaurant," said Cordelia, pulling a plastic Pepsi bottle out of her coat pocket and taking a couple of swigs. It was almost as if she'd read Jane's mind. "But he's not listed. Here." She handed Jane a piece of paper. "That's got the address of Mickey Freeman's friend on it. All we have to do is find it, and the house next to it—I don't know which side—belongs to Roland."

The address said 2327 Maple. Jane looked up at the street sign. "We're already on Maple. And that house is—" She squinted to get a better look at the number over the door. "—Two-zero-one-six. So, three more blocks and we're there."

"Lucky us," groaned Cordelia, holding out her hand and watching the snowflakes accumulate and then melt. "When I get back to Innis-hannon tonight, I'm going to soak my feet. All evening. That is, after I get through reading my sister the riot act."

They walked with more purpose in their steps now, knowing that they were mere blocks from their destination.

"There it is," said Cordelia finally. "That's Carla Roebling's house. The dirty yellow one with the brown trim."

It was a spooky looking place, thought Jane. As they got closer, she could see an old black hearse parked in the backyard. "The hippie nation is alive and well and living in Wister." She surveyed the houses on either side. "You want to pick? Or should we go together?"

"Together," said Cordelia. "We make more of a statement."

They climbed the front steps of the house closest to them. It was a white clapboard building with two second floor dormers jutting off the front. The house actually looked like a large cube, almost perfectly square. The front door was on the left, and a small deck and three narrow windows on the right.

Cordelia pointed to the mailbox, looking smug. "It says Lesney."

Jane stepped across to the first floor windows and peeked through the blinds. The front room looked like any other living room. A couch. A couple of chairs. A TV set. Some end tables and lamps. Nothing special. Nothing out of the ordinary. It almost looked like a movie set. When she tried the handle on the front door she noticed two deadbolts. That was interesting. "Let's walk around the back."

As they came around the side of the house, she nodded to the bars on the basement windows. The only thing missing from the picture was a full blown security system. But then, in a neighborhood like this, installing a bunch of high tech anti-burglar gadgetry would be like sticking a neon sign on the top of the house with a blinking arrow pointing to the door.

An enclosed porch jutted off the back of the house. Taped to the door was a sign that said, "Deliveries."

Jane followed Cordelia inside.

Several boxes were stacked next to a wicker chair. On a bench by the back door they found a packet of UPS shipping labels and instruction forms.

Cordelia checked the address on the boxes. "These were mailed from

New York on the twenty-second, the day we arrived at Innishannon. I'll bet that's where Roland was."

"What's the return address?" asked Jane.

"There isn't one."

Again, that fit her theory. Roland mailed them to Wister from the post office in Times Square. "Open one and see what's inside."

While Cordelia busied herself trying to rip off the strapping tape, Jane sat down on the bench and looked at the UPS material. The labels were all blank. So were the instruction forms. She fanned through them quickly, but stopped when she found a piece of paper that didn't belong. "Hey, look at this." It was a receipt that had been inadvertently left in between two of the unused labels.

"What's it say?" asked Cordelia, still fighting with the tape.

"Roland shipped three parcels last summer to Chaumont, Belgium. Thirty-seven Rue d'Alembert. My God, Cordelia, this must be Roland's warehouse."

She snatched the paper out of Jane's hand. "Octavia is going to lose her mind she'll be so excited!" She nodded to the box she'd finally opened. "Film canisters."

"He processed them here. When he was done, he'd send them off. This porch was probably always left open for pickups and deliveries." She glanced over at the back door and saw another deadbolt. "The problem is, how do we get inside?"

"We *have* to get inside, Janey. We've just discovered Shangra La! The Lost Ark! The Holy Grail! The Golden Fleece! The cure for the common cold!"

Jane put a finger to her lips. Two men had just emerged from a house across the alley. They stared in the direction of Roland's house for a few seconds, then got in a truck and left.

"I agree," said Jane, lowering her voice. "But maybe it's time to call Toscano. Breaking and entering isn't a speciality of mine."

Cordelia had started digging through the box, but she now rose straight into the air. "It's not breaking and entering, Janey. Octavia owns the place now. It just—we can't let anyone know about it! Not until we have our own security in place."

"Our own?"

"I'm speaking for my sister."

"Oh."

"I am!"

"Keep your voice down."

"It belongs to her, Janey. We have to tell her, then let her make the decisions."

Jane supposed she had a point. "Okay, okay. But if we are going to break in, we'll want to do it at night. And we better do it soon. We're living with a murderer at Innishannon, Cordelia. If that person gets wind of what we know, we're dead. And I don't mean metaphorically."

38

Leonard had just finished bringing Cordelia's luggage up to her bedroom when Octavia appeared in the doorway. "What took you so long? I expected you back hours ago."

"What? No 'welcome home'? No affectionate hug?"

"This hasn't been one of my better days. Don't push it."

Cordelia ignored her sister's irritated look and opened her suitcase. "Aren't you at least going to ask me if we had a good time?"

"Did you?"

"Fascinating, Octavia. Utterly fascinating."

"You better change."

"Why?"

"Because we're meeting Dad for dinner in an hour. He borrowed my car this morning and drove into New Haven. We're supposed to meet him at the Cornwall Inn at six. I'll expect you downstairs in half an hour."

Cordelia was about to suggest that they have a little sisterly chat first, but when she looked around, Octavia was gone.

"How was he last night?" asked Cordelia, turning her father's Lincoln onto the I-95 on-ramp. The weather had turned nasty. A stiff wind was blowing snow across the highway, making it difficult to see.

"I can't tell anymore," said Octavia, looking out the side window. "He read the paper after dinner, then played a game of chess with Christian and eventually went up to bed. I didn't see him for the rest of the evening. After he left this morning, I checked his room. He had four fifths of vodka in his suitcase. Three of them were empty. I think he must be drinking pretty much all the time."

"How could you let him drive off alone this morning?"

"How was I supposed to stop him?"

"Throw your body in front of the car!"

"He'd probably just drive over me." She looked down at the gloves in her lap. "You're the one he loves. No matter what I do, what I accomplish, what I try to give, it's always been that way. I should just accept it."

"Yeah, and Mom always loved you best."

"A hell of a lot of good it did her."

Cordelia's attempt at humor fell flat. How could it not? Their relationship was a mine field. Octavia seemed unusually discouraged tonight. While Cordelia resisted the emotion, she still felt a pang of sympathy for her. You'd think that by the time a woman turned forty, she'd have a handle on all this family stuff. Except that Cordelia had flunked Happy Family 101. With each passing year, matters only grew more complex. More layers were added, more feelings repressed. Each member had his or her own take. Her own opinions. His disappointments. And each person kept a mental list of the slights, the insults, the perceived favoritism, the misunderstandings, the rude behavior, the malicious disinterest, the unkept promises, and the good intentions that went nowhere. Factions developed. History was rewritten. Stories were repeated, analyzed, and embellished. In Cordelia's humble opinion, it often felt as if the nuclear family, that pillar of civilized society, was nothing but a mini Bosnia waiting to erupt.

The sisters rode in silence until they reached the outskirts of New Haven. It was a few minutes to six when they finally pulled into the Cornwall Inn's parking lot. Cordelia was determined to have a talk with Octavia before they went inside, but she didn't want to do it at the risk of life and limb. The driving had been too treacherous to concentrate on anything other than the road in front of her. They might not have much time now, but it would have to do. She eased the car into a narrow parking space and left the motor running. She might be dying to tell her sister everything she and Jane had found out, but before they got to that, Octavia had some explaining to do. "Don't get out just yet."

"Why not? Dad doesn't like it when we're late."

"Isn't there something you've been meaning to tell me?"

"Like what?"

"Can we *please* stop with the games?"

"Look——"

"No, you look. I don't like being lied to. First, you tell me you're done with booze and drugs. The next thing I know, my mother is lying in a hospital bed fighting for her life. Why? Because *you* were driving drunk."

"I thought we agreed to table that discussion. How many more ways can I say I'm sorry? Honestly, Cordelia, I've come to the conclusion that apologies are pointless. And regrets come way too late. All any of us can do is move on—try to do better in the future."

"Nice speech. Is that what you were doing when you lured me here with the promise of being in your wedding? Your *bogus* wedding?"

"I explained all that."

"Hell-o! Am I speaking to a wall here?"

Octavia clenched her jaws.

"The secret? Don't make me drag it out of you."

"I don't know what you're talking about."

"Okay, I'll give you a hint. Jane and I talked to Sir Jefferey Gorham when we were in New York. Remember him? He asked how you were feeling. I thought he was merely inquiring about the general state of your health, but as it turns out——"

Octavia's face went suddenly blank.

"You're pregnant. Why couldn't you just tell me?"

Her gaze drifted out the window.

"Answer me!"

"Because I couldn't!"

"Why?"

"Because . . . because Roland swore me to secrecy. I made a promise, one I couldn't break. And then, after he was gone, I wanted to tell you. I was going to the other day, when we were in the billiard room, but then Dad came in——"

"And of course, you have to keep secrets from *someone*. You can't just let any old Tom, Dick, or Harry off the street know you're pregnant."

"No! But I had to pick the right time."

"I see. The right time. Okay, you've got the perfect opportunity tonight to fill us all in on the happy details."

"It's not that simple." Even in the darkness, Cordelia could see her sister's face had gone pale. "Think, Cordelia. I surprised Dad with the wedding and it nearly pushed him over the edge."

"A feather would push him over the edge right now. By keeping secrets, all you do is heighten the effect when he does learn the truth. God knows, this family doesn't need any more drama."

"That's not what I want either. But . . . I can't stand to cause him more pain. I've already done enough. Mom's death nearly killed him. I hate myself for what happened. I've relived that moment every day since it happened. I know I shouldn't have been drinking, but . . . it was such a wonderful celebration. I was on top of the world. And then—"

Cracking the car door open, Cordelia said, "You're going to tell him the truth tonight."

"Can't we have *one* normal evening together before he leaves?"

"What the hell is normal? For the sake of peace, are we going to sit and watch him drink himself into another stupor?"

"No. Of course not. But—"

"I'm beginning to think Dad never quit drinking. He lied to Mom. He lied to all of us."

"That's not true. He did stop . . . for a while."

"Mom protected him for years. Now the torch has passed to us. We can't follow in her footsteps, Octavia. If we do, he's a dead man. Damn it, you're going to back me up for once. We're going to lay it all out on the table. No more secrets. No more lies."

"This is a restaurant, Cordelia. It's much too public for a discussion like that."

"Right, just like Innishannon's too public. And oh, dearie me, tomorrow won't work because you'll be having one of your headaches. And then there'll be another excuse, and another. I don't care if we have the conversation under that street lamp over there." She pointed. "We're not putting it off another minute. If you don't tell him about the baby, I will."

"You grew up to be a freaking battle ax, you know that?"

Getting out of the car, Cordelia muttered, "I will assume you mean that in the kindest possible way."

Entering the dining room, Cordelia asked to be seated in one of the booths in the back. The weather had thinned the ranks of diners, and the table she selected gave them maximum privacy within the limits of a public space.

They'd just finished ordering coffee when their father came charging into the room, his expression exuberant, waving a stack of papers over his head.

"I wonder if he was in the bar?" whispered Cordelia, trying to gauge the state of his intoxication by the way he walked. He seemed as steady and sober as the proverbial judge. "We should have looked."

Slipping into the booth next to Octavia, Hiram dumped at least a dozen brochures in the center of the table.

"What's that?" asked Cordelia, gazing at the pile with open suspicion.

"Vacation brochures. I picked them up this afternoon. Went to three different travel agencies."

"Why?" asked Octavia.

"Because I'm taking my two beautiful daughters on vacation. If this last week has taught me anything, it's that we need to spend more time together."

Cordelia felt herself stiffen and pull away from the table. He wasn't "asking" to take them, or "hoping" to take them. He was simply "taking" them. In his mind, it was a *fait accompli*. On the face of it, what could possibly be wrong with such generosity? A father wanting to do something special for his daughters. Except, it was all based on a lie. He was playing the good father while his drinking was causing his family to crumble around him.

"Look at them. They won't bite." His laugh was hearty. "Not one of them is the usual trip to Paris or London. We Thorns are more adventurous. There's an exotic cruise up the Nile. Or we could visit Turkey, see the Whirling Dervishes in Istanbul. One brochure is all about a tour of the cliff top monastery at Meteora—that's in Greece. It sounded so peaceful. And then—" He selected one out of the pile and tossed it in front of Cordelia. "Timbuktu. How many people can say they've been to Timbuktu?"

"How many people would *want* to say it?" she mumbled.

"Now, don't spoil the fun. I bet you two don't even know where Timbuktu is."

"The end of the earth?" said Octavia. She wasn't smiling.

"It's in West Africa. Just think." He spread his hands, creating the scene for them. "Sunset on the Sahara Desert. Living in a tent. Mixing with the natives."

"Sounds just peachy, Dad," said Cordelia, folding her arms over her chest. "I'm sure I'd simply adore watching all those odd West African bugs crawl up my legs, infest my bedding, my clothes. Not to mention the intense heat, the freezing cold nights. No shower. No hot and cold running water. Boiled bush critters for dinner. And all that luxurious sand, the kind that gets in your clothes and hair and won't come out. Yup, it sure is my idea of a good time."

"Where's your sense of adventure?" He'd moved into irritation mode.

Cordelia looked him straight in the eye, waving to get his attention. "Hey, remember me? Cordelia? I'm your oldest daughter? The one who thinks there should be cushions on park benches. The one whose favorite exercise is reading. The woman who climbed into thirty-seven bathtubs before she found one that was comfortable enough to be installed in her loft. I don't *do* outdoors. I never have, at least willingly. I'm not the pioneer type. I find it bizarre beyond belief that people would risk their lives to climb a mountain. I am not, I repeat *not,* Ernest Hemingway!"

"Stop ranting," said Octavia, straightening her silverware. "We know who you are."

"Good. For a minute there, I thought I was being clasped to the bosom of the wrong family."

"Okay, okay," said Hiram, unwilling to give up on the idea. "Then we'll do a culinary tour of France. Or an architectural tour of Budapest."

"Or a pastry tour of Austria," offered Octavia.

Well, at least they had her attention now. Except that traveling with their father, even if they could work out the timing, would be a nightmare if he didn't deal with his alcoholism first.

The waitress arrived with the menus and the coffee. Before she left, Hiram asked for "another" double vodka on the rocks—stat. Apparently, he thought he could issue orders the same way he did at the hospital.

326

So he *had* been in the bar, thought Cordelia. She didn't say anything. First things first. "Dad, Octavia has some good news she wants to tell you."

"It can wait," said Octavia, stirring cream into her coffee.

"No, it can't." She smiled through clenched teeth.

Adjusting his glasses, Hiram glanced at the menu. He read through it for almost a minute before saying, "What news?"

"I think I'll have the steak and lobster," said Octavia.

"That makes sense," said Cordelia, "since you're eating for two now." Octavia flashed Cordelia a look of warning.

"Eating for two," repeated Hiram, glancing up with a puzzled look. It finally hit him. "Octavia, you're not pregnant?"

"Actually, Dad . . . I am."

All expression died in his face. "Who's the father?"

"It's Roland's child."

The waitress arrived with his double vodka. It didn't sit on the table for more than a second before it was in his hand, on the way to his lips.

"Roland and I planned it from the very beginning," said Octavia. "I've wanted a child for years, but it was never the right time. Now it is. I'm very happy. So is Cordelia, and I hope you will be too."

"But . . . to have a child with a man—a gay man—who . . . who was so old, who wouldn't live long. It's ludicrous."

"It's my life. If you find it ludicrous, I'm sorry. Roland would have made a wonderful father." She looked down at her coffee cup, adding, "If he'd lived."

It was probably too much to ask Octavia to explain about Roland's promise of wealth and power in return for the child. It put the entire interaction on a distinctly unflattering basis. Then again, perhaps Octavia did want a child. The offer probably appealed to her romantic sensibilities, or at the very least, her sense of the absurd. Within the context of the moment, it had no doubt seemed like a good idea, not that their father would ever understand. For all of his intelligence, experience, education, and sophistication, he'd become a rather stodgy New Englander.

"I don't understand you," said Hiram. He sat back in the booth, looking defeated. "The world must have gone crazy when I wasn't looking."

Cordelia braced herself for an explosion, then said, "You know, Dad, things might make more sense if you stopped drinking."

His face flushed a deep red.

"This isn't easy for me to say, but you're in trouble. Before Mom died, she told me you'd stopped drinking. Octavia and I were both so proud of you. But you started again. I don't know when, although I assume it had something to do with her death. I know how hard it hit you. I haven't come to visit you as much as I should have in the last few years, and that's my fault. But someone's got to tell it like it is. I love you too much to keep quiet. You're hurting yourself and you're hurting your family. You're heading for a disaster, Dad, if you don't get some serious help."

Octavia reached for his hand. "She's right, Dad. You made a promise to yourself, just like I did. And just like I did, you broke it. But I haven't had a drink in years. You *can* change. There are lots of people out there who want to help you. Let them. Let *us*."

"I can't believe my daughters are talking to me like this." He looked shaken. Rattled. All the bluster and good humor had dropped away. In its place was a sad, vulnerable old man.

Cordelia found the look on his face so painful, she had the urge to turn away, but she knew she couldn't. "We should have said something a long time ago, but we didn't. For all the wrong reasons. Same as Mom."

He tried to pull his hand away, but Octavia held on tight. "Cordelia's right, Dad. I turned a blind eye. And I did it *for all the wrong reasons*."

He looked at her with fear in his eyes. "I refuse to sit and listen to this."

"We're not playing, Dad," said Cordelia. "If you don't agree to check yourself into an alcohol rehab, I'll talk to the head of your hospital. I'll tell him you're in no shape to continue your duties there."

"How dare you threaten me!"

"It's not a threat, it's a promise. I lost Mom because of Octavia's drinking. I won't lose you too."

Flustered, he yanked his hand free and stood up. "When the two of you get a grip on yourselves, when you can behave like rational human beings, again, we can continue this conversation. I admit, I may have a problem, but I won't be shamed like a small child. And I won't be bullied!"

"Dad—" said Octavia, looking shocked. Before she could say another word, he turned and stomped away.

Cordelia watched his disappearing back. "That went well."

"What did you expect? You've got all the finesse of a wrestler!"

"It didn't matter what I said or how I said it. He wasn't going to like it. At least the truth is out in the open now."

"The truth? The *truth*. My God but you live in a simple world."

"Excuse me?"

"There are a lot of things more important than the truth, you moron! Why the hell didn't you become a tent evangelist and leave us the hell alone?" She pushed her coffee away and got up.

"Where are you going?"

"To catch up with Dad. Tell him I'm sorry."

"For what?"

"For everything. For nothing. Because I love him. Who cares! He's been drinking, Cordelia. And he's upset. I don't think he should be alone."

Cordelia didn't like the implication that she'd done something wrong. She'd merely stated the obvious, set the ball in motion. Getting their father into rehab might be a long process, but it had to start somewhere. Somebody had to be the bad guy. It took courage to do what she'd just done. Why couldn't Octavia give her some credit? And yet . . . in this one instance, maybe she was right. He shouldn't be alone, or more specifically, he shouldn't be driving around by himself in the state he was in. "I'll come with you," she said, tossing some cash on the table.

"Fine," said Octavia. "You can drive my car home. And I'll drive Dad's. He can ride with me. No arguments, Cordelia. Otherwise, you walk."

When they got out to the parking lot, they saw the rear lights of Octavia's Volvo disappearing down the street.

"Damn," said Cordelia, hands rising to her hips. "Why didn't he take his own car?"

"You've got his keys, remember? And he's got mine. Come on, we're wasting time."

They both worked quickly to scrape the snow and ice off the windows. On this monster of a car, it seemed to take forever. Finally, slipping behind the wheel, Cordelia started the engine and turned the defogger on and the defrost up to high. The weather wasn't any worse, but it wasn't any better either. By now the roads had to be in terrible shape. Since the car was so large, it took several minutes for the inside of the windows to clear.

Once she was able to see well enough to drive, Cordelia backed out of the parking space, then turned left out of the lot, skidding onto the street. "Do you see his car anymore?"

Even before she said it, she realized it was a stupid question. Every car was covered with snow. Nothing was particularly recognizable. When they finally left the tangle of slow traffic and reached the highway, Cordelia breathed a sigh of relief. The traffic on the interstate was light. Then, a thought hit her. "We're assuming Dad's heading back to Innishannon."

"Where else would he go?"

Cordelia looked over at her sister. She could tell they were thinking the same thing. "A bar."

"He wouldn't do that," she insisted. "Just keep going."

For the next half hour, they passed every car they came to, but not one was a Volvo C70. "Where could he be?" asked Cordelia, banging on the steering wheel in frustration.

"He's probably driving too fast."

"Oh, just great." She squinted at a highway sign. "We'll be off the freeway and onto a county road in less than a mile."

"Drive faster," ordered Octavia.

"I'm driving as fast as the conditions allow."

"Just stuff the caution, okay? I've got a bad feeling."

To be honest, Cordelia did too. The mixture was lethal. Bad weather, booze, and bad temper. When they finally came to County Road 37, they left the interstate lights behind and entered a world of winter darkness. The road to Innishannon was winding and narrow, bordered by woods and an occasional open field. Without the moonlight to guide them, all they had were their headlights. It was like driving into a tunnel with all the road markings erased.

Octavia kept wiping away the fog on the side window with her bare hand while Cordelia did her best to keep the car on the road. The interstate had been plowed and sanded, but the side roads were drifted and treacherously slippery. At times, she wasn't even sure where the road was.

"If he's sitting in some cozy little bar getting plastered while you and me and my baby are taking our lives in our hands rushing back to Innishannon, I'm going to kill him."

"I'll help you," said Cordelia. At last, a little healthy anger.

"I see car lights," said Octavia, her voice growing excited. "Up ahead to our right."

Cordelia could see them too. "It's probably a car traveling down a side road."

"There aren't many side roads out here. Besides the car's not moving."

Cordelia felt her pulse quicken. "I better slow down."

"No! Just keep going—as fast as you can."

"Octavia, it isn't safe."

"There," she cried, rolling down the window to get a better look. "It's my car. And it's off the road, halfway into the field, but the car lights are still on. Move it!"

"He spun out."

"Come on! You drive like an old woman. He could be hurt!"

A second later, the headlights caught the tracks where he'd tried to stop. Cordelia glanced at the speedometer. She'd slowed to forty, but it was still too fast. Applying the breaks as gingerly as she could, the car slowed a little more, but instead of stopping, it started to swerve and then to skid.

"God," she yelled, turning into the skid, trying to regain control of the car. Instead of the field, they were hurtling toward the woods on the other side of the road. "Hold on."

Octavia screamed just as the car slammed into a tree.

39

As soon as Jane finished unpacking, she returned to the mansion's first floor to see about dinner. She hadn't eaten anything since breakfast and was starting to feel the effects. Leonard informed her that Mrs. Gettle had left no instructions for a formal meal, but that he would ask the cook's assistant to make her a sandwich. He suggested tuna salad on wheat, potato chips, and a pot of tea. Jane asked that a tray be brought to the library. Ever since she'd had the conversation with Salvador Barros last night, she'd been itching to do some research on film preservation. She hoped that Roland's collection would include a book or two on the subject.

Once she'd located a volume entitled *Our Vanishing Past: Hollywood Film Preservation and the Race Against Time,* she made herself comfortable in one of the easy chairs, adjusted her wire-rimmed glasses, and began to read:

It may come as a shock to many Americans, but over 90 percent of our silent movies no longer exist, and far more than half of the feature films made before 1950 are gone as well. It is a fact of life that all film self-destructs, more often than not, rapidly. If we are to save what is left of our movie heritage, we must act now. Make no mistake. This is a race against time.

Just because a movie exists on videotape, because one can see it on TV, or rent it at a video store, doesn't mean it has been preserved. This is one of the hardest concepts to get across to the American public. Movies were meant to be shown in theatres, and if a print or a negative doesn't exist in superior condition, it simply isn't possible.

In the early days, film was made of cellulose nitrate, or simply, "nitrate." This type of film had superb photographic capacities and dominated the industry until the 1950's. Most believed it to be the perfect medium to record the dramatic light and shadow used so effectively in black-and-white movies. In the 1930's, the three strip Technicolor process was developed using the very same nitrate film, capturing the full color spectrum equally as well.

And yet, along with all its desirable qualities, nitrate was found to have severe limitations. The chemical nature of the film was unstable. Stored in a dark vault, the movie reels would undergo a slow decomposition. Before they finally turned to powder, they would become extremely volatile—nitroglycerine in a can. Film canisters eventually came to be viewed as mini-explosives that could spontaneously combust at the relatively low temperature of 105 degrees. In fact, nitrate film fires in the late nineteenth and early twentieth century resulted in hundreds of disasters all across the country. No wonder cellulose nitrate came to be looked upon as a liability.

Since old films were dangerous and expensive to store, many of the studios simply burned them. There were no ancillary markets like TV or video, so once a film had made the rounds of the movie houses, its value was considered nil. Many independent filmmakers were operating on a shoestring, so selling the used reels for their silver content made financial sense. Finally, because piracy was a widespread problem during the silent film era, many of the prints were destroyed to prevent them from being copied, recut, retitled, and reissued. The more modern notion of "preservation for posterity" was never even thought about.

As Jane turned to the next page, she heard the library door open. Leonard carried in the dinner tray and set it down on a low table next to her chair. She thanked him, picked up half the sandwich, and continued reading.

During the final years of the 1940's, a rash of nitrate-caused fires eventually pushed the motion picture industry to abandon the use of cellulose nitrate altogether. Another kind of film, cellulose triacetate, more commonly referred to as "acetate" or "safety" film became the medium of choice, primarily because it was far more stable. "Acetate" had been developed before WWI and had been used in the 8mm and 16mm format, but within the industry it was considered to have two serious drawbacks. First, it was far more costly. Second, it produced an inferior image. Still, because it posed no threat to moviegoers, projectionists, and theatre owners, and appeared to be a huge step forward to the growing ranks of film preservationists, its use was adopted.

In recent years, however, as archivists opened the stored "safety" films, they found a new threat to preservation: The Vinegar Syndrome. As with nitrate film, acetate was subject to decomposition. In this case, the reels would literally cook in their own juices. It is now widely believed that cellulose triacetate is even more short-lived than cellulose nitrate.

Another potential step forward came when Kodak introduced Eastman Color in the 1950's. This was a far less costly process than Technicolor and needed less light during photography. Unfortunately, as time passed, archivists discovered that it was prone to serious fading. In fact, color fading has become the single most costly aspect of film preservation today.

The Whitney Film Institute recently announced a staggering statistic. At least 7 billion feet of film contained in private collections, libraries, and various motion picture archives around the world are in desperate need of restoration. A good 100 million feet of that film are American movies on cellulose nitrate. The cost of restoration if we could start tomorrow would far exceed three billion dollars. Every year, thousands of feet of precious, irreplaceable film disappears forever. Up until recently, the crisis has been a silent one. Today, however, preservationists from all over the world are demanding to be heard. We must heed their warning if we are to preserve this vital, vibrant, visual link to our past.

Pouring herself a cup of tea, Jane's thoughts turned to Ellie. She finally understood Ellie's anger at Roland, her desire to uncover the full truth and document it for the entire world to see. Not only had Roland maneuvered her family out of a financial gold mine, but he'd kept the formula a secret from an industry in desperate need of a miracle. Further, Roland had cheated Ellie's grandfather out of his place in history as the inventor of the formula.

To be fair, a deal had been struck between Wallace and Strong. It wasn't as if the process had been stolen. On the other hand, if Strong hadn't been an immigrant, a poor working stiff, if he'd had more clout within the industry, perhaps his discovery would have been taken more seriously. As it was, he was just a guy down on his luck, a man who drank too much, possibly bragged a bit too loudly. Maybe the studios even thought of him as a little crazy. Inventors didn't always follow the tried and true roads to success. Because of that image, he may have been given short shrift by the powers that be. Since nobody back in the thirties was particularly interested in preserving films, Strong had developed a world-class idea that nobody wanted. Perhaps the chemists that tested it did a less than adequate job because it was essentially just nuisance work.

And yet, by the late forties, when Roland first got his hands on the formula, he knew how valuable it might be. He probably took more care when he had it tested—or perhaps he tested it himself. Whatever the case, when he found that it worked, he must have known it was an immense discovery. And yet, he told no one. Instead, he set about creating his own private collection, one he intended to pass on to his daughter—along with the formula. And now it all belonged to Octavia, except that she was missing the most vital piece. Roland hadn't lied to her. He really was offering her the key to wealth, power, and fame beyond her wildest dreams. The more Jane thought about it, the more certain she was that the house in Wister held the key. She couldn't wait to get inside. As soon as Cordelia and Octavia returned from dinner in New Haven, she intended to drive back with them and find some way to break in. It was Octavia's house now. Maybe, if they looked through Roland's keys, they'd find one that fit the back door. But even if they didn't, what would a couple of broken windows matter in the scheme of things?

As she set her teacup back down, Verna sailed into the room, bringing with her a cloud of cigarette smoke.

"Jane," she said, stopping with a start. "I thought you and Cordelia were in New York."

"We just got back."

She seemed tired tonight, her heavy makeup a little less carefully applied than normal. "Having some dinner, I see."

Jane had just about finished her sandwich and chips. "Would you like some tea? I could go get you a cup."

"No thanks." She removed the cigarette holder from her lips and blew smoke out of the side of her mouth. "I guess I'm feeling kind of lonely tonight. It was a monumentally depressing day." She tapped some ash into the ashtray she was holding, then sat down. "Ellie's father and brother drove out to the estate this afternoon. They flew in from California this morning. They wanted to see the tack house, so Buddy took them down there."

"I'm sorry I wasn't here to meet them."

"The police are releasing the body tomorrow. Her father is taking Ellie back home, but the brother is staying. He's a very angry man. He's demanding answers. Wants to know how something like this could have happened."

"So do I," said Jane. "Have you heard anything more? Do the police have any leads?"

"Just me," she said bluntly, exhaling a puff of smoke.

"You?"

"Don't tell me you haven't heard? My Virginia Slims gave me away. As if I had anything to hide. Sure, I went down to talk to her that morning. I don't deny it. But I had no reason to hurt her. I hardly even knew her. I agree, with her death following so closely on Roland's, something sinister is going on in this house, but it's not because of me."

"What did you two talk about?"

"Lots of things. The documentary. Her family."

"Did she tell you about her grandfather?" Jane watched her reaction.

"Not that I recall. Mostly, we talked about New Year's. Do you realize tomorrow night is New Year's Eve? Another year gone, and not many more left." She stared up at the bookshelves for a few seconds, her high, sculpted cheekbones every bit as majestic as they'd been as a young woman. "After a day like today, I really feel the years. I know I'm headed for the departure lounge, as my late husband used to say."

"You don't look that way to me."

She smiled. "You're kind, and too young to understand. I've been weepy all day, crying at the oddest moments, even before Ellie's family arrived. I'd like to think it's because of Roland's death, because I'm a sensitive soul and I'm in agony over a dear friend's loss. But the truth is, I'm not feeling sorry for him, I'm feeling sorry for me. When you get to be my age, your friends leave the planet every day. You stop counting. Maybe you even stop caring. The present may *be* real, but it's the past that *feels* real. I suppose I'm crying for that, mostly. It's hard to believe the world I knew is all gone now. All gone."

"But not forgotten."

"Yes, but you had to be there to understand how it felt, how it smelled, how it tasted and glittered, how luminous some of the moments truly were. Words can't begin to describe it." With a contemplative puff on her cigarette, she continued, "You know, back in the dark ages, when a woman got to be middle-aged—a little worn in the face, as they say—cameramen would slip gauze over the camera. After a while, people began to notice that the close-ups were very soft, while the rest of the film wasn't. Friends would say, 'I see they're using the gauze on you.' It was embarrassing. Naturally, the actresses would go to the cameramen and complain. And what was the answer? Diffuse the whole picture. I remember someone telling me once that a famous actress was sitting in front of the camera, the gauze over the lens for a close-up. The cameraman lit a cigarette, looked through the finder and reached around to burn the gauze right where the eyes were. Very clever. That actress didn't dare move a muscle, but when you saw the finished film, what you got was a soft face and these sparkling eyes." She laughed, tipping ash into an ashtray. "I need the gauze pretty badly these days."

It must be a very different way of life, thought Jane, always having to think so critically about your appearance. Most women felt that pressure to one degree or another, but for an actor or an actress, careers lived and died based on looks.

Verna was wearing a gray silk lounging suit tonight. She fussed with the collar for a moment, then continued. "I'm always surprised to find out people don't know the MGM lion was defanged and toothless. Roland and I used to laugh about it all the time. What struck us, I suppose, was the irony. Reality verses image. The lion seemed to be the perfect Hollywood symbol." She removed the cigarette holder from her mouth and used it to punctuate her words. "When I was young, I always played the girl next door. The upright virgin. The paragon of female goodness. Later, I became the long suffering wife, or the noble mother. Occasionally, I'd play a career woman, but I always bit the matrimonial dust by the end of the movie. The odd part is, not once during my entire career did I ever play a villain on-screen. I'd been typecast, of course. I wanted to stretch, take on other roles, but producers and agents constantly told me that nobody would believe I could be bad. Two-faced. Evil."

"And . . . the irony is, you are?"

Verna didn't seem upset by the question. Instead, she considered it briefly. "I don't know, really. I suppose we all act based on self-interest. I will say, I'm not the impulsive type. I always had good reasons for what I did."

Jane sipped her tea. "I don't know if Octavia mentioned this to you or not, but the other night she found several boxes of Roland's personal papers in a vault in the projection room."

Verna's eyes narrowed ever so slightly. "Really?"

"There was an interesting letter from a man named Byron Vance, an editor at Random House. It was all about the autobiography Lew Wallace had written. *In the Belly of the Beast,* I believe it was called. You said that Lew never wrote a book."

"Did I?"

"That's what you told Ellie when she interviewed you."

Verna's expression grew remote. "Yes, I may have."

"But you did know about it."

"Of course."

"Why did you lie?"

She sat quietly, eyes averted, thinking very hard about something. Finally, returning her gaze to Jane, she said, "It was a reflex, I suppose." She paused, stubbing out her cigarette. She took her time lighting another. "How much do you know about the book?"

"I know that Random House wouldn't publish it because of libel considerations."

A smile crept around the corners of her mouth. "It was explosive."

"You've read it, then?"

"Many years ago." She waved her cigarette holder dismissively. "You know, people in this country think of Hollywood as Sin City—a bunch of shallow, immoral people hopping from bed to bed. The truth is far more interesting than that."

"What is the truth?"

Verna laughed. "You don't want much, do you?"

"What was Lew's truth, then?"

She brushed a flake of ash off her slacks. "I'm always amazed that, with all the trumpeting that goes on today about gay liberation, times have changed so little."

"But they have changed."

"You think so? I had lunch with a young friend of mine a few weeks ago. Young . . . I assume she's close to forty, but that's young in my book. She was in Atlanta for a couple of days and wanted to get together. Understand, this woman is box office, the kind of actress that can make or break a picture deal just by agreeing to be in a film. She's also a lesbian. People in Hollywood know the score, but nobody talks, at least they don't talk to anybody who counts, and that means the rest of the world can live in blissful ignorance. Again and again, as we sat talking, she referred to her name in the abstract, as if it had nothing to do with who she really was. I finally called her on it and she said, yes, her agent, a man she's known for years and trusts implicitly, said she had to view her 'star persona' that way. 'Jane Doe' was a commodity, something to be bought and sold. It was an image, one that needed to be positioned correctly within the industry, promoted with intelligence and a clear sense of purpose. It wasn't that she was lying, her image was something apart. I didn't really get it, but she seemed to. You have to understand. At the level she's working at, the radiation is toxic. It affects the brain. This woman isn't dishonest. On the contrary, she has a great deal of integrity. But on this one issue, she seems to buy the convoluted, Byzantine logic necessary to maintain the falsehood. It gave me a headache fifty years ago, and it still gives me a headache today." She drew on her cigarette, blowing smoke high into the air.

"And yet, you kept quiet just like all the rest."

"Of course I did. I play by the rules. People of our generation, whether heterosexual or homosexual, think homosexuality is still an untouchable subject. I suppose our attitude helps make it so, but that's just the way it is. Today people let almost everything hang out. There's no distance, and very little dignity. In my opinion, some things are private, and should remain private. Roland surprised the hell out of me when he said he was going to tell that Saks woman the whole truth about himself and Lew. Sure, I loathe homophobia, but people today are notoriously sanctimonious about the past. They want to know why we all didn't rise up and defend our homosexual brothers and sisters. They have no real sense of the times in which we lived. All they want to do is condemn, and in the process, feel superior. If people today knew about the book Lew had written, they'd probably make him into some kind of saint. Lew was many things, but never that. In fact, by the time he wrote that autobiography, he'd become careless and self-destructive."

"So you think what he did was wrong?"

"It was worse than wrong, it was stupid. Reckless. It didn't matter to him who he hurt."

"Maybe he couldn't stand the charade any longer."

"It was just fine as long as it paid the bills. Don't get me wrong, I adored Lew. But I hated what he'd become. By the time he finished that book, he'd grown so cynical, I hardly knew him anymore. I understood his reasons as well as anyone did, but the book was a mistake."

It was her opinion and she was welcome to it. Still, Jane couldn't help but wonder if it wasn't motivated by a certain self-interest. The autobiography probably talked about Verna as well. Maybe she didn't like what it said. "Are there any copies of Lew's manuscript still in existence?"

"No. Maybe he had a right to risk his career, but he didn't have a right to destroy others'. And that's what the book would have done."

"Was he murdered because he wrote it?"

"How should I know?"

Before Jane could ask another question, Leonard burst into the room carrying a cordless phone. "It's Ms. Thorn," he said. "It's urgent. She asked me to find you right away."

Jane took the phone and said, "Hello?"

"Janey, it's Cordelia. I'm at New Haven General. There's been an accident."

"Are you all right?"

"Yes. No. I mean I'm not hurt, but I'm not all right. Get here as soon as you can, okay? Oh, God, there's the doctor. He's about as communicative as a mushroom. I've got to talk to him before he disappears again. Just come, okay, Janey? I need you!"

40

Aren't we going the wrong way?" asked Jane.

Buddy had volunteered to drive her to New Haven. He was the only one at the house with a four-wheel drive vehicle and he said that, with the weather as bad as it was, his Explorer had the best chance of making it to the hospital safely. Except, as they were about to pull out onto County Road 37, Buddy turned right instead of left.

"You're used to going through Asbury," he said, turning up the defroster. "It's about ten miles to the interstate that way. Normally, you're right. That's the most direct, quickest route. But in this weather, we'll catch I-95 faster heading east."

Jane didn't remember seeing it on a map. As she cupped a hand around the seat belt, she wondered if it had been smart to get in a car with a man she considered a prime suspect in a homicide. But waiting for a taxi would have taken forever.

"Do you know what's wrong with Cordelia?" asked Buddy, adjusting the rearview mirror.

"She said she was okay, so I assume the problem is with her sister or her father."

"I'm sorry to hear it." He hesitated. "I don't mean to speak out of turn, but Dr. Thorn seems to be having a rough time of it." Glancing at Jane, he added, "The drinking, I mean."

"His daughters are pretty concerned."

"I hope the three of them will be able to make it to Roland's memorial tomorrow. His ashes arrived this morning. I plan to scatter them in the sound just before dusk. Everyone at the house is invited to pay their final respects on the eve of a new year."

"Thanks. I'll let them know."

They rode in silence until they came to the interstate. Jane breathed an inward sigh of relief. Buddy didn't seem dangerous, but then, at this point, what did she know? Under other circumstances, she might have asked him some leading questions, tried to get him to open up about his confession, but riding alone with him in a car, she felt too vulnerable. She decided to ask him about Gracie instead. "I haven't seen your granddaughter around much."

His eyes shifted to her, then back to the road. "She hasn't been feeling very well."

"She must be upset about losing Innishannon."

"She told you about that?" He seemed surprised.

"Not in so many words. But when she invited me up to her apartment for pizza the other night, I got the impression she was really looking forward to the day when the property would be hers."

He gripped the wheel more tightly and stared straight ahead. "My brother could be such a bastard sometimes. In this case, he acted without considering the repercussions. Grace is so upset, half the time she won't even talk to me. I'm an old man. I've seen a lot with these two eyes of mine, and that kid's in trouble. It's wrong to speak ill of the dead, but it's all Roland's fault."

"You don't blame Octavia?"

"Octavia? Hell, no. I'm hoping, when all the dust settles, that she'll let me buy the house back from her. Gracie and I can live there together."

That was interesting, thought Jane. Apparently, he didn't think he was about to be arrested for Roland's murder. Did that mean he was innocent, or was he simply betting they'd never find enough evidence to convict? "Who do you think poisoned your brother?" The words just slipped out. She couldn't take them back now.

He grunted. "Don't get me started."

"No, really. I'd like to know."

"You mean, you don't think it was me? Everyone else does."

"No, Buddy. I don't think you did it." It wasn't a complete lie. She didn't know for sure.

"Why?"

"I have a brother of my own. I could never hurt him."

"Even if he hurt you?"

She nodded.

"At last, a sensible human being." He considered her question silently for a few moments. Finally, he said, "Okay, I'll tell you who poisoned Roland. You may not believe me, any more than the police did when I talked to them yesterday, but it was Christian Wallace. He's been circling Roland like a vulture for years, just waiting for the carcass to get cold. Did you know he was blackmailing my brother?"

She shook her head. Of course, she did know, but she wanted to hear Buddy's take on it.

"He was. Ever since Lew died. Oh, he didn't call it blackmail. Neither did Roland. But they both knew what my brother's yearly 'gift' was for. He was paying for Christian's silence."

"So he wouldn't tell what he knew about Roland's relationship with his father?"

"Exactly right. And, of course, there was Roland's guilt. That was another reason he paid."

"Roland felt guilty? Why?"

"Lew's murder. It was a perfect opportunity for Christian. At between fifty and a hundred thousand a year for over forty years, you do the math. But, the night before my brother died, he told him to pack his bags and leave. In other words, no more money. It seems pretty clear to me what happened. Christian blew a gasket. He thought he had Roland in his pocket, and, turns out, he didn't. Did you know the police found Christian's fingerprint on the bag of jimsonweed they discovered in my room? They didn't find any of my prints, but Christian's was there, big as life. He was the one who planted it—to implicate *me*. I should have suspected him right away. Maybe I'm a little slow sometimes, but let me tell you, as soon as I heard about that fingerprint, I knew."

And Jane bet it was the exact point where he stopped trying to convince the police that he'd murdered his brother. It made sense.

"All I can say is, if the police don't put him behind bars, he's going to have to answer to me."

That sounded ominous. "Did you see him anywhere near the teapot that morning?"

"I wish I had. Hilda brought it up on the tray just like she always

344

does. Eight sharp. I made it to Roland's room around eight-thirty and brought it inside. And then I poured him the tea. Over the course of the next hour, he drank nearly the whole pot."

"You didn't have any?"

He shuddered. "Never touch the stuff. All tea tastes the same to me. Like wet grass."

So, thought Jane, whoever put the poison in the tea knew Buddy wouldn't drink any.

"I did lie to the police about a couple things. I'm sorry about it now. I can't take what I said back, otherwise they'll know something was fishy. But I had a good reason for my actions, I just don't want to explain myself."

After this last comment, Buddy seemed to shut down. Jane asked a few more questions, but received only half-hearted answers. She finally gave the conversation a rest. They rode in silence until they reached the hospital.

It was just after nine when Jane thanked Buddy and said good night. He offered to stick around to drive her back to Innishannon, but she said she'd catch a ride with Cordelia. She stood and watched his Explorer pull away into the snowy night, then went inside.

The first order of business was to locate the emergency room. Jane figured it was the best place to start. As she approached the information desk, she heard someone call her name. Turning, she saw John Toscano breezing down the hall toward her. She was surprised to find him there. When she saw the look on his face, her surprise turned instantly to worry. "What are you doing here?"

"Same reason you are," he said, drawing her over to a quiet corner of the front lobby. "The accident."

"What accident? All I know is that Cordelia said I had to get to the hospital right away."

"She didn't tell you what happened?"

"No." She searched his eyes, bracing herself for the worst.

"On his way back to Innishannon, Dr. Thorn spun his car out into a field. He wasn't hurt badly, but he was dazed, so he just sat there."

"What about Cordelia and Octavia?"

"As I understand it, they were on their way back to the estate when they spotted Dr. Thorn's car in the field. They tried to stop, but they were going too fast."

"Who was driving?"

"Cordelia. The car skidded across the highway and smashed into a tree. The air bags deployed, which allowed them to walk away from the crash. They both rushed into the field to see if their father was okay. That's when Octavia started having these pains in her stomach." He hesitated. "I had no idea she was two months pregnant."

"Oh, my God," said Jane, realizing what must have happened. "The air bag."

"They've stabilized her in the emergency room now. The doctor thinks she's going to be okay."

"And the baby?"

"He wants to keep her overnight, but they think the child will be fine. She was lucky on two counts. Her father is a doctor, so he knew what to do, and he had a cell phone. They called nine-one-one right away. A squad car was dispatched, and that's how I found out. Since I was right around the corner having dinner, I met them at the emergency room entrance."

Jane wondered if that's all it was.

"I thought you might be here," said Toscano, the humor in his eyes noticeably absent.

"What's wrong?" asked Jane. "There's something else."

He rubbed the back of his neck. "It's Dr. Thorn. They brought him into the hospital because he had a rather deep cut on his leg. Since he was here, we requested a blood test."

"We? The police? Why?"

"The officer at the scene thought he smelled alcohol on his breath. He had a PBT with him—" At Jane's questioning look, he added, "It's a portable Breathalyzer. He asked Dr. Thorn to take the test, but he refused."

"Oh, God. I should have known it was something like that."

"He was way over the legal limit. As soon as his wound's been tended to, we're taking him down to the station. Charging him with a DUI." Toscano paused again, this time lowering his voice and bending his head closer to Jane. "I thought you'd like to know, we're about to make an arrest in the Lester homicide."

"Who?"

"I can't say. By tomorrow, we should have all our ducks in a row."

"What about Ellie? Her death's got to be related."

"I agree, but we can't wait on this."

"Is it Buddy?"

"We can't play twenty questions either, Jane."

She thought for a moment. "Look, just so you can make sure all your ducks are cooperative, I found a piece of information you should have. Roland was being followed before his death, remember?"

"Right," said Toscano, narrowing his eyes.

She reached into the back pocket of her jeans and took out a small notebook. Flipping through the pages, she came to the one she wanted. "Here's the license plate number of the man who was tailing him."

"How on earth did you get your hands on that?"

"Oh, well, I happened to be talking to Roland's limousine driver, and—"

"You just *happened* to be talking to him?"

"Don't look a gift horse in the mouth, John. The driver got a good look at the guy's plate number and copied it down. He was going to give it to Roland, but he never saw him again."

"And he just *happened* to give it to you."

"What can I say? I've got a face you can trust."

Now he smiled.

She tore off the page and handed it to him. As she did, his beeper went off.

Toscano pulled back his coat and checked the message. "I'm sorry, but I've got to run."

"Which way to the emergency room?"

He gave her directions and then said, "I'll see you tomorrow."

"When you come out to the house to make your arrest?"

"Correct me if I'm wrong, but I doubt it's something you'll want to miss."

Cordelia paced back and forth in front of the curtain separating her father's cubicle from the rest of the emergency room. The cop who'd arrested him was standing guard by the admitting desk, waiting to take him into custody. Before they left, Cordelia intended to talk to her dad. And it wasn't going to be pretty.

The nurse who'd been treating his wound came out and told her that she could go in now. Turning to the police officer, Cordelia said, "Give me a few minutes?"

The man nodded.

As she walked in, she saw that her father was sitting on a gurney, his bare legs dangling over the side. All he had on was a hospital gown and his black socks. Without the normal accoutrements of power—the suit, the vest, the tie, money clip, expensive shoes, the sophisticated "look" he so carefully crafted—Cordelia felt she had the edge.

"Feel better?" she asked, pulling up a chair and sitting down.

"Give me a minute, honey. I want to get dressed."

"No, let's talk first."

He didn't say anything, he simply examined the dressing on his wound.

"The cop's outside. As soon as you're ready, he's going to take you over to the station and book you. You're going to be spending the night in jail."

He looked up at her, then away. "How's Octavia?"

"She's okay. No thanks to you. I sat with her until she fell asleep."

He stiffened. "I did nothing to hurt her."

"Your drinking hurt her, Dad! It's why we hit that goddamn tree! If you don't get help, I swear, I wash my hands of you. The judge will probably order some kind of therapy, at least I hope he does, but he can't *make* you want to change. Only you can do that."

He looked at her, his expression defiant. Suddenly, covering his face with his hands, he collapsed into tears. "God, look at me. I'm so scared I can't even spit."

It wasn't what she'd expected.

"Don't hate me," he choked out. "Promise you don't hate me." Tears were streaming down his cheeks.

"I don't. I love you. I'm just not going to stick around and watch you destroy your life."

"I never meant to hurt her."

She got up and put a hand on his shoulder to steady him. He seemed so utterly unhinged, she wasn't sure what to do. This was what she wanted, wasn't it? He needed to face the truth. It was just . . . she'd never seen him like this before. Not even at their mother's funeral.

Through his sobs he mumbled, "I lied."

"I know," said Cordelia. "You've been lying to us ever since you came. You kept telling us you were going to stop drinking. Octavia found the bottles of vodka in your room."

"It's . . . the pain," he stammered.

"Of Mom's death?"

"I can't help it."

She started to melt a little. "I know you blame yourself."

"Of course I blame myself."

"You need to talk to someone, Dad. A professional. Somebody who isn't in the family."

"I can't," he said, his eyes pleading for her to understand.

She didn't. "You've got to talk about your feelings. Sort things out. It's the only way."

"No!"

She shook him by the shoulders. "Stop making excuses."

"Stop pushing me!"

Now she was getting mad. "I am *so* close to walking out that door." She glanced at the curtain. "Or whatever."

"Go ahead. If that's what you want, leave."

"It's not what I want."

He broke into tears again.

She realized she was getting nowhere. "Look, I have to check on Octavia." She didn't really, but she needed an excuse to get out of the room.

"Fine," he said, twisting away from her.

She watched him suddenly begin to shake, only one hand covering his face now. She desperately wanted to help him, to reach him, but she didn't know how. She felt guilty leaving, but maybe that's what he needed. Finally, to have someone walk out. As she turned to go, she heard his voice rasp, "Don't you get it, Cordelia?"

As she turned back to him, he got up off the gurney, hunched over, like an old man. "*I* was driving that night. *Me.* Octavia lied to the police to protect me. *I* killed your mother!" He was sobbing even louder now, almost wailing, biting at his lips, refusing to meet her eyes.

Cordelia was dumbfounded.

"Don't hate me, *please,* Cordelia. It was a mistake. I didn't mean to. It was a celebration. What's wrong with a couple drinks at a celebration? I didn't mean it. It was a mistake!"

He crumpled into the chair, holding himself, rocking back and forth. He was terrified and pathetic. Probably still high as a kite. And he was her father.

Struggling to keep her mind focused while her emotions took off in a hundred different directions, Cordelia said, "Are you telling me . . . you let Octavia take the heat for Mom's death?"

"Yes."

"You were behind the wheel?"

"Yes!"

"Do you realize what you did?"

"Of course I realize! My wife is dead because of me!"

"And what about your daughters? Do you know what you did to us?"

"No," he said, crouching even lower. "I didn't know. We haven't been together since . . . since the funeral. I knew you were angry then. I wanted to tell you the truth, I came so close once, but I couldn't stand the idea that, when you found out what really happened, I'd lose you too. I'd just lost your mother. I felt like everything in my life was coming apart. Octavia knew about my other DUIs. She also knew my career might be on the line. When she offered to help, to take the rap for me, I wasn't strong enough to say no. But I took care of it, Cordelia. I have lots of friends in the Boston police department, and I play racquetball every week with a couple of judges. I made sure it was . . . handled. Octavia didn't suffer for my mistake."

"I didn't speak to my sister for eight years!"

"I never realized. She never said anything to me. Neither did you."

"You couldn't have guessed?"

"I didn't!"

"We were both trying to protect you."

"I know," he whimpered, looking up at her. "I'm sorry! I'm a terrible father. Don't hate me, Cordelia. You can't hate your father." He grabbed her hand. "I called the hospital this morning. Tendered my resignation. I was going to tell you and your sister at dinner tonight, tell you that I planned to check myself into a rehab unit in New Haven, but then you got so pushy. And Octavia hit me with the news about being pregnant. It was too much. I had to get away. Clear my head." He held onto her hand, refusing to let go even when she pulled it away. "You forgave your sister, can't you forgive me?"

"I never forgave my sister."

"Oh, God," he said, dissolving into his pain. "I know what I am. I'm a goddamn drunk. What have I done? Oh, God, what have I done?"

At this moment, it was the same question Cordelia was asking herself. All this time and Octavia had never said a word. They'd been getting closer before their mother's death—as close as motor oil and rose water could ever be. Her family was in crisis and all she could do was blame. She couldn't make that same mistake now. She just couldn't.

Smoothing back her father's hair, she bent down and cradled him in her arms. Closing her eyes, she said, "It's going to be okay, Dad. You told the truth. That was the hardest part. Now, God willing, it's time to heal. It's time for all of us to heal."

41

NEW YEAR'S EVE

Jane had walked in on quite an emotional scene with Cordelia and her father last night at the hospital. She felt guilty for interrupting them, but Dr. Thorn said it was all right, that if he didn't get dressed soon, he was afraid the cops would haul him off to the station in his hospital gown. After he'd left with the officer, Jane and Cordelia remained in the room and talked for a few minutes. Still a bit stunned, Cordelia explained what had happened. She seemed exhausted and yet hopeful. Before leaving to go rent a car, they stopped by Octavia's room to check on her. As it happened, Octavia was awake, in good spirits, and eating her third piece of toast. The doctor had just been in to see her, giving her a green light to go home in the morning. As long as she took it easy for the next few days, the prognosis for the baby was good.

Sitting down on the hospital bed, Cordelia explained what had happened in the ER, that their father had finally admitted he needed help with his drinking, that he was checking himself into a rehab program in New Haven, and that he'd been driving the car the night their mother died. At first Octavia couldn't believe it. The sisters sputtered for a while, throwing "How could yous" and "Don't give me that fish-eyed looks" at each other. But as the sparing quieted down, Cordelia apologized. So did Octavia. They hugged, spoke melodramatically of forgiveness, then seemed to grow embarrassed. After they'd insulted each other a couple more times, Cordelia got up and said she had to go. All in all, it had been quite an evening. Jane doubted that would be the end of it. Their conversation provided the closure Cordelia had needed last night, but only time would tell what scars would remain.

Standing in the mansion's living room now, looking out the front window at the statue of Venus, Jane wondered when Toscano and his men would arrive. It was after four. The memorial service was scheduled for four-thirty. Cordelia had been talking on the phone on and off throughout the afternoon with the powers that be at the Allen Grimby. She was trying to negotiate another few days of vacation. Buddy had spent most of his afternoon dealing with reporters and people in the media, all wanting the latest scoop on his brother's murder. Verna had taken a few of the calls, but had given up in disgust when someone from an entertainment magazine had brought up the Wallace homicide.

The outward show of busyness at the mansion belied the sense of inertia and depression that had settled over everyone. Jane would be happy to get away from the estate tonight after the memorial service. The plan was to head off to Roland's house in Wister as soon as it got dark.

Just as she was about to move away from the front window to go find her coat, she saw a mail truck pull into the drive. Leaving the motor running, a man jumped out, hurried up the front steps and knocked on the door. She wondered what it was about. The regular mail usually came in the morning. She watched as the driver got back into the truck and drove away.

"Special delivery," said Leonard, entering the room a few minutes later. He handed her a letter. She thanked him, then sat down on the window seat and looked at the postmark. It was from Paris. An overnight letter from Julia. Opening it quickly, she read:

Dear Jane,

I thought I should let you know that I've made a decision about helping my Canadian friend mount an education campaign in South Africa. I've been giving it a lot of thought this past week, and I finally decided that I'm going to do it. It will be good to get involved in meaningful work again, especially something that's important to me, something I'm good at, and something where I believe I can make a difference.

I feel as if this last month has given me some much needed perspective. As hard as I've tried, I can't change what happened between us. After talking to you last week, I finally admitted to myself that what we had together is probably over. And yet, it feels so wrong to say good-bye in a letter. I have to see you one more time, Jane. Look you in the eyes. Maybe you can't understand, but it's the only way I'll truly be able to let go.

I have no idea how long I'll be staying in South Africa. I need to get all the legalities squared away—a work visa, etc.—but I've been assured it won't be a problem. My plan is to fly to Johannesburg in the next week or two and find a place to live. My Canadian friend has already returned to Botswana. I'm going to meet him in Durban later in the month for an AIDS conference. If I like the work, I may stay on. I just wish you and I could have spent some time together in Paris. My French is getting better by the day, and I do love it here, but I know it's impossible now. It was just a dream, but it helped me through some very lonely nights.

So, I guess we both go on with our lives. We'll date, perhaps even fall in love again. I do hope that one day you'll find a special someone who'll love you the way you deserve. I just wish that someone could have been me. You may think this is simply sour grapes talking, but I don't believe that special person is Patricia Kastner. She's not good for you, Jane. She's a user. You'll do what you want, no matter what I say, but do think long and hard before you let a woman like her into your life.

Till I see you again, be safe and well, and know that you are in my heart, always.

Love,
Julia

As Jane put down the letter, she felt tears burn her eyes. Her throat felt dry and she had an irresistible urge to throw something large and dramatic at a wall. She couldn't have hoped for a more adult response, a more amicable ending. It had been inevitable, the only way it could ever be between them, and yet if that was true, why did she feel as if one more tether holding her safely to the earth had just snapped?

"It's days like this that make me think about asteroids," announced Cordelia, drifting into the room a few minutes later, a gloomy look on her face. She dropped down in a chair.

Jane quickly stuffed the letter into her pocket. "What about asteroids?"

"Scientists think one will eventually hit the earth, ending all life as we know it."

"Maybe that's good."

Cordelia snorted. "Hey, your mood's about as cheerful as mine." She was wearing her black jeans, a black turtleneck, and a black wool jacket. In other words, her "breaking and entering" outfit. "You all ready for our visit to Wister tonight?"

"All set," said Jane. She was glad Cordelia hadn't pressed her about what she'd been reading. Normally, she would have. Something in Jane's expression must have warned her off. Cordelia had grown more careful with her lately. It wasn't that Jane didn't appreciate good manners, but this felt more like reticence. She wasn't quite sure how to read it. "How's Octavia feeling?"

"Raring to go." She checked her watch. "It's just about time for the service. Why don't we walk down to the beach together?"

With all the new snow, Jane was glad to have a steady arm to lean on.

As soon as they stepped out onto the terrace, Jane could hear the murmur of Long Island Sound coming up to them from below. The lawn, now covered with a fresh blanket of snow, stretched down to the water. A fringe of trees helped guide them along the shoveled path. In the growing dusk, the water looked like a vast sea of gloom.

Once down on the beach, they found that Buddy, Verna, and Christian were already there. Buddy was holding a brass urn, looking suitably grim, and he was wearing chest-high wading boots over his pants.

Octavia arrived a few minutes later, carrying a single red rosebud.

"Is Gracie coming?" asked Christian, kicking a rock into the water.

Buddy searched the grounds for a sign of her. "She'll be here," he said, scowling. He cradled the urn protectively under his arm and looked back out at the water.

Jane sat down on a fallen tree trunk, making room for Cordelia and Octavia as they followed her lead. The dusk had turned the evening sky a deep purple.

After finishing another cigarette, Christian said, "Shouldn't we get started?"

"No," said Buddy. "We have to wait for Grace."

"You did tell her four-thirty, right?"

Buddy didn't answer. He hadn't said more than a few words to anyone and wasn't about to start a conversation now.

"Maybe I should go get her."

"She'll *be* here," said Buddy, his voice sharp.

"Fine. Whatever." Christian tapped another cigarette out of the package. He and Verna talked quietly a few feet away while Buddy continued to stare at the sound.

"I'm freezing to death," muttered Cordelia, shifting her weight closer to her sister.

"Don't crowd me," said Octavia, pushing back. "Buddy, I think we should get started." Before she could get up, the sound of crunching snow caused everyone to turn around.

There in the distance, walking out of the mist that was hugging the shoreline, making her way slowly toward them, was Grace. As she walked up to her grandfather and gave him a kiss on the cheek, his expression finally relaxed.

Jane hadn't seen her in days. She seemed so somber, not at all like the cocky, ebullient Gracie who'd invited her upstairs to her apartment last Friday night. The twilight had washed the color from her face, making her seem very pale and thin.

"We can begin," said Buddy, his voice formal.

"What about Hilda?" asked Verna, drawing the cigarette holder away from her lips. "We can't start without her."

Strange, thought Jane, that no one had missed her until now. She was always around the house somewhere, making coffee or tea, polishing the silver or puttering with the china in the china cabinet.

"She said she wanted to watch from the terrace," said Buddy, pointing.

Everyone turned to look.

Standing like a sentry, framed by the yellow light of the tall windows behind her, stood Hilda, her head tilted downward toward the beach.

"She looks different," whispered Cordelia, standing up to get a better look.

"Different how?" Octavia whispered back.

"Her clothes, for one. She's not dressed like an anchorwoman anymore."

"I didn't know you thought she dressed like an anchorwoman," whispered Octavia. "I thought so too. No style at all. When she left a room, you could never remember what she'd been wearing."

"But tonight, she looks like . . . my God . . . the Queen Mum! It's not much style, I grant you, but it's *something*."

As Jane stood, she could see that Cordelia was right. With her short, dumpling figure, the suit, the proper hat, she did look like England's Queen Mother.

"She's so . . . imposing," whispered Octavia. "She has an aura."

Now they'd crossed the line. As they always did. Still, it got Jane to thinking. "Octavia?"

"Hmm?" She and Cordelia seemed transfixed.

Jane kept her voice very low. "Was Hilda mentioned in Roland's will?"

"Are you kidding? Of course. She gets some stocks and bonds, and a yearly income until her death. Roland also insisted that she be allowed to remain at Innishannon for as long as she wants. I've got nothing to say about it." She was clearly annoyed.

As the murmuring died down, Buddy cleared his throat, then began to wade slowly out into the choppy water. Because it was low tide, he had to walk a good twenty feet before the water came up to his thighs. "I'm not very good at this sort of thing," he began, holding the urn in front of him as the waves slapped against his body. "Roland told me many years ago that, if he preceded me in death, I was to scatter his ashes in the sound. I'm not a minister, so I won't say a prayer, but I thought we could have a minute of silence. You can each say what you want to the good Lord, or to my brother." He bowed his head.

Jane probably should have offered up a prayer for Roland's soul, but she'd never been very religious. At best, she considered herself a kind of reverent agnostic. She did hope that, wherever he was, he was at peace. Instead of focusing on the dead, her thoughts returned to the living—specifically, to Hilda Gettle. In a way, she was like the phantom of Innishannon. Her presence was such a given that she could move about the mansion almost without being noticed. She did have something to gain from Roland's death, though that didn't seem overwhelmingly significant. In this group, who didn't? But Verna's comment came back to her now—the implication that Hilda had been in love with Roland. If that was true, what had happened to her feelings for him when she found out he was gay? Had she felt betrayed? What if Roland *had* let something slip about his film archive or the formula? Who would have been in a better position to put it all together than his house manager? A woman he trusted. A woman he'd known since his days in Hollywood, and a woman who was around him every day. Hilda was the person who took his calls when he wasn't home and who probably cleaned out the pockets of his suits before she sent them to the cleaners. As Jane thought about it, she realized how easy it would have been for Hilda to put the poison in his tea. Had Toscano done more than a cursory investigation of her? Had he investigated her at *all*? Jane felt a moment of guilt for suspecting such a sweet, loyal old woman of doing something so heinous, and yet, the more she thought about it, the more it made sense.

"All right," said Buddy. "If I can have your attention again." He lifted the cover off the urn. "I thought about preparing a Bible verse to read, but neither Roland nor I were much for Bible reading. This morning, after breakfast, I stood in front of that statue of Venus. I hadn't really looked at it in years. You all know they called my brother the Merchant of Venus. When I read the quote by Titus Lucritius Carus again, I figured Roland had already picked his epitaph. I believe it says a lot about the way he viewed life and love. Right then and there I decided that, when I committed his ashes to the sea tonight, I would repeat that quote. So . . . here goes." Clearing his throat again, he began pouring the ashes into the water, intoning the words, "From the heart of this fountain of delights wells up a bitter taste to choke us, even amid the flowers. Good-bye, Roland. Till we meet again, godspeed."

"Amen," said Octavia and Cordelia, wiping tears from their eyes.

As Buddy waded back to the shore, Octavia moved forward and tossed the rosebud into the water. Jane waited a respectful few seconds, then turned to look up at the terrace. To her surprise, she saw two police officers making their way down the shoveled path. Toscano wasn't with them. Even so, this had to be it. They were here to make an arrest.

"What are you doing here?" demanded Buddy, stomping up to them as soon as they reached the beach. He looked flustered. Gracie followed him to where the officers were standing. Putting his arm around her, he drew her close.

One of the officers switched on his flashlight, shining it at Buddy's face. "Evening, Mr. Lester."

The other officer used his flashlight to scan the crowd. The beam washed back and forth a couple of times, finally coming to rest on Christian.

"Christian Wallace?" asked the first officer.

Christian looked startled. "Yes?" he said.

The officers moved quickly toward him. Once he was cuffed, one of the men said, "Mr. Wallace, you are under arrest for the murder of Roland Lester. Anything you say can be used against you in a court of law."

"But . . . I didn't do it," he protested. "I'm innocent!"

As they dragged him away, they continued to read him his rights.

Everyone watched in silence as he was hauled up the path to the terrace, then further up to where the squad car had been parked.

When they'd finally driven away, Verna moved closer to the group and said, "My God. Can you believe it? And to think I was standing right next to him!"

Gracie whirled around, nailing Verna with her eyes. "He didn't hurt Roland and you know it!"

"Grace," said Buddy, holding her back by one arm.

"You did it. I saw you coming out of Roland's study the night his files were stolen. You were carrying a whole bunch of his journals and papers. I told Christian about it, but he wouldn't let me tell the police. He was protecting you. He's always been protecting you."

"I don't know what you're talking about," said Verna, her voice calm, her manner poised.

"His father! You murdered Lew, and then you murdered Roland to cover it up. You couldn't trust him anymore—not after he'd decided to admit to the world he was gay. Oh, that part was okay. Maybe you even agreed with it. But what if he got pressured to talk about Lew's murder? The truth might finally come out! You couldn't have that."

"The girl's delusional."

She broke free of Buddy's grip. "I'm not a *girl,* you dried-up old prune. And there's nothing wrong with my mind. Christian's feels some weird kind of loyalty to you, I can't imagine why. You're a has-been— the original black widow spider. You're going to let him take the rap for you, aren't you? Admit it! You're a coward. You don't care about him, or anyone else. You never have."

"I'm not going to stand here and listen to this. She's . . . making this up." Verna laughed, as if it were all a joke.

"I'm going to tell the police what I know. And then we'll see if the great Verna Lange is still laughing." She stormed off down the beach.

Jane continued to watch Grace for a moment, then stepped back as Verna brushed past her. The actress had put up a good front, but right now, she was rushing up the path as if her life depended on it.

When Jane glanced up at the terrace, she saw that Hilda was gone.

42

Jane, Cordelia, and Octavia sat across the street from the house in Wister for a good ten minutes before leaving their car and finally going in. Even though the house was dark, Jane wanted to make sure nobody was inside. Since it was New Year's Eve, the normally quiet neighborhood was crowded with cars. Music blared loudly from several houses, the deep, throbbing base pulsing right through the walls out into the cold night air.

"I wish we could have found a key," grumbled Cordelia.

"I looked everywhere," said Octavia. "Buddy said Roland didn't take his keys to the church. He didn't need them, and he didn't want them in his pocket, ruining the look of his tux. We both assumed he left them in his top desk drawer, where he always keeps them, but when I went to look, they were gone. I searched all over the house. I can't produce them out of thin air."

Jane turned around to look at Octavia in the back seat. "But you own the house now. We could call a locksmith tomorrow morning and you'd be inside in a matter of minutes."

"What if the neighbors saw us?" Octavia bit her fingernail. Ever since they'd left Innishannon, she'd been a ball of nerves. "No. I don't want anybody to think there's anything unusual going on at old Mr. Lesney's place. Not until we get in there and see for ourselves what Roland was up to."

"I found a crowbar in the garage and tossed it in the trunk," said

Cordelia, restuffing her auburn curls up under her black knit cap. "In case we needed it. But I still wish we had a key."

"We do," said Octavia, touching the chain hanging around her neck. "We're just not sure what it fits."

"Come on, let's get this over with," said Cordelia, opening the car door.

On their way up to the house, Octavia hid the crowbar under her coat.

"Okay," said Jane, taking the lead as they came around the side of the house. "The basement windows are out. Roland had bars put on them. I think it's safe to assume there's no security system. I didn't see signs of one the other day. In a neighborhood like this, it would be an open invitation. Our best bet is the back door. At least, I think we should try that first. The porch will give us some cover. Who knows? We may get lucky."

"Lucky how?" asked Cordelia, bringing up the rear as Jane and Octavia stepped inside the back entrance.

Jane took out her flashlight. Just as she'd remembered, the lock on the interior door was a deadbolt. The top third of the door was a window covered by an opaque curtain. "If we break this window and stick our arm through the opening, we'll find one of three things. If it's a single deadbolt, we can just flip the lever and we're inside. If it's a double deadbolt, the lock on the inside of the door will require a key. Sometimes, people leave a key in the lock."

"And sometimes they don't," said Cordelia.

"Only one way to find out," said Octavia. She held up the crowbar.

Everyone ducked as she tapped the glass. It didn't break.

"Don't be such a sissy," said Cordelia. "Use some muscle."

Giving her sister a nasty look, Octavia tapped harder. This time, the window shattered. After chipping off the jagged pieces nearest the lock, she reached inside. "Damn. My arm's not long enough."

"Step aside," said Cordelia, edging her sister out of the way. Since she was the tallest of the three women, she had the advantage.

"Can you feel the lock?" asked Jane.

Cordelia's scowl turned slowly to a smile. "It's a double deadbolt and the key's in the door."

Jane heard a click. The next moment, they were inside.

"Is it safe to turn on a light?" asked Octavia.

"Shhhh," said Jane. With her flashlight pointing the way, they all crept into the kitchen. Everything seemed quiet enough. "Is it me, or does it feel awfully warm in here?"

"It's not you," said Cordelia, unzipping her jacket. "It's like . . . summer on Miami Beach. Without the piña coladas and the oiled bodies, of course. Why would Roland keep the heat so high?"

"Maybe something's wrong with the furnace," said Octavia.

"Oh, just great," muttered Cordelia. "Let's get this over with and get out of here."

"We're never going to make any progress if we can't see," said Octavia.

A second later, the lights burst on.

Cordelia stood next to the wall switch. "Let's risk it," was all she said.

With Jane in the lead, they moved cautiously into the living room.

Cordelia turned on a lamp. The oversized chartreuse shade bathed the room in a kind of sleazy, flop house glow.

It was pretty much the way Jane remembered it from the other day. What furniture there was, was tattered and shabby. The brown shag carpeting was matted and dirty, threadbare in spots. A half-eaten bag of taco chips rested next to a beer can on the battered coffee table. A few magazines were scattered on the couch. And the TV set was old. No other electronics were visible. It gave the impression of a trashy hotel lobby.

"Why don't we do a quick reconnaissance?" said Octavia.

"Good idea." Cordelia marched through the living room and up the stairs. A light came on up on the second floor. Octavia hurried after her.

It took Jane a little longer to make it to the second floor. She hadn't brought her cane with her tonight. She hoped it wasn't a mistake. Reaching the upper hallway, she saw that it was another world entirely. The hardwood floor was beautifully polished, the woodwork painted a light coral to match the deep coral in the walls. Several small but expensive gilt-framed oil paintings hung between the two doorways. The overhead light looked as if it might be antique brass. This was where Roland actually lived when he was here. She'd been right about the living room. It was just a stage set, a way to tell potential burglars that they might as well look elsewhere.

Just as she was about to enter the closest bedroom, she heard

Octavia gasp and Cordelia shout, "Paydirt!" They were in the next bedroom over.

Rushing to the door, Jane found a room filled with film canisters. She'd already suspected they might find quite a stash. Roland hadn't been away from Innishannon during the entire time Octavia had been living at the estate, not until last week. During that time, he'd probably received more than a few films. Which meant they'd piled up. As she moved further inside, she saw that along one wall, Roland had set up a small, self-contained processing lab. It looked like a fairly simple affair. He'd modified an old projector. On one hub he must have put the film to be processed. On the other side was the empty reel. When the projector was turned on, the film was dragged through a small basin he'd affixed between the two reels. The basin was empty now, but Jane assumed that when he was working, it was filled with liquid—the formula.

"It stinks in here," said Octavia, wrinkling her nose.

"Must be the chemicals," said Jane. Neat rows of bottles, some glass, some plastic, sat on another, smaller table. They were labeled with numbers, but no names. Underneath, inside a wooden box, were beakers, measuring cups, a couple boxes of wooden safety matches, and a large bowl containing at least a dozen eyedroppers. Paper towels, the kind used in commercial bathroom dispensers, were stacked against the far wall. And there were two stools. One pushed under the mixing table, the other sitting next to the processing area. "I'll bet he prepared the chemicals fresh each time." That way, if anyone ever did break into the house, Roland could be sure all they'd find were a bunch of bottles. Except, the formula had to be here somewhere. If it wasn't, Jane had no clue where to look next.

Cordelia and Octavia had already flung off their coats and were busy ransacking the room, looking for anything that might require a skeleton key. As Cordelia opened a closet door and began to examine the contents, Jane took the opportunity to return to the first bedroom, the one closest to the stairs. The overhead light had already been turned on. This room contained a single antique sleigh bed covered by an applique quilt. Everything was neat, almost obsessively so. The clothes in the closet were perfectly arranged. A pair of comfortable leather slippers peeked out from one end of the bed. A Queen Anne nightstand held a tall Tiffany lamp, a clock, a telephone, and a book. Nothing else. The top of a matching chest of drawers was partially covered by a round, tatted doily and a small picture frame.

As Jane stepped closer, she saw that the photo inside the frame was an old black-and-white snapshot of Roland and Lew. They both looked so handsome and tanned in their white shorts and polo shirts, as if they'd just come off the tennis court, their hair windblown, broad smiles on their faces. They were standing in a garden, a pool off to their left. The photo captured such a sense of youth and sunlight and joy. It was hard to reconcile this picture with the quote Roland had placed under the statue of Venus. Was this the beautiful setting, the fountain of delights, where a bitter taste welled up to choke him, even amid the flowers? Did Roland feel that way on the day this photo was taken, or was it only in retrospect one could understand a life?

The rest of the bedroom was used as a kind of mini packaging store. Once the films were processed, Roland must have packed them himself, called UPS, then carted the boxes down to the back porch. As Jane stood looking around, she realized he'd developed quite a streamlined operation.

And yet, with a man so concerned about order and detail, there had to be some rhyme or reason to where Roland had hidden the formula. Old houses always had nooks and crannies where things could be stashed with relative ease—and privacy. Perhaps he kept it somewhere else as well, but it seemed logical that he'd have a copy on the premises. The house was small. Then again, when it came to an exhaustive search, it seemed vast. Unless they got lucky, they could be here for days.

Feeling suddenly overwhelmed by the task before them, Jane sat down on the bed and stretched out her injured leg, massaging the muscles around the knee. The only object even slightly out of place in the room was a braided wool rug. It was almost centered, but maybe a foot or so off.

"This is no time for idle reflection," announced Cordelia, looming suddenly in the doorway. "This is . . . I mean, unless your leg is bothering you."

"No, I'm okay," said Jane. "I take it you haven't found anything."

"We've covered the room from top to bottom. Nothing." She stepped over to the rug and pulled it a couple feet to the right. Now it was off in the other direction.

"I think one of us needs to go find the thermostat and turn the heat down," said Jane, shrugging out of her coat.

"I'll do it. Why don't you crack a window in here?"

"Good idea." As Cordelia left to run downstairs, Jane crossed to the window, unlocked the latch, then opened it wide. Crisp, invigorating air whooshed into the room. She stood for a moment breathing it in. On her way back to the door, she pulled the rug straight. As she did so, she noticed a small gap between two of the boards. So that was the reason for the rug.

On her way to the processing room a thought struck her. Hurrying back to the bedroom, she knelt down and fiddled with the board. She realized immediately that it wasn't merely a flaw in the flooring, the impression it gave from several feet away. Up close, she could see that someone had cut a small door into the floor, then tried to cover it up with dark brown paint.

Removing the top, Jane gazed down at an ancient metal strong box. "Oh my God! Octavia? Get in here!"

When Octavia didn't answer, Jane called again. Louder, this time.

"What!" shouted Octavia finally, her voice muffled.

"Where are you?"

"In the closet."

"I think I found something."

Octavia rushed into the room.

"Help me up first." Once Jane was standing, she held the box while Octavia tried her key. To their amazement, the box opened easily.

Inside was a shoe.

"Jeez," said Octavia, hands rising to her hips. "We get this close and what do we find? And old cordovan wing tip. That's really a big help, Jane. Really a spectacular find."

But Jane had tuned her out. She was remembering the conversation she'd had with Salvador Barros about the card game. All the crazy things the men had bet. In the end, Salvador said that all Roland had kept was Lew's shoe and the formula. Nothing else. "It's in here," she said. "I'm sure of it." She removed the shoe, tossing the box on the bed. Pressing her hand down carefully into the tip, she touched what felt like an envelope. As soon as she'd pulled it out, Octavia grabbed it.

Inside was an old piece of paper. The writing had faded and the edges of the note had darkened and curled. But it was unmistakably a chemical formula.

"This is it!" shrieked Octavia, rushing back to the processing room. "Cordelia, we found it! Where are you? Cordelia?"

Jane closed the window, then limped across to the other room. "Let's get out of here, okay?"

"How am I supposed to interpret this gobbledygook?" Octavia was sitting on one of the stools, studying the note. "All these bottles. None of them are labeled."

"It doesn't matter. You can buy whatever you need later. We should go. The longer we stay here, the more danger we're in."

She looked up. "Danger? From whom? They arrested Christian hours ago, remember? Cordelia!" she hollered. "Get in here and help us celebrate!"

Jane felt deeply uneasy, and the feeling was growing more intense by the second. Why was Octavia being so obstinate? Just because the police made an arrest didn't mean they had the right man. Or woman, as the case might be. Someone was having Roland followed before his death. That meant there was a good chance that same someone knew about the house. If it was Christian, great. If it wasn't, they could be in big trouble. "We should leave now. Take that formula and put it someplace safe."

"It is safe."

"How can you be so sure?"

Glancing up with a satisfied smile, she said, "You worry too much."

"And you don't worry enough."

Cordelia appeared in the doorway, an odd look on her face.

"We got it," said Octavia, rubbing her hands together excitedly.

"Cordelia, help me out here," said Jane, turning toward her. "I think we should go." Her friend's facial expression was so strange that Jane added, "Are you okay?"

"I've been better." Her eyes flicked to Octavia and then back to Jane.

"We should have brought some champagne," said Octavia, examining one of the smaller bottles.

"Where is it? The piece of paper?" Cordelia spoke almost like a robot. Low and expressionless.

"What is your problem?" said Octavia, holding it up. "It's right here."

"Excellent," said a voice from out in the hall. Jane knew immediately who it belonged to, and what Cordelia's peculiar look was about.

As Cordelia was shoved forward into the room, Jane saw the gun.

Octavia jumped off the stool. "What are you doing here?"

"Same thing you are," said Buddy. "But it looks like you beat me to it." He nodded to the table. "Put the paper down, and then . . . all of you, stand back by the film canisters."

"No!" said Octavia. "This doesn't belong to you. It belongs to me!"

"Do what he says," said Jane, backing up.

"Of course it belongs to me," said Buddy, raising the gun and pointing it at her chest. "Who the hell do you think you are? Huh! Did you think I was going to let some goddamn bitch take my inheritance away from me? I've worked my entire adult life building that film library. I was a trusting, loyal brother. I had no idea Roland would double-cross me in the end. He never told me about the formula. Can you believe that? I had to find out about it myself."

"It's mine! Roland gave it to me!"

"Right, like I didn't even exist. He *had* a family! Mine! He didn't need to start a new one." He pointed to the piece of paper in her hand. "Put it down on the table and stand back against the wall. *Now*. I've killed two people to get what I want. I won't hesitate to kill another."

"Give it to him!" demanded Cordelia. She backed up next to Jane.

Slowly, carefully, Octavia put the paper down. She inched away from the table, keeping her eyes on the gun. Because she wasn't looking, she bumped into a stack of canisters, sending them crashing to the floor.

The noise shattered what was left of Jane's composure. She felt herself begin to panic. She fought the feeling as hard as she could, but it was immense, like a tidal wave coming straight at her.

"What are you going to do?" asked Cordelia.

He shook his head, wiping the sweat from his forehead. "God, that idiot friend of mine must have turned up the heat. Roland probably kept it cold in here."

"What friend?" asked Jane, trying to sound normal, to ask a sensible question just to prove she could. When she looked down at her hand, she saw that she was still holding Lew's shoe. Not much of a weapon. Her stomach clutched. Her hands began to shake. She flashed on her study back home in Minneapolis. A different gun was pointing at her. She struggled to stay in the here and now.

"None of your business," snapped Buddy. "None of this is *any* of your business! Your interference . . . it's all your fault. My back's against the wall. What else can I do?"

"You've got the formula," said Octavia. "Take it and get out."

"I can't."

"Why not? What else do you want?"

"I want to be a free man. If I let any of you leave this room, I'll spend the rest of my life in prison."

"But we won't breathe a word," said Cordelia. "Really. The formula's all yours. Octavia will just trundle herself on back to Broadway and leave you alone. Me, I never was much good at science projects. And Jane does whatever I tell her."

"Shut up."

"Pardon me?"

"I said shut up!" He jerked his hand toward the table and picked up the piece of paper. After glancing at it, he turned his full attention on the movie reels. "This has to look like an accident."

"Please," pleaded Octavia. "You may think my sister is trying to feed you a line, but she isn't. Let us go and none of us will ever bother you again. I swear it on the life of my unborn child."

"You," he said, pointing at Jane. "Read me the names on the canisters right next to you."

"Why?" asked Cordelia.

Using every ounce of willpower she possessed to stay focused, Jane bent down and started at the top. *"The Man from the Diner's Club. Tell Me You Love Me, Junie Moon. Justine."* She stopped and looked up.

"Keep going."

She moved to another stack. *"The Blue Bird. Her Cardboard Lover—"*

"That will work." Motioning with his gun he said, "Open a couple of reels of that last one. *Her Cardboard Lover.*"

Jane glanced at the release date. 1942. Suddenly, she had a sickening feeling she knew what he was planning.

"You three are about to make movie history," he said almost proudly. "You're going to die in the last cellulose nitrate fire in the U.S. Seems fitting, somehow. Don't worry. It won't take long. With all these old movie reels, the room will go up like a firecracker."

This is it, thought Jane. Once he'd tossed a lighted match on top of one of the exposed reels, it would all be over. She had only seconds to make a decision. As he bent down to retrieve the safety matches from the wood box under the table, she lunged at him. He hadn't expected it, but reacted quickly, bringing the gun up hard into her stomach, then up again, slashing it across her face. She crashed back against the stool, falling to the floor.

"Not smart," he barked angrily, cocking the gun at her. "Not smart at all."

It took her a moment to regain her bearings. When she did, she saw that Buddy had forced Cordelia and Octavia into the far corner of the room. She wanted to get up, try it again, but without the advantage of surprise, she didn't have a chance.

Removing a match from the box, Buddy scraped his thumbnail across the tip.

"No," screamed Octavia. "We'll do anything you want. Anything!"

The match burst into flame. Tossing it on the reel, he backed out of the door. The film caught instantly. "You leave me no other choice!"

If it was a choice of burning to death or dying by a gunshot, Jane chose the latter. Buddy had backed far enough into the hallway that she couldn't see him. That meant he couldn't see her either. As the next reel caught, flames rushed up the curtains toward the ceiling. The temperature in the room was rising fast. It wouldn't be long before other films started to spontaneously combust.

Crawling toward the door, Jane assumed a crouching position, then hurled herself forward, catching Buddy around his ankles and slamming him back against the wall. They scuffled, all arms and legs, pushing and shoving, both struggling to gain the upper hand. Buddy dropped the gun. Jane felt his hands at her neck. She fought to get away, to grab the gun herself. When he brought his hand up to her face, she bit his index finger hard. She could taste blood, feel the bone crack. He howled in pain, reeling backwards. She twisted around and was mere inches from the gun when he slammed the heel of his shoe into her side, knocking her backwards. Reaching the gun himself, he fired at her, then whirled around to the door where Octavia and Cordelia were rushing at him. The gun stopped them dead.

"I don't want to shoot, but I will," he shouted.

370

Jane lay on the floor, breathing hard. She'd felt the bullet whiz past her ear, but she wasn't hurt.

"*Be* a hero," he screamed, turning to Jane again as he stumbled to his feet, "but make another move and your friends die first. Painfully, I'll make sure of that."

As she tried to sit up, she heard an explosion. She ducked away from the blast and covered her face. When she looked up, she saw that, in a matter of seconds, the processing room had become an inferno. Cordelia and Octavia were in the hall. The sleeve of Octavia's sweater was on fire. Cordelia was trying to force her to the floor so she could roll it out. The scene was pandemonium.

An instant later a fireball burst into the hallway. Jane was on one side of it, Buddy and the sisters on the other. Lunging backwards away from the flames, Jane strained to see what was happening. Buddy was backing down the hall, screaming obscenities, shouting at Octavia and Cordelia, telling them to stay where they were. To die. To burn. Cordelia was calling for Jane. The air was growing thick with smoke. Suddenly, there were more people. Other voices. Then gunfire. Buddy screamed. "Get away from me."

"Stop him!" shouted Octavia. "Oh, God, no! Buddy, don't! Please don't!"

Jane realized she'd backed all the way to the far end of the hall. She was trapped. She'd never make it through the flames to the stairs alive. But she had to do something. Otherwise—"I'm toast," she said out loud, amazed that she could make a joke at a time like this. She dove into the bathroom.

Jumping into the bathtub, she turned on the shower. It only took a few seconds before she was soaked to the skin. Next, she grabbed the shower curtain. The liner was plastic, but the curtain felt like cotton. Yanking two bath towels off the wall rack, she wet everything down until it was dripping with water. Covering herself with the curtain and one towel, she hugged the other to her face and bolted back into the hallway. She had one chance. Get to the stairs.

Forcing her head down, she prayed that her leg would hold. She burst into the wall of flames. In seconds, she was through it. On the other side, the smoke was so thick that she could hardly see. It burned her eyes and choked off her breath, but she kept moving. She had to get out. She felt along the wall for the head of the stairs. As she started down, her leg wobbled. "God," she cried out, stumbling forward. "Help me!" That's when she felt the hands. The arms. Reaching for her. Holding her steady. Then, up into the air.

Moments later, she was outside. In the snow. The soft, cool snow. A woman and a man in paramedic gear were bending over her. Talking to her. Asking if she could hear them. Behind them, she could see the house. The upstairs windows had burst out. Flames shot upward into the night sky. They looked like human fingers, grasping and hungry.

"I made it," she rasped, coughing, sucking in the fresh air.

Behind the paramedics, she could see Toscano. He looked scared. Cops shouldn't look sacred. He knelt down next to her.

"Cordelia?" she asked, coughing, wiping a hand across her face. "Octavia?"

"Cordelia twisted her ankle, but she'll survive. Octavia has a burn on her arm. They're in the paramedic van."

"Buddy?"

"He's in custody."

She nodded. The paramedics were examining her. She wanted them to go away. "It was you in there."

Someone called Toscano's name. Looking up, he shouted, "I'm coming." Glancing at one of the paramedics, he asked, "She's going to be okay, right?"

"She'll be fine," said the woman.

Jane reached out and gripped his hand. "Thanks, John. You saved my life."

"You saved your own life. And everybody else's."

She didn't know what he meant, but she closed her eyes, letting the paramedics do their job. "I'm alive," she whispered to herself. "I'm alive."

43

NEW YEAR'S DAY

The following morning, Jane was getting dressed when she heard a loud rap on her bedroom door. Throwing on her robe, she limped over to open it. It was a bit early for Cordelia to be up, but there she was, big as life in her brown turtleneck, faux fur vest, and jeans, a thermometer stuck in her mouth.

"How's the ankle?" asked Jane.

"The pain is *excruciating*." She whipped out the thermometer and hopped into the room. "I think I have a fever."

"Sprains don't usually cause fevers."

"Cordelia Thorn is *never* the norm." She plunked down on the bed, holding the back of her hand dramatically to her forehead. "How are you feeling after your ordeal?"

"Actually, pretty good."

"None of us are good, Janey. Tell me the truth."

"No, really. I inhaled a lot of smoke, so my chest is sore, but all in all, I made it through okay. How's the burn on Octavia's arm? And the baby?"

"My sister and the spawn of the devil will live. Unlike me." She fell back against the pillows, groaning. "Thank God that burly detective showed up when he did. Be a dear and stuff a pillow under my foot, will you?"

Jane used the small throw pillow from the armchair.

"That's better." She sighed with contentment, then glowered. "I can't believe what that horrible, evil bastard did."

"You're speaking of Buddy now."

"Of course Buddy."

"Destroying the formula."

"Octavia is furious! She paced back and forth in my room half the night. She would have strangled him right then and there in the hallway if one of the cops hadn't pulled her off."

"Tell me again what happened," said Jane, sitting down on the window seat. She'd been trapped on the other side of the burning doorway and hadn't witnessed it firsthand.

"It was a travesty of justice! An act of insanity! I heard him say something like, 'If I can't have it, nobody can.' Then he dropped the paper in the fire. It was gone in a millisecond. Nobody could have prevented it—it was too quick. And unexpected. I keep telling Octavia that Roland must have kept a copy somewhere else."

"That would be my guess."

"But where?"

Jane wished she had an answer. "Octavia will just have to take it one step at a time. Look through Roland's papers. See where it leads."

"Right." Cordelia snorted. "You don't know my sister. She is *so* not into patience—or deferred gratification. Oh, look at the time." She stole a sideways glance at the clock on the nightstand. "I've got to hop downstairs. I feel like a freaking bunny."

"Are you going somewhere?"

"Octavia and I are driving to New Haven this morning. That's why I'm up at such an ungodly hour. Dad checked himself into rehab yesterday. We need to visit him, tell him how glad we are that he's finally taken the plunge, and that we're behind him one hundred percent. And then, of course, we have to fill him on all the details of Octavia's sordid new family."

"But you'll be back in time to take me to the airport." Last night, after they'd been treated at the hospital and driven back to Innishannon, Jane had made a decision. She wanted to go home. She'd had enough of mansions and millionaires to last her a lifetime.

"Never fear," said Cordelia, slipping her arm around Jane's shoulder for support as she bobbed back to the door. "Your limousine, such as it is, will be here at the stroke of four."

"You're still planning to stay another week?"

"That's the idea, but don't be surprised if you get a call from me in the middle of the night telling you that *I'm* at the airport." Rolling her eyes, she added, "Sisters. The gift that keeps on giving."

Jane grinned. "If you need me, I'll be there."

"Oh, I almost forgot," said Cordelia. As she bounced through the door, she reached around and grabbed Roland's cane.

"Just what you need," laughed Jane.

"No, Janey. It's for you. Octavia wanted me to give it to you as a thank you gift. She thinks it has much more style than that piece of orthopedic kitch you've been using. Who knows? You may grow to like the look of a cane. Kind of eccentric. You're a born eccentric, you know."

"I am?"

"Absolutely. You just haven't mastered your personal style yet."

"I knew something was wrong." She ran her fingertips lightly across the gargoyle's golden head. It had to be hollow. It wasn't heavy enough to be solid metal.

"But you're right on the cusp. I was thinking last week that maybe you should lean towards the Margaret Mead look. Bangs. Tweeds. Sensible shoes. But hey, that's not you. This is better. More glamorous."

"Thanks, Cordelia."

"Don't mention it." She socked Jane on the arm, then hugged her. "Later, babe," she called as she hopped her way down the hall.

Jane spent the next half hour packing. Once everything had been safely tucked away in her bag, she carried it downstairs and set it next to the front door. Drifting quietly through the empty rooms, she realized that in last few weeks, Innishannon had become a sepulcher. Octavia and her child held out hope for a resurrection, and yet the house would forever remain full of uneasy ghosts.

Standing for a few minutes in the solarium, with its broad windows looking out on the distant shimmer of Long Island Sound, her somber mood turned a bit more personal. As much as she fought to keep her own sense of fragility at bay, at times like this, when the rush of life quieted down, it resurfaced. This morning, everything she'd experienced in the past three months was all mixed together in her mind. Roland and Ellie, Lew Wallace, Julia, the weakness in her leg, her growing sense of anxiety and disconnection. No matter how hard she tried to put the past behind her, the memory of the awful night she'd been assaulted in her home was always there, lurking around the edges of her consciousness like a haunting. She assumed it would get better over time, that the memory would recede. Instead, it was getting stronger. Maybe Toscano was right. Maybe she would look into this post traumatic stress thing. But she refused to dwell on it now. Thinking about it, talking about it, only made it worse. Stronger. More real. She wanted the feelings to fade. To disappear. Maybe they would fade in time.

All things considered, she felt she'd handled herself well last night. Fighting for her life and winning actually gave her quite a buzz. And frankly, that confused her. If she could survive last night with nary a scar—physical or emotional—what was different about the assault in her home? She'd always loved the thrill of the chase, relished a mystery because it engaged her so totally. Buddy was behind bars and she'd helped put him there. That felt good. She'd slept well. No bad dreams. And yet, this morning the nervousness had descended once again like a thick, gray thundercloud, cutting out the light.

"Oh, Jane," said Hilda, bustling into the room. "You're still here."

Jane turned to face her. The older woman was wearing her winter coat and carrying a small suitcase.

"I thought I should let someone know that I'm leaving for a few days. A shopping trip to New York. I have to get out of here for a while."

"I'm leaving this afternoon myself," said Jane.

"Well, bon voyage, then, to both of us. Christian left this morning to fly back to L.A. The police released him last night after Mr. Lester was arrested. When he got home, he received a call from some actress he was hoping to sign for his new movie. She said yes. He's terribly excited. And Verna's leaving tomorrow. Everyone's scattering to the four winds."

"So it seems."

"Such a sad time." She shook her head. "Nothing will ever be the same again. By the way, I let Leonard go this morning. We won't be needing him any longer. Same with the cook's assistant. If you see Octavia before you go, will you tell her? I'm sure she'll want to hire her own staff." Hearing the doorbell, she said, "That must be my taxi. Have a safe trip, Jane."

"Thanks. You too."

Jane stayed in the solarium for a few more minutes, then wandered into the kitchen. She'd always loved the smell and feel of a kitchen, especially the commercial kind. It was so familiar, so comforting, and at the same time such an exciting place to be. When she'd first opened her restaurant in the early eighties, she'd spent several years working the line, making sure that every plate sent out was exactly the way she wanted it. Those had been good years. Perhaps that's what she needed now—to reconnect with the Lyme House's kitchen. She'd always found cooking both meditative and energizing. After finally hiring an executive chef, she'd slowly left the line behind as she moved out into the dining room to meet and greet guests. She still kept a close watch on the cuisine, still created what she hoped would become new signature dishes, but it wasn't the same. Maybe this would be the key to help her through this rough patch. At least, it was something to consider.

Jane had been ravenous last night when she'd returned from the hospital, devouring two turkey sandwiches and several beers, but this morning her appetite was nil. Even so, she spread some cream cheese on a bagel, poured herself a mug of coffee and was about to sit down at a large butcher block table when the phone rang. Since nobody was around to answer it, she picked it up. "Hello?"

"Jane Lawless, please."

She recognized the voice. It was Toscano. "John, hi. I'm so glad you called."

"First, tell me how you're feeling."

"My lungs are a little sore, but otherwise, I'm good. I need to thank you again for carrying me out of that house last night."

"Like I said, you got your own self out. I just gave you a minor assist."

"Okay, okay. Be self-deprecating. Really, I'm glad you called. I've got so many questions."

He laughed. "I assumed you would. You being *you*. If you've got a few minutes, I thought I'd fill you in on some of what's happened. I spent most of the night interrogating Buddy Lester. He's hoping to get the judge to go easy on him—I smell a plea bargain—so he's been pretty cooperative."

Jane took her coffee mug over to the table, pulled out a stool and sat down. "That's about what I expected. I wish we'd had more chance to talk last night."

"I'm sorry I had to rush off."

"No, I understand completely. It's just . . . how come you showed up at the house in Wister when you did? Not that I wasn't thrilled to see you."

"It was all your doing."

"Mine?"

"Sure. You gave me that tip about the guy who was following Roland Lester before he died. We checked out the license plate number. Turns out, it belonged to an Irv Keegan. He lives in Naugatuck. A friend of Buddy's. That's where I was yesterday when my men came out to Innishannon to arrest Christian Wallace. I had to lean on this Keegan pretty hard, but once he understood he could be arrested as an accessory to a murder if he didn't cooperate, he sang like a birdy."

"What did he say?"

"Well, he and Buddy have been pals for years, so when Buddy came to him with the story of how his brother had double-crossed him, he was eager to help."

"But . . . how did Buddy find out about the formula?"

"Buddy said he was in Belgium this past November looking at several old movies he wanted to buy for the film archive he and his brother were developing. The archive was stored in a warehouse outside Brussels. Buddy had stopped by the building once before, many years ago, thinking he should take a look at it, but he was turned away. Roland had left strict orders that he was the only one who was allowed in. Of course, Buddy didn't like that much, but I get the feeling he did what he was told. Didn't ask a lot of questions. Except that, when he was there in November, he was angry at Roland because of his budding relationship with Octavia. He knew he and his family were being edged out. So, he tried it again just to piss his brother off. Only this time he bought a cane that resembled his brother's, wore a dark fedora and dark glasses. It worked. The guard thought he was Roland. When he got inside and started checking out some of the film canisters, he smelled a rat. Even with the climate-controlled air, there should have been some deterioration in the films, I guess, but there wasn't. If anything, the films were in better shape than when he bought them. It didn't add up. That's when he remembered a conversation he'd over-heard years ago between Lew Wallace and his brother. They were laughing about some chemical formula some guy had invented that was supposed to revolutionize the film industry, make films last forever. Buddy asked his brother about it later. Roland told him it was a hoax. Just a big joke."

"It wasn't," said Jane.

"I know. After his last trip to Belgium, so did Buddy. He came back to the States and had this Keegan follow Roland. Buddy knew his brother had to be processing the films somewhere. He'd always been so secretive, Buddy figured he was doing it himself. Except, during that time period, Roland only left the house with Octavia, and they never did anything except go shopping or out to dinner. But then, Buddy got lucky. Octavia flew back to Minnesota to see her sister. While she was gone, Roland had his limousine service drive him to New York. Keegan said he followed him every step of the way. The limo driver left Roland off in front of the post office in Times Square. He mailed some boxes, then took a cab to Grand Central, and Metro North to New Haven. The final cab ride took him to the house in Wister. Once Buddy found out about that, he knew he was close. He'd already borrowed Roland's keys and had copies made, so he gave the set to his friend and told him to go into the house and look around. Keegan reported back that it looked like there was a lab upstairs. That cinched it. From that moment on, Roland's fate was sealed, Buddy wasn't going to see his life's work go to a stranger. He was furious at his brother, but if he was going to get rid of him, he knew he had to use his head. He remembered the poison his granddaughter had told him about. Jimson-weed. He went to the library and looked up some information on it, then went to New York and found a place that sold it. The rest is history. Buddy put the poison in his brother's tea before the wedding, then waited for him to die. Frankly, I think he had some real remorse about it after the fact, but he couldn't change anything. And the re-morse didn't last long."

"I still don't get it. Why did he confess that first night?"

"Because he knew that when we searched the house, we'd find the poison in his room. Like a lot of criminals, he wasn't very smart. Since Roland was an old man, he figured the emergency room doctors would assume it was his heart. End of story. When they nailed the cause of death correctly as poison, Buddy was shocked. But by then, we were at the house. He couldn't go upstairs because we wouldn't allow it. That meant he couldn't hide the evidence. It was right there in plain sight. He must have thought about it for a while, then decided to tell the truth. Except, as he was about to give his confession down at the station, his lawyer inadvertently overheard the news about Christian's fingerprint and passed it on to Buddy. The fingerprint muddied the waters for us, but it was a stroke of luck for Buddy. He started giving wrong answers to our questions. And that confused us—since he *was* confessing to a murder. We couldn't arrest him with a confession that wasn't accurate, so we had to release him. But, like a lot of people who break the law, Buddy has a problem with overconfidence. And impulse control. Once Christian was implicated, he figured he was home free. But he also thought we might've put a tail on him, just in case. So he couldn't go to the house in Wister. He had to wait. That gave you time to put it all together. Ellie Saks was getting close too. When he found out she was about to expose Roland as a thief, and inform the entire world that the formula existed, he 'did what he had to do.' His words."

"He was the one who took the tape from the tack room. The documentary Ellie had done on her grandfather."

"He said he'd been down there snooping around several times before. Apparently, she'd stolen a reel from the screening room. Some silent movie—*A Daughter of the Gods,* I think the name was. Anyway, Buddy discovered it on one of his snooping expeditions. He kept a close eye on her after that. He had this very protective attitude toward his brother, which didn't seem to end with his death. When he discovered the videotape, he knew immediately that it was dynamite, and that it could blow his own plans sky high. He was also smart enough to know it wasn't the only copy of the documentary that existed, but he had to buy himself some time. He didn't have the formula in his hand yet. But he knew where it was."

"At the house in Wister."

"You got it. The fact that he couldn't go there drove him nuts. But he had to wait. Play it safe. He felt confident that Octavia knew nothing about it, so he could afford to be patient. When we arrested Christian last night, he figured the heat was off. Unfortunately, you'd found out about the house too. And you picked last night to break in."

"It wasn't illegal. Octavia owns it."

He laughed. "I'm hardly going to quibble about legalities."

"How did Christian's fingerprint get on the sack of poison?"

"Buddy took the plastic sack from one of the kitchen cupboards so he could store the jimsonweed in it. He used gloves, just to be on the safe side. Christian told us he'd taken this dog, Busby, out for a couple of walks while Gracie was taking care of him for a friend. He brought plastic bags along to clean up any mess the dog made on the property. If he didn't use the bags, he'd put them back. It was just a fluke that Buddy picked one that had Christian's fingerprint on it. It's the kind of crazy thing that happens sometimes. Who knows? It might have been the detail that tipped the scales, sent Christian to prison for a murder he didn't commit."

"Lucky Christian."

"You said it."

"But why did you come to the house in Wister last night?"

"On the way back from Naugatuck, I called Innishannon. I guess I was worried about you. Buddy was a murderer and he was, as of that moment, still on the lose. When Hilda Gettle told me that you, Cordelia, and Octavia had just left, and that the Thorn sisters were dressed strangely—all in black—well, just call it a gut feeling. We drove straight to Wister. I could see the house burning from several blocks away."

"Thank God for your gut feeling."

Again, he laughed. "That's it, Jane. The full story. I called Ellie Saks's brother a little while ago, told him we'd caught his sister's murderer and that he was being arraigned tomorrow morning."

"He must have been so relieved."

"He is. He said he wanted to call his parents right away. So, what's your plan? I suppose you're going to stick around a while longer. See if you can help Octavia find another copy of the formula."

"Actually, I'm leaving this afternoon."

He didn't respond right away. "I'm sorry to hear that," he said finally. "I was hoping we could have dinner together before you left."

"We'll have to do it at my restaurant—when you come to Minnesota."

"I'm not much of a traveling man, I'm afraid, but I rarely turn down invitations when they involve food."

She smiled. Feeling a bit awkward, she added, "I'm sorry . . . I couldn't . . ."

"Don't worry. Friendship's fine with me. If I flirt, just ignore it. Hey, maybe you've got a sister you can set me up with."

"No sisters, but I do have friends."

"Are they anything like you?"

"Nobody's like me, John."

"They broke the mold, right?"

"Thankfully, yes."

"Hey. You take care of yourself, you hear?"

"I will. You too."

"It's the Lyme House, right?"

"Dinner on the house. Anytime. I owe you."

"All right, all right. And don't you forget it."

As they said their good-byes, Jane felt suddenly sad. She wished Toscano didn't live all the way on the other side of the country from her. They could be friends. Good friends. Maybe they still would be.

Dumping her cold coffee in the sink, Jane wandered into the dining room. Most of her questions had been answered now, and yet there still remained the matter of Lew Wallace and his death. Perhaps it was a mystery that would never be solved. The only two people left who might know the truth were Christian and Verna. Christian was gone. And Verna wasn't talking.

Or was she? Surely she'd heard by now that Buddy was in jail for the murder of his brother. Did that change anything?

It was only polite to say good-bye. Jane hoped to find Verna in her room. Knocking on the door a few minutes later, she heard a familiar voice say, "It's open."

As Jane stepped inside, she saw that the older woman was sitting in one of the easy chairs, dressed in a paisley silk robe, her fiery red hair done up in a knot at the back of her neck. And, as always, she was smoking. Several stacks of papers rested next to her on an end table, with a few files scattered on the floor. The blinds were open, and the sun streamed in, making the room seem cheerful and bright, even though Verna's expression was anything but.

Waving Jane to a chair, she said, "I can't think without sunlight. It's the curse of living too long in California."

"I wanted to say good-bye, tell you how much I enjoyed meeting you. I'm leaving in a few of hours."

"Riding a mule cart back to Lake Woebegone?"

Jane grinned. "Something like that." She nodded at the papers. "You've been doing a lot of reading."

"I have."

When she didn't say anything more, Jane continued, "I suppose you heard about Buddy."

"Oh, yes," she said, an eyebrow arching ever so slightly.

She was a movie star, thought Jane, not a stage actress. On screen, such a minute reaction probably indicated great emotion. "Did you suspect him?"

"To be honest—" She withdrew the cigarette holder from her mouth. "—no. I can see it all very clearly now, what was going on behind the scenes, but I thought Buddy loved his brother far too deeply to ever harm him. They'd been through so much together. But then I didn't know about Roland and his magic formula. When you're talking about something like that, all bets are off."

"But you read Lew's book. It was all in there about Ellery Patrick Strong and his invention."

"I beg to differ. All Lew wrote about was a silly card game. I thought that whole business about a formula was a joke."

Jane tapped her fingernails on the arm of the chair. This could take forever. "Look, Verna, you may feel that this is none of my business, but Ellie Saks was a friend of mine. She spent the last few years of her life trying to figure out the mystery of Roland Lester's life. I hated what happened to her, and I guess it makes me hope there are answers to her questions. She thought Roland murdered Lew Wallace because of that formula. I think you know more about Lew Wallace's death than you've ever let on."

"You're right. I do."

Her bluntness put Jane off.

"Ellie or no Ellie, you're just itching to know, aren't you?" She laughed throatily, then stubbed her cigarette out in a bronze ashtray. Lighting up another, she said, "If I tell the truth, I wonder if I can be arrested. I didn't tell the truth back in 1957, but then since it never went to trial, at least I didn't commit perjury."

"If you're worried about legal issues, I could call my father. He's a defense attorney. He could answer all your questions."

She waved the idea away. "At my age, I guess I can take a few risks. Sometimes I'm too cautious for my own good. And I owe it to Roland. I've been thinking about it for days now. After what's just happened, I believe he'd want the facts put on the table."

"You mean . . . you'll tell me?"

"Not just you, I'm going to tell the whole world." She nodded to the papers. "These all belonged to Roland. Notes. Journals. Letters. Fascinating stuff. I figure quite prominently, if I do say so myself."

"Where—"

"I *lifted,* as they used to say, all this from the files in Roland's study. Yes, I admit it. Gracie was right. I am a common thief. At the very least, I deserve the rack." As she exhaled a puff of smoke, she burst into laughter. "Close your mouth, dear. I know this is all very serious business, but at the moment, it strikes me as damned funny."

"You were the one who jimmied the filing cabinet."

"And I did one hell of a professional job. I couldn't let that information land on some police officer's desk. Because—" She leaned forward to pick up a file on the floor, "—I'm finally going to attempt something I swore I'd never do. Write my memoirs."

"And you're going to tell the truth about the Wallace homicide?"

She gave a defiant nod.

"You were there the day it happened."

"Of course."

"Who murdered him?"

She paused dramatically. "People always want good guys and bad guys, Jane. Hollywood built an empire on simple, unsophisticated stories. We like our morality easy, our endings black and white. When the world finds out Roland and Lew were gay, that they were lovers, some people will be disgusted, others will want to be proud. The gay community, like any group under fire, requires heroes. Okay, no problem. Roland and Lew were both heroes in my book. They were both good men, the best friends I ever had. But they weren't saints. In my opinion, there's a big difference between a hero and a saint. Roland and Lew did bad things. Neither were kind men. Both made big mistakes. And, in the end, if simple answers and half-truths are what people want, if they're looking for deification, then they won't be happy with my memoir."

"Tell me the story," said Jane. "The real story."

Verna puffed contemplatively on her cigarette. "You already have a good part of it. You know, for instance, about the op ed piece Lew wrote to the L.A. paper. The one about George Cukor and *Gone with the Wind*. That was the beginning of the end for Lew. It started a chain of events that culminated in his writing *In the Belly of the Beast*. He gave Roland a copy of the book in early April of 1957, hoping to get some positive feedback. Roland was scared to death. Both for himself, and for what the publication of a book like that would do to Lew. I read it next. My reaction was the same. We all tried to talk him out of sending it around to New York publishers. When Random House turned him down, we figured it was a good sign. Maybe that would be the end of it. But then Lew started toying with the idea of self-publishing. He started contacting cover designers. I hardly knew him that last year. He was so bitter. So full of hate. He couldn't wait to get back at the people who'd taken his career away from him. If he had to destroy other careers in the process, so be it.

"I'd just come back from shooting a film in Mexico that last month. Since I didn't have a place to stay right then—I'd sold my house and hadn't found another, and I've always hated hotels—Lew insisted I move in with him. I was leaving the next month for Italy, where I was doing some location shots for another film, so it made a certain sense. I thought we'd have fun, like the old days. But all Lew did was sit in his study and brood. He was depressed, and he depressed me.

"The morning of the day Lew died, Roland called and invited him out for dinner at Chasens. His birthday was coming up. Roland told me that he had a present he was going to give him that night that would lift his spirits immensely. In fact, Roland thought it would end all talk about his autobiography."

"Do you know what it was?" asked Jane.

She shook her head. "But it was something really big. I wonder now if he wasn't going to tell Lew about the formula, maybe even give it back to him. Knowing what I know now, that would be my guess, but I suppose we'll never know for sure. Anyway, I was sleeping a lot right then. I was exhausted from the shoot in Mexico, and

I'd also picked up some sort of bug, so I rarely went out. I think that's why nobody knew I was staying with Lew. Christian had come by a couple times that day to yell at his father. He knew about the book too, and he thought Lew was going to publish it just to ruin his life and his forthcoming marriage. That's Christian. Everything is about him. I always felt sorry for the kid. He had a rough time growing up. Lew didn't help much. I tried to do what I could, but it was never enough.

"That night, Lew was getting ready to go to dinner with Roland when the doorbell rang. I was in one of the back bedrooms watching TV, so I didn't pay much attention until I heard shouting. It started to sound rather explosive, so I got up and crept down the hallway toward Lew's study. Buddy was standing a few feet away from him, screaming his head off. How could Lew do it! Publish that goddamn book? He was trying to ruin Roland's life! Maybe he didn't care about him, but Buddy did. Lew was a goddamn bastard—etc., etc., etc. Of course, Lew tried to calm him down, but he eventually got just as mad as Buddy. That's when Buddy pulled out a gun. He asked Lew if he had any more copies of the book around. Lew said no. It was a lie. There was one in his bedroom, but I think Buddy believed him. I'll never forget what happened next. Buddy just looked at Lew. Just stood there and stared while Lew babbled on and on about the Hollywood machine, about the blacklists, about how two-faced people were. He was trying to get Buddy to understand why he'd written the book. Right in the middle of a sentence, Buddy pulled the trigger and shot him point blank in the chest. I've never been so horrified by anything in my entire life. I stood in the shadows and watched as Buddy bolted for the front door.

"When he was gone, I hurried into the study to see if I could help Lew. He wasn't moving, and the pool of blood was immense. I'd just jumped up to call an ambulance when I heard the front door open again. As you can imagine, I was terrified Buddy'd come back. So I rushed back to my hiding place just as Roland entered the study. I didn't know what to do. I was paralyzed. Roland knelt down next to Lew and felt for a pulse. Then he said, 'Lew, can you hear me?' Lew opened his eyes. He lifted his arm so that he could touch Roland's face. Roland wanted to call an ambulance, but Lew said no. Roland was crying, trying to get away, but Lew gripped his arm. He said, 'I'm dying. Don't leave me alone.' Roland could see he was right, so he sat down next to Lew and held his hand, stroking his beautiful blond hair back from his forehead. It was so difficult to watch. Two men who'd loved each other for so many years. And now they had to find a way to say good-bye. Roland said, 'Who did this, Lew?' Lew didn't answer right away. Instead, he told Roland how much he loved him, and how happy he'd made him. Finally, he said that Buddy had come by, angry about the book. Roland made a sound I've never heard a human make before—or since. He just bent over and wailed. He kept repeating, 'It's all my fault,' over and over and over again. But Lew told him, no, it was *his* fault. And that maybe it was better like this. He told Roland to forgive Buddy. And then asked him to forgive him. They were both choking on their tears. So was I. Roland held Lew's hand to his lips, kissing his fingers so gently. They sat like that until—" She cleared her throat. "—until it was over. I wanted to go to Roland then, but . . . it was such a private moment. I didn't want him to think he had an audience. It just wasn't right. As he was sitting on the floor crying, I crept back to Lew's bedroom, removed the last copy of the book from the drawer of his dresser, then slipped out the back door, jumped over the neighbor's fence, and took off into the woods at the back of the property." She tapped some ash into the tray. "Roland must have removed my clothes before the police arrived, but he forgot a negligee, or some such thing. The police never traced it to me, thank God. So, that's what you wanted, and now you have it. The story of how Lew Wallace died."

"But what about his dying words?" said Jane. " 'Gideon, dumb son-ofabitch. He never had a chance.' "

"Oh, that." She gave a contemptuous wave. "Roland came up with that when the police were interrogating him. It was just a red herring—to throw them off the track."

"You mean, there never was a Gideon?"

"Oh, sure there was. Gideon had been Roland's dog when he was a little boy. He was an old dog. A mutt. His father called him 'Useless.' Said all he did was eat and sleep and get in his way. One day, Roland came home from swimming and found that his father had taken the dog out behind the garage and shot him. Something about the way Lew looked the night he died reminded Roland of Gideon. He said that more than once."

So, that was it. The end of the story. "You never told Roland that you knew? That you'd been there that night?"

"Never. But he knew I knew the truth. It was so obvious—to everyone but the police. Roland bought Innishannon less than a month after Lew died. And he sent Buddy back to Connecticut to caretake the place for him, out of harm's way. I don't think he could stand to have Buddy anywhere near him after what happened, and yet he couldn't just turn him over to the police. Roland spent the rest of his life trying to forgive his brother, but I doubt he ever succeeded. They had a bond. Earlier in life, I might have called it love. But later, it was something else. Something far less healthy. Amazing as it may sound, I think Buddy always thought he'd done Roland a huge favor by getting rid of Lew. He expected gratitude. When he didn't get it, it confused him. He wasn't an Einstein, but he wasn't stupid either. And yet, he never understood Roland's relationship with Lew—how a man could love another man so totally. Their world was incomprehensible to Buddy— just the way it is to so many others. In the end, Roland and Lew paid dearly for their love, and for their mistakes."

Jane sat for a moment, digesting the story. Finally, she asked, "Do you still have the copy of Lew's book? The one you took with you that night from his home?"

She took a quick puff on her cigarette, then nodded.

"What are you going to do with it?"

"I haven't decided. All I know for sure is that I won't publish it. But I won't destroy it either. It's the document of a life and a time. Who knows, maybe I'll give it to you one day. You'd certainly be a better choice than my closeted actress friend—who shall remain nameless for now." She laughed. "What would you do with it?"

The comment took her by surprise. "I don't know. I'd have to think about it."

"Do that. If you come up with any ideas, write me. I'm always open to suggestions."

Jane figured it was time to leave. But before she got up, she saw that Verna had begun paging through the folder she'd picked up off the floor.

"Here," she said finally, handing Jane a piece of typing paper. "It's the quote Lew wanted to use at the beginning of his book. It's by his

favorite poet—Edwin Arlington Robinson, from the poem 'Cassandra.'
Read it."

Jane glanced down at the page.

> *Are you to pay for what you have*
> *With all you are?*

"It's a good question, don't you think?" asked Verna, blowing a lazy circle of smoke into the air between them. "I intend to give it a good answer."